# CHOSEN BY DESTINY

## Finding Sanctuary Book One

Natasha Madden

Magic Mist Publishing

For all those who believed in me.
You are my everything.

# BOOKS BY NATASHA MADDEN

**Finding Sanctuary Series**
Chosen by Destiny
A Night of Shadows and Death (Novella)
Marked by the Gods
Wicked Desires
Fractured Souls

**Crescent Moon Series**
His Light in the Dark
A Spark of Madness

# CHOSEN BY DESTINY

A hidden bloodline, an ancient order out to destroy it.

Twenty-eight-year-old Nesrin left everything she knew behind in hopes of a fresh start. Building a new life and remaining anonymous is a balancing act, one she thought she had perfected. That was until a series of run-ins with the Pacific Northwest Pack brings with it a protector who will defend her no matter the cost, whether or not she wants his protection. Forbidden desires have Nesrin questioning her sanity. She trusted very few and no one enough to reveal her secret. Her only priority was to keep her last remaining family member hidden and safe from those who wouldn't think twice about killing either of them.

Her journey of self-discovery brings new friendships and unexpected allies. The more she uncovers about herself and her family, the more questions she has. Things are not adding up.

All Nesrin cares about is protecting those important to her, even if that means sacrificing herself.

The Finding Sanctuary series is a gritty, sexy, action-packed urban fantasy, and paranormal shifter romance. *Chosen by Destiny*

NATASHA MADDEN

is a full-length novel recommended for mature readers due to language, sexual situations, and graphic fighting scenes.

# PROLOGUE

My breath comes out in short, sharp bursts as my feet pound the dirt track beneath me. My heart crashes against my ribs, as if it were trying to escape the confines of my chest. As terrifying as this is, running for my life, and I won't admit this to anyone, I love the thrill of being chased. That rush of adrenaline that infuses every part of your body, the kind that makes you feel you can do anything, is incredible.

My focus remains steady on the path in front of me. The forest is hard to navigate this late into the night, the shadows taking on different shapes as they stretch across the ground in front of me, playing tricks on my eyes.

Glancing up, I'm able to make out the full moon overhead. A slight smile adorns my lips as I notice a rise in my power. I've always found comfort and power with the moon. Still, I know better than to enter Forest Park after dark, especially on a full moon. But I have no choice.

Well, that's a lie, the little voice inside my head whispers. I have this insatiable pull to aid those who need it. My plans may often go awry, and sometimes they can be impractical, but I always get the job done. I just don't have it in me to say no, a shortcoming I blame on my birth date. I was born on the twenty-seventh of August along with my twin sister, Niamh. We're both restless, impulsive, compassionate, and born fighters who refuse to tolerate injustice. Mom used to say we had hearts of gold. We just didn't know when to concede, when to accept things for how they are.

I dodge to the side, ducking to avoid a branch that's in my path. Not much further. I can totally make it. A chill snakes down my spine and my scalp prickles as those tiny hairs on the back of my neck lift. A low growl has my heart skipping a beat or two, while anticipation twists my stomach. Beads of sweat drip down my back, making the shirt under my leather jacket stick to my skin.

They're getting close.

A branch snaps to my left. I don't dare look. I knew I shouldn't take my eyes off the path in front of me. Still, I let my gaze drift from the path, and I could just make out the flash of black in between the trees. I jerk my attention forward again. Nope, don't look.

I force myself to stay focused. If I give in to my temptation to look again, I'll likely end up running into a tree and knocking myself out. My long auburn hair streams behind me, having become loose from my braid. My head grazes the wood as I dip under a low-hanging branch. Losing my footing, I slide in the mud, my arms flying out to steady me. My breath falters, fear slamming into me as I regain my footing. I sprint down the track to freedom, a snarl echoing close behind me.

I am going to make it out of here. There is no other choice. Astraea is relying on me to come home in one piece. A vision of her big blue eyes, wide and innocent, and her cute little face hits me, taking my breath. Which is already becoming ragged, my legs burning from the effort to keep my feet steady in the muddy path. The rain has been relentless all day, but that's nothing new for Portland. It just means the path is covered in mud that I now feel flinging up with every step, coating my new jeans.

"Fan-fucking-tastic," I mutter, then roll my eyes because now is not the time to be upset about my new jeans.

The creatures chasing me aren't likely to stop if they catch me. I am the prey now and their sense of logic will probably be gone, taken away by the urge to hunt and kill. Not all are like this, but most are, and as I don't know the pack here personally, I can't say for sure what they would do with me. Plus, the witches and the shifters aren't exactly on good terms.

My stomach dropped as the ground beneath me disappeared, my feet slipping as I slid down a steep hill and slammed hard into a tree.

"Mother trucker!!" I curse, jumping up. I don't waste time looking around. My palm lands on the rough bark of the tree as I push off, darting forward again. The jolt of adrenaline that shoots through me spurs me on faster than before. My bracelet flares bright, giving me that extra boost of speed I need.

The wolves are gaining ground. I can almost feel their hot breath on the back of my neck, causing an icy shiver to coat my skin. Terror rips through me at the low, menacing growl so close behind me, I feel like they are close enough to snap at my heels. I bite back a whimper as another branch snaps to my left, then another to my right. Fuck, they're closing in, herding me.

Up ahead, I see the barrier. Not a physical barrier, a magical one. My salvation. The barrier is an invisible border that surrounds the entire park, and if I can make it to that border, I'll be safe.

The witches created the barrier as a sanctuary for magical and supernatural creatures. It keeps them concealed from human sight without the need of their own magic or glamor. While the humans can still enter Forest Park through the barrier, they cannot see what hides amongst them. The magic won't allow it. Some of those creatures choose to live here in the forest, safe inside the barrier. They wouldn't dare reveal themselves to humans, none of us would. Humans are the worst beings out there, killing and imprisoning anything they don't understand or can't control.

I don't slow as I run through the barrier. It shimmers a beautiful pale blue as I cross through, my skin tingling slightly from the magic. A thundering growl, followed by a hair-raising howl echoes through the park a moment later. As I slow down to a jog, I risk a glance over my shoulder. My blood freezes, and I stumble at the sight of several sets of gleaming yellow eyes looking at me from the darkness. Even though I am sweaty from the run, small, prickly goosebumps break out across my arms and stomach, sending a small, icy shiver through me. I let out a slow breath, relieved, when I realize they've stopped the chase. At least they have enough sense and awareness to stay hidden within the barrier, even though there shouldn't be any humans about at this hour.

What was I thinking going into Forest Park? Especially on a full moon with the pack out on a run. Tonight was close. Marcus will kill me himself when he finds out where I was tonight. The man seriously has a stick up his ass and most days, and I love to see just how far it goes. Not that anything I do is any of his business, but there is no way he won't hear about this. No way the Shadow Lake Coven won't know I broke the rules tonight. Again.

I've kept my distance from the coven as much as possible. My parents always warned us to stay as far away from them as possible. From a young age, they taught me many things. I learned how to harness the sun and the moon. That nature itself is an element to nurture and guide us. Our magic comes from the elements, and how we harness that energy depends on how much control we have. Even crazier, I've always thought there might be magic locked way inside of me, which is impossible. We draw our magic from all around us, not inside us. But still, I feel something just out of reach, something pure. Above all else, they taught me to keep all of what I learned a secret. Who we are a secret. Not only from humans, but from our own kind. Other witches. Trust is something I find hard to deal with. Which was made worse after my twin Niamh's death last year.

I still have a little further to go to get back to my beat-up old car that is parked just past the cemetery at one of the many entrances to Forest Park. A shiver runs through me as a gentle wind picks up my hair, tossing it around my face. I pull my leather jacket tighter around me. The weather is a little cooler than usual for this time of year in Portland. Well, it's always cool in Portland, but as it's the end of June, the wet weather and chill should have abated by now. I moved here with Astraea around ten months ago, having fallen in love with the beauty of Portland. Not so much the city, but the suburbs and countryside are beautiful. I guess it reminds me of home a little.

Astraea and I moved here needing a fresh start. We couldn't stay where we were any longer. It didn't feel safe anymore. My twin Niamh and I talked about moving here after the death of our parents when we were fifteen, but never made it happen. Now, at twenty-eight, I'm here without her. I rub at my chest, hoping to ease the pain there. I miss my sister. It always amused us that people who looked at us together rarely thought we were sisters, let alone twins. Niamh was all light and happiness, with long, wavy blonde hair and stunning blue eyes that practically turned violet when she was mad. I am the opposite, the dark to her light with my wavy waist-length hair in shades of fall colors, a mixture of browns and reds. My amber eyes that are a little too big for my face are what stands out, along with my pale skin that showcases a small array of freckles. I could never compare to Niamh. Her inner light had everyone gravitating to her. I was the odd one out most of the time. If it wasn't for Niamh, I wouldn't have had any friends growing up. But truth be told, the only genuine friend I had was my sister. My heart aches at the knowledge of never seeing her again, never staying up watching terrible rom-coms, eating way too much chocolate, discussing the latest book we read, who our fictional boyfriends were, or just having someone to confide in.

Tears well up at the thought of Niamh and what happened to her and my brother-in-law, Hunter. My stomach clenches in anguish, as it does every single time I think of my sister. I quickly block out the rising feelings of despair.

"Get your shit together, Nesrin," I mutter to myself, crossing my arms over my chest and picking up my pace, not having realized I'd slowed. My boots crunch over fallen leaves as I make it to the dark abandoned parking lot.

Up ahead, I see my car, and I sigh in relief. The quicker I can get out of here, the better. I sense eyes on me the moment I reach the driver's door. I know at least one of them is watching me.

My hand automatically flies to the dagger strapped to my thigh, my fingers brushing the hilt. They won't be able to follow me, not in wolf form, so I'm not too worried. That doesn't mean they can't snatch me now, if they so choose. I need to get out of here, like yesterday. If they happen to be smart enough to take note of them trying to track me down, the fake license plates will lead them out of state.

I take a deep breath, reaching for the door handle to my old beat-up VW. My hand just closes over the cool metal when pinpricks of awareness skate over my body. Sucking in a breath, my chest constricts as I glance around. At first, I see nothing, but then I spot him standing at the edge of the path, only thirty feet away.

How did I miss him?

Even from this distance, I can tell he's well built, strong, and attractive. He seems to be tall, and broad across his shoulders and chest. The man is extremely intimidating. I can feel the power emanating from him despite the space between us. I swallow over the lump in my throat as we stare at each other. He stands there at ease, his hands in the pockets of his jeans. He tilts his head to the side, and some of his dark hair falls over his forehead. I wish I was closer so I could see the color of his eyes. They are mesmerizing, and seem to pierce right through me, stealing my breath. There's a slight jolt in my chest, then a small tug pulls at my body, wanting to propel me toward him.

Well, that's a first. Since when have I ever wanted to go *toward* a dangerous man?

He continues to watch me, his eyes narrowing on me. A slight glow appears behind his eyes, making them seem even brighter. He's studying me, and I'm not sure I like the idea of that. I stare back in silent challenge, praying he doesn't decide to kill me on the spot. Finally, he blinks, and I'm able to take a breath.

Fuck, what was that?

A smirk pulls at his lips. I swallow hard and take that as my chance to get away. I open my door and slide into the seat of my car, hands shaking as I try to put my key in the ignition. Finally, I get it and send a prayer to my goddess, Hecate, as I turn the key.

Please start, I beg silently.

Thank Hecate, she starts without a fuss. I really need an upgrade on my car one of these days. A quick glance in the side mirror reveals the stranger has disappeared. I take several deep shaky breaths before putting the car into drive. Tonight wasn't a total bust. I managed to heal the Puca before the wolves detected my presence. The wolves of Portland do not like witches, and don't tolerate us trespassing on their land, especially at night. The relationship between the two factions is hostile at best. Even though I'm not part of the coven, I am still a witch.

My apartment is on the south side of Portland, close to the river. It's small and cramped, but it works well for Astraea and me. Parking my car on the street, I trudge up the steps to my apartment, my legs protesting the whole way. Huffing out a breath, I curse myself. I am unfit, even with the charmed bracelet I wear to help with speed and agility. Then again, less than an hour ago, I was running for my life. Still, I really need to get back to the gym. I let loose a sigh. Just one more thing to add to my ever-growing list of things to do.

Unlocking the door, I take a deep breath before entering my apartment. Grace stands from the lounge, worry coating every inch of her face. "You're home," she says, the relief easy to read in her voice.

"Sorry I'm late, Grace. Things didn't go as planned . . . How was Astraea? Did she go down alright?" I shut the door behind me and drop my keys and phone on the table near the door. The apartment is simple, an open living area with a kitchen off to the side and a hall down to the only two bedrooms and bathroom. Grace is standing in front of my favorite piece of furniture, the biggest lounge that could easily be mistaken for a bed. It takes up a great deal of the room. Right now, I'm fairly sure I am looking at it with longing.

Turning to Grace, I find her intense blue eyes studying me. I squirm under her gaze, her eyes fixing on my hair, which I'm sure is a tangled mess. Grace is my older downstairs neighbor, a quiet lady who lives alone. She's a tiny little thing, with long thick gray hair that falls past her lower back. She always wears it braided over her shoulder. Grace's eyes are such a deep blue, so unique, the color reminding me of a midnight storm. Most of all, Grace is someone I feel I can trust. We had an instant connection and Astraea took to her straight away when we met.

"Astraea was a perfect angel, like always, but are you okay, Ness?" she asks in a voice a concerned mother would use. Her gaze then travels down to my mud-coated jeans. Fudge sticks. How do I explain that? I look down at my clothes and shake my head.

Goddess, they are going to be a pain to clean.

"Yes, yes, of course. I had a flat and dropped my phone in some bushes while I changed it. Hence why I'm such a mess." I wave at my general appearance, and even I cringe at that terrible lie. The look Grace gives me says she knows I'm full of shit but won't not call me on it. At least, not this time.

"Well, I will let you get some rest. It's already past midnight," she says, moving to pass me, leaning in to kiss me on the cheek before continuing on out the door.

Grace helps me out as much as she can with Astraea. I would be seriously lost without her. Still, she doesn't know about my heritage. I feel awful lying about it, but humans don't always react well to finding out magic is real and supernatural creatures are living among them. So, I am reluctant to tell her and risk ruining what we have. It may be selfish, but I can't bring myself to tell her just yet.

Once she leaves, I walk around my apartment, checking that the door and windows are locked, then checking if my protective wards are strong. Then I make my way to the bedroom, quickly peeking in on Astraea.

"Sweet dreams, Astra," I whisper, her nickname falling from my lips as I gently kiss her on the head. She is fast asleep on her stomach, her blonde curls scattered around her head and her stuffed wolf tightly tucked under her arm. At least she's safe and sound, just like I promised. I check my protection and cloaking spell I placed on her. Then I quietly make my way down the hall to my room, planning to take a shower, but change my mind as I pass through the bedroom door, my bed calling to me. The shower can wait till morning like the rest of my problems.

# CHAPTER ONE

B ang, Bang, Bang . . . What the? I jolt up in my bed, still dressed in last night's clothes. I check the clock next to my bed. *Oh, for the love of . . .* It's only seven in the morning. Who in the hell is banging on my door this early? I look at the baby monitor and see Astraea sitting patiently in her bed playing with some toys, her curious eyes drifting to her bedroom door.

The banging comes again, louder this time. "I know you're in there, Nesrin," yells the angry male voice, and I growl loudly, tipping my head back to the ceiling.

"Bloody Marcus," I mutter. How he even found out where I live in the first place is beyond me. And to even risk bothering me before my morning coffee. He has to have a death wish. I drag myself out of the bed and look over at the mirror, startling at my reflection. Anyone would think I was dragged backward through the forest last night, and is that . . . *Oh my god, yes!* I have a twig in my hair. No wonder Grace was looking at me with concern last night. I reach up and pull it out as another round of banging starts.

"I'm coming!" I yell, maybe a bit more harshly than necessary, but seriously, it is early. The sun has barely risen. What does he expect? I stalk down the hall, probably stomping my feet more than necessary, and throw open the front door, glaring at Marcus. He stands there in his usual black suit. Today, he has on a light blue shirt. Marcus is a few years older than me and stands at least a foot taller with a lean swimmer's body, close-cropped black hair, and even blacker eyes. Marcus is a good looking guy, don't get me wrong, but his personality sucks balls. He is tall, brooding, and bossy.

"What do you want, Marcus? It's a bit early to be making house calls, don't you think?" I snap. I know why he's here, but I want to see how much he knows before I give anything away. You know, innocent until proven guilty type thing. No way am I admitting to anything just yet.

"God dammit, Nesrin. You know why I'm here. What were you thinking? Are you really that stupid?" Marcus whisper-yells, pushing past me into the apartment.

That just pisses me off even more. I don't like people in my space. Grace is the only exception. I grit my teeth and slam the door shut, storming after him. Marcus makes it a few steps before he rounds on me, pinning me with a lethal look which I'm sure would have most grown men running for their lives. But not me.

"Well, are you going to answer me?" he demands, hands going to his hips.

I wave my hand in front of me. "Oh, I'm sorry, I thought it was a rhetorical question," I mock.

Throwing his hands in the air, annoyance coats his features. "Do you always have to be a smart ass?"

"Better than being a dumbass," I mutter, leaning back on the door frame and crossing my arms defensively over my chest.

Marcus gives me a dark look. "What was that?"

Letting out an exaggerated breath, I pin Marcus with a scowl. "Nothing. You're being dramatic. What are you even talking about?"

It is none of his business what I was doing last night. Plus, it is far too early in the morning for this bullshit. I'm not a morning person. I'm not even a people person, and especially not a coven person. Anything to do with the coven immediately has me on the defensive.

My mother's words float through my mind. *They cannot be trusted.*

"Don't play games with me. You know what I'm talking about. Do you know what they would have done if they caught you?" Marcus growls.

I push off the wall and take a step forward. Rolling up on my toes, I push a finger into his chest. "I don't answer to you or your coven, Marcus!"

Movement from the hall catches my eye. I turn my head to the side where Astraea now stands looking between the two of us, her stuffed toy wolf held up to her face like it can shield her. I take a step back from Marcus, shooting him a glare, and turn to scoop her into my arms.

"Good morning, gorgeous girl," I whisper in her ear, then rub my nose on hers. Astraea grabs the hair on either side of my face, pulling me closer so she can nuzzle my neck. This girl. Goddess, I love her so much, and she's mine. My sweet girl. She pulls back and looks at me, her big blue eyes—my sister's eyes—blinking once. That sharp pain pierces my chest again. Is it ever going to get any easier?

I turn back to Marcus and give him my best resting bitch face. "We have nothing to discuss right now, so you know where the door is. As you can see, I have more important things to take care of than bossy men who have absolutely no right to be banging on my door."

I've been holding Astraea in a way that kept her out of Marcus' line of sight, something I'm sure he's noticed. I don't want the coven knowing about her, and have somehow managed to keep Marcus from knowing about her until now. I hate that the cat is out of the bag, so to speak, but there's nothing I can do about it now. I just hope he'll keep his mouth shut. I won't be able to avoid dealing with the coven if they choose to push this further.

Marcus's black eyes flare at my words, at the clear dismissal. I see the argument brewing in the depths of that dark gaze before they flicker to Astraea, and he hesitates. Before he has a chance to say more, I turn and walk down the hall with Astraea.

"You know where the door is," I call over my shoulder as I close her bedroom door behind us.

I stand at the door, listening to see if he decided to leave. A moment later, I hear the front door open, then close, the locks engaging. He must have locked them magically. I loose a breath I didn't realize I've been holding, then turn, resting my back against the door, and look down at Astraea to find her studying me in a way that always freaks me out.

It probably wasn't the smartest move turning my back on Marcus and leaving him in my apartment like that, but the man infuriates me. Ever since I moved to Portland and ran into him at my bookstore, he has been a constant shadow in my life, trying to get me to meet with his coven.

*No, thank you!*

Looking down at the little girl in my arms, I plaster a smile on my face that feels so fake. I hate it.

"What should we do today?" I ask sweetly.

Astraea smiles up at me and nuzzles back in my arms, gripping her wolf tight. My throat closes up, making it hard to swallow. Her father got her that teddy when she was born, and it has never been far from her reach.

"Okay, sweet girl. Hugs it is. I'm perfectly happy with that," I say hoarsely, my emotions running high after last night's close call and barely any sleep. There is a chair in the corner of her bedroom, and I make my way over to it. We both love this chair. It's big and white with so many pillows you could get lost in it. I look down at my still-dirty clothes and wince, reaching for a blanket and tossing it over the white fabric before taking a seat. That's where we stay most of the morning until our bellies are grumbling.

# CHAPTER TWO

I take the stairs two at a time down to the street. It's quiet this time of the day, with only a handful of people milling about. Our apartment may be small, but I love where we live. The trees that line the streets have beautiful purple flowers this time of year, and the petals scattering the ground adds to the soft look of the street.

As I make my way toward the river where the houses start, each has its own color door with distinctive carvings on it. I love that. In this modern world, everything is the same. It wouldn't surprise me if people accidentally walk into the wrong house or apartment on occasion because everything is identical. But here in this part of Portland, each front door is different. I feel it tells a story of the people that live there.

Taking a deep breath of fresh air, I let it fill my lungs fully before releasing it. I have the afternoon shift at the bookstore I opened ten months ago, using up a good chunk of my savings. Naming it was harder than I expected, but I ended up going with Scarlet Charms. It's a cozy spot for people to come in and find a quiet corner and enjoy getting lost for a while in whatever world they chose. What most don't know is that I also run a small side business as well, selling potions, charms, and spells for those who need them in the magical community. I have a talent for creating spells and potions, and am also exceptionally good at healing. I'm one of the best at these things because I can also see magic, which comes in handy. Not a lot of witches or mages can see magic in its raw form. Most can feel it to a certain extent, but to see magic in a rainbow of colors flowing and weaving together through the air, is an extremely rare and amazing gift. When I first saw pictures of the aurora borealis as a child, I thought it was a spell until my mom explained it to me. That's when she found out I have magical sight. Because of the gift, I can see any gaps or holes in my work. So, all my spells and potions are airtight. I can also decipher the spells of others and unravel them, picking at the threads until it falls apart.

I have to keep all my activities secret from the coven in Portland. If they thought I was an active witch in their territory, they would be even more persistent in getting me to join them.

And Marcus is part of that coven, a lackey for the High Priest, and for some reason, he thinks I belong to him. He couldn't be more wrong. From my time here in Portland so far, I have heard nothing good about the coven. My parents always told us to avoid the covens, and I never understood why at the time, but I'm starting to. Deep down I have a niggling feeling I can't trust them, especially with Astraea. I have to stay under the radar. I can't risk the coven finding out what Astraea is. If they ever found out about her, there would be no future for either of us.

I push open the door to my favorite coffee shop, shaking off the dark thoughts. Little Bites is small and quaint and smells just like grandma's after she'd been baking all day. I bask in the smell of the coffee and fresh pastries. This is heaven. I never go to work without a coffee from Blue's shop.

A wistful smile overtakes my face, and I gaze around, spotting Blue at the coffee machine. "Hey, Blue."

"Morning, Ness. Just the usual today?" comes his cheery reply. Blue is in his fifties and is the warmest, kindest person I know. There is just something so inviting about him, so much joy in his bright blue eyes that earned him the nickname Blue.

"Yes, please," I say, rubbing my hands together to warm them up. I glance around the café and notice it's very quiet today, which is unusual. Blue's café is always one of the busiest on this side of the river.

Blue's voice reaches my ears, pulling me from my thoughts. "Hmmm?"

"Where's my girl today?" he repeats, starting on my order. I grin, recalling Grace and Astraea elbow deep in dough when I left ten minutes ago.

"She's at home baking with Grace today."

Blue laughs like he can just imagine the mess that will be. "Promise to bring her by soon. It's been too long."

Shaking my head, I look over at the old man. "I had her here two days ago, Blue."

"Yes, see, too long," he grumbles, drawing another laugh from me. I throw a twenty on the counter as Blue hands me my order.

"Keep the change, Blue." With a wink, I turn for the door.

Astraea has Blue wrapped around her little finger and he doesn't bother to deny it, either. Anything she wants, Blue gets it. It's like they have their own language going on. As I push open the door, I call out over my shoulder, "I'll bring her by tomorrow,

I promise." I walk down the street to the corner where the local homeless man, Merve, sits. He has been living down this alley since I moved in. I've kind of gotten into the habit of bringing him lunch on my way past. As I approach, he looks up, his thick shaggy brown hair falling all over the place. There is the usual twinkle in his brown eyes as he smiles up at me. It amazes me how he's always so happy.

"Hey Merve, I got the usual cappuccino and blueberry muffin warmed up just how you like it," I say as I bend down, kissing him on the bearded cheek and handing him the food.

"Ness, you're too good to me." He laughs, opening the bag and taking a big whiff of Blue's amazing muffins. I laugh at the dreamy look on his face. Blue's muffins are incredible. No one could resist them.

"Nah, not even close. I wish you'd take me up on the job offer to get you off these streets," I reply, giving him a stern look which he just chuckles at. Why he's so happy living on the streets of Portland, I do not know.

"Now, now, Ness. Who would look after these streets if I wasn't watching?" I just roll my eyes at his candid reply. It's always the same story with him.

"Oh! I have something for you," I say, juggling my coffee and trying to reach into my handbag. My fingers close around a knitted beanie, and I pull it free. "Aha! Here it is."

I place my coffee on the ground and lean over, placing the beanie on Merve's head, his brown hair poking out the bottom. The wrinkles around his eyes crinkle as he smiles up at me.

"Aww, thanks Nessy," he chuckles.

I wave off his praise, feeling my cheeks heat. Picking my coffee back up, I grin. "Grace was teaching me how to knit. It's my first beanie. So, you are my guinea pig."

Merve snorts and grins up at me. He has the kindest eyes and soul. I wonder for the millionth time how he ended up on the streets.

"Thanks," he replies, shifting around under his blanket, trying to get comfortable.

The smile drops from my face when I feel the hairs on my neck stand on end, and straighten, knowing someone is watching me. Looking around, my eyes catch on a stranger across the street. He is casually leaning back on the wall outside the florist with his arms crossed over his wide chest, one foot lifted and pressed into the wall behind him. It's difficult to tell from here, but he looks close to six feet tall. He has his dark blonde hair pulled back at the nape of his neck. Age can be tricky, but I'd put him in his early thirties. He's not even trying to hide the fact that he's staring directly at me, so I stare right back. Frowning, I narrow my eyes at him, but he continues to stare back at me with a blank look.

*What is his problem?*

A car goes past, breaking our staring match. He shoves off the wall, sending a smirk my way before turning and walking down the street and disappearing around the corner.

*Right. Okay, then.*

Bringing my attention back to him, Merve says, "You know that man Ness?" He sounds a tad concerned as he looks to where the stranger disappeared.

"No, I don't think so," I answer warily, an uneasy feeling drifting over me. "Well, I better be off. Work and all."

"Take care Ness," he calls after me.

"Always."

The shift at the bookstore is dragging. I lay my head down on the counter and sigh. I just want to go home. There is barely anyone around tonight. I wonder where everyone is? It's a lot quieter than normal. It's probably time to call it a night. Walking over to the front door, I flip the sign from open to closed, then turn the lock. Rubbing my hands over my face, I pivot and make my way over to the register, the last twenty-four hours playing over in my head. I haven't heard from Marcus again, which could mean several things I honestly don't want to think about.

Three steps from the door, something in the air changes, making my magic swirl under the surface. The air pulses with unease. But I can't figure out where this feeling is coming from, so I make my way around the store, turning out the lights. With the shop plunged into darkness, I make my way to the register. That's when I hear a soft scuffling and a whimper coming from the rear of the store. Halting my steps, I listen. A muted thud of a book hitting the carpet has me on alert.

*What the hell was that?*

I haven't had a customer in over an hour, and I locked the back door before Suzy, my employee, left for the night. Making my way slowly toward the back of the store, scenarios run wild in my mind. I really should give up watching horror movies. They do nothing to calm my imagination, especially because I know the things that go bump in the night do indeed exist.

"Come on, Nesrin, get a grip," I mutter to myself. I really wish I would have left the lights on now, but I always turn them off when I lock the door. As I round the last stack of bookshelves, movement catches my eye from the shadows. I approach slowly, raising my hands in a gesture that I hope says, *I don't pose a threat. Please don't hurt me*, while I call on my magic, wrapping it lightly around me like a coat.

"Hello?" I call out, my heart thumping wildly in my chest. At the sound of my voice, I hear something scramble further into the dark. "I won't hurt you. I can help."

I see a pair of tiny feet and tilt my head to the side in surprise. There, huddled in the dark corner of one of my reading nooks, are two children no older than five and eight.

"What on earth?" I mutter, taken aback by the sight of the children.

"How did you two get in here? Are you okay? Are you hurt?" I ask, rushing toward them.

Both stare back at me, terrified. Then their large brown eyes are fixed on the door behind me. That door leads to the alley behind my store, and I rarely leave it unlocked, so I'm unsure how they got in without me noticing. A loud bang startles us as the back door shudders. I spun around, my body locking up. The children cry out as another bang echoes through the store. Something or someone is trying to get in. I spin to face the children.

"You need to follow me. I will take you out the front door and get help." I haven't checked my wards in a while, so I can't be sure they will hold up. It's been on my list to redo them, but kept getting put off. I have a feeling I'm going to regret that now.

Before I can even get the children to stand, the door explodes inward, shards of wood flying everywhere. Without thinking, I launch myself over the children, covering them as best I can with my body, while throwing up a quick shield to protect us from flying debris. As everything settles, I slowly stand up, turning to face whatever just burst through the door. The children whimper and push at my legs to get out from behind me. They want to run, but I have a better idea. As quick as I can, I cast a cloaking spell, wrapping it around them, blending them into shadows.

I twist at the waist to look back at them, and am startled by two sets of glowing yellow eyes.

*Shit, wolf shifters.*

There are shifter pups in my store. This is so bad. I raise my finger to my lips, widening my eyes at them. They both stop trying to push past me and stare in shock at me. Needing them to be quiet and trust me, I wink, hiding my unease, and spin back around to face the threat. That threat is in the form of two hunters. I am so screwed. They stroll into the store like they don't have a care in the world. Like they didn't just blow up my back door.

*Assholes.*

"Hi there, pretty. We're looking for two children. Seems my nephews took a wrong turn and we got separated," the older of the two says.

I curl my lip in disdain, crossing my arms over my chest and surveying the damage behind them before looking back.

"I hope you plan to pay for that damage, as I'm sure you're aware I have a front door," I reply , ignoring his question as I hastily tie off the last of the threads on my cloaking spell, enveloping them in darkness.

There is no way I am letting those hunters leave with these pups. Hunters are the evil they think all magical beings to be. Humans fear what they don't understand, what they can't control. If they can't control it, it must be evil, so they attack it. Fear is born from a lack of knowledge and being too ignorant to learn, and turns them into monsters worse than those they choose to hunt. They had my own family and many others fleeing across Europe in what they called The Great Hunt, in seventeenth-century Germany, then Wales and Ireland.

"We know they came this way, there is no use hiding them from us." The hunter is in his sixties and is at least a foot taller than me, which isn't too hard to achieve. I am a meager five feet. The other looks to be in his teens, smaller and skinnier, so that could work in my favor.

"I think you better leave before I call the cops. There is no one else here but me," I snap, walking toward them, trying to muster as much bravado as possible. I am unprepared and outnumbered, not to mention I've been putting off my training in favor of spending time with Astraea.

The older one sneers, "See, we think you're lying. We saw them come this way."

"Does it look like I give a shit what you think? There is no one else here," I grind out.

The older one takes a quick step toward me, his hand reaching out to grab me. I dart to the side, his fingers just brushing my sweater as I run back through the store, hoping to draw them away from the pups. They are my only concern right now. I won't let anything happen to them. My hand automatically goes for my dagger, which, of course, isn't strapped to my leg right now. I can't outright use my magic against them, either. I'd give myself away for sure and I can't afford that. These men hunt us in the name of their god so they can justify killing innocents. To them, all supernaturals are abominations that need to be exterminated. Apparently, we have no soul. *Blah, blah, blah.*

They consider witches to be pagans doing the Devil's work. Don't get me wrong, there are some who practice black magic, but they are very rare.

"You won't get away, you little bitch. There is no point running. Just tell me where they are!" he yells, chasing after me.

I run behind the counter where I keep a baseball bat and my bag. Reaching inside my bag, I fumble through the contents until I find what I want. I grab the bat with my other hand and turn toward the oncoming threat. I didn't have to wait long. As soon as the hunter appears, I swing with everything in me. The shock vibrates up my arms at the impact of the bat striking his face. I cringe at the sound of bones crunching under the force of the hit.

"Argh, you fucking bitch!" he screams, dropping like a sack of potatoes.

I can't help the smile that spreads across my face. Crouching low, I bring the bat back again as the other hunter rounds the corner and swings again, getting him across the shins. He goes down hard and fast, cursing. I cast a quick magical net over them, which shimmers a beautiful blue, weaving the net over them, pinning them in place.

*That should hold them for a few minutes.*

Then I turn and run back to the pups. I have to get them out now, but to where? I left my car at home, and even then, I don't know where they live. I round the last shelf and skid to a stop, noticing someone else coming through the door. He is huge, his broad shoulders taking up the width of the door frame, tapering down to trim hips. He is the picture of strength and power.

That's the first thing I notice. The second thing is how tall he is. A lot taller than me. I'd be lucky if the top of my head reached his shoulders. Third is how his white t-shirt strains against his biceps and chest. He is built like a damn god. Tattoos snake up one arm and peek out of the top of his t-shirt at his neck. I can feel my body responding to this man. Whether in fear or desire, I'm not so sure, and that just pisses me off.

Finally, I manage to drag my eyes away from his body, looking up as he walks into what little light there is in the shop. Recognition slams into me. His eyes have a deadly calm to them, unlike last night's stark curiosity. He is gorgeous and absolutely terrifying, those green eyes glowing like emeralds, the yellow spark behind them intensifying the color. Now that he is closer, I can see his hair, so dark it's almost black, has a slight wave to it and curls around the nape of his neck.

It's the wolf shifter that was watching me leave the park last night. *Double shit.*

"Could the night get any worse?" I mutter under my breath just as three more figures appear behind him.

*Alright, then. Spoke too soon.*

The fact that I now have four wolves in my store, and they are in human form, does absolutely nothing to dispel the fear clawing at my insides. I reach into my pocket, wrapping my fingers around the taser I got out of my handbag. I doubt it will work on a shifter, but it's worth a try. *Right?*

I'm not ready to reveal myself as a witch just yet, although I'm sure the shifters in front of me know exactly what I am. Using another spell to defend myself is out of the question. I am already working two spells.

The leader seems somewhat agitated at the sight of me as he takes another step forward. "You! Why am I not surprised?" he growls, and a thrill goes through me at that deep rumbling voice.

*Wow, totally inappropriate Nesrin.*

I hold my head high as I gaze back at him, shocked by the raw intensity in his eyes. I refuse to take a breath, fearing they would hear the shudder, giving away my unease. He sounds pissed. I am in so much shit.

I slowly, as casually as possible, move in front of the pups that are still hidden by my spell. Lifting my shoulders in a shrug, I discreetly pull the taser from my pocket. My fingers spasm around the handle, I hate the fear that clogs my throat. Shifters and hunters have taken over my store. I need a plan.

What a way to spend a Saturday night. I squeeze the taser tightly in my hand.

"I wouldn't use that if I were you. It would only serve to piss him off more," says someone from the doorway. His voice holds an amused tone, which confuses me. This is not an amusing situation.

My gaze moves to the other shifter. It's the stranger from earlier. The one watching me from across the street when I was with Merve. He shoots me a wink when he realizes I've recognized him.

Throwing my hands in the air, I make an exasperated noise. "What the hell?" Obviously, I am easier to track than I thought. His eyes are the brightest blue, reminding me of Blue's eyes.

"Tonight has been a shitastrophy," I groan, my head tipped to the ceiling. I am seriously crying invisible tears at my predicament. Honestly, how bad is my luck this week?

"Shitastrophy? That's new." The blue-eyed stranger laughs.

My eyes snap to his, and my frustration spikes. "What would you call tonight? Other than a fuck up or epic fail." At his amused look, I mutter, "Whatever." Now isn't the time to explain my vocabulary. The two shifters look at each other in confusion and I sigh, sucking on my lower lip, trying to think of a way out of this.

There is a sizzle and pop that only I can feel as my spell on the hunters breaks. Then the two of them charge around the corner, so lost in their fury that they don't notice the shifters until it's too late.

Quicker than I thought possible, the shifter from the park darts forward, intercepting the hunters before they can reach me. His hands shoot out, grabbing them both by the throats and lifting them off the ground. Their feet dangle and their bodies squirm in his hold. I can see them gasping for air, eyes wide with shock and fear.

I tilt my head, as I watch from a few feet away with genuine fascination, admittedly captivated by the way his green eyes ignited with wrath. And the way his muscles flex and tense under his shirt.

*Shit, I need to keep my head together.*

"Are you the two hunters terrorizing my people and taking pups as you see fit?" he growls, his voice so animalistic it makes my muscles lock up.

The hunters are struggling against his hold and promptly turning purple. Surely, he doesn't plan to kill them right here in my store. Does he? I make a move toward them, to do what exactly, I'm not sure. One shifter steps forward, letting loose a low growl. Goosebumps scatter across my body. A warning for me to stay where I am.

"Lukas. I mean Alpha, let us take them to holding where we can question them. We need to know what they are up to," says the blonde from this morning to the man named Lukas, who is currently choking two hunters to death. At least I got a name, Lukas. Even worse, he is the fucking Alpha.

*Seriously, can this night get any worse?*

Lukas throws the two hunters toward the door, where they are swiftly dragged away by the other two shifters. Which leaves me with Lukas and the blonde stranger from this morning. The Alpha slowly turns to me, his eyes still glowing with power and dominance. I fight the fear that worms its way through my body, lifting my chin higher and narrowing my eyes. There is no way I will cower and let him see the effect he has on me.

"Where are my pups?" he demands, power rolling off him in waves. I almost stumble back a step from the unexpected force of it, but manage to hold my ground.

*Yeah, he's pissed.*

My stomach sours at the thought of them being his pups, and my chest aches to the point I wanted to rub it. But I have no clue why, which only annoys me more. Placing my hands on my hips, I glare at him, not saying a word. *The least he could do is say please.*

Lukas raises an eyebrow and the other wolf lets out a small, huffed laugh.

*Shit, did I say that out loud?*

"Yes, you're speaking out loud," Lukas replies. Looking a bit confused, he tilts his head back, gazing at the ceiling, like it might offer him patience. I wonder if he's counting to ten?

"Look, it's been a long night. They are here. I can smell them." Then, more softly, he adds, "I just want to get the pups back home to their family. I promised my friend she would have her boys back." As an afterthought, he implores, "Please."

I let out a breath I didn't realize I was holding, the ache easing in my chest. I should be more worried about how much relief I feel at his words, but I can analyze that later when I'm alone in the comfort of home.

Nodding, I casually turn, letting the spell fall away, and the two little pups calmly move from the shadows, their eyes back to normal. I smile softly as they come toward me, but before I can move out of the way, they both launch themselves at my legs, crying. I am so shocked by the action, I can't help but to squat down, embracing the poor terrified pups. When I look up, Lukas is watching me with an intense look on his face, his jaw clenched, eyes hard.

"Right," I say, standing up, rubbing my hands on my jeans. Lukas averts his gaze and rubs a hand over his dark hair, looking just as exhausted as I feel.

"What is your name?" he asks. His voice warms me and I answer without thinking.

"Nesrin."

His eyes freeze me to the spot as we stare at each other for a long moment. His scent drifts over to me, invading my senses, reminding me of rain and the forest.

Blinking, he breaks our connection and turns, leading the pups outside. Stopping, he glances over his shoulder at me. "Zee, my Beta, will fix the door and get you home safely."

I take a breath, ready to object, but Lukas beats me to it. "We already know where you live, so no arguments," Then he disappears into the darkness of the alley. Well, that's just great then. I turn and storm to the front of the store, tossing my taser inside my bag before marching back.

Zee comes sauntering back through the door with a toolbox in hand. His gorgeous smile stretches across his face, which only serves to irritate me more.

"So, it's quite a week you're having," he says, amusement coating his words.

"What does that have to do with the price of eggs?" I snap back, my anger getting the best of me.

Zee looks at me and cocks his head in confusion. "Eggs? Who said anything about eggs? Did you hit your head or something? Should I take a look?" he asks, stepping toward me. I hold my hands up, my chest so tight I think I might suffocate.

"No, I'm fine!" I shout, then cringe. Now that the adrenaline is fading, I can feel my body waning, my mood dropping with it.

Zee grins, making the dimple on his left cheek appear, but that smile falls into a grim line as he takes in my mood. "Look, honey. I know you're nervous. It's written all over your face, and your heartbeat is, like, crazy fast."

"Don't knock a good ticker," I retort, crossing my arms.

He continues as if I didn't interrupt him, "But nothing is going to happen. I'm just going to fix the door and see you home safely. Nothing to worry about, yeah?"

I shrug, looking away. "I have a taser and magic, so I'm not worried about anything. It's you who should be worried."

"Right," Zee replies, moving out into the alley and then carrying in a new door. A *bright pink* fucking door. Where did he even get a new door at this time of night?

"Um. What is that?" I stand up straight, pointing at the monstrosity in front of me.

Zee stops moving and looks over at me, his eyebrows furrowing, then looking at the door he carried. "Your new door?"

"Does this look like a five-year-old girl's bedroom to you?"

Zee smirks. "No."

"Then why are you replacing my door with a bright pink one?" I all but shout.

"It's all they had on short notice. Lukas got one sent straight over."

"No. Nope," I object, shaking my head. I refuse to have a goddamn pink door in my store. I am *not* a pink girl.

"You can paint it, but it needs to be replaced. Your door is in pieces."

I know he's right, but frustration wells up inside of me anyway. Of course, I can always paint it. I look longingly at the shards of my original door lying around me and sigh.

"I liked my door," I mutter. I'm sure the Alpha could have gotten a better suited door if he wanted to. But I need to count my blessings. Someone is fixing my door, which means I can get home to Astraea earlier than I would have otherwise.

"What was that?"

"Fine. It's fine." I smile at Zee. "Thank you."

Zee chuckles as he gets to work. "Sarcasm?"

"No. Honestly, I'm grateful. Thank you, Zee."

# CHAPTER THREE

The fire is so hot I can barely stand it. Smoke is everywhere, making it nearly impossible to breathe. With my throat burning, I gasp, but I can't get enough air to fill my lungs. Flames suddenly burst skyward, running up the walls and across the ceiling. I burst from my room, falling to my knees in the hallway. I crawl forward on my hands and knees, doing my best to push my building panic down. All I can do is stare in shock and horror at the flames as I try moving forward, pain piercing my body with every move.

My eyes blur, and I wipe at them with the back of my hand. I try once more to take a deep breath, only to choke on smoke. My whole body feels like it's shutting down, my movements slowing. Everywhere the air touches my skin it burns. The heat is unbearable. What happened? Where are Niamh and Hunter? Did they get out of the house? Is Astraea with them?

These thoughts are what's driving me forward.

Up ahead, I can just make out the sound of a baby crying. Pushing aside the pain each movement brings, I crawl forward as fast as I can. The smoke is growing thicker, my eyes burning with tears now tracking down my face. Opening my mouth, I try to call out, but no sound comes from my throat. It's like I'm drowning on smoke. But I continue up to the baby's room. If Astraea is still in there, I have to get her out. I'm sure the crying I heard was just my imagination, but I need to see for myself. I need to be sure.

I try to cast my magic outward in search of anyone else who may be in the house, but I am in too much distress and it just fizzes out. I propel myself forward as fast as I can manage on my hands and knees, trying to keep below the smoke. Pushing open the door, I crawl into the room, the smoke and flames biting at my heels.

I quickly shut the door behind me and smoke starts billowing in through the crack at the floor. I blindly reach for the towel hanging behind the door and throw it down to cover the crack. The fire itself hasn't reached this room yet, but that won't last. Any minute, the flames will engulf us. I force myself to stand and run over to the crib, cursing my weak legs as I stumble forward. Astraea is there, staring up at me with her big blue eyes. Without hesitation, I reach for her and bundle her in a blanket then run for the window. That's when I feel it for the first time, the magic stirring the air, moving with the fire. It swells, and a surge of power lifts the hair from my shoulders. I drop to the floor as all the windows smash, glass flying everywhere as I curl myself over Astraea, shielding her with my body, too weak to form a magical one. I barely notice the sting of tiny cuts across my back as I climb up onto the ledge of the window. There is a trellis covered with a vine on this side of the house that I might be able to use to get down, but the tremble in my limbs has me questioning it. With the heat of the fire at my back, there is no other choice. I sit on the ledge and slowly lower myself down into the vine, holding Astraea as tightly as I can.

My heart is thumping wildly in my chest to the point of it being painful. I hear sirens in the distance coming closer. Help is coming. But the relief is short-lived. I make it to the ground and stumble onto the lawn, carefully adjusting Astraea in my arms. Looking around, I see a few neighbors out watching the scene unfold from the street. I can't make out anyone's faces with the tears burning my eyes. Heat from the flames still licks at my skin. My whole body feels like it's on fire. I turn and turn, searching for my sister, but I don't see her. Where is she? Icy dread fills my veins as realization hits. She would never escape without Astraea; she is our priority.

"No, no, no, no, no, Niamh!" I scream, spinning around and running back toward the house. People are now trying to stop me, holding me back, keeping me from reaching my sister. Twisting, I tear free from their hold and run, a choked sob escaping me. I look down to the bundle in my arms as I run. Astraea, all of eight months old, is staring at me, eyes wide with fear. I stop running, my knees slamming to the ground. Pain radiates through my body, as another sob works its way up my throat. I softly grasp Astraea to my chest, hoping with all my heart Niamh will make it out alive.

A heavy hand lands on my shoulder, squeezing painfully. I jolt up in bed, a scream lodging in my throat. I sit there panting, trying to steady my heart as it thumps violently in my chest. My fingers pluck at the wet shirt stuck to my skin. I grimace at the cold sweat that covers my body, the sheets wrapped around my legs. My hand rubs at my chest, hoping to ease the pain there, and maybe hold my heart in one piece. The pain of losing Niamh and Hunter rolls through me. I hate these nightmares. I don't understand why I keep having them. Why does my brain refuse to let that night go? Why does it keep forcing me to run through it over and over?

I push the sheets from my legs to stand, then realize I'm not alone. Laying at the end of my bed is Astraea. Reaching over, I brush the curls from her face and smile. She always knows when I'm having a nightmare and comes in to comfort me. I reach down and pick her up, moving her under the blankets and tucking her in. Astraea's grip tightens on her stuffed wolf, and she snuggles deeper into the blankets. My heart fills with warmth as I stare down at her. She is perfect. Astraea was named after the Goddess of Innocence. I have no doubt in my mind she will live up to the title.

I stand and make my way to the kitchen in search of some water, when a flash of movement outside the window catches my eye. I freeze, my body locking up as I wait, watching for any movement on the balcony. We are on the third level. But I 've watched enough parkour videos when I was bored to know it wouldn't be all that difficult for something to get to our balcony. Even humans with no supernatural grace could make it up here. Which is why I have my apartment warded against anything or anyone meaning us harm. I don't know how long I stand there holding my breath, but when nothing else moves on the other side of the glass, I run a shaky hand through my hair, blowing out a long breath. My imagination is running amok and I am on edge. I have this crazy feeling that my quiet life in Portland is about to end.

Unable to go back to sleep after that, I just lie there next to Astraea, soaking in the comfort she offers. Her soft snores bring a smile to my face. At least she's safe, I think as my worries circle my mind. I check our shields and find that they are as strong as ever. No one would know she was anything but a normal toddler.

# CHAPTER FOUR

I push off the sink where I've been leaning, throwing the washcloth behind me. "Okay, beautiful girl. What should we do today?" I ask Astraea the next morning. Her big blue eyes blink back at me from her spot at the tiny kitchen table where she's finishing her Sunday morning pancakes.

"Nothing?" I hedge, giving her a soft smile. Astraea is almost two, and she is growing so quickly. She is also extremely smart. I just haven't been able to get her to talk. Not a peep. I've taken her to see several doctors, and according to them, everything is working fine. One doctor said it was selective mutism, which usually occurs because of a rare psychiatric condition. That her ability to speak and understand spoken language is not impaired and she may talk when she is ready. I would love nothing more than to hear her speak or laugh just once. Even her tears are silent. It breaks my heart.

"How about a walk down the river to the park?" Her little eyes flare wide. "You like that idea?" I question and she nods, jumping down from her chair and running for the coats hanging on the wall near the door.

"Okay, the park it is." I laugh, following her.

It's still cool out, so I pop a beanie on Astraea's little head. Tilting her head up, she smiles at me, showing off her two dimpled cheeks. My heart just about explodes every time she smiles like that. That look makes me feel like I'm not completely screwing things up. I take her small hand in mine, as we head down the stairs, then follow the quiet street toward the river.

It's a lovely day. Even though the sun's out, there is a bite of cold in the air. But we don't live too far from Willamette Park. We love this part of the city and all the parks it offers. The walking paths along the river always keep us entertained for hours. As we near the park, I can see that it's extremely busy. Everyone is making the most of the sunshine. Letting go of my hand, she runs straight for the swings. As she climbs on, she looks over her shoulder at me, her cheeks flushed rose red and a look of anticipation sparkling in her eyes. Letting out a small laugh, I reach for her, giving the swing a gentle push.

This little angel means the world to me. She is as completely dependent on me as I am on her. I am determined to make a good life for her. All we have in the world is each other, no other living relatives left to speak of. Some days, I feel that loss so badly I can't breathe. Losing Niamh is the worst. How am I ever supposed to recover after losing my twin? It's like I've lost a piece of my heart and soul. A piece I will never get back.

The night Niamh died, I screamed so much I damaged my vocal cords. It took four weeks to recover fully. Even though those weeks were a blur, all I can remember is the despair and confusion. I hate it, hate feeling that way. I have nobody I can talk to about it, and even if I did, how do you tell someone about the worst day of your life?

I remember the desperate need to run, to take Astraea as far away as I could, and I did. All the way from Pittsburgh to Portland. The drive was long and tiring, a grueling thirty-five hours on the road. We made a lot of stops along the way, sleeping in motels or in the car when we couldn't find one. I trusted my gut, and it led me here. Now my priority is this little girl, and her safety and happiness. I have to keep our secret safe. That has to be my first priority because if the wrong people find out about her, they won't hesitate to kill us both.

Shaking off the thoughts hanging over me like a storm cloud, I look around the park, taking in the river and the trees. Astraea pumps her little legs in time with the swing, doing most of the work for me. She would happily stay right here on this swing all day if I let her.

I turn my gaze toward the river, remembering my father's love for fishing and how he always used to get Niamh and me to go with him. We always used to play along and indulge him, even though we both hated it. My chest warms as the memories filter through, even as I feel a sharp pinch in my heart. It's always been there, ever since I got the news my parents died in that car crash. That sharp stab of pain between my ribs every time I think of them. It didn't seem real at the time. Niamh and I were in shock. Both our parents were gone. They had once seemed invincible to us. Especially my father. He was an unstoppable force, loyal and brave. As time went on, it still didn't seem real. It had to be a mistake. I remember thinking that a lot in the days that followed their deaths. Some days grief struck us down like a tidal wave and kept us pinned beneath the waves, but we at least had each other.

But now she is gone, too. Tears spring unbidden to my eyes, and I quickly wipe them away before Astraea notices them.

I look down at her and clear my throat. "Ready to try something else out, Astra?" She shakes her head, and I can't help but laugh at the way she grips the chains a little tighter.

After a good half hour on the swing, I notice she is finally growing restless, and stop the swing.

"Should we . . . " I start, but Astraea's feet hit the ground and she is off running. Shocked at how fast she moved, I stand motionless for a moment before chasing after her.

"Astra, where are you going?" I call after her. Her blonde curls fly like ribbons behind her as she runs. Her beanie is now clutched tightly in her fist. Up ahead, I see a dog walker and chuckle. How Astraea spotted the dogs from where we were, I do not know. She loves dogs, or any animal for that matter. It doesn't matter what size they are. I catch up to her as we near the dogs and grab her hand. She looks up at me, pointing at the dogs, hope shining in her bright blue eyes.

"I know, sweet girl, but you can't be running off like that," I say gently, then turn to the dog walker, flashing the teenager a bright smile. He looks slightly alarmed, and I try to stifle my laugh.

"Hi, is there any chance we could have a play with the dogs just for a bit?" I ask. He looks around and then back at me, seeming a little flustered. Hesitating, he looks down to find Astraea already in the middle of four large dogs. He seems speechless, looking at me with wide, worried eyes as Astraea plays with what looks like a German shepherd, a couple of labradors and a ridgeback. I am actually quite surprised all these dogs can be walked together and the young teenager can maintain control, because they are some powerful dogs. I cast some of my magic out to see if he is more than he seems, but nothing. He is a human who just happens to be incredible with animals.

I shrug at his surprised look. "She likes animals."

"Uh huh," he replies, looking baffled.

Looking down at the dogs, I notice one of the labradors has a slight limp. Frowning, I crouch down and call it over. The dog comes to me without hesitation. Noticing Astraea gazing at me, I send her a wink and grab the dog's leg, gently lifting it off the ground. Peering up at the teenager, I catch the look of impatience crossing his face, but as he turns to watch a group of young women as they pass, I take advantage of his distraction. I cast my magic into the dog's leg, searching out the injury. It only takes a couple of seconds to find the old injury that didn't quite heal properly and a few more seconds to heal it. I drop the dog's leg, *done*. Good as new. Before I can stand, the dog jumps at me, bowling me over in excitement and gratitude. I let out a laugh, unable to help myself. The dog's joy is infectious.

I push through the door of my bookstore, seeing Suzy sitting behind the counter, book in hand, and grin when she looks up. "Hey Suzy," I call out, ushering Astraea in and closing the door behind me.

"Nesrin, Astraea, what are you doing here on your day off?" She greets us, coming around the counter. Her vibrant purple hair is up in a messy bun today, the color setting off her blue eyes. I absolutely love her bohemian style, it suits her bright and cheery personality. Nothing I would ever be able to pull off. I am more of a jeans and jacket person. Throw in a dagger and some boots as my accessories, and I am ready to go.

Astraea's grip tightens on my leg, peeking her big blue eyes up at my college student employee. Suzy is eighteen, and studies art history at the local university. I enjoy listening to her ramble on about Plato and his theories of art.

I smile warmly at her, tucking my hair behind my ear. "I just wanted to check and see how things are going today?"

"Good. It was a busy morning, but this afternoon is quiet. I did want to ask about the new door though?"

I tilt my head back and let out a long, pained groan. "Don't remind me."

Laughing, she turns for the counter and takes her seat again. Resting her chin in her hand, she raises a perfectly manicured eyebrow, her bangles jingling.

"This sounds like an interesting story," she says in a light tone.

My chest tightens as I think back to the night before, but I put on a smile, for Suzy's sake. "No, not really. Some young kids tried to break in last night. But I scared them off."

She sits up straight, concern shining in her eyes. "Seriously? Are you okay?"

I wave off her concern. "I'm fine."

"You're tiny and alone here most nights, Nesrin," she deadpans.

"I can protect myself,"

"With your faithful taser?"

"Hey. Don't knock my taser. It works in a pinch," I retort.

Suzy looks unconvinced. "Uhhhhhuhhhhh."

I shake my head. People assume because I'm small, that I must be defenseless. But Suzy is a human. She doesn't know I have magic to protect myself. "Look, let's shut up early today and I'll take you for a coffee?"

Suzy's blue eyes light up. "Really?"

"Yes. My treat."

Snatching up her bag, she swings it over her shoulder and holds a hand out to Astraea, who just stares at it. Laughing, she bends down, winking at Astraea. "One day soon you will like me. I won't give up on you."

I pat Suzy on the shoulder. "Don't take it personally. She's just shy."

"I know. Kids usually love me," she says, blowing out a breath and I watch with a grin as Astraea takes a step closer to her and slowly reaches up and takes Suzy's hand. And Suzy, to her credit, swallows her surprise and widens her eyes at me.

I turn to hide my grin, opening the door. "To Blue's."

The walk doesn't take long, and my stomach rumbles as soon as we get to the door. Which is absurd, because we had pancakes for breakfast and that usually keeps me full all day.

"God, I love the smell of this place," Suzy groans.

Laughing, I agree and hold the door open for them.

Blue's voice booms through the café, startling a few customers. "There's my precious girl."

Astraea runs around the counter and into Blue's arms. I shake my head and glance at Suzy.

"I want that reaction from her," Suzy pouts.

I hook my arm in hers and lead her over to a booth. "Just you wait, she is already warming up to you."

Blue knows our order and gets to work with his pint-sized sidekick. A young boy with a head full of green hair and warm brown eyes brings our coffees over as Blue takes Astraea into the kitchen to help prep tomorrow's muffins and cakes.

"So, how are classes going?" I ask, nodding my thanks to the boy.

"It's okay. I love the work, but my professor is a jackass," she grumbles.

I smile over the rim of my coffee cup. "He can't be that bad."

"He is the worst. I'm not a violent person, but he gets me so mad I could smack him right in that smug face." Her face goes a little flush as she speaks.

Snorting, I cough, almost choking on my blueberry muffin. I hear the door open and an icy breeze follows. Suzy splutters, choking on her coffee, my eyes flying to hers and I follow her wide gaze to the door. There, standing just inside the door, is the Alpha, Lukas. It's entirely unfair how gorgeous he is. And dangerous, I remind myself. I watch as he lifts his head slightly and slowly turns my way. *Oh no.* When he spots me, surprise flashes across his face before he can mask it. He makes his way toward us, never breaking eye contact.

I swallow the last bit of the muffin in my mouth as Suzy leans closer and whispers harshly, "You know that gorgeous man?"

I see a small tug at the corner of Lukas's mouth. He heard her. Of course he did. My face heats under his open gaze. I try my best not to notice how his black shirt stretches across his chest and biceps.

My heart is already pounding in my chest when Lukas stops in front of our table, his eyes burning into mine. "Nesrin."

I clear my throat to make sure I can manage actual words. "Lukas."

Tipping his chin down, Lukas stares at me through sparkling emerald eyes and thick eyelashes. I can't tell if he's annoyed to see me or simply entertained. I shift uncomfortably under his gaze. Suzy clears her throat, bringing me to my senses.

I drag my gaze back to Suzy. "Suzy, this is Lukas. He helped scare off those teenagers last night."

Suzy's eyes widen. "Oh. Oh. . . well, nice to meet you. Lukas," she stammers.

His eyes move off me and I can breathe again. "You, too, Suzy. I just wanted to say hi and make sure you were okay," he says, bringing his eyes back to me, his deep voice sending butterflies fluttering.

"Oh, I'm fine," I reply awkwardly. Reaching up, I twist my hair over my shoulder and play with the strands, needing something to do with my hands. His deep green eyes track the movements.

His gaze moves back to my face and he smirks. "I hope your new door was up to standards."

Suzy chokes on her coffee, and I want so badly to kick her in the shins. "Yes, it was exactly what I was hoping for. Thank you," I reply, plastering on a sweet smile.

Grinning, as if he can tell I'm full of shit, he nods and turns to leave. "Have a great day Nesrin, Suzy."

He makes his way back to the counter and orders a coffee to go. For some reason, my eyes follow his every movement. I look to Suzy, who is observing me with eyes as wide as saucers. Leaning forward, she whispers, "He is hot! Go get his number."

I jolt in my seat. "What? No."

"Yes!" Seeing my look, she rolls her eyes. "Why not?"

"He's way out of my league," I say, even as a fluttering starts in my chest, and excitement builds. I am being ridiculous.

"Bullshit!"

"What?"

"I call bullshit."

"Whatever," I say, taking another sip of my coffee. The young boy who served our food walks over and I watch Lukas stroll from the café. Suzy doesn't understand. Even if there were an attraction there, I couldn't follow through. I couldn't forget he is a shifter. And not just any shifter, the Alpha.

"Excuse me, Miss. Your order has been taken care of and I was told to give this to you." Holding his hand out, I look down at the card and reach out for it.

"What is it?" I ask, flipping it over in my hand.

The young boy smiles, a twinkle in his eye. "It's a voucher. Free coffees for a year."

My mouth drops open as I stare at the card in my hand. I'm not tight for money, but free coffee is like offering a girl diamonds. Well, to me it is. "Free coffees?"

He nods and starts to turn.

*Why?*

Stopping, the boy looks at me again. "He said it was to say thank you for helping him."

*Shit, I thought out loud again.*

"You do that a lot," Suzy laughs.

"Argh!" I groan as the boy heads back to the counter to serve the next group of people who walk in.

"Yep, I told you! Go get his number! And what did you help him with? I thought he helped you?" Suzy asks, her blue eyes filled with excitement.

"He did, but I found his nephews who were lost, and he came to get them from my shop," I explain, giving her the human version of the story.

Suzy smiles dreamily, her hands going under her chin. "How romantic. Sounds like a fairytale in the making," she muses. I roll up my napkin and toss it at her, laughing.

"Hardly. It was not romantic," I retort. I'm glad it was me working last night and not Suzy. She wouldn't have stood a chance against the hunters. Human or not, having the pups in the store would have put a target on her back.

"Go see if he is still outside and thank him," she urges. I can see her little matchmaking dreams swirling around in her head.

"He won't be out there."

Suzy smirks, "I bet you he is."

"Fine, I'll go," I relent, knowing she won't leave me alone until she gets her way.

"Go on then," she laughs, waving her hand toward the door, her array of bangles jingling.

With a very unladylike huff, I stand and walk to the door, pushing outside into the cool air. I won't be getting his number, but I will give him the voucher back. My gaze automatically goes left and I spot Lukas leaning against a sleek, black Ducati, his eyes focused on me like he was expecting me to come looking for him. I walk over, trying to control my breathing and hold out the card for him.

"This isn't necessary."

"I know."

I raise an eyebrow. "I appreciate it, but I can't take it."

Lukas takes a sip from his coffee and studies me. I can't help but squirm a little and I feel my temper rising.

"Seriously, take it!" I snap, thrusting the gift card toward him again.

"No." He doesn't seem concerned by my tone. If anything, he looks entertained.

"No?"

"Yes. Take it. Use it to buy the homeless coffees each morning on your way to work."

"How?" Then I remember Zee watching me from across the street yesterday when I was with Merve. "Nevermind." I huff, crossing my arms and eyeing Lukas and his motorbike. It is a nice bike. I've never ridden a bike before. I wonder what it would be like having my arms wrapped tightly around him. Nope. I halt that train of thought right there.

"Thank you for taking care of my pack's pups until I could get there. I didn't say it last night and I want to make it up to you," he says. "Coffee seemed like a good start."

Though my heartbeat remains loud, it slows, my body and mind relaxing with the thought that he is trustworthy.

Don't ask me where that belief comes from. I've been wary of strangers my whole life, thanks to my parents. But after what happened in Pittsburgh last year, I am completely distrusting of anyone I don't already know. Which is why, for the life of me, I don't understand myself right now.

"Okay. Well, thank you," I reply softly. I feel awkward and uncertain, and before I can say anything more, I turn and make my way back to the café. I can feel Lukas's stare on me the whole way, and force myself not to look back.

# CHAPTER FIVE

Nervous energy buzzes through my veins as I gaze at myself in the mirror. I can't pinpoint where the feeling is coming from, which only frustrates me more. After a great Sunday off with Astraea, it's back to work. The late shift again, which I prefer. I'm more of a night owl than a morning person. I need a few hours to get myself sorted in the morning. Whenever I'm feeling off, I go for my comfort color: black. I put on a tight black long sleeve thermal with black skinny jeans and boots, then wrinkle my nose at my reflection. This will just have to do. I braid my long auburn hair over one shoulder, the only splash of color to be seen. Sighing, I reach for my favorite leather jacket, and tug it on as I make my way downstairs.

Grace already came by for Astraea this morning, so alone I make my way out of the apartment building onto the street. I shift my gaze from the sidewalks to the busy street full of cars and yellow cabs. I feel antsy, and I'm not sure why. As I walk into Blue's, my mind tries to sort through the odd feelings swirling through me.

I push open the door to the cafe, and stop short. One look at Blue's concerned expression has my stomach dropping. "What's wrong?"

All sorts of scenarios spin through my head. I know Blue's wife is out of town visiting family. I haven't met her yet, but I hope she's okay.

Blue's worried eyes lock on mine. "Merve's gone. I can't find him."

My body tenses. "What do you mean, Merve's gone?"

Running his hands nervously over his apron, Blue looks at me, his mouth turned down. Worry fills his bright blue eyes.

"I haven't seen him since Saturday afternoon, Ness. It's highly unusual for him to disappear. I have owned this store for twenty-five years, and he has been on that corner for the last six," Blue replies.

Saturday afternoon? An icy chill sweeps over my body. The hunters. Could they have done something to Merve? Or maybe the shifters when they were looking for their pups? I look at Blue. He is really concerned. Merve is more than the homeless man on our street. He is a friend.

"I have a few ideas. Let me ask around and I'll let you know what I find out." I turn, heading for the door.

"Be careful, Ness," he calls after me.

"Always," I respond, pushing out the door.

Out on the street, I let out a deep breath. Leaning against the wall, I tilt my head to the sky, closing my eyes. I have to figure out how to approach the shifters and find out what they know, if anything at all, but that is going to be difficult. They hate witches, and witches hate them. Times have long since changed and witches don't hunt wolves anymore, but the relationship remains strained. I'm not like most witches though. I've never had a problem with the shifters back in Pittsburgh. I'm not sure where the shifters live in Portland, but I can find out.

Anticipation curls in my stomach at the thought of heading to Forest Park after dark again. Am I really thinking I can just walk in there and ask to talk to the Alpha? I should have gotten his number like Suzy said. Pushing off the wall, I turn and start walking toward my bookstore. If I am going to pull this off, I'll need a few special items from my office.

Walking into my store, I take a deep breath, inhaling the sweet aroma of books. If I could bottle the scent of book pages, I'd be rich. I spot Suzy with a customer and give her a wave before heading for the back of the store. It's dark when I unlock the door to my office and slip inside. No one is allowed back here. I am the only one with a key, and I keep it locked at all times. Shutting the door behind me, pinpricks of awareness scatter across my scalp. Someone either is or has been in my office. Stepping further into the room, I turn in a slow circle, looking for anything that's out of place. Everything seems untouched and in its rightful place, but I can't shake the feeling of being watched. I'm not alone.

I summon my magic and cast a wave outward, sweeping over the room. It rolls across the room in waves of color and swirls around my desk. That's when I notice a faint glow coming from behind some books and potions on my worktable. Slowly, I approach the table and feel stupid for not spotting the light when I first walked in. I gather my magic close to the surface, just in case I need it, feeling it warm my chest and hands.

I peek over the books and my gaze locks on a set of wide, glowing, violet eyes. They look up at me from a tiny delicate elven face. Her long brown hair floats around her as if she were in water. Her wings are shimmering and translucent, fluttering quietly, keeping her an inch from touching the table. She wears a sparkling green and yellow dress that seems to move and flow like water over her body.

I draw in a sharp breath. "You're a sprite," I breathe. I've never seen a sprite before. They're rare and almost never leave the forest. So, what is one doing in my store? The sprite moves out from behind the books, and I awkwardly fall into my chair, staring at the beautiful creature in front of me, letting my magic wisp away.

"Daughter of light," she whispers, bowing at the waist.

I feel a shock jolt through me at the name. I was called that name the night I was in Forest Park being chased by the wolves. The Puca I was tending to whispered it to me in my head along with its thanks before galloping off, the beautiful black horse gleaming in the moonlight. I'll never forget those luminescent, golden eyes. The sprite flitters anxiously as she lowers herself to the table, regarding me warily. I shake my head, clearing my thoughts of the Puca.

"What are you doing here? This is the last place I'd expect a sprite to show up," I say, puzzled. I relax a fraction now that the shock has worn off.

She nods her head as if she assumed as much. "I don't mean to be forward, but you need to come with me now." The demand rushes past her lips as she takes flight. I jolt back in my chair, surprised by the sudden movement.

"Why?" I question, pushing the hair that came loose from my braid out of my face.

Her expression hardens slightly, her eyes frosting over. She isn't used to being questioned. "You will see. There is no time to waste. He sent me to you and said you could help him." She turns and flies to the door.

I stand my ground. This is breaking all my rules. "Who? And where will we be going?" I demand.

The sprite spins around, flying back at me as I stand up. "All will be answered when we get there, but we must leave for Forest Park now."

My mouth drops open, but before I can ask any more questions, she murmurs, "Please."

Relenting, I spin and grab my knife belt and travel potions—some for healing, others for protection. The sprite seems troubled, and I am curious enough to follow. Besides, the park is where I was planning to head anyway.

On the way out, I ask Suzy if she can stay a bit later and close up early. I'm so lucky to have her around. I have never seen her with anyone, so I don't think she had many friends. But she is great with my customers, and very outspoken. Plus, I never have to guess how she's feeling because she always lets me know.

Pulling into the parking lot, I turn the car off, letting out a huge breath. With trembling hands, I yank out the keys from the ignition then lean forward in my seat to peer out the windshield. The sky has just started darkening, dusk is upon us. The colors that streak across the sky are a beautiful array of purples, pinks, and oranges against the backdrop of blue sky. Pushing open my door, I get out, walking around to the trunk. I snatch up my leather jacket, tugging it on, then load it up with potions. Grabbing my knife belts, I secure one around my waist, the other on my thigh. Quickly I send off a text, letting Grace know I am going to be home late. I look around for the sprite, seeing her faint glow waiting for me at the edge of the forest, but not near any of the paths. I take several deep breaths, and before I have a chance to change my mind, I jog over to the waiting sprite.

The barrier around the park has a soft pale blue shimmer to it. I lift my eyes as we pass through, watching the magic ripple and form around us. It is beautiful to watch. I sense the slight tingle of magic floating over my skin, making me squirm. Still, I can't help the smile that forms on my face as I look over my shoulder to watch the magic reform where we just passed through. Turning back around, I see the sprite watching me with a curious look.

Shrugging, I murmur, "Lead the way." I don't like sharing that I can see magic. It isn't that common a gift. Most magical beings can feel magic to some degree, even some humans, but being able to see threads of magic in colors is extremely rare. And quite useful.

"What's your name? I mean, what should I call you? Sorry, I'm a little nervous. I shouldn't have asked. It's just I have a sprite leading me into the woods after dark." I half laugh, pushing some branches aside so I can squeeze past some trees. The sprite barely casts me a glance over her delicate shoulder. I know that the pure fae don't give out their real names freely, and to do so is a great danger to them. I shouldn't have asked her name, but a nickname would be nice to know.

"This way," is her curt reply.

"You don't like me that much, do you?"

"I don't particularly care for witches," is her honest response.

Pushing a branch out of my way, I step closer. "Ah, but you don't even know me, and I'm not with the coven."

"Yes, he said that. I can also see you are different from the others."

The 'but' wasn't spoken, but I can feel it hanging in the air between us.

As time passes, the woods start to change, growing more dense, some plants becoming shades of blue and purple, a slight glow of magic floating off them. Birds and insects are humming and chirping about still, which I find a little odd for this time of day. Lifting my hand, I summon a small orb of light. This magic comes easily to me, just like clicking my fingers. I smile at the small orb floating an inch from my palm. I always love summoning light.

"There are those who would give anything to see you fall. Never give them the satisfaction. If you do, you'll become the victim of your story." The sprite's eerie voice floats on the wind. My head snaps up, alarmed by her words.

"What's that supposed to mean?" I demand, feeling my pulse quicken. Those bright violet eyes glow as she takes me in, the tension between us growing.

"You have quite a journey ahead of you," she says, turning and continuing forward. "You have the power to change the narrative, if you so choose." I wait, but she says nothing else. Having no other choice, I follow after her.

"What are you talking about?" I ask, pushing branches out of my way as I try to follow her through a thicker part of the forest. We are getting deeper into the woods, and it's growy darker by the minute. As the last of the light disappears, I feel a shudder in the air. Everything falls silent, the night becoming unusually unsettled. The spine-chilling howl of a wolf sounds and I freeze. "Who exactly are we going to see?" I whisper.

A ghost of a breeze circles around me, coating my skin with goosebumps, my jacket doing nothing to ward off the chill. My heart is thumping in a tandem of fear and anticipation. Adrenaline courses through my body, and I glance at the sprite who is still watching me with those eerily glowing eyes. Have I made a mistake in following her willingly into the woods? I recall tales from my childhood about wisps, a type of sprite said to appear as a strange ball of light. They are seen mostly at night to lure travelers off the road and into swamps or graveyards.

"Not far now, don't worry. The wolves and other creatures won't bother you," she says, reading my mind.

Sure. Like I could be that lucky.

We come to a small clearing in the trees and a faint glow pulses on the far side of the clearing, looking as if there are fireflies everywhere, but as I draw near, I realize the glow is coming from more than a dozen other sprites. I look down to see a larger lump on the ground. The sprites move away as I approach, and with the path cleared, I realize the lump is actually a person.

"Merve!" I race the last few yards and slide to my knees at his side. My hands run over him, looking for the injury I'm sure I'll find, but come up short.

*"What the fuck!?"* I fall backward, staring at Merve's lower half. That can't be right. Maybe I'm hallucinating, my imagination running rampant again. Wouldn't be the first time. I reach my hand over and poke his leg. Oh god, they're hooves. Merve is a satyr. I sit there, dumbfounded. How did I miss that? Looking back now, Merve has always had a blanket over his legs and never stood up around me. It didn't even seem odd at the time.

"Ness?" His voice is weak, and kind of slurred.

"I'm here," I choke out, still unable to tear my eyes from his hooves. Were the situation different, the look on my face would probably be considered comical.

"What's wrong? What happened to you? Blue and I were worried. Why can't you get up? Are you drunk?" I blurt out in a rush, remembering satyrs' need for alcohol. Merve lets out a strangled laugh, which seems to take a lot of effort.

"So many questions, Ness. And a wee bit stereotypical, don't ya think?" he replies with a gentle smile.

I roll my eyes at his tone. He can't blame me right now for jumping to conclusions. "Please, Merve. What's wrong?" I ask, a bit more calmly this time.

"Seems my lack of fermented drink has weakened me more than I realized, and my usual tasks drain all my energy. I can barely muster the energy to talk," he explains, his words nearly incoherent. I sit there a moment, blinking at him.

"So, you called me here to what? Bring you wine?" I question incredulously.

"No. No, I need help to get home, and maybe some herbs to help restore my energy. Much to everyone's disbelief, I'm not like most satyrs. I don't actually *like* alcohol all that much," he adds gruffly. Seeing that my comment bothered him, I feel like a bitch. I hate that I've hurt his feelings. Determined not to do so again, I rack my brain, thinking of what I know of satyrs. As the days go by without a drink, their health deteriorates. Like water for humans, the satyr cannot go more than three days without a full drink.

"I'm sorry. I didn't mean to jump to conclusions, Merve. It's just I'm more than a little shocked right now," I say, feeling a wave of embarrassment go through me. "I mean, you're a satyr," I point out, gesturing to his legs as if he doesn't know they're there.

"Yes, I am." Merve chuckles.

I move to grab some of my potions, sure I have something here to help restore some strength to at least get him to the car.

"Here, take this." I hand him a glass vial containing a mixture of all-spice, cinnamon, angelica, poppy seeds, chamomile, and a few personal touches. He doesn't hesitate to gulp it down. Honestly, it shocks me he didn't even question it. He gives me a slight nod and his usual cheeky smile. I feel all the tension from the last few hours drain out of me as I smile back, resting a hand atop his.

The potion seems to be working. Some color has returned to his face from what I can tell with only the faint light of the surrounding sprites. I reach down and grab the beanie I made for him off of the ground beside us, brushing the dirt and leaves off of it. For the first time, I notice the small horns and pointed ears as I place the beanie back on his head, then give him a weak smile and nod my approval when it's in place.

"What were you doing out here, Merve?"

"I tend to the forest once a month, making sure plants and trees are being cared for. I help the tree sprites and the water nymphs. Using my magic when I'm already depleted was stupid. But us fae creatures have to stick together in this world."

A noise sounds from behind me, making me jump. I stand, taking a protective stance in front of Merve and the sprites, even though I'm sure the sprites can handle themselves. It's instinct.

My hand goes to my dagger, easing it from its sheath at my thigh. I know that all the creatures dwelling in this place will only make a noise if they want me to know they're there.

Though, I don't know if that's a good thing or not. I peer into the darkness, searching, and see nothing. My chest feels tight, my breath strained with the pressure of staying calm. I wait a moment, then straightening up, I let out a ragged sigh. Sheathing my dagger, I turn back to Merve.

"Merve, I think it's time to go. Do you think you can make it to the car if I help you?" I ask as I spin around, coming face to face with a set of startling green eyes. A flare of bright white light erupts in front of me as I let my magic go on reflex.

"Shit! What the fuck?" Lukas's deep voice barks as he jumps back, eyes wide with shock.

I cringe, then lean forward, getting into his personal space. "Well, that's what you get for sneaking up on me in the middle of the forest at night! Who does that?" I snarl back, embarrassment making me lash out.

Both of us are doing our best to regain control of our breathing while simultaneously having a stare down. I know he's an Alpha and I shouldn't be challenging him like this, but he scared the shit out of me. In times of danger, we are nothing but reflexes and instinct, reacting without thought. Suddenly, I realize we are standing less than a foot from each other, and when Lukas's gaze drifts to my lips and his eyes darken, my pulse races for another reason entirely.

I hear a subtle cough coming from behind Lukas and look down to Merve, who seems completely fascinated with our interaction. "You two know each other?" he asks, intrigued, the empty bottle of potion spinning in his fingers before he tosses it back to me.

Catching it, I slip it in my pocket, brushing my hands on my jeans as I walk past Lukas. "Yes," I bite out, pushing my fingers against my chest in an attempt to slow my heart. He can definitely hear it.

Lukas turns, giving me a devilish smile. Obviously, I don't shock him hard enough if he's over it already. "You say it like it's a bad thing," he teases.

I blink at him. What the hell is happening right now?

"Well . . . " I shrug, dragging the word out, feeling my cheeks heat under his stare. I am at a loss for words. Unable to keep eye contact any longer, I turn back to Merve. "Can we go now?"

*Goddess, I sound like a child.*

"Sure thing, Ness. Thanks for coming to my rescue. I promise next time I will be more careful," he says in earnest, moving to get up. Rushing to his side, I help him the rest of the way, one arm slipping around his back, the other pulling his arm over my shoulders. We move to start walking and once again face Lukas, who has been silently watching our exchange.

He raises one eyebrow at me. "Interesting company you keep, Ness," he says, drawing my nickname out.

"It's Nesrin," I reply, glaring at him.

He only laughs before his deep voice drops an octave and turns rough. "Okay, Nesrin." His voice wraps around my name. The power of it rolls down my spine, and I suppress the urge to shiver. I might be mid panic attack, but I kind of like the way he says my name in his deep voice.

*Shit. What is wrong with me lately?*

Lukas grabs my free arm and we both look down to his hand on my arm. Slowly, he loosens his grip. "Let me."

I pause, eyeing him. "No."

He releases my arm, but not before his fingertips trail over the sensitive skin on the inside of my wrist, just under the cuff of my jacket. Goosebumps break out and, even with layers of clothes, I shiver in response. I hope to Hecate that he doesn't notice, but he's a shifter. No such luck. His amusement at my body's reaction to his touch is easy to see, which just pisses me off more.

Just then, I feel something light land on my shoulder and peer over to see the tiny violet-eyed sprite now resting there. She is glaring daggers at Lukas. I can't help but smirk at him, raising my eyebrow in return. Lukas just grins at me, his well-defined arms crossed over his broad chest, feet planted wide. His eyes flicker to the sprite, and he bows his head.

Then, his sparkling emerald eyes lock on mine again, causing my breath to catch. "I'll help you back to the car." Lukas starts moving in to take Merve from me, but when I go to protest, both males shoot me a look.

"Fine," I mutter, letting Lukas take hold of Merve. I trail closely behind as we make our way back through the woods. It won't take long to get back to the car with Lukas's help. I couldn't help but notice how well his clothes fit to his body and how his muscles bunch under his shirt as he helps my friend over the uneven ground. As we emerge from the woods and approach my car, I am still staring at Lukas's form—more precisely, his ass—when I realize they've stopped and are waiting for me to unlock the car. I jerk my eyes up to Lukas's and he winks over his shoulder at me. Embarrassment floods me at having been caught staring.

Goddess, how embarrassing. Like that man needs an ego boost. I cringe and move to open the door so Lukas can help Merve into the car, then quickly I round the car, ready to make my escape. But not quick enough. A large hand lands on my door as I go to open it and I turn my head, glaring at Lukas. How the hell does he move so fast?

"Yes?!" I snap, still flushed with embarrassment, my head feeling slightly foggy with the close proximity. This man is a shock to all of my senses. He moves in closer, bending so we're nose to nose, our lips a breath away. I inhale a shaky breath. Rain and sandalwood. I can feel his body heat through my clothes. It seems to wrap around me in a comforting way, along with his enticing scent.

With humor coating his words, Lukas speaks softly, "We need to talk. And, you know, a thank you would be nice, as well." His lips twitch as he pulls back just a little to look at me, one of his hands reaching up and tugging on my braid.

"I'm busy," I bite out. "Now, I have things to take care of. Thank you for your help getting my friend back to the car," I quickly add.

Lukas moves back a step, letting me open my door and get in, but before I can shut the door, he leans in close. "I'll be in touch soon." He straightens up and closes the door. Then, with a wink, he turns on his heel and strolls for the woods.

Tight coils spring up in my stomach. What on earth could he want to talk to me about? Blinking, I look over at Merve to find him smirking at me. Letting out a huff, I roll my eyes, starting up the car.

"Don't say a word," I mutter, driving us home. I don't care what he says. He will not be sleeping on the streets tonight.

# CHAPTER SIX

The next week went by uneventfully, which only made me more anxious than usual. I still hadn't heard anything from Marcus or the coven, which most would consider a blessing, but I knew deep down they were brewing something. There were no other solitary witches in Portland, which I found weird. There were no laws dictating that we needed to be part of a coven, so I didn't understand their persistence. I had changed my last name when we moved, so I couldn't be tracked from Pittsburgh. It hurt to change my name from Carson to Locke. I had kept our first names, figuring we'd be fine. No one knew about Astraea. I kept her hidden, so I figured a single mom would go under the radar. Since no one knew of her, they wouldn't be looking for a mom.

My family was originally from Germany generations ago. I know through the family grimoire they had fled Germany through Europe, where my great grandmother ended up in Ireland. It's where my grandparents met, as well as my parents. Germany had the highest witchcraft execution rate, while Ireland had the lowest. I think that was why my family had been running for so long.

As I moved around the shop putting books away, my mind drifted from my family to Lukas and his deep green eyes that reminded me of the ocean waves during a storm. Our last encounter had left me a little shaken. What did he need to talk to me about? Astraea popped into my head. I shook the thoughts away.

*Not possible.*

My cloaking spells were solid and intact. There was no way he or anyone else would be able to detect her. The upside of being able to physically see my magic, I knew when they were fading or weakening. Astraea was fully cloaked, completely hidden. Her magic, when it evolved, would be as well. I would teach her everything I knew so she could protect herself.

I move around the shelf, only to walk into a hard wall of muscle and bounce back, stumbling over my feet. "Crap!" I exclaim books falling from my hands as I tried to regain my balance.

Massive hands landed on my arms steadying me, startled I looked up into the deep green eyes I had just been thinking about. Quickly I take a step back, putting some much needed space between us, his hands falling from my shoulders and moving to the pockets of his jeans.

My cheeks heat. Feeling flustered, I scowled. "What are you doing here?"

"Hi to you too, Nesrin," Lukas said, grinning down at me. He is so tall I have to tilt my head back to look at him. I'm used to being short, but next to him I felt like a mouse.

Neither of us spoke for a moment. I wasn't sure what to say.

Goddess, how awkward could I be? Why did this man always put me off kilter? I looked around uncertainly, and tug at the hem of my jumper.

His gaze slowly roamed over me, and I flushed, trying not to think about how he saw me. I was suddenly very aware of the oversized jumper I threw on this morning, with food on it from Astraea's wayward breakfast. At least my black leggings and boots were clean. I really wanted to hide under a stack of books right now, instead I looked down at the floor, avoiding those piercing green eyes.

My eyes instantly snag on his black combat boots, then slowly unable to stop myself. I raised my eyes, following his muscular legs encased in dark jeans up to his trim waist, over his wide chest and broad shoulders in a long sleeve black Henley. My eyes travel up his face along his strong jaw with a few days growth on it. His dark hair was falling over his forehead, the color bringing out the green in his eyes. Lukas really was a gorgeous man. Too bad we weren't well suited. I had to keep reminding myself he wasn't for me.

"I told you we needed to talk," he replied, his lips curving up into a soft smile as he reaches over, tucking a piece of hair behind my ear. I was so mesmerized by that gentle smile, I didn't even flinch when his fingers grazed my cheek. Shaking my head, I went to walk past him, but he gently clamped a hand around my wrist, stopping me from moving past. I looked up to find those green eyes swirling with an emotion I couldn't name.

"It's important," his voice wrapped around me, making me sway slightly towards him. When I didn't reply, he continued. "When do you close up? I can meet you back here, then we can take a walk, maybe get coffee?"

I look down at the hand that's clamped gently around my wrist, his thumb rubbing circles on the back of my hand, a total contradiction to the power I felt rolling under his skin. This was the most powerful shifter in the Pacific northwest, and he was being gentle and kind to me. He could just demand a meeting right now and drag me away, but he was choosing to be nice.

I nodded dumbly, unable to speak while he was rubbing those circles on my hand. My mind becoming fogged under his touch. I hear Lukas' chuckle, and my eyes snap to his. "Going to be needing a time, sweetheart."

"Huh?" My mind caught on, *sweetheart*, and stalled embarrassingly.

He flashed me a devastating smirk, causing my butterflies to take flight in my stomach. He knew exactly what he was doing to me.

*Bloody wolf.*

"What time do you want me to meet you back here?" he asks, his voice was colored with amusement.

Blinking several times, I feel my face heat, shaking off the effect he had on me. I pulled my arm free, rubbing at my wrist. "I'm closing at seven, so come by around then." I replied, shifting around nervously on my feet.

Lukas smiled, "Beautiful." Then he turned and walked out the door.

*What just happened?*

I was a mess. It was six thirty, and I was glancing at the door every other minute. I didn't know what to think when it came to Lukas, and I was really worried about people finding out about Astraea. The sound of rain drew my attention to the window. When had it started to rain again? The water was calling to the magic in me, the smell in the air calming me slightly from the scenarios that were running wild in my head. I really needed to calm the fuck down. Lukas had not indicated that this was about anything bad. Plus, if Lukas knew about me, about Astraea, there is no way he'd be this calm or nice to me.

Turning the lights off at the back of the store, I make my way to the front door to flip over the open sign when Marcus came strolling in, halting my steps. I watched as he pushed past me, an unreadable expression on his face.

*Fuck, what was he doing here? This wasn't good.*

"Marcus, what do you want," I sigh, I was tired and exhausted. I was over being hounded by the coven.

Marcus walked up to the counter, leaning against it casually, crossing one ankle over the other. His black eyes were gleaming with dry humor, like he knew something I didn't. He picks up a book, flicking it open, ignoring me. I storm over and snatch the book from his hands and close it.

"What are you doing here?" I snap, trying to hide the tremble in my hands. My stomach drops as he stared back at me. His eyes always unnerved me with the lack of color and warmth, but I would never show it, never let him see how he affected me. The coven's persistence was wearing thin, and I didn't trust them one bit.

"I have been waiting patiently for you to come to me and explain what you were doing that night in Forest Park, only to get reports you visited again," He accused.

I barely suppressed my growl. "I don't owe you an explanation, Marcus. Wait. Are you having me watched?"

Marcus pushed off the counter, coming towards me. I stood my ground. I would not back down, not ever. "So, what if I am? You know the high priest wants to meet you. He is worried you will upset the balance we have here if you don't join us."

My fist clenched as annoyance rolled over me. "If he wants to see me, tell him to get off his lazy ass and come see me himself." I was fuming.

My mother always told me to never dismiss your gut instinct. She would tell us girls all the time to trust in ourselves. *"You are not paranoid. Your body can pick up on bad vibrations. Listen to them."*

And Marcus, in this moment and his coven, were sending me a ton of bad vibes. I know something deep inside me says nothing about this situation is right. I need to trust my instincts.

"Nesrin, you will come with me tonight and see him. Put him at ease. You don't have a choice this time."

"Oh goodie, I get to see the wonderful high priest. How exciting," I replied dryly. This was bullshit. Of course I had a choice. There was always a choice.

"I can hear sarcasm, Nesrin," he shot back instantly.

I roll my eyes at him. "Good, because I was laying it on thick."

Marcus shook his head. "Stop putting up these pathetic attempts to avoid us because that's what they are, pathetic." He said, coming to stand a foot away. I had to tilt my head back to keep eye contact. Slowly, I blinked. I'd never seen him so furious before. Okay, yes. He was always annoyed with me about something, but there was never hostility in his eyes, not like there was now. He was practically vibrating with anger. What had gotten into him, he has never been this aggressive in his attempts to get me to go with him to meet the high priest before. It didn't make sense.

I narrow my eyes as heat rose to my face. "Fuck off Marcus, I'm not going anywhere with you."

"Why? Why keep fighting this, fighting us?" He asks.

I throw my hands up in the air and glare. "You're an askhole. You know that, right?"

His brows drop as he watches me. "May I dare ask what exactly is an askhole?"

"You are always asking pointless, obnoxious and stupid questions."

His eyes widen before he growls. "I'm not asking anything, I'm telling you."

"You need to leave me alone. Tell your precious high priest I'm not interested. Ever," I seethe, stepping forward and thrusting my finger in his face. "Also, you don't tell me what to do. No one controls me. And I will certainly never join your coven, so forget it!"

I was slightly out of breath when I finished, but relieved. Marcus' expression darkened further at my outburst. My eyes widened, and I tried to take a step back, but he moved quickly. Rushing forward, he grabbed my arm in a painful grip, twisting it slightly. A small yelp escaped my mouth. Fear shot through me, twisting my stomach. My fight or flight mode kicked in and my mind whirled with escape routes. I started drawing in the surrounding energy, gathering all the magic I could. I didn't want to use magic against him, but I would if it came to that.

"Like I said before. You don't have a choice this time," Marcus growled, turning towards the door pulling me with him, only to stop suddenly as a tidal wave of raw power rolled through the store. I looked up to see Lukas standing there, blocking the doorway. His eyes drew together as he looked between Marcus and I. His gaze went down to where Marcus had a firm, painful hold on my arm.

The air rippled and shook and I jolt as another wave of power accompanied by a loud growl ripped from Lukas' throat. I felt the blood drain from my face. This was bad.

Lukas' gaze was now locked on Marcus, who let go of me like he'd been burned. The power in the room pricked at my senses. Making my skin tighten and tingle uncomfortably.

Rubbing my arm, I stepped away from Marcus, my stance turning defensive, my muscles tense, ready to fight if I had to. Marcus' hands went up in surrender. "Alpha, anything I can help you with? You're interrupting a personal matter." His voice was full of arrogance as he regarded the pissed off shifter. He thought he was untouchable. The entire coven did. They thought themselves rulers of the whole fucking magical community here in Portland. Well, they could think again. "Not to mention the wet dog smell is terrible. Is there something you can get for that?" Marcus' nose wrinkled as he adjusted the cuffs on his shirt. His words finally penetrated my mind.

*Holy Fuck, he did not just say that.*

My eyes squeeze shut at Marcus' statement. I didn't breathe or move. I didn't dare. I can't believe he'd said that!

There was a strained silence, and I open my eyes. My gaze swiveled to Lukas, who just stood there breathing heavily. I could see his chest moving, his muscles coiling with restraint, fury lined his eyes and his answering growl was more animal than human. "What did you say to me Mage?" the power in the room became stifling. I had to defuse the situation before my store ended up ruined, or somebody got hurt. Not that Marcus didn't deserve what was surely coming his way.

"We are done here, Marcus. You need to leave now!" I was shaking as I moved towards Lukas. I needed him out the way of the door so Marcus could leave.

"Don't be stupid, Nesrin. You need to come with me," Marcus snapped, taking a step toward me, which was a dangerous move. Before anyone could react, Lukas had Marcus pinned on the ground. My eyes went wide, I couldn't help the shriek that fell from my mouth. How had he moved so fast?

A heavy hand landed on my shoulder. I spun around so fast I almost fell over, my hands flaring with magic, ready to attack.

"Easy there, honey," a gentle voice said.

I relaxed just a little. Zee moved in front of me, shielding me from the situation taking place a few feet away. I put a hand on his back to help steady myself. His shoulders tensed for a moment, then relaxed under my touch. I peeked around his large form to look at the two males on the floor. Lukas was leaning over Marcus, whispering something in his ear, the color draining from his face rapidly. When Lukas pulled back, he looked over his shoulder, his eyes clashing with mine. He seemed to be making sure I was okay. I gave him a small nod. His deep green eyes darkening a few degrees as we stared at each other. I startle as my phone vibrates in my pocket. I duck back behind Zee and pull it out, looking down at the screen.

Weird, Grace never calls me. "Hi Grace-" was all I managed before she cut me off.

"Nesrin. Thank god, you answered. Where are you? You need to come back right now." She sounded panicked. Grace was never panicked.

Moving further away from Zee, I drop my voice. "What's happening? Is Astraea okay?" My body seizing up at the thought of something happening to her.

"Yes, we are fine. Well no, I mean someone is trying to get in the apartment, your wards are holding up for now but it's not stopping them from trying and they are determined to get in here, Nesrin," Grace whispered into the phone. Her voice held a note of fear.

*Wait, Grace knew about my wards?*

I looked up to see Zee watching me, concern filling his features. Obviously, with his heightened sense of hearing, he could hear what Grace was saying.

"I'll be there in five minutes, Grace." Hanging up, I spin to the others. "I need to leave, like, right now." My voice is surprisingly calm compared to the panic building inside of me.

I grab my jacket from the counter and quickly make my way to the door with Zee right on my heels. Clutching my hand, he pulls me towards a motorbike on the curb. "This will be quicker," he said, handing me a helmet. Just then Lukas appeared getting on the bike first. He started up the bike, and I didn't hesitate to get on after him.

"Zee, take out the trash and lock up. Meet us at her place," was all he said before we were off. I didn't even spare Marcus a second thought. The ride to my apartment was barely a minute. Lukas had just pulled up to the curb, and I was off running, tossing the helmet at Lukas. I heard a curse behind me but didn't slow. Anger swept through me like wildfire, chasing away any fear I had for my own safety. All I could think was someone was trying to get to my sweet girl and Grace.

I took the stairs two at a time. When I reach our floor, there was a witch in front of my door at the end of the hall. She had long black hair and was wearing black leathers. I hated to admit it, but she looked badass. I also noticed that she had put a containment spell around the area where she was working, so no humans could see or hear her.

"Excuse me, can I help you?" I strolled towards her as she spun around. A look of shock flashed across her face for a split second, then it was gone, a smirk taking its place. She looked familiar. Tilting my head, I studied her features.

Her arms crossed over her chest as she stood there smugly. "I see Marcus failed."

Marcus? Her eyes went past me, focusing on Lukas as he moved around me. I appreciated the chivalry, I did, but this was my fight. They came after the only family I had left.

"I see the rumors are true." Her voice carried a mocking tone that made my skin crawl, but I forced myself not to show any signs of irritation.

"What rumors?"

"Poor Marcus, he will be heartbroken," she pouted.

"You and Marcus can burn in hell for all I care." I shot back, stepping around Lukas.

*Don't stab anyone. It's illegal to stab people for being stupid,* I thought as I approached her.

The witch just laughed in my face. I'd obviously spoken that out loud. I reacted without thinking. I strike out with the heel of my palm straight to her nose. Her head whipped back, and she fell into the door behind her. The glare she sent my way said I was going to pay for that. She raised her foot to land a kick, but I managed to move in time. I lunged sideways as her boot glanced off my thigh.

"My brother said you were feisty," the witch mocked. She was Marcus' sister? Now I know why I thought she looked familiar.

I heard scuffling behind me and risked a look over my shoulder to see Lukas fighting a mage. They had come prepared. A flash of silver appeared in the mage's hand. A rope made of silver. Though silver is not deadly to shifters, it can still hurt them. Unlike iron and wolfsbane, that was lethal. But then again, wolfsbane is not just poisonous for wolves. It contains a neurotoxin, aconitine, that can kill almost anything. And why I was thinking about that now, I had no idea. Lukas let loose a growl that shook the walls and raised the hair on my arms. He was the Alpha, he would be fine.

With a second to spare, I broke out of my thoughts. Raising an arm to block the oncoming blow and dodging the witch's knee. I struck out, aiming for her throat, but she deflected me easily. We circled each other. The witch's eyes glittered dangerously. Moving faster than I thought I was capable of, my right fist connected with her face, before either of us had realized I'd struck out. Pain exploded in my hand as her head snapped back. She stumbled, but recovered quicker than I thought she would. Fists clenched, she stormed forward. I duck to avoid the punch that would surely have me seeing stars. As I pop up, I pivot on one foot. Lifting my right leg, I aim a well-placed kick to her midsection, knocking her off balance. I was so focused on her I hadn't noticed the other mage creeping up behind me. A hard hit landed on the back of my legs, and I stumbled forward, landing on one knee. Biting back my surprise, I take advantage of the position. Quickly reaching into my boot, my fingers wrap around the cool handle of my dagger. I spin around on my knee, flicking my wrist as I let the dagger fly. The mage drops to the ground, a bellow of pain and rage coming from him as he held his leg where the dagger protruded. I didn't allow the smile to grace my lips as I focused my attention back on Marcus' sister. She had returned to my apartment door. I muttered a few words, sending a spiral of magic her way. Her feet are swept out from under her, and she lands hard on her back. I take a step towards her, but movement from the mage catches my attention. I turn in time to see the mage pull the dagger from his leg, glaring at me as he did. Raising an eyebrow at him, I wait. He doesn't disappoint. The mage charges me, roaring like an enraged fool. I sidestep him easily, considering the cramped space. Muttering a few words, I draped my magic over him like a blanket and trapped him. I smirk as he struggles against my spell.

A body slammed into me, knocking me to the ground. My teeth snapped together on impact as a head collided with mine. That was going to hurt tomorrow. Laying on my back, I stare up at the ceiling dazed for a moment. I went to push up, but hands clamped around my throat, pushing me back onto the ground, squeezing painfully. Tears built, burning my eyes while I tried to get precious air into my lungs. Fear flooded my body, making my limbs tremble as I looked into Marcus' sisters empty black eyes. I struggled to loosen her grip on me. Fighting the light-headedness, I reached deep down inside myself and dragged up my defensive magic. Placing my hands on her chest, a bright white light flared. It exploded outwards, sending her flying off me to land ten feet down the hall.

The witch landed in a heap on the floor, stunned. I gasped for breath, coughing as I rolled over onto my stomach. Slowly, I pushed up on weak, trembling arms. I looked to where the witch had fallen to see she was gone, turning I looked the other way and notice Lukas, and the other mages were gone as well.

*Where the fuck did they go?*

I grabbed the wall to steady me, my legs felt like noodles as I stood. I made my way to the apartment door, using the wall to keep myself upright. With shaky hands, I unlock it and push inside. "Grace, it's me. I'm here," I rasped, shutting the door behind me. I turned to the small living area where Grace and Astraea huddled in the corner behind my giant lounge.

Astraea saw me and pushed out of Grace's arms, running as fast as she could towards me. Dropping to one knee, I took her in my arms, squeezing tightly.

"I'm here sweet girl, I'm here."

She made no noise, arms just squeezing me tightly around the neck. Grace approached, looking warily at the door. "They're gone," I reassured her.

Grace nodded, wringing her hands, "I'll give you a minute" before heading for the kitchen.

A loud bang sounded at the door, startled we all jumped. "Nesrin, it's Lukas and Zee," Lukas' deep voice called through the door. I exhaled softly and rose, taking Astraea with me and moving to the door.

Wanting to be sure I look through the peephole seeing the two shifters standing there waiting patiently, I unlocked the door and stepped aside so they could pass. Lukas and Zee just stood there, making no move to enter. They were both staring at Astraea, shock and confusion on their faces. Lukas shuts his face down pretty quickly, but I saw the look of longing there, as well as hurt?

Letting out a long exhale which stung my throat, I murmur. "Are you planning on standing here all night, or do you want to come in?"

Both seem to shake out of it at the sound of my voice and enter my apartment. I shut the door behind them and turn. These two huge shifters make my apartment seem so small. There was really nowhere to put them besides the couch. Lukas' gaze roamed over me, stopping on my neck. His eyes flashed yellow, a growl slipping from his throat. Astraea's grip on me tightened and she let out a tiny whimper. My heart sped up. That was the closest thing to noise I've heard her make in nearly a year.

I sent a glare at Lukas. "Would you calm down? I'm fine but you're scaring Astraea." I seethed, holding her a little tighter. At that, Lukas looked at the little girl in my arms and his eyes soften. Zee seems to be mesmerized by Astraea as well. It was like they'd never seen a toddler before. I peer down at Astraea, who was now peeking out from my arms. Lukas stepped closer, reaching his hand up to run his fingers gently over my neck where I'm sure bruises were appearing. Shivers ran across my body, scattering goosebumps at the touch. "It looks worse than it is," I whisper.

"It should never have happened," Lukas replied.

*No, it shouldn't have.*

"They are gone. They took off pretty quickly when they saw Zee coming." Lukas informed me. I look down at Astraea, running a gentle hand over her head.

"Is she yours?" Lukas asked softly as he motioned to Astraea. I smile at the blonde head rested on my shoulder before I meet his gaze.

"Yes, she is." Because she was mine, in every way that counted.

Zee was looking around my apartment, taking in the small space. I wasn't ashamed of my apartment or what it must look like to them. It was home, and I had worked hard for what we had. Lukas must have seen something in my expression and whispered gently, "It's perfect." My heart may have skipped a beat at his words.

Astraea had turned in my arms and was eyeing Lukas with curiosity. "Astraea, my sweet girl, this is Lukas, my friend, and over there is Zee. Lukas, Zee this is Astraea." She looked at me with shy, curious eyes. I nodded silently, telling her everything was okay. Astraea slowly turned back to Lukas, who gave her a sweet smile. One I didn't think he'd be capable of. She lifted her arms to him. The shock of her going to him so willingly rolled through me. Even Grace gasped from the kitchen. Lukas' eyes darted to mine, silently asking for permission. I nod, and he gently lifted her from my arms into his. My heart rapped against my ribs almost painfully as I watched her go to him. Apart from me, Astraea had only ever really gone to Grace and Blue willingly. Zee came up next to me, nudging me with his elbow, and I looked over to find him smirking at me. Whatever. I elbowed him back. I turned back to Lukas and Astraea to see her snuggle her tiny body into his massive chest and my heart melted. Lukas looked up at me and I saw that longing in his eyes again. I hadn't imagined it.

I cleared my throat, which hurt like a bitch. "Take a seat and I'll get us some drinks and we can talk."

"No need dear. I'll get the drinks. Is coffee good for everyone?" Grace asked, looking as nervous as I felt. I'd forgotten all about her knowledge of the wards until now and I need to ask her how she knew. That could come later. I had a feeling it was going to be a long night.

# CHAPTER SEVEN

I make my way over to the opposite end from where the shifters are sitting on my giant corner sofa with Astraea, after having taken her back from Lukas.

"Soooo . . . " I say, drawing the word out as Astraea gets comfortable on my lap with her stuffed wolf teddy, her eyes barely staying open as I stroke her hair. I chuckle softly at her attempts to stay awake. I love watching her fall asleep. Some nights I could sit there for hours and just stare at her, my heart swelling with love at her precious face. She reminds me of an angel. So sweet and innocent.

"How do you know Marcus?" "What did Marcus want?" both Lukas and Zee say at the same time, drawing my attention away from Astraea. They don't bother to look at each other, just keep their intense gaze locked on me. Waiting. It's totally intimidating. To have them both stare at me with so much intensity, it has my stomach tumbling with nerves.

"The coven has been harassing me since I moved to Portland. I refuse to join them, and they aren't too happy about it. Seems I'm upsetting the balance." I roll my eyes at their ridiculous notions.

Grace lets out an angry huff from where she sits beside me, and I glance at her with a raised eyebrow. "You know of the coven?" I ask curiously. Grace looks sheepishly at me, wringing her hands once more, her long gray hair coming loose from its braid.

"Yes. They are, I mean, they govern all of us magical creatures here in Portland. That high priest considers himself a king." Disdain drips from her voice, taking me by surprise. I have never heard her sound anything but sweet.

*Wait what?*

"Wait, magical creatures? Grace, what are you? Because I'd notice if you had a glamor spell on you," I add, turning more fully toward her. Grace doesn't know of my ability to see through magic spells, glamors, and enchantments. I thought she was just some harmless old lady who was kind enough to help a single parent. Seems I'm not the only one hiding things.

Grace looks nervously at Lukas and Zee, who are both just waiting silently for her response. She takes a seat next to me, seeming to gather herself before speaking. "Well, I'm a Banshee." At the shock on my face, she rushes to reassure me, but I hold my hand up, stopping her. I feel like the ground has fallen out from under me.

Banshees only appear to warn a family that a loved one is going to die. "Why here, why us?" I breathe, unable to move, scared of her answer.

"It's not what you think, Nesrin. I knew your Grandparents, Emrick and Guinevere. I made them a promise before they were murdered. Then your parents left Ireland before I could contact them. I followed them to America so I could keep that promise, but I failed them." Grace is looking at me with so much earnestness I can't bear it.

I look away, taking a moment to rein in my emotions. "Murdered? My grandparents weren't murdered," I hiss, sliding a sleeping Astraea onto the lounge so I don't disturb her. I have so many questions that I don't know which to ask first. My parents never told us why we had to leave Ireland, only that bad people were looking for us.

"Yes, they were. There is so much you don't know. I don't understand why such details were kept from you. After all, you can't have justice without the truth," Grace says, moving a little closer before she continues, "I swear I knew your family. I thought I could help your parents, but I was too late. After their deaths, I realized it wasn't over, so I followed you and your sister, watching from afar until I thought the time was right to make myself known." Grace was wringing her hands again and casting nervous looks toward the two wolves occupying the other half of the lounge.

"Wait, you knew what wasn't over?" I question, a sense of dread washing over me like icy cold water. What isn't she saying?

Blinking rapidly, I try to sort through my thoughts. I am so confused. My grandparents died in a fire and my parents died in a car crash, helping another witch. Or so I thought. I stand and start pacing in front of the tv, my mind going over all the details my parents ever told me.

"Them hunting you, when your sister was ki–" Grace starts, but I cut off her words.

"Hunting us!? No." I shake my head, refusing to believe what she's saying. No one is hunting us. *Then why did you leave*

*Pittsburgh in the dead of the night?* a little voice in the back of my head whispers.

"Nesrin, you have to know they are coming for you."

"Who's coming for her?" Lukas's deep voice startles me.

Grace's eyes dart his way and she visibly swallows. Looking back at me, her voice quivers. "Nesrin, I'm sorry. Niamh–" my heart thuds painfully at the name.

"That's enough. I can't talk about this yet, Grace. Not about that. I need you to leave."

I am pleading with her to stop talking. I realize I am being unreasonable, but I don't want to hear this right now. Betrayal is running hot through my system. Why didn't she tell me the truth before? With Lukas and Zee here, I just won't expose myself like that.

I send Grace a look, hoping she understands. "Grace, I can't talk about it," I whisper.

I want answers. I really do, but not with an audience. The glimpse of hurt on Grace's face is something I hate. Grace stands slowly, as if she were trying not to startle me.

"I understand. When you're ready I'll be waiting," she says and turns to leave.

Astraea, having woken during the commotion, slides off the lounge and walks up to Grace, hugging her legs. A lump forms in my throat and an ache in my chest as I observe the two of them. Grace has become part of our lives and I know I'll need to talk to her soon, just not right now.

"Grace," I choke out. She looks over at me as she nears the front door. I can't get anything else past my lips. I just hope she can read my face well enough to know I'm sorry. Tears burn my eyes as I glance away, my emotions getting the better of me. I feel a few tears fall down my cheek and I quickly wipe them away as I hear the front door click shut softly, the sound resonating through the apartment.

Taking a few deep breaths, I get my emotions under control, blinking away the tears in my eyes just as a low whistle follows. I turn, looking at Zee in question.

"What?" Zee says, leaning his elbows on his knees, looking between Lukas and me. "She is a Banshee. That's . . . wow. I have never met a banshee before," Zee admits with a shrug. Lukas hasn't taken his eyes off me, regarding me very closely. I can't even pretend I'm okay right now, so I don't try.

I flop back down on the couch dramatically and stare at Lukas. "It's been a long night," I mutter, feeling the weight of today dragging me down.

"Do you want to talk about it?" Lukas asks from his spot on the sofa, hands clasped in front of him as he leans forward.

Clearing my throat, I mumble. "No."

"I do," says Zee, resting back in the chair, getting comfortable, feet landing on my coffee table. My eyes widen at his shamelessness, and I cast him a glare.

"Of course, you do," I retort, rubbing my temples. I can sense a headache forming and it's the last thing I need. All I want is to curl up in bed and forget tonight even happened.

"Well, it's not every day this kind of shit happens," Zee says casually.

"Well, should I get us some snacks and we can laugh and joke over the calamity that is my life?" I snap.

Zee's eyebrows shoot up. I deflate immediately, letting out a sigh. I glance toward my room. Would it be rude to just turn around and go to bed? They can do whatever they want, but this conversation is not happening tonight. This shit can wait till morning.

Lukas and Zee share a look. I don't like that look. They are silently communicating, which is rude. I cross my arms over my chest and tap my foot, waiting, doing my best to bite my tongue. Astraea walks over, grabbing her wolf from the lounge, and lifts her arms. I pick her up and look at the two men on my couch.

I have my out. Thanks, Astraea.

"I'm putting Astra to bed," I announce and turn abruptly, walking down the hallway and into Astraea's room. I get her settled into the bed, closing the curtains and turning on her night light. A beautiful rainbow of colors dances around the room. Astraea sighs and snuggles deeper into her blankets. I can't help but smile and sit down next to her. I run my fingers through her curls and sing her an old Irish nursery rhyme my mother sang to Niamh and I when we were little. Astraea is fast asleep before I'm halfway through, but I finish the song, needing this moment with her. I lean down, pressing my lips to her head. "I love you, sweet girl," I whisper gently into her hair. Reluctantly, I stand and slowly make my way over to the door. I close it most of the way and turn back toward the kitchen.

My steps are heavy as I make my way back to the living area. I frown, looking around. "Where is Zee?" I ask, finding the apartment empty, bar Lukas, who is in the kitchen, putting the last of the dishes in the sink. I watch him in silence, waiting for his reply. Finally, he turns, his eyes catching mine. I could get lost in their deep, stormy green depths.

"I sent him home."

Lukas moves closer, standing a foot in front of me. He reaches up, running his fingers lightly over my cheek. "I thought you could use some rest," he explains. I want to move those last few steps into his arms. If I do, I might never let go.

*Shit, where did that thought come from?*

"Okay, well, I guess you better go, then." I go to move around him, but he steps to the side, blocking my way. Tilting my head back, I peer up into his handsome face. There is concern in those green eyes, and determination. I can see it in the set of his jaw.

*Oh man, what's he up to now?*

Lukas smirks before his expression grows serious. "I'm staying here tonight, Nesrin. I need to make sure you're safe, you and Astra," he says in a way that means he's not asking but telling me. Alphas!

Damn him for saying Astra, but I have to admit, I will sleep better knowing he's here after what happened tonight.

"You look tired," Lukas says, moving even closer, so close I have to crane my neck to keep eye contact. "I'll sleep on the sofa." His voice is deep and warm, and I feel my heart pick up with the sound of it.

"Okay," I agree.

The shock on his face must mean he thought I'd put up a fight, but I don't have the energy. I shrug.

"What? I'm not that dumb to not appreciate the protection." The realization that I'll be sharing a space with this gorgeous man hits me and my eyes widen. Suddenly, I feel very self-conscious. I just hope the blush I feel working its way across my pale skin isn't visible in the dimmed lights. There is something about him that sets me on edge, leaving me feeling off balance.

"I'll get you some blankets," I blurt. I turn, hurrying down the hall to the linen closet and return with a blanket and pillow. I hand them over to him and say goodnight. Quickly, I head down the hall to my room, not waiting for him to reply. I take a quick shower, wondering if I should have offered one to Lukas, but the thought of him naked in my shower makes my brain short circuit and my skin flush with heat. I jump into bed and fall asleep the quickest I have in a long time.

# CHAPTER EIGHT

A ll I can feel is the suffocating heat. Smoke is wrapping its way around me as if it were alive and trying to steal the air from my lungs. I open my mouth and try to scream, but no noise comes out. The smoke just fills my lungs. I start kicking my legs out, thrashing around to get the thick plumes of smoke away from me, but the more I struggle, the tighter its hold on me becomes. Like a snake curling its way around me, squeezing the air from my body, the life from my soul. It threatens to drag me down into the depths of unbearable heat. Fear and frustration war inside me, my body fighting for all it is worth.

A woman's laughter echoes in the distance, sounding cold and cruel. Suddenly, a loud bang has me jerking in my binds, the smoke seeming alive, coiling tighter, refusing to let me go. I can't tell where any of the noises are coming from. All I see and sense is smoke. I am trapped, completely helpless. I hate it.

Suddenly I feel a coolness sweep over me, fighting away the burn of the heat. I become weightless for a moment. The binds around me loosen, then release. The smoke recedes slightly, my consciousness being tugged away by a deep, soothing voice filled with concern. My eyes twitch at the touch of fingers gliding through my hair, the strands falling through fingers, so much like I do with Astraea. I struggle to open my eyes, my eyelids heavy, but I manage to get them open. I'm met with a set of startling green eyes looking down at me. Blinking slowly, I realize my head is on Lukas's chest. He is stretched out against the headboard of my bed, one arm wrapped around me, the other is brushing away the sweaty hair sticking to my face.

He dips his head closer so he can look me in the eye, "Hey, it's okay, you're okay," he whispers softly. His voice is so tender and full of concern. I want to scream, cry, and rage for Niamh and Hunter who left this world too soon, for Astraea who will never know her parents, for me losing my best friend and sister all in that terrible fire.

"I'm sorry," I choke out, my throat still raw from my nightmare. My muscles were trembling from the tension that holds me captive. Lukas's hand continues to run over my hair in soothing motions, and I can feel myself slowly relaxing, melting into him and the comfort he is providing.

"You have nothing to apologize for, sweetheart," Lukas says, drawing me closer to his chest, wrapping me in his arms. I let out a sigh, grateful to have him here with me. We lay here in silence for so long I drift back off to sleep, letting the exhaustion from the day drag me under.

Morning comes too quickly. I don't want to move. I'm soaking in the warmth of my bed as I snuggle down deeper under the covers. My eyes fly open as I notice something tighten around my waist. Embarrassment has my cheeks heating. And I realize I'm still wrapped in Lukas's arms. He is only in his jeans, which are unbuttoned and dangerously low on his hips. My head is still resting on his warm, bare chest. My fingers twitch, wanting to explore the dips and swells of his body. Curling my hand into a fist, I refuse to give into temptation. Biting my lip, I do my best to keep my breathing even. I can just make out the edge of a tattoo on his side that trails down and under the waistband of his boxer briefs. I really want to know how far down it goes, where it stops. I know it goes up and over his shoulder, trailing down his left arm to his wrist. This man is perfection. He is dangerous, and he seems to push all the right buttons. I want to push him away and hold on to him as tight as I can. I wish he could be mine.

What, now? Where the hell did that thought come from? Get yourself together, Nesrin. He is only comforting you. You can't have him. He is not for you.

Letting out a sigh, I know I have to make my escape. I slowly try to untangle myself from him. Holding my breath, I push up on my elbow and slowly raise my eyes to look down at his face and startle. His vibrant eyes lock on mine and I draw in a deep breath, my chest tightening. He is staring at me with a soft smile on his lips. His arms tighten around my shoulders, drawing me back into him.

"Morning, Nesrin." Lukas's deep voice is rough with sleep. It resonates through me, coiling in my stomach, making me blush.

"Morning," I mumble, breaking his hold on me and sitting up, avoiding eye contact. Staring at him is like looking at the sun sometimes. Big, bright, and warm. I'll get burned if I'm not careful. I feel his fingers slide up my neck and pull my chin back to look at him. Concern has now replaced the easy-going smile from before.

"Are you okay?" Lukas whispers like he is afraid if he speaks too loudly, I'll run, and you know what? I probably would right now.

"I don't know. I'll let you know once I've had a coffee," I say with a smile, needing to lighten the mood. My nightmares are the last thing I want to think about or talk about.

I clear my throat, looking up at him. "Thank you for last night, for being there. Handling Marcus and helping scare off the coven." I don't mention saving me from my own nightmares.

A hard look crosses his face, and I feel my pulse quicken. His fingers toy with the ends of my hair. "You're welcome," he murmurs softly, eyes fixated on my mouth. My throat goes dry, and I unconsciously lick my lips and regret it the moment his eyes flare, igniting with desire.

At hearing the bedroom door push open, I sit up, grateful for the interruption. I see Astraea standing in the doorway, blinking her large blue eyes at us.

"Morning, sweet girl," I say, pushing off the bed. I stand on sore legs and stretch, doing a quick check of my body. Apart from stiff legs and my bruised throat, I'm feeling surprisingly good. I let my arms fall back down to my sides, and realize I'm only in my favorite black panties and a tight singlet. I peer over at Lukas and find him staring at my bare legs. His eyes roam up my body like a physical caress, and I suppress a shiver. His eyes make it to

mine. A lazy grin takes over his face, the smug ass. I reach for the
bed, picking up a pillow and throwing it at him. He catches it
before it hits his face. Amusement lights his eyes, and he laughs
as he gets up, reaching for his shirt on the floor, muscles and skin
rippling as he tugs it over his head.

Does he know the effect he has on me? The cheeky smirk he
sends me over his shoulder says he does.

He walks over to Astraea. "Good morning, beautiful," he says
and swings her up in his arms with no hesitation whatsoever. Her
laughter rings out, drawing my eyes to her. Shock freezing me
in place.

She laughed. *What the actual fuck?*

A barrel of emotions tumbles through me. I can't seem to get
a grasp on any of them. My chest heats with magic and my eyes
burn with tears. My hand shoots out, gripping hold of the dresser
so I don't stumble. Astraea is looking at Lukas like he hung the
moon just for her. My girl is smitten.

Not that I can blame her.

The shock slowly wears off, and a smile overtakes my face. My
heart aches something fierce because this is the first time I have
heard her laugh since the fire and it's a beautiful sound. A lump
forms in my throat. I turn quickly, grabbing some clothes from
the drawer and pulling them on before either can notice. Once
my emotions are in check, I turn around and find I'm alone. I
slowly make my way to the kitchen where Astraea is standing
on a chair watching Lukas with a keen eye making coffee. Lukas
turns to me, concern clear on his face. He must have seen my
moment in the room.

Before he can ask about it, I clear my throat. "You said you had things to discuss with me, that it was important? We never got a chance last night,"

"It can wait. I don't want to burden you right now. Not with the coven breathing down your neck," Lukas replies, turning back to finish the coffees. I see how stiff he has gone. Whatever he wishes to talk to me about is important. At least to him.

"I'm alright Lukas, you can tell me. I won't break."

"I know that, Nesrin. You are strong, loyal, and fierce. Anyone can see that, if they look close enough, but I don't wish to burden you right now, is all. It can wait, I promise." He seems sincere, so I drop it. I walk over, giving Astraea a kiss on the head and sense Lukas come up behind me. I turn to see a large coffee in front of me.

Smiling, I reach for it. "Thank you." I take a mouthful, and close my eyes, humming at the rich taste that fills my mouth. *Coffee is life.*

When I open my eyes, Lukas is looking at me with a weird expression. I shrug. "I love coffee."

"I can tell," Lukas chuckles. He takes a sip of his own, leaning back against the bench. Astraea chooses that moment to launch her cup across the table. My magic flares without thought, catching it at the same time as Lukas. Man, he moves fast.

We stare at each other for a moment and I can't tell what he's thinking. The guy has an impressive neutral face. As for Astraea, that girl never has accidents. I turn to stare at her, and she is smiling at Lukas. Kid just wants his attention. I let out a loud laugh that startles both of them, which in turn has me laughing harder. I'm hysterical now, and I can't stop. Tears are streaming down my face, and my stomach aches. Then I realize I'm crying.

These are real fucking tears, and I cannot stop or catch my breath. What the fuck is happening to me?

A heavy hand lands on my back, rubbing in circles as I'm leaning over with my hands braced on my knees, trying to get a grip on my emotions. I've built walls around myself, not allowing people to get close, because I'm afraid. Afraid of what they see, of getting too close and losing someone else. Astraea only met Lukas last night and already she is trusting him and laughing at him.

*I feel like such a failure.*

"You're not a failure, Nesrin," Lukas whispers, still rubbing circles on my back.

And now I'm talking out loud, dammit.

"I have come to understand that people don't always build walls around themselves to keep others away. Sometimes it's done out of pure necessity and self-preservation to protect whatever is left within. When you trust me, I will be here to listen to your story. I want you to tell me it all, because I see you've been through a massive amount of heartache in your short life. I want to be the one to make you whole again."

My heart lurches at his words. I take several deep breaths, the tears slowing. I don't think that it's possible for me to feel whole again. The last year has been a nightmare and Portland was supposed to be our safe place, our fresh start. I don't feel safe with the coven acting this way and Grace lying to me, hunters breaking into my store, and the wolves taking an interest in my comings and goings.

What am I supposed to do now? I glance over at Astraea, who has made her way over to us. She looks at me with concern on her beautiful face. It makes me feel guilty all over again. I have her to protect. She is my priority. Nothing else matters but her. I need to figure this out. I sink down to the floor, putting my back to the cupboards and bringing my knees to my chest.

Maybe we should leave . . . Right at that moment, Astraea starts shaking her head. She takes my face in her little hands, staring into my eyes, her blue ones glowing with emotions. A soft but firm "*No*" rings out in my head. I jerk back, my head hitting the cupboard behind me as I gape at her.

Did she? Did she speak in my head?

"What happened?" Lukas asks , squatting down next to us. I am frozen for a moment, then blink away the haze that has overtaken me.

My voice is hoarse when I whisper, "I don't know." I am losing my mind in front of this gorgeous man and my adorable toddler. *This is just great.*

Lukas's brows furrows. "What is?"

I swear under my breath. I really have to work on not blabbing my thoughts out loud. Taking a deep breath, I don't take my eyes off Astraea. I push to my feet and dust my pants off. I squint my eyes at her, trying to work out if her voice sounds in my head or if I'm going crazy.

Crazy is more likely.

Some of what Lukas has said starts registering in my head. It then hits me square in the chest. "Okay. Wait. Did you say you wanted to make me whole?" I stammer, fixing my stare on Lukas now.

He reaches up, muscles flexing, as he scratches the back of his neck. "Yeah, I want to be here for you, however you need me," he replies. I stare at him dumbly.

"Why?" I blurt, I am really curious.

If the question surprises him, he doesn't show it. His eyes roam over my cheeks to my eyes, which I'm sure are red and puffy from crying. "Because you're a very intriguing woman, Nesrin Locke," Lukas says, turning to grab his coffee and walking over to the sofa, Astraea joining him. I guess that's the end of the conversation.

"Okay. I need to write a plan. I need a list," I murmur to myself. I open several drawers before I find what I'm looking for. Grabbing the notepad and pen, I take a seat at the table. "I'm done running. I feel like I've been running my whole life," I continue murmuring to myself.

Lukas quirks an eyebrow at me from his spot on the sofa. "I will not let you run or face anything alone," he says simply, and I yearn to walk over and hug him. I know I can't get caught up in whatever is happening between the two of us. That spark in my chest that lights up when he's near.

I send a genuine smile his way. "Thanks."

"Why a list?" he questions.

"I need to figure out how to handle everything, the things that are priority. Like I need to redo my wards on this place and the store, sort out staff, see Merve, and find out what Grace knows." I throw my hand up. "See, this is why I need a list. It helps calm my mind. I like to prioritize and cross stuff off. Makes me feel like I've accomplished something."

I am so wrapped up in my tirade I don't hear Lukas approach. Firm hands land on my shoulders, squeezing lightly. "You need to take a breath before you pass out, and may I make a suggestion?"

"Sure," I say, dragging the word out warily, earning a chuckle from Lukas.

"I want you and Astra to come and stay with me."

I open my mouth to interrupt but he puts his hand over my mouth, my eyes flare in warning and I'm tempted to bite him.

"Let me finish." When he sees I'm not going to say anything, he removes his hand. "No one will look for you there. You will be surrounded by my pack. It will give us time to figure out what exactly the coven wants from you. Astra will be safe and have plenty of room to run around. The pack lands are secluded and cover a vast area of forest."

I can feel my eyes go wide. "The pack lands." I shake my head, "No. Nope. No way, Lukas, the wolves hate my kind. You can't possibly think we would be safe there?"

"Of course you will. You are under my protection. No one will touch you. I promise. I'm offering you my home and protection. You have a safe place with me." Lukas touches his chest. He really means it, but he can't speak for all the shifters. I mean, he is the Alpha and can order it, but some still won't listen.

"Why are you helping us? We are no one to you," I say, trying to understand his motives. The fact that my own feelings are confusing me is bad enough, but his.

Lukas's face softens. "Because I want to," he replies, stepping into my space. He lifts his hand, tucking some hair behind my ear, his hand lingering there. My heart is thrumming wildly in my chest. What is it about this man that has me so worked up all the time? I have to keep my head on straight.

"I'll think about it," I say, taking a small step back, my legs hitting the kitchen table where Astraea is seated, silently watching our exchange.

"I will have someone watch over you and Astraea until you decide. If you choose to stay here, I can organize a bodyguard," Lukas says, giving me a nod, as if to say that's final. Before I have time to respond, his phone rings. He lifts it to his ear and turns on his heel, walking away.

Alright, then.

# CHAPTER NINE

From my spot in the kitchen, I watch Zee and Astraea doing a puzzle on the floor in the living area. I sigh, pushing off the sink, and make my way over to them. Lukas left an hour ago to take care of pack business and Zee came barreling in like he was a lifelong friend, taking over my apartment. He seems at ease with everyone. I don't know how. As much as I wish I was, I will never be like that. I wouldn't say I'm shy, but I definitely struggle with social norms. My only friends are a homeless man, a teenager, a sixty-year-old woman from downstairs, and the sweet man who serves me coffee every day. I have no friends my age, not since Niamh and Hunter.

I walk over to Zee, who is sitting on the floor with his back against the sofa, and stare down at him. His head falls back onto the cushions as he looks up at me. His eyes seem familiar to me, but I just can't place them.

"What's up honey?" he asks.

I shift on my feet. "Want to watch a movie?"

"Sure," he replies, his lips lifting in a smile.

Astraea jumps to her tiny feet and runs toward the tv, a bright smile on her cute little face.

"Okay, sweet girl, you can pick. Why don't you run and grab your blanket and wolf, and I'll get the popcorn," I suggest. She flashes me a massive grin, running for her room. I watch her go, a smile pulling at my lips. I turn, making my way to the kitchen to get some popcorn started.

Zee stands and follows me into the kitchen, resting his hip on the bench next to me, arms crossed over his chest. His tall frame towers over me. It's funny how comfortable I am with both him and Lukas, considering how long it usually takes for me to warm up to people. I should feel uneasy and a little threatened, but I'm not. They have done nothing to suggest they mean Astraea or I harm. I look at Zee out of the corner of my eye. He hasn't said a word yet, and that makes me slightly edgy.

"What?" I ask, opening the microwave and putting the popcorn in. I shut the door and copy his pose.

Zee glances down at me, frowning. He's hesitating.

"Spit it out Blondie," I tease.

"Blondie?" he chuckles lightly.

"Sorry, continue."

His smile drops and a serious expression crosses his face again. Oh no, I don't like that look.

"Why haven't I heard her talk? She's, what? Nearly two, right?"

My breath stutters and I push off the bench, turning to get a bowl from the cupboard, buying myself some time to gather my thoughts. I wasn't expecting that question to come out of his mouth. I knew it would come, but not right then. My hands grip the bench in front of me and I take a deep breath, staring at the chipped paint on the shelf.

"I didn't mean to sound rude. I was just curious," Zee whispers, bringing my attention back to him. "Please don't kick me out. Lukas will have my ass."

Glancing over, I give him a small smile. "Really?" I wiggle my eyebrows and his face pales as he realizes what I was implying.

"No, not like that. Geez, honey," he exclaims, raking a hand through his hair.

I hum, doing my best to fight my smile. "Thy doth protest too much, methinks."

Zee rubs his hands over his face, blowing out a breath, a smile tugging at his lips. "You're deflecting."

"Yeah, maybe." I sigh, looking over my shoulder.

Astraea is now arranging herself on the sofa with her blanket. Her stuffed wolf is tucked under her arm, and her wild blonde curls are in a state of disarray. A pang of pain shoots through me at the sight of her wolf and how tightly she always holds it. I wonder if it reminds her of her father. She must miss them so much.

The microwave beeps at me, pulling me from my thoughts before they can overwhelm me and drag me under. How many times have I let them consume me? Pull me down, and drown me in my own misery? I grab the popcorn, and tip it into the bowl before whispering an incantation under my breath, subtly weaving a silent bubble around us, so Astraea won't hear me.

"Astra hasn't ever spoken. The first time I've heard a noise from her in eleven months was last night." I let out a painful breath. "Lukas made her laugh this morning, Zee," I choke, tears burning my eyes, but I refuse to let them fall.

I turn, brushing them away before he can see the humiliation sweeping through me. Pulling myself together, I pick up the popcorn only to have it plucked from my hands and put back on the bench. Zee puts his finger under my chin, tilting my head up to glance at him. He stares so hard for a moment, then pulls me into his chest. I go willingly, needing some comfort for once.

"She hasn't laughed out loud in almost a year, Zee. A YEAR. And she did for Lukas. What am I doing wrong? Why am I even telling you this?" I groan as I push way from him, wiping at my face, making sure no stray tears have escaped. This isn't me. I am not a crier. I don't open up to a practical stranger about these things. Grace is my outlet for these things. But I can't go to her right now. It sucks.

"Don't cry. I can't deal with crying," Zee says, looking frantic. So help me, I can't stop the laugh that bubbles up and bursts from my lips at the panic on his face. Zee's lips twitch then he looks over at Astraea, frowning. "Can she not hear us?"

"No. I've put us in a silent bubble," I reply nonchalantly, waving away his concern as I look at her through the bubble. The shimmering dome around us distorts my view of Astraea slightly.

His eyes widen as they swing back to me. "Okay, that makes sense, and is an extremely nifty trick," Zee replies, letting out a sigh. He runs a hand over his blonde head, and I watch in fascination as his hair falls perfectly back into place. "Look, I don't know what to tell you, but I'm here if you need to talk, okay? Sometimes, I might have some wisdom for you, other times a shoulder to lean on, but I'm here. As for Lukas, he is great with kids. They all love him. Lukas would do anything to keep you two safe, and maybe Astra can pick up on that. That's why she is trusting him."

Biting my thumbnail, I eye him warily. "Maybe," I mumble, my own insecurities eating at me.

"You have a great kid, honey. Don't be too hard on yourself. You're an amazing Mom," Zee says, not realizing what he has said and how it's ripping my heart to pieces. He picks up the popcorn and walks over to sit next to Astraea, giving her a megawatt smile. I let out a deep breath, then another before I follow him over to the lounge where the three of us watch a story about a girl and her mission to find a dragon. We move on to the next movie, and must all be more tired than we thought because next thing I know, we are being woken by banging on the door.

Squinting my eyes, I look at the clock. It's already four in the afternoon. I look over at Zee, who is now standing, making his way over to the door.

I scramble up quickly, stepping in front of Astraea to block her from whoever is at the door. Zee reaches the door, swinging it open without checking. There stands Lukas, freshly showered and looking gorgeous. Man, the guy is built like a god. He is also holding four pizza boxes in front of him. My stomach betrays me by rumbling loudly at the sight. Even without their heightened senses, they would have picked up on that. Lukas and Zee both chuckle.

"I thought you all might be hungry," Lukas says. Astraea, having heard Lukas, was already dashing around my legs for him. Lukas hands off the pizzas to Zee without missing a beat, scooping her up and throwing her in the air, and catching her. Astraea let out a squeal of excitement and my heart speeds up at the sound I've longed to hear for so long. Zee catches my eye, giving me a small, gentle smile. I manage to send a small smile back, barely.

"Thank you, I am starving, as you all heard," I say, walking to the table to make room for the boxes.

Pulling my hair back into a messy bun, I turn, eyeing my little girl, who is staring at the handsome man holding her. There's a dreamy look on her cute face. I let out a chuckle. Lukas's eyes meet mine, a brilliant smile on his face. I suck in a sharp breath at the sight, then quickly turn back to the table where Zee has placed the pizza boxes and was in the process of opening them. I sneak a peek back at Lukas, who is whispering to Astraea. I don't know what he's saying, but she is just staring back like she can't believe he's here, that he's real.

Well, you and me both, sweet girl. I might not be able to have him for myself, but sooner than later, Astraea will need to find a pack to be a part of, and maybe that would be Lukas's. I'm still not sure how her shifter side will manifest, if at all, but she is going to need other shifters around to help guide her. Which will also mean trusting others with our secret.

After stuffing our faces with pizza, we decide to take Astraea for a walk before getting her ready for bed. I'm putting Astraea's coat on when Zee comes over to us.

"I'm going to head out, honey. Lukas will be here with you two tonight."

Butterflies take flight at the thought of another night with Lukas. "Oh, okay. Thanks for today, Zee. For everything," I say, standing up straight. I hesitate a moment, but . . . fuck it. I step in close to Zee and wrap my arms around his waist, giving him a quick squeeze.

Surprised, Zee freezes for a moment before returning the hug. "Anytime," he replies, stepping back, and not a moment later, he's out the door.

Lukas and I make our way down onto the street with Astraea on Lukas's shoulders. She looks so happy up there. Although she does have a death grip on poor Lukas's hair. I chuckle. "Is she pulling too much?"

He flashes a smile my way. "Not at all," he says, adjusting her slightly.

Zee's right. Lukas is good with kids. He's great with Astraea. I just can't help worrying that he's using me somehow. No, I know that can't be it. Lukas doesn't seem like that type. But for the life of me, I can't understand why he would hang around and offer his protection to us. For one, I'm a witch, and so is Astraea, as far as he knows. Shifters and witches don't always get along because of our long and bloody history. And two, we don't know each other. You don't just become someone's bodyguard out of the goodness of your heart. When it comes to Lukas, I don't know what to think. My gut tells me I can trust him. My heart wants to, but my mind is wary.

When I was growing up, my parents said nothing about not trusting other magical creatures. It was just our kind. I wish they would have told me why they steered clear of the covens for all those years. I understand there are a few bad eggs, but not everyone is bad or untrustworthy. Still, their fears seeped into me, becoming my own.

We make it to the park in record time. Lukas reaches back, lifting Astraea off his broad shoulders. Wasting no time, she runs off to play with a young brunette girl who looks to be around five. Astraea always gravitates to the older kids even though she's a toddler. She fits in with them. Her advanced understanding helps. I smile as she gestures to the slide, and the girls run off together.

Lukas turns to me, but keeps Astraea in his line of sight. I love how protective he is of her. "Zee told me what you told him this morning, about Astraea not speaking. Don't be mad."

Startled by his choice of topic, I swivel, staring up at him. "I'm not mad. It's just . . . What did he say?" I ask.

"That Astra hasn't made even a peep in almost a year until this morning,"

"Oh." I breathe, looking over at Astraea as she climbs up the ladder to the slide. I understand Lukas is going to want more answers than that, but what am I supposed to tell him?

Proving me right, Lukas sighs. "That's it? Just 'oh?'"

I can feel myself getting frustrated. "What do you want me to say, Lukas?"

"I want you to tell me what happened that sent that beautiful little girl mute?"

There is no accusation in his tone. If anything, he sounds concerned, but I immediately go on the defensive.

"Not that it is any of your business, Lukas, but I don't want to talk about it," I scowl, taking a step away. My cheeks flush and I can feel my anger rising. I'm like a cornered animal when I get like this.

Grabbing my arm gently, he pulls me back and softens his tone even more. "I didn't mean it like that, Nesrin. It came out wrong. I'm sorry."

Deflating, I look over at the sweetest little girl I know. Can I tell him? Would it hurt to give him more information? Just not the secret I have to guard with my life. Astraea's life depends on it, at least for the time being.

Taking several deep breaths, I prepare myself. I can do this. I focus on a spot in the distance. "Eleven months ago, we lost my sister and her partner in a house fire. Astra and I barely escaped," I say slowly, almost detached, so I don't choke on the words. I glance around, quickly deciding a silent bubble is a good idea right now, and get to work weaving my second bubble for the day. I watch as the bubble slowly forms around us, like ice spreading in a dome around us. Of course, I'm the only one who can actually see it.

"Fuck," Lukas swears, running his hand through his hair as he glances over at Astraea.

"Yeah," I agree, pushing past the lump forming in my throat, and willing the tears not to fall and my heart not to race the way it always does when I think about that horrible night. "Astraea and I had to bury the two most important people in our lives on the same day. Then I decided to start fresh here. Astra hasn't made a peep since it happened. She was only a baby, still is only a baby, but I think it stuck with her. She is hurting and I can only imagine her loss," I murmur barely above a whisper, the lump in my throat preventing me from speaking any louder. Looking down, I let my hair cover my face, needing a moment to gather myself again. Not giving me that chance, Lukas cups my face in both his hands, tilting it up, so our eyes meet, his fingers sinking into my hair. I close my eyes briefly, savoring the touch.

"I'm so sorry for your loss, Nesrin. I couldn't imagine losing a sibling." His eyes search mine. "If you ever want to talk about what happened or about your family, I'm here for you. You know that, right?"

I open my eyes, blinking. How is this man real? When was the last time someone held me like this, like they actually cared?

I'm not so sure I can talk about that night with anyone. How could I possibly describe the worst day of my life? How I lost a part of my soul that night Niamh perished in the fire. I will never get her back, never talk to her again, laugh or cry with her. How do I tell someone that I am barely holding it together most days? That for the first month after her death, all I wanted to do was follow my sister into the afterlife, but I had to be better, stronger for Astraea, she needed me. I am all she has left in this world, and I can't fail her. That's why I run head first into danger to help or heal anyone I'm able to. Maybe it's because no one helped me when I needed it the most?

"I don't think I will ever get over the loss of Niamh," I croak. His thumb brushes the tears from my cheeks. I don't even try to stop them. At this point, there's no use, the floodgates have opened.

Lukas pulls me into his chest, holding the back of my head. "Let it out, sweetheart," he murmurs into my hair. It's as if we were the only two people here.

"She was my twin, and I couldn't save her. She deserved to live. Niamh was the one who should have lived. I love her so much, and I just want her to be here with me, to hear her voice again. Even if it's teasing me about my freckles or to yell at me for using all the hot water. I want Astraea to trust me enough to talk. I don't know what to do. Lukas, I am so lost. What do I do?" Oh, goddess, I am a mess. Today has been a fucking disaster, and it's all these bloody wolves' fault. I was doing just fine before they came along with their warm touches and soft looks.

Pulling back, Lukas puts space between us, trapping my face with his massive hands once more. "We will figure this out, Nesrin."

"I want my sister back, she should be here with Astraea," I sob, my heart breaking at our feet. Confusion pastes over Lukas's face. I realize what I've said. *Shit.*

"Hey, it's going to be okay. I promise, sweetheart. I will do everything I can to help you. You deserve to be here too, I know it's unfair but I'm glad you're here, Astraea needs you too," Lukas breathes, bringing our bodies closer. He still has my face cupped in his hands, swiping at the endless tears that stream down my face. At some point, I lift my hands and grab hold of his wrists. He didn't know that Astraea isn't my daughter, that she deserves to have her mother with her.

"Is this what the nightmare was about the other night?" He asks.

With my face still in his warm hands, I nod as much as I can. I'm feeling a little lighter now since I've opened up to him. I have told no one how I've been feeling. Who is there to tell? I will miss my sister every day. That will never change, never go away, but maybe I can heal from this loss. Lukas's gaze locks onto mine, holding me so still I can barely breathe. Lukas moves his hands up to run his fingers over my hair, pushing it out of my face. His eyes drop to my mouth and darken. My mouth goes dry. Does he want to kiss me? I am a mess and have just ugly cried in front of him. There is no way he would want that.

Next second Astraea barrels into our legs, breaking the spell. Startled, I glance down as Lukas scoops her up. I can't stop the smile that takes over my face. I lift my arms to take her, but she holds tight to Lukas, throwing one of those little arms around my neck. We end up in a group hug, Lukas's arm wrapped around my waist and my face pressed against his hard chest. This is nice.

# CHAPTER TEN

I love it when the kitchen is tidy. I look around, admiring my nice sparkling clean kitchen. Then, reaching down, I pluck some lemongrass room spray from under the sink. This is one of my favorite smells. It always seems to help relax me and make me seem lighter, somehow, like there was less weighing me down. Before I can start spraying, I hear Lukas's phone vibrating. I glance over at it where it lays on the bench, seeing Zee's name flashing on the screen.

Lukas is with Astraea in her room, so I swipe it up and press answer, "Hey Zee, what's up?"

"Nesrin, I need to speak to Lukas now," is Zee's rushed response. The urgency in his voice has me on alert.

"Okay, I'll go get him. Is everything alright?" My stomach twists with nerves as I rush down the hall to Astraea's room. It's none of my business, but I am starting to care for these guys.

Zee lets out a deep, growly sigh. "No," is all he says, all he needs to say.

I quietly push open the door, finding both Lukas and Astraea sleeping on the small bed. Her stuffed wolf is tucked under one arm, while her whole body curled into Lukas's side. He's holding one of her story books open on his chest. Some of his dark hair has fallen over his forehead. I halt at the sight. My heart melts and aches at the same time.

I'm still holding the phone to my ear when Zee growls. "Nesrin. Lukas. NOW!"

I jolt. "Shit! Sorry, Zee," I say, snapping out of it. Lukas is now wide awake, having heard Zee's voice through the phone, most likely.

Lukas pushes off the bed, careful not to wake the sleeping toddler as he does. In a few steps, he is in front of me, motioning for the phone. I hand it over, staring at his disheveled hair, parts of it still scattered across his forehead. My hand itches to brush it away for him. Lukas moves past me and out of the room.

"Zee?" he barks into the phone. Cringing at his Alpha tone, I turn and follow him out into the living area. I stop at the doorway and lean against the frame, crossing my arms as I watch Lukas pace a few times, his bare feet making no noise at all. He runs a hand through his hair, messing it up further. The conversation is brief and tense. Lukas has his back to me as he hangs up the phone. I can see the muscles in his back tense and strain against his shirt.

He takes what looks like several deep breaths before turning to me. "I need to go, but I can't leave you here alone." He runs his hand through his hair again in aggravation. I'm beginning to realize this is what he does when he is frustrated. It's cute. But I hate he thinks he is responsible for us. I don't need him to protect me. I have gotten by so far.

"If you have to go, Lukas, we will be fine. I have this place well warded, you know that. What happened?" I add softly.

Lukas blows out a breath and starts pacing again. Whatever it is, it has him worked up. "Two of my wolves were out on patrol and have been found unconscious. They can't be woken. It looks like some illness."

"I'm a healer, Lukas. Let me come with you. I might be able to help."

Lukas stops pacing around the room. His gaze capturing mine, he tilts his head as he contemplates my offer. "I would feel better if you did. This could be a trap to get you alone. I don't want to take that chance."

My heart beats a little faster at the thought of that. I don't think the witches would care either way if Lukas was here or not. They would come for me anyway. Whenever that may be.

Agreeing it would be best for me to come along, we load Astraea up in Lukas's truck, still sleeping soundly, and head to the outpost close to where Lukas's property ends.

Forty minutes later, we pull off the main road onto a dirt track, then continue on for another ten minutes. The drive is silent, both of us lost in our own heads as we go down the bumpy track leading to the outpost. I glance over my shoulder at Astraea, a smile stretching across my face when I see she is still sound asleep.

When we arrive at the outpost, there are at least a dozen shifters waiting outside the small cabin, half of them in their wolf forms, pacing the area. My breath stalls in my chest. This is a piece of cake, easy-peasy. I will not shit my pants. I take a deep, fortifying breath and let it out before slowly reaching for the door handle. My hand is trembling when I peer down, and I clench my fist several times to dispel it. The last thing I need is the shifters sniffing out my weaknesses, fears, and a bunch of other private shit.

"Everything will be fine, Nesrin," Lukas's voice says, breaking the silence of the car. "No one here will harm you or Astraea. You have my word."

I nod, not trusting my voice to hold steady. Pushing the door open, I can't help but flinch as several sets of glowing yellow eyes lock on me.

"Hmmm . . . safe," I hum, not completely convinced. But you know what? I've been in weirder and worse situations than this. I can do this. A chill creeps down my spine, starting at the base of my neck. I do not enjoy having their focus on me. Still, I understand their hostility, especially when Lukas comes to my side, placing his hand on my lower back, and leads me forward. My hand lingers over the dagger I strapped to my thigh, hoping I won't need it. Lukas nods to a young male who looks to be of Asian descent and tosses the keys to him, a silent order: watch the car. Astraea will be fine. No one would dare touch her. I see Zee step out the door of the house, coming straight for us, and let out a relieved breath at the sight of him, but it's short-lived. When I get a good glimpse at his face, I can see that Zee is on edge, stress weighing him down, his face grim in the moonlight. From the couple of days I've gotten to know Zee, he has been so laid back he is basically horizontal. But now his usual good humor has evaporated. This is the face of a second in command, a Beta. His blonde hair is in a mess around his face, not pulled back like it usually is.

"I have them both in the main room. I cleared as much furniture as I could. Lukas, man, I don't know what's going on. They were both fine when they left for patrol, then when they didn't check in, we sent others out looking. We found them passed out and unresponsive. Mark's mate Sara is in there. She won't leave his side," Zee tells the Alpha as we approach.

Lukas moves around Zee, storming toward the house, leaving me to follow. The power rolling off him is intense, making my skin crawl with awareness. Zee reaches the door first and holds it open as we pass through. I immediately sense icy fingers pinching at my skin. Something feels incredibly wrong here. I move around Lukas to get a good look at the room, a loud gasp escaping me as I take in the two silvery gray wolves laying on the floor in the middle of the living room. Dark, angry red magic swirls around both wolves. But it's the black magic gathered around their hearts, swirling like a mass of misty shadows, that catches my attention.

"I haven't seen a spell this complex in . . . well, ever," I whisper, stepping closer. Lukas and Zee spin around, watching me, but I haven't taken my eyes off the two wolves on the floor. I tilt my head, studying the spell, it's mesmerizing. I have never before come across something that looked and felt so horrible. The spell surrounding them throbs with malicious intent.

"What do you mean, spell?" Lukas demands, grabbing my arm and stopping me from approaching the wolves. I didn't realize I was moving.

"How can you see it?" Zee inquires, and I ignore him. My stomach drops as I look up to Lukas. His eyes hold questions, but they will have to wait. There is no time to think about my slip-up. If I don't undo this spell now, they will die.

I point down at the two wolves on the floor. "They have been hexed."

Although they are unresponsive, their pain radiates off of them in waves. The thing with my healing abilities, which really bloody sucks, is that I can feel the pain of others. Not fully, but enough. It's how I'm usually drawn to where I need to be. A wave of nausea has me sucking in a sharp breath. Sweat beads my brow as I try to filter what I am feeling.

Sara turns to me, growling long and low. I raise my hands in a placating gesture, moving forward a step. "I can help them, but you have to trust me. They don't have much time."

Lukas moves to intercept me again, but Sara is quicker in her desperation. She grabs my hand, pulling me closer to her. "Please save him. We have a pup on the way. I haven't told him yet. I was going to surprise him. He's going to be a dad," she wails, holding my hand in a death grip. She is small for a shifter, with soft brown eyes and short, light brown hair that floats around her delicate face. The despair in her eyes breaks my heart. Lukas and Zee both move forward to stand at my side. I half expect them to drag Sara or me away, but they both nod at me, and a warmth fills my chest. They trust me. A witch, an outsider.

Clearing the emotion from my throat, I focus back on Sara. "I will do what can." I extract my hand from her grip and move over to the two unconscious wolf shifters. Kneeling between the two, I wave my hands over the red magic swirling just above their bodies. Placing a hand over each of their hearts where the magic is the worst, I summon my healing magic. It stirs awake from deep inside my chest, warming me as the light pulses through me. The pain from the shifters recedes and I can breathe a little easier.

I whisper a few words to Hecate to help guide me in the undoing of this spell. Since I can remember, I have been worshiping Hecate. She is my chosen goddess. I feel closest to her, as a goddess of magic and witchcraft, as well as a goddess of protection and the underworld. She is shrouded in mystery. For centuries, there have been debates about her name and origin. Facts support the theory that she originated outside Greece, but no one can say where.

I stare at Lukas, trying to convey with my voice and expression the seriousness of what I'm about to say. "You can't touch them when I start. Please allow me to work. I will do everything I can to save them. But I've never had to work a spell this complex before," I warn them. Lukas and Zee grunt in response and Sara nods her tear-stricken face. I feel Lukas and Zee move in closer behind me. Support and protection surround me. I can sense it rolling off them in waves. They are trusting me, and I them. I've never thought of having wolves at my back as being a good thing, but they make me feel safe.

Closing my eyes, I sink my hands into the wolves' soft fur, making contact with the skin underneath. I open myself up to the surrounding elements, pulling from that magic as well. Knowing I will need all I can get to save the wolves. I feel the warmth of magic flow from my hands into their bodies. The depth of magic weaving around their hearts is tightly constructed. This is no ordinary spell, worked by any ordinary witch. This spell is ugly. Done by someone who practices in dark magic and witchcraft, someone who doesn't mind paying the cost of such a spell.

I get to work, letting my magic sweep through their bodies, following thread after thread. Sweat beads my face as I work. I pull more magic from the elements around me, keeping the flow open and replenishing myself as I work. I have my own magic that hums inside of me, which is rare. Most witches have to rely on the elements around them for their source of magic. The magic I draw from deep within me never lasts long, though. I always burn out too quickly. The elements are always around and ready to use. That magic doesn't burn out as easily. Though, when fatigued, it gets more difficult to control the flow.

The threads of magic turn purple, or rather a purple haze coats each of the threads. I frown, squeezing my eyes closed to concentrate. Even with my eyes shut, I can see the threads of the spell. "Sleeping nightshade," I say under my breath. This is not good.

"What is it?" Lukas asks, but his voice sounds far off in the distance.

Grimacing, I shudder as I fall a little deeper into the spell. I pull at a thread and watch it unravel, revealing more of the spell. The wolves twitch under my hands and I push down harder.

"Dark Magic," I mumble, my attention focused on the weaving of the spell, following the intricate lacing of threads.

Lukas shifts closer to me. "No, I mean sleeping nightshade, what is it?"

Before I can answer, Zee snaps, "Let her work, man."

I'm panting now, and I hear Sara gasp. The sound is so distant I barely notice. I'm hoping nothing bad is happening, as I keep my eyes squeezed shut, focusing on the spell. I am almost there. I just need that one sweet spot to pull. Then it will all fall apart. Gritting my teeth, I shove my magic deeper, feeling the structure of the spell. *Uh-huh.* I locate it. A sudden pain explodes in my head, and I double over, hands forming fists in the fur of the wolves so I don't break contact.

An unexpected blackness surrounds my mind, and the threads of magic disappear. "What the—" I stammer, my mind frantically looking for anything in the darkness, something to grasp onto. I open my eyes and  see nothing but darkness. "Shit," I curse, squeezing my eyes closed again, my heart rate tripling. Now is not the time to panic. I must have hit the black threads of magic around the heart. Maybe the caster added a failsafe to stop someone from undoing the spell. Well, I'm not just anyone, and I am not giving up. A woman's laugh echoes through my mind, taunting and teasing. It was faint, but I know it was there. Whoever cast this spell is watching.

"Nesrin, what is it?" Lukas's concerned voice reaches out to me. He can tell something is troubling me, but I'm unable to answer as something tugs at my mind, threatening to drag me down. I know it's not a place I want to go. I will end up like the two shifters I'm trying to save. Knowing what I have to do next, I steel myself. This will require Lukas's trust, and it scares me to find out if he really trusts me. But if I don't do it, these shifters will die, and I may follow.

I grit my teeth against the pull. "Lukas, I need more magic. I need you to help me."

"Anything," is his quick reply.

"Put your hand on my shoulder and open yourself up to me. You're an Alpha. You have a lot of magic in you."

I'm struggling to hold on to the flow of magic. I am grasping at nothing, the magic falling through my hands like sand.

Another voice sounds from the room somewhere. "Alpha, you can't. What if this is a trap? The witch cannot be trusted."

Lukas's answering growl rattles the windows, his power blasting through the room, silencing any further objections. I can sense my magic draining quickly. We need to move now.

"Lukas!" I yell urgently. His warm hand lands on my shoulder as he kneels behind me, his other strong, muscled arm circling my waist and tugging me back against his warm, broad chest. The hand on my shoulder moves down my arm slowly, his hand sliding on top of mine that is still gripping the fur of the shifter beside me and linking our fingers. Only when I feel that connection open, the magic encasing me in its warmth and flow freely, do I chant an incantation my mother taught me. My full concentration is on the words and the flow of magic. I block everything else out.

"I am a healer to all, the one who fights to right the wrongs. To make the weak stronger and the proud humble. I help inspire the voices of those silenced. I am justice tempered with mercy. Call for me in the darkest hour so you may awaken in the light. By my power, I will illuminate and heal your body and soul, washing away darkness, bringing forth the light."

Slowly, the blackness retreats, my mind clearing with it. I sigh in relief when the threads of magic reappear in my mind. Instantly, I start pulling on that last thread. It's time to deconstruct this cluster fuck of a spell. I feel it the moment the spell falls apart, disintegrating into nothing.

My body sags against Lukas's grip, my arms falling uselessly to my sides. Groaning, I open my eyes and am immediately blinded by the glow of light in the room. As I lift my hands to cover my eyes, I realize it's me. I am glowing. I peer down at the two

121

shifters, finding them back in human form, moving to sit up. Sara launches herself at her mate, laughing and crying, covering him in kisses.

I did it. Holy shit, I did it. A broad smile takes over my face as the light starts to fade. I'm left staring at a group of shifters who have their mouths hanging open. My eyes capture Zee's. He seems in shock, a dazed expression on his face.

I tilt my head at him and quirk an eyebrow, grinning. "What?"

A growl erupts from the man near the door. My eyes fly to his. I'm startled by the amount of hostility in them. "What has she done?" he snarls, striding closer to me, his blue eyes flashing yellow.

*Huh? Does he mean me?* I just saved these two wolves, asshole.

"Yes, you!" he snarls.

My eyes dart back to Zee, but he is still standing there staring at me like I'm some sort of alien unicorn. I realize then that Lukas is no longer holding me up. Quickly, I twist my body around and almost choke on my gasp. Lukas is lying unconscious behind me. I spin around, ignoring the dizziness that hits me and reach for his face, my hands grasping his cheeks.

"Lukas!" I yell, patting his cheeks, probably a little harder than is necessary, but he's tough. He can take it . . . I hope.

"Get away from him." The man growls again, lunging toward me, but he doesn't make it far. Zee bursts into action, finally coming out of his shocked state.

"Back down, Ryan." The order comes through crisp and clear as Zee steps in front of me, going nose to nose with the other man. My attention returns to Lukas. I must have taken more magic than I should have.

Dammit. I have no magic left to help him, either. I am depleted, exhausted. My face grows hot as I feel tears building in my eyes. I slump forward and rest my forehead on Lukas's chest. I blink, my eyelids feeling heavy. It's a struggle to keep them open. The arguing around me fades as I turn my head on Lukas's chest, letting my ear rest over his heart. I can hear its strong, steady beat and feel the rise and fall of his chest. I breathe a soft sigh. That is such a beautiful sound. I give in to the urge to rest, taking several deep breaths and letting my eyes fall shut as sleep takes me.

# CHAPTER ELEVEN

I wake to voices speaking in hushed tones and let out a groan. My head is pounding like a mothertrucker.

"Would you all be quiet?" I say gruffly, rolling over to my side. I feel like I have the world's worst hangover. Pounding headache, dry mouth, and dizziness. The voices stop and I hear a door shut somewhere in the room.

For a moment, I think I'm alone, but the bed dips, and a warm body slides in behind me. A muscled arm is draped over my waist, pulling me firmly into his body. I take a deep breath and smell sandalwood and rain. Lukas. I snuggle deeper into my pillow, too tired to even process the fact that Lukas is cuddling me. My whole body aches like I ran a marathon. That was the most magic I've done in a long time. No, ever. I've never done a spell that complex. I shiver. All that malice.

"Are you alright?" Lukas mumbles into my hair and I'm one hundred percent sure he just sniffed it.

"Did you just smell my hair?"

Lukas chuckles behind me, giving a soft shake to the bed. "Yes, I love the smell of your hair. And the color. It's the shade of fall leaves—red, orange, brown, some blonde streaked through. It's mesmerizing, truly beautiful," he says, taking another sniff. I have to laugh over the fact he didn't even try to deny it.

"Where is Astra? Is she okay?" I ask. My heart speeds up at the fact we are in a strange place, and I'm not with her.

"She is fine. I have Zee watching over her," Lukas replies, squeezing me a little tighter in reassurance.

A vision of Lukas laying unconscious flashes through my mind and a wave of guilt hits me square in the chest. "Wait, are you okay?" I roll to face him. Smiling at me, Lukas brushes the hair from my face. I'm doing my best not to let my eyes close at the touch.

"I'm fine. Back to full health again." His reassurance does nothing to ease the guilt. I narrow my eyes at him, biting my thumbnail, and considering all that happened.

"Are you sure? I'm sorry. Truly, I didn't realize how much I'd taken from you. I should have stopped," I blurt out. A sense of shame washes over me at the thought of having drained Lukas of so much power. I didn't mean to take so much. With the hex almost broken, those last few steps required all my focus.

"I promise I'm fine. We saved my men, so it was worth it." He sits up, leaning his back against the headboard, and pats the spot next to him. With a sigh, I move to mirror his position, sparks of energy prickling my skin where our arms are touching.

"Can you tell me about the spell? How did you know it was a spell that had my men in that state and not something else?" Lukas asks, looking over at me. My eyes widen, and I swallow around the lump forming in my throat. I forgot, with everything that's happened, that I didn't censor the fact I could see the spell. Averting my gaze, my mind goes blank. Lukas's hand reaches across my face, cupping my cheek and turning my head back to meet his intense gaze.

"Nesrin, you can trust me. I need to know anything you can tell me about what you saw. It almost killed two of my shifters last night. I need to be aware so I can prepare for whatever's coming. How did you know they were hexed?"

I pull my face from his hold and glance down at my lap. I twist my mother's ring on my finger, shifting uncomfortably. My brain tries to process how I might explain my ability to him. "It's nothing, just a rare gift. I can see magic. I can see many spells, like wards, hexes, and glamors. They float on the air like water currents of color, weaving, entwining, joining together. It's quite beautiful to see. Because of this, I can follow the threads and unravel most spells. Last night when we entered the house, I could sense the dark energy of the spell in the air, and when I saw your shifters, red magic surrounded them. A kind I've never seen before. It was bad, Lukas." I release a big breath.

I scrub my hands over my face, leaving out the fact that the spell could have dragged me down with the two shifters. If it wasn't for Lukas, I'd most likely be dead.

"That's an amazing ability, Nesrin. Could you tell whose magic it was? Who cast the spell?"

"Like a signature?" I question. At his nod, I shake my head. "No, I can't tell that. I can only see the workings of the magic."

"The hex. How was it placed? You said last night something about sleeping nightshade. What is that?" His voice takes on a serious edge. Reaching over, he grabs my hand, halting my movements from twisting my ring. His thumb caresses the back of my hand in slow movements. I draw in a deep breath and launch into my assessment.

"Sleeping nightshade is one of many plants with sleep-inducing properties. When consumed, it makes people waver between sleep and death. It's an extremely dangerous plant. It has only ever been used in the direst of situations. Whoever used the nightshade mixed it in with the incantations to lay the spell on your men. They went into a death sleep. It was giving them a slow and painful death. Though unconscious, they were in a lot of pain. The poison would have killed them without a trace. They would have taken the night shade and then the spell would have activated. It's odd though, I felt like I was being watched, tested maybe. I heard a woman laughing."

Lukas is so silent and still next to me. Even his thumb has stopped its movement over my hand. I glance over to see if he's okay, waving my hand in front of his face. "Are you okay?" I ask, worry eating at me. His eyes take a far-off look. I've seen this before. He must be communicating telepathically with someone in his pack.

I lurch back as a sense of panic washes over me. Something isn't right. That isn't my panic, I'm sure of it. Rubbing my chest, I can't shake the feeling. My unease ripples through me.

"Nesrin?" Lukas's voice sounds far away.

Without answering, I jump from the bed, rushing for the door. I hear Lukas following close behind. I push out the front door of the cabin, coming to a stop in the yard and lift my arm, running a shaky hand through my hair, looking around frantically, my stomach churning with dread.

"Astraea," I whisper. Then, louder, I yell, "Astra!"

Zee jogs over to me, concern lining his face. "What's wrong?" he asks as Lukas puts his hand to the small of my back. Panic is building now, both mine and I'm pretty sure Astraea's.

"Zee, where is Astraea?" I demand, grabbing his arm desperately.

Zee places his warm hand on top of mine. "Sara took her for a walk."

"Shit." I drop his arm, spinning in a circle. I reach up and grip my hair with both hands.

*Where is she?*

"Which way?" Lukas demands. Before either can say a word, a pained howl rises from the woods behind the house. I take off in that direction without hesitation. I can still feel Astraea's panic alongside my own. It takes me seconds to reach the edge of the woods. I don't think I have ever moved so fast in my life. I don't care how much noise I make as I crash through the woods in the direction of the howl. Lukas and Zee are suddenly there, flanking me in their wolf forms, their presence oddly comforting. Lukas is a stunning black wolf, his head the same height as my chest, and Zee is a slightly smaller gray wolf with one black ear. Both are huge, powerful, magnificent wolves, but I don't have time to admire them right now. We race through the trees, leaping and dodging everything in our path.

"Astraea!" I shout, though I know it's no use. She won't answer me. Lukas lets out a long, thundering howl. Not a second later, another howl follows. I veer toward the howl, my foot slipping on loose rocks, and I brace myself for a hard fall that never comes. Lukas is by my side, his large furry body leaning into mine, righting me. I gasp, getting my balance again. Relief floods me. That was close. A sharp pain shoots through my foot and I realize then that I'm not wearing shoes. I don't dare look at my feet to survey the damage. That can wait till later. I grit my teeth and pick up my pace. They can't be much further.

Up ahead, I see Astraea crouched down on the forest floor. Her white nightgown is covered in dirt. As we get closer, I realize she is patting a small brown wolf, Sara.

Breathing heavily, I skid to a stop just in front of Astraea, dirt and leaves flying everywhere. I land hard on my knees, wrapping my arms around her tiny body, pulling her into my chest.

"Astraea, are you okay? Are you hurt?" I ask, squeezing her a little tighter to me. I can sense Lukas's worried eyes on me and glance over my shoulder. Lukas is right there at my back. He nudges my arm with his nose, then trots around my body to get a closer glimpse at Astraea. A whimpering draws my attention to Sara, who is lying next to me.

"Goddess," I mutter. Lukas and Zee shift suddenly, looking over Sara's back leg which is being crushed inside a bear trap.

Lukas glances around as if looking for something. "What the hell is a bear trap doing on my land?" he growls, anger vibrating the air, making the hairs on my arms stand on end.

"Fuck. Do you think the witches put it here? How could they without us knowing?" Zee snarls, kneeling down, stroking Sara's side.

Lukas is studying the trap intently. He lifts his eyes to meet mine, and I draw in a sharp breath at the fury in them. "You can take her back to the cabin. We will meet you there," he says.

I stroke Astraea's hair and shake my head. "No, I can help."

Just then I notice several sprites floating around us, one in particular standing out from the rest. The one who took me to Merve.

"What happened?" I ask her.

She glides forward, stopping a foot away, and bows slightly. I hear a tinkering from the other sprites at the action. Ignoring them, I focus on the sprite in front of me, her wings beating as fast as a hummingbird's.

"The wolf saw the trap before Astraea, and she pushed the girl out of the way, getting caught in the process," the sprite says in her musical voice. Her brown hair is woven in flowers today, her blue, shimmering gown near translucent. Her violet eyes seem to harden. "There shouldn't be traps in this forest," she seethes. I never thought something so small could sound so menacing, but pure wrath shone in her eyes.

Astraea looks up at me, and I notice the tears streaking down her face. I wipe them away, tilting her face up to mine. "Astraea, it's going to be okay. I'm going to help Lukas and Zee. I need you to wait over with the sprites, okay?" She looks up into my face, and the tears filling her crystal blue eyes break my heart. Moving to stand, I help her up and guide her over to where the sprites are waiting. "I'll be right back," I whisper softly. The sprites move to surround her. The one who seems to be in charge nods to me before moving to rest her hand on Astraea's arm.

Turning and making my way back to the others, I stare down at Sara's poor leg. "What do you want me to do?" I ask, looking up at Lukas.

"I will push down hard on the springs to compress them. As the springs compress, they will lower and relieve pressure on the jaws. I need you to open the jaws while Zee pulls her away," Lukas says, clear and full of authority. He is in Alpha mode. I don't blame him. Someone is messing around on his territory and hurting his pack.

Zee is quietly whispering into Sara's ear, while stroking her side to keep her still and calm. I move to kneel behind the trap, ready to pry them open, when Lukas gives me the word. Sara won't be able to heal properly until the jaws are off her and then I can help speed up the process. Lukas pushes down on the springs and Sara whimpers anew. Startled, I reach for her and lay a hand on her flanks, my magic seeping into her, sending warm calm waves through her body. Sara's head lifts and looks at me, and even in her wolf form, I can see the gratitude shining in her eyes.

"Now, Nesrin," Lukas says.

I spin back to face the trap. Grabbing hold of the cold metal, I pry them open, surprisingly easy. Moments later, Sara is free. I let go of the trap and crawl over to her, looking at her leg. I'm amazed by how quickly it's healing, but just to be sure, I let my hands hover over it for a moment, feeling for damage. Once the healing is complete, Zee lets out a breath. His whole body sags in relief and he reaches over, ruffling my hair. I bat his hand away, chuckling softly. Lukas is helping Sara, who's back in human form, to her feet. How are their clothes still intact? Where do they go when they shift?

Zee breaks me from my thoughts, his voice cool and calm. "That's one way to start the morning. Now, who's hungry?" He stands, brushing the dirt off his clothes before looking at each of us. Startled by his abrupt change in subject , I blink up at him, and I can't help the laugh that escapes me. Astraea comes walking over and wraps her arms around Sara's legs. I'm happy to see Zee back to his unruffled self, and Sara is fully healed and smiling down at my niece. Lukas comes over and holds my elbow to help me up. I look at him, puzzled.

"Your feet," is his clipped response. He is angry, and I don't blame him. Someone put a dangerous trap on his land and messed with his pack. I try my best to ignore the pain throbbing in my feet, as I glance at Sara. "Thank you for protecting her."

"It was nothing."

"It was everything."

A blush coats her cheeks, and she nods, tucking her hair behind her ear. "Thank you for healing me and my mate. I hope I didn't drain too much energy from you."

That tiny bit of healing would do nothing to my energy levels. Lukas's hand hooks around my waist as he helps alleviate some of the weight from my feet. I want to protest, but I enjoy his touch, so I keep my mouth shut. Astraea releases Sara and runs for me, and I scoop her up in my arms as we all head back to the outpost. I do my best not to wince at the pain each step brings. Even with Lukas taking some of the weight, it hurts like a bitch. I have a quick look and notice quite a few deep lacerations on the bottom of my feet. When we get back, I would have to bandage them. For some reason, I have never been able to heal my own wounds.

Soon I'll need to have another conversation with Lukas. I hope the wolves don't think I'm too much trouble and get rid of me. This last twenty-four hours has not painted witches in a good light, and even with me helping, I fear the pack will not want me around. I know I should leave so no one else gets hurt, but I can't. When I'm with Lukas, I feel safer than I ever have before.

# CHAPTER TWELVE

I want to scream, to cry and rage, but I am strangely numb as I push through the door of my bookstore. My heart is already building a protective armor around it, preparing me for what I am about to see. My heart sinks as I walk a few feet into Scarlet Charms.

"I can't believe it," I murmur, looking around me. It is all gone, everything lying in ashes around me. A tiny crack forms in my chest as my breath catches in my throat, and I swallow, pushing down the tears. All my hard work has been destroyed in a matter of minutes. All those precious books now lie in ruins. I can still feel traces of magic in the air, causing my magic to crackle along my skin in response. I know who did this. What I don't understand is why.

We woke this morning to the police knocking on my door, informing me my bookstore was gone. I got dressed and put on my comfiest boots because my feet were still in bandages. My tender soles were not yet healed from the run through the forest yesterday. I left Astraea with Zee and gave them strict orders not to leave my apartment. Then Lukas and I followed the police to my store on Lukas's motorbike. The drive went by so quickly, I don't recall it at all.

A slight tug in my chest alerts me that Lukas is close by. I have become oddly aware of where he is at all times. He has a deep frown on his face as he talks in a quiet voice with the fire marshal.

I glance down when my foot catches on something, a growl working its way up my throat.

"Gary couldn't find where the fire started or how," Lukas says, coming up behind me. I bend to collect a half-burned copy of The Wind in the Willows. I love this book. The moral of the story is one I choose to take into my own life. That you should always try to do your best at all times, forgive others, and make the world a better place. It doesn't always seem to work that way though, because I'm not sure I can forgive the coven for this.

"Huh?" I shake off the thoughts swirling in my mind.

"Gary, the fire marshal," Lukas says, indicating to the short stout man with a balding head standing by the front door of the store. "He said he can't see where the fire originally started, which is strange."

"Because someone created it magically," I state.

"The coven?" Lukas's face darkens with fury.

"Yes, it was a warning." I spin to face Lukas. I realize the coven can't possibly know what Astraea is, and my magic isn't so special that they would go to all this effort to get me. Yes, my healing power is getting stronger, and yes, I have magic sight, but still. The only reason I can think that they would come after me would be Astraea, but they can't know about her. If they learned about her being a hybrid, they would execute us on the spot. Witches are not allowed to be involved with the wolves, or any shifter or other magical race, let alone mate with them. Still, things are escalating, and I don't know why.

"Why me? What do they want?" I whisper into the burned-out room, even though I know Lukas won't have the answers I want.

"I don't know, Nesrin. I really think you should consider staying at my house at least until we can figure this out. It is the safest option at this point."

I nod my head as I look around at my destroyed bookstore, unable to form a verbal response.

What has my life come to? I feel like I've been running from something my whole damn life.

I make my way to the back of the store and pull out the key for my office before unlocking the door and pushing inside. The wards I have on this room are stronger than those on the rest of the store and have saved it from the fire. I breathe out a sigh of relief at the sight of my family's grimoire sitting on the desk, untouched. Its old brown leather cover is still in perfect condition. I walk over, running my finger over the engravings. I always thought my family originated from Germany, as that was when the grimoire was first started by Blanchette. She was a healer like me. Many called her the witch in the red cloak. She wore it to let the magical community recognize her as a healer. I stare at the markings on the cover and wonder for the hundredth time about the markings etched there. They are from ancient Greece, so I can't help feeling that maybe that is where my family's story truly began.

Lukas comes up behind me and looks at the mess on my desk. Potions, charms and spells are laid out everywhere, my own organized mess. I pick up my grimoire and wave my hand, summoning an orb of light. I walk over to get a box, placing my grimoire at the bottom and bringing it back to the desk to start packing up my supplies.

"We can move all this to my house. It will be safe there," Lukas tells me.

I nod, not looking at him. My mind whirling, my concentration focused on what I'm doing. If I let myself feel any emotion but anger in this moment, I will lose it, and I can't—won't do that. Not here. Maybe when I am alone I will allow myself to break down, let it all out.

"That would be great. I can't leave all these potions and spells here. I don't want them to fall into the wrong hands."

Lukas doesn't answer. He just gives my shoulder a gentle squeeze, and then I feel him leave the room, probably to go talk to the fire marshal again. I move around, gathering things I want to take now and putting them in the box. The rest I can come back for later today. I make sure to grab extra sleeping potions. I have a feeling I'm going to need them.

When I got the news, I called Suzy. She was devastated and wanted to come down to help me, but I told her I couldn't have anyone in here as it was a crime scene. She made me promise to tell the police about the teenagers who tried to break in, but she doesn't know who they really were, or what is actually happening.

I huff out a long, suffering sigh and pick up my box. I make my way back through the store, the tug in my chest guiding me toward where Lukas should be. As I make it around some shelves, I see Lukas standing outside with a woman. Her hand is resting on his chest as she smiles up at him. A growl works its way up my throat, and my fingers clench the box in my hands. Her long honey blonde hair flows down her shapely body, as her other hand moves to his arm. Lukas's frown is firmly in place as he listens to whatever she is saying. Jealousy courses through me, tearing at my insides, causing my magic to flare in response. I try desperately to claw it back to me, but it's no use. It senses my emotions and is reacting in a primal way, out of instinct to protect me. I watch as she leans up, and whispers in Lukas's ear. My body locks up. Anger burns in the pit of my stomach, and I want to vomit. Is it totally irrational to want to tear her limbs from her body so she can't touch him again? Goddess, what is *wrong* with me?

Lukas laughs at whatever she's said to him, and something in my chest fractures, sending out a wave of raw magic. The ground shakes violently, and everyone yells as the windows explode outward. Lukas's head whips up, his eyes finding mine through the broken glass window. His gaze narrows on me, and the woman turns to see what he is looking at. Seeing me standing there, a smirk claims her face, and she runs her hand up Lukas's arm. Lukas says something and pushes her hands away, but I'm already turning away from them. I have no right to feel this way, but I can't help the hurt that worms its way into my heart. I let out a deep breath. What is wrong with me?

# CHAPTER THIRTEEN

I take a deep breath and knock twice on the door in front of me. I left Astraea in my apartment upstairs with our two self-appointed shifter bodyguards. After my display of magic earlier outside of what remains of my bookstore, Lukas tried to get me to talk, but I refused. My embarrassment and anger hasn't fully settled and I know I can't trust myself not to say something I will regret later. To my relief, the woman responsible for sparking my irrational fit of jealousy left after my outburst, which was probably the best decision, for her sake and mine. Still, things were tense until Zee showed up.

I smile as I remember how the three of them looked when I left the apartment moments ago—Lukas and Astraea sprawled out on the floor with a puzzle, while Zee lay on the sofa behind them, throwing a ball into the air. They've become so comfortable with each other so quickly that I can barely wrap my mind around it. It's as if the two shifters have always been in our lives. They seem to have just fallen in with us so easily, and I've never had that kind of connection with anyone before. Not even with Hunter.

The door slowly creaks open, and Grace's blue eyes shine at me as she stands in front of me, looking just as she always does, her long gray hair hanging braided over her shoulder, a soft smile on her face.

Nervous, I run my hands over my jeans and give her a small smile. "Hey, Grace. Can we talk?"

Grace nods, stepping aside so I can enter. Her apartment, the exact same setup as mine, is neat and tidy. "You smell like smoke, Nesrin," Grace observes, scrunching up her nose.

I glance down at my jeans and sigh as I notice the black marks smeared across them. My clothes have been doing it tough lately. At the rate things are going, I'm going to end up needing a new wardrobe soon.

A lump forms in my throat as my thoughts turn to my store. "That's because I just came from my bookstore . . . Someone burned it down."

Grace gasps, covering her mouth. Her eyes are wide, expressing every bit of her shock as she stares at me. Grace knows how much I loved that place. How much work I put into opening it up, into building a dream. For most people, reading is a way for them to escape their lives. It was my escape. Somewhere I could hide from the troubles of my life, if only for a moment. I opened the store so that I could share that feeling with others. Not to mention the fact that the smell of books is magical in itself. That a book, new or old, can trigger emotions difficult to describe. For the most part, it has a calming effect on those who inhale the aroma.

"Oh no! Was it . . . you know . . . the coven?" she whispers, moving to take my hands in hers. I squeeze her hands and let go, turning and sitting down at the kitchen table. Grace takes the chair next to mine.

"I think so. They're sending a warning." A warning that I have no intention of heeding. I will not join their stupid little coven. Especially after what they have done.

"They are definitely persistent," Grace muses.

"Do you know why? You said last night that *they* were hunting us. Who are *they*? The coven? If so, why would they be after us? My parents were always so adamant that we stay away from other witches—the covens—but never told us why."

Grace looks uneasy at my questions, shifting in her seat and turning her head away to look out the window. I can't shake the feeling that she is hiding something more. I realize that I shut her down last night, but I need her to answer my questions. Questions my parents should have given me the answers to. With a deep sigh, her blue eyes flicker toward me, their usual spark gone, replaced with sorrow.

"I don't know why the coven is after you, Nesrin. All I know is that the Order of Tartarus has been tracking your family for a long time. And by a long time, I mean centuries. They would use the covens to get to you. It's why your family stayed clear of the covens and others like them. I would love to know what drives them to be so covert in their plans to eliminate your bloodline. They are hell-bent on making sure none of you live."

My mouth drops open and my chest tightens at her words. I've never heard of this order before, and the name does not fill me with warm fuzzy feelings. I start to ask about them, but Grace holds up a hand to stop me.

"I can't answer any questions about the Order of Tartarus. I'm sorry, Nesrin, but I know nothing about them. If I did, I would tell you. I have tried for years to get answers, and have been blocked at every turn."

And yet I know there must be more she knows about them, and I can't understand her hesitancy.

"What I can tell you is they have spies hiding within the covens all over the world. They keep to the shadows. They are secrets and myths. Fire is their specialty, and they are merciless in their goals. They won't stop until every last one of you is gone. They are evil through and through."

I open my mouth and snap it closed again. Tilting my head, I frown at her. "Why? What is so special about my family?"

Grace is silent. Surely, she will tell me if the information was important. Right?

"Grace?" I prompt.

She looks anxious as she finally responds, "I can't be sure, and I don't want to speculate. All I know is that it has something to do with your bloodline."

She is being beyond vague. I'm not sure why that is, but figuring I can try again later, I ask another question, "You said you were friends with my grandparents?"

Her shoulders tense as if I've caught her off guard with my change of topic. "Yes, we were. Your grandmother and I were best friends growing up. We drifted apart as young adults, as most do, but we found each other again later in life," she explains, a wistful expression on her face.

I rest my chin on my hand, leaning on the table. "You said you made them a promise. What was it?"

"You understand, I'm a banshee, and with that comes horrible knowledge of when a loved one is going to die. Most people think we banshees are something to fear. A bad omen. But that is only because they misunderstand us. Don't get me wrong, there are some of us who have turned to a less favorable path, but most are like me. I tied myself to your family's bloodline so I could watch over them and warn of dangers to come. I promised your grandmother the night of her death that I would watch over her kin and protect them for as long as I lived. A promise I failed to keep."

I feel a tiny bit of guilt slither through me because I misunderstood as well. I thought banshees brought death with them, but that isn't the case at all. To be able to see or sense someone's death in the near future doesn't mean you made it happen. "You were there the night my grandparents died? What happened? Mom and Dad refused to talk about them or Ireland after we left."

"I was. I tried to warn them about the fire, what it meant, but they knew it was their time, and they sacrificed themselves for–" She halts, the words seeming to stick in her throat.

"For what?" I press, shifting forward in my seat.

She falters, placing a hand on her throat as she continues, "For me. So I could watch over those who remained."

She is lying. I have no idea how I know, but I do. I keep my face neutral and sit back in my chair, idly tapping my fingers on the table as I eye Grace carefully. Once again, she is leaving something out, withholding something important. I am fully aware of my growing frustration, but I push it back down. There is still something I am dying to know. Something I need to understand.

"Where were you when Niamh died?" I breathe the question out, bracing for the answer.

I lost so much that day. But Astraea lost even more. She lost her mother and father. I am not sure I've been doing the best job of raising her, and the way she has instantly bonded with Lukas and Zee gives me the distinct feeling that I've been holding her back. An enormous task has been placed on my shoulders to raise and care for this beautiful girl, and . . . What if I fuck it up? What if I've *already* fucked it up?

"I felt nothing until they started the fire. There were no warnings, no signs. Nesrin, I'm so sorry I didn't make it in time. It's something I regret every day." Grace looks stricken, tears falling down her face. I lean forward, reaching out to cover her hands with mine. It's apparent that this guilt has been weighing her down, a struggle I am all too familiar with.

"It wasn't your fault. I don't blame you," I say, and mean it. Grace would never hurt us like that.

"I see the look in your eyes, Nesrin. It wasn't your fault, either." Her words are gentle, as if she's trying to convince me, though I'm not so sure. If I would have tried harder, woken up sooner, something, anything . . . everything could have been different.

"Astraea deserves her mother, not me. I'm so afraid I'm going to fail her."

"You have a lot of internal strength, Nesrin. Don't sell yourself short. Being sensitive to these issues is okay, and it means that you're going to be a wonderful mom, because every good mom has those thoughts. Astraea is a hybrid. She is half-witch and half-wolf. With that will come challenges."

My stomach bottoms out at her words, words no one should know. Noticing my shock, she smiles and continues, "Yes, I know your secret, and trusting only a few is wise. Astra is looking for a pack whether or not she realizes it. Even you have the urge to fit in, Nesrin. Every wolf needs a pack. You have the eyes of a wolf, you know." I frown, but she keeps going, unfazed or unaware of my confusion. "Nesrin, you can't be the only one she ever has, all because you're too afraid to open yourself up. You are strong because you've had to be. You've had no other option. But true strength is taking a leap of faith, to trust the blood which flows through your veins. Plus, Astraea is stronger than you think."

Goosebumps spread across my body and my heart speeds up, but I am utterly confused. What is she talking about? I'm not the hybrid, Astraea is. She's the one I have to protect.

"You can't do this on your own. Haven't you heard the saying it takes a village to raise a baby? And, from what I've discovered, Lukas runs a loyal pack and is a great Alpha. His pack follows him because they respect him, not because they fear him."

I bob my head, trying to keep my emotions at bay. The lump forming in my throat feels like it will choke me. I have been so alone. I shut everyone out in order to protect Astraea, but really it was to protect my own heart from more loss. A stuttered breath heaves from my mouth and I rub my hands over my face, feeling tears on my cheeks. I didn't even realize I've been crying.

"Thank you, Grace. I needed to hear that." My voice is barely above a whisper.

"It's the truth. I will always be here if you need me." She reaches over and pats my cheek. "You look so much like your grandmother." Her eyes begin filling with tears again.

Ignoring that last part, because I don't think I can go there right now, I fill Grace in on my plans. "I have decided to stay with Lukas for a while until we can sort this coven stuff out. Will you be okay here on your own?"

"That is the best idea I have heard. Lukas will keep you and Astraea safe. I will be fine here, and I'm just a call away if you need me."

A small sigh of relief leaves me. I needed to hear *that*, too. That going with Lukas is a smart idea. I don't fully trust my feelings where he is concerned.

"Okay. Well, I best be going. Lukas is waiting for me." I stand up, pulling Grace into a hug. We embrace for a long moment before I release her, moving toward the door.

"Wait! I almost forgot. I have something for you." Then she races off toward her room. When she returns, she is holding a small wooden box, the sides carved with intricate patterns of vines and roses. She holds it out for me to take and I give her a puzzled look before reaching out to take it from her. As I do, my fingers brush the top, tracing the patterns.

"It's beautiful," I whisper, running a finger over the carvings. They're the same as those on my family grimoire. My hand trembles as soft vibrations come from within.

"Open it," Grace urges gently.

Lifting the lid, I suck in a sharp breath. Nestled inside on blue velvet is a silver chain necklace with a pendant that seems to glow, pulsing with its own magic. The pendant is in the shape of a bright silver star with a blue stone in the middle. It dangles from a crescent moon which is laced with intricate designs. It is absolutely stunning.

"It was to be given to you on your twenty-first birthday," Grace explains.

My gaze shoots to hers. "What?" I choke out, lightly touching the pendant. A warmth flows up my arm and I pull my hand back.

"Your grandparents asked me to give this to you." I am so confused.

"How do you have it?" I ask.

"Your grandmother gave it to me to pass it along. It was important to her that you get it," she replies.

"Why wait so long, then? You've known where I was for a while now and it's been a few years, Grace." The anger burns in the pit of my stomach. I've only known Grace for the eleven months since I moved to Portland, but she knew even then where I was in Pittsburgh.

"The time never seemed right," she answered with a shrug.

If it was meant for me, she should have passed it along straight away. Yes, I would have had questions. Any normal person would. But instead this feels like another secret she's kept from me.

"And *now* seems right?" My voice comes out harsh. I really don't know what to make of this conversation with Grace. She doesn't want to answer my questions. She just wants to create more. I find myself beyond baffled, and the sting of betrayal nips at my chest.

"Yes."

The hum of magic from the pendant draws my attention again. I gently pick up the chain, lifting the pendant from the box and holding it up at eye level. As the silver star slowly spins around, the light catches the blue gem and flashes my eyes. I blink, and when my eyes open again, I'm standing in a field of white flowers. I blink again, confused, and am now standing in a forest. A flash of movement to the left catches my attention, and I turn my head to see a teenage girl running and laughing, her long blonde hair floating behind her. Two brown wolves flank her as she darts between the trees. Suddenly, the scene shifts and I'm standing in Grace's apartment once more. Quickly, I drop the pendant back into the box and shut the lid. Grace frowns at me, clearly confused by my reaction.

I clear my throat. "Can you feel that energy coming off it?" I ask, curiosity getting the better of me.

A strange look crosses her face. "No. But it's not meant for me. Your grandmother was rather vague about the whole thing, but over the years, I have discovered rumors regarding this necklace."

"What rumors?"

"Rumors saying it belonged to a goddess. That she gave it to her daughter as a gift of magic and protection when her daughter took a mortal as a mate, choosing to live in this realm. It's been passed down for generations, waiting for the daughter of light to unlock her power."

I stare at Grace, unblinking. Daughter of light? Well, that's weird. It's the belonged to a goddess part that has struck me speechless. Why on earth would it be given to me, then?

I recall the start of my family's grimoire. It was first written in by Blanchette. Then by her daughter, Alisa. There is no mention of the pendant that I've ever seen there. Maybe they have the wrong person?

Grace smiles, patting my arm. "I'm sure you'll figure it out. You're a smart girl." She turns me toward the door, ushering me into the hall. I turn, raising my eyebrow at her. Is she kicking me out? "Wait. Grace, don't you think–"

"Now, you better get going. Take care, Nesrin." She shuts the door, and I stand there, staring at her door for a few moments, unmoving. Then I stumble from her apartment in a daze, making my way back up the stairs to my apartment to pack. I have no idea what is happening, and the more questions that get answered, the more I find I need to ask.

# CHAPTER FOURTEEN

Walking into my apartment, I feel lighter than I did hours ago. I still had so many questions swirling in my head. Grace did not give me any answers, just more questions. My bookstore was a pile of ash, but Astraea was safe. That was the most important thing. I turn, locking the door. My apartment is silent, the absence of noise almost deafening. It kicks my anxiety levels up a notch.

"Guys? Astra? I'm back." I call out but there's no reply. The apartment is empty. With shaky hands, I pull out my phone but remember I haven't exchanged phone numbers with the guys yet. I turn to go back out the door and spot a note on the small table next to the door. Putting down the box, I pick it up reading over it. I'm pissed. I feel tears prick my eyes with the rush of emotions barreling through me.

*Nesrin, Gone for ice-cream at Little Bites.*
*Lukas.*

Within seconds, I'm out of the door and racing down the stairs. I put on an extra burst of speed, hurrying through the lobby towards the front doors. I get hit with a bitter breeze as I exit the lobby door out into the cold, having forgotten my jacket in my haste. Crossing my arms tightly over my chest, I storm towards the café. I couldn't bring myself to turn back and get it. Yes, I was angry, and I knew I should use the walk to calm down and think rationally, but they took Astraea from me, well technically they didn't really take her from me, but they took her without my permission. I weave past a group of teenagers on the sidewalk and feel my phone vibrate in my pocket. Quickly pulling it out, I glance down at the screen. It was Suzy.

I take a breath and gather myself. "Hey."

"Nesrin, where are you?"

"On my way to Blues, why?"

"Okay, I'll meet you there."

Before I can respond, the line goes dead. I frown and look down at my phone. *Weird.*

Pocketing my phone, I see Blues café up ahead, my emotions bubbling over. Astraea was all I had left. I couldn't let anything happen to her. I couldn't believe they thought a note would be enough with everything going on. My anger heated my cheeks even though I was shivering from the cold. Gripping the handle, I swing open the door and step inside. The gust of wind that followed me in sent my hair flying all over the place. Sighing, I let the warmth of the shop soak into me. Pushing hair from my face, it was a knotted mess from my brisk walk here. I turned to my left, where six tables lined the front windows and another four booths covered the far wall. I spotted them straight away in one of those booths and stopped short.

Astraea was perched on Lukas' leg with Zee sitting across from them, laughing behind his hand, the spoon dangling from his fingers. That's not what had me frozen to the spot, though. It was Astraea feeding ice cream to Lukas, like he wasn't the most powerful Alpha on this side of the country. She had the biggest smile on her face and Lukas only had eyes for her, like she was his entire world as well.

"Quite a sight, hey Ness." I jumped, startled at the voice, not having noticed Blue coming up next to me.

I cleared my throat. "Sure is." I barely manage to get out. My anger had simmered down at the sight of them. Now I'm just plain upset.

"Didn't know you knew the Alpha?" Blue eyed me curiously, his blue eyes assessing. I took a step back, confusion rolling through me.

"How… how do you know who he is?" I stammer.

"Well, considering he is my Alpha, I should know." Blue had spoken slowly, gauging my reaction closely. He said it like he thought I knew.

"What?" I exclaim, putting my hands on my hips and facing him. It seemed I was not very good at identifying magical creatures around me at all, unless they used magic to conceal their appearances. I had no clue. First Merve, then Grace and now Blue.

*What the actual fuck.*

"It's okay, Ness." Blue looked stricken by my response.

I gave him an apologetic smile to reassure him I wasn't going to lose it or run away, at least not because of what he was. It's just wolves hate witches. There was only mild tolerance between the two. So why would Blue be so nice to me? What made me so different from the other witches? Why was I so trusted with the shifters? Not to mention the trolls, sprites, elves, the Puca. The list went on with the creatures I had helped since coming to Portland.

Blue held up a hand as if he could sense my rush of thoughts and building panic. "It's okay Nessy. I thought you knew," He repeats softly, moving closer.

I glanced at him, giving him a small smile. "I know, I'm sorry. You just surprised me, that's all."

"Everything okay?" Lukas' deep voice sounds from behind me. I spin around and stare up at his handsome face, and the concern in his eyes ignites my anger again.

"I can't believe you took Astra without asking me first. I was so worried when I got back, you were all gone." The words coming out sharp then fade into a croak as my anger withers away and I'm swallowing over the lump in my throat.

Goddess, I was a mess.

Regret flashed in Lukas' eyes. He reached for me, grabbing my arm gently and pulling me into his chest, then wrapping those powerful arms around me. I relaxed in his hold and rested my head on his chest, my hands resting on his sides, drawing warmth and strength from him.

"I'm sorry, sweetheart, I wasn't thinking. It won't happen again." He murmured into my hair and promised. Deflating, I let myself enjoy the hug a moment longer and pulled back, stepping out of his embrace before I started snuggling in like I belonged there. I would never belong in his arms, no matter how much I enjoyed being there. I reined in my emotions and put them in a tight little box.

Clearing my throat, I looked up at Lukas. I was still upset with him. His apology seemed sincere, so I'd let it go. He lifted a hand and tucked some of my wayward hair behind my ear. He smiled down at me with bright green eyes, his stare turning thoughtful as he scanned my face. "Did you get the answers you were looking for?"

My heart skips a beat or two at the question and I shake my head. I looked around the café and noticed several families watching our exchange.

*Nosey much?*

I heard Lukas smother a laugh and frown. Damn it, I hope no one heard me. I looked to see where Blue had gone and noticed he was back behind the counter. Zee and Astraea were coloring in and finishing up their ice cream in the far booth. I bring my gaze back to Lukas and shrug, "I got some answers, but not all the ones I was hoping for."

"We will figure this out. Come sit down. I'll get you a coffee." Lukas offered, taking a step closer. I sucked in a breath at his close proximity. With a sigh, I take a step back, and glance around again. "No, you guys stay. I will go back and pack some things to take with us to your place. Meet you there?"

"You sure? Did you want me to come with you?"

"No, that's okay."

He sighed deeply. "Are you sure?"

Heat pooled in my stomach at the intense look in his eyes. "Yes, I'll be fine."

Turning, I make my way to the door, trying my best not to glance back. I push out the door, walking into the cool, fresh air. The air whipped across my face, throwing my hair everywhere again. I take a deep, cleansing breath of fresh air. I let the coolness of it soak into me. When I open them again, I feel much more relaxed. This time, I start back towards my apartment at a slower pace. I close my eyes, listening to the noises around me, drawing in the elements to recharge and trying to center myself again. I can't believe how worked up I got, and Lukas, with his dumb handsome face and great hug, melting away my anger. Argh.

*I probably needed therapy.*

I hear a car approaching faster than usual. Opening my eyes, I watch as a black escalade sped down the street towards me. I shake my head at them. *Idiots*, I mutter under my breath. I really hope they got caught by the cops for speeding in a populated area like this.

As they drew closer, I realized they were angled towards me on the sidewalk. I halt my steps and stare at the car. I have a deer in headlights a moment before I'm scrambling to throw up a wall of magic. Raising both hands instinctively, I start humming my incantation. Suddenly, powerful arms wrap around me from behind, throwing us to the side as the car screeches past, barely missing us. I land on a muscled body, then I'm rolled to the side and my back is on the cold ground as a massive hand cups the back of my head, keeping it from hitting the pavement. My breathing is heavy, my heart has the pace of a galloping horse, and I'm just a little bit in shock at how quickly that escalated. It couldn't even have been a minute since I left Blue's. I tilt my head back and look up. I already know who has me cradled gently against them, but Lukas isn't looking at me. He is watching the escalade speed around the corner. I reach up and stroke Lukas' cheek to draw his attention to me. Slowly, so slowly, he tilts his head down to look at me. My breath catches at the rage on his face, the fury blazing in those emerald eyes.

Lukas lets go of me, getting to his feet. I envy the grace with which he moves. He holds out a hand, helping me up. His gaze roams over me as if looking for injuries.

"I'm okay, Lukas." I try to reassure him. "Thank you, I don't know if my shield_" I start but Lukas has other plans. He raises his hand, stopping me mid-sentence. Lukas looks down the street to where the SUV had disappeared around the corner. He shakes his head, blowing out a deep breath. I could still see the rage simmering under the surface in the way he held his body.

"Nesrin, what were you thinking? You were just standing there. You didn't even try to get out of the way." He growled, his hands clenching and unclenching at his sides.

Taken aback by his accusations, my defenses went up. "I wasn't just standing there," I snap.

"Yes, you were." He shot back, instantly cutting his hand through the air in front of us, in an angry gesture.

Annoyance flashed through me, feeling the need to defend myself. "No, I wasn't, I was putting up a _" I started, but Lukas steamed on over the top of me, again. Fury flashed in his eyes, flecks of yellow lighting the green depths. I couldn't stop the tremor that ran through me.

"I came out, and you were just standing there, Nesrin. I thought you might be cold, so I came to give you my jacket and you were watching that car come for you. I was calling your name."

*He was?*

"You didn't hear me. I've never been so scared." Lukas was furious, his whole body shaking. Flecks of gold shot through his emerald eyes. It was terrifying and beautiful. I wasn't sure just how close to the edge he was, so I took a step back and another. I clenched my jaw to stop myself from saying something to make the situation worse, then turned around, walking away.

"Nesrin," Lukas called, but I just lifted my hand and flipped him off. How dare he yell at me like I was a child. I stormed the rest of the way home and packed up mine and Astraea's stuff and sat there waiting.

# CHAPTER FIFTEEN

"Hi. You've reached Suzy. I can't answer the phone right now, but please leave a message."

I groan, tipping my head back. "Hey, Suzy. It's Nesrin. I've left you like three messages. Please call me back."

I hang up and pace the living area. Where is she? I've been trying to call her since I left Lukas standing on the sidewalk, and she still hasn't answered. I hope everything is okay. I turn, plonking down on my lounge unceremoniously, and open my phone to find something to distract me from worry. Ten minutes later, a knock sounds at the door. I stand, pocketing my phone, and make my way to the door. I push onto my tiptoes and peek through the spyhole to see Zee alone in the hallway, running a hand through his mass of blonde hair. I swing the door open and peer behind him, but still don't see Astraea or Lukas.

"Lukas needed time to cool down. He is in the car with Astra," Zee answers my unspoken question, rubbing his neck. He looks almost contrite, which amuses me to no end.

I arch an eyebrow at him and shrug. "Okay, whatever." Spinning around, I head for the piles of bags in the middle of the room, but Zee stops me, putting a hand on my shoulder and turning me to face him.

"Are you okay? Lukas told me what happened."

Shrugging his hand off, I glare at him. "Yes, I'm fine. I'm more pissed at Lukas right now," I snap, regretting it straight away. He doesn't deserve my anger. I'm not mad at Zee. But I want this conversation over with. The situation with the Shadow Lake coven is wearing me down enough as it is. I wanted it resolved so I can get back to normal. But have things ever been normal?

"Well, he can be over the top, but he means well," Zee says in earnest. He nudges my arm, making me sway.

"I don't care. It's been a fucking long week for me, Zee. All I want is some time to process, a bath, and chocolate. Lukas promised me a bath, and I promised myself chocolate. If you want to promise me wine, it will be a trifecta." I don't mean to pout, but it happens.

Zee lets out a laugh that softens his entire face, making my own smile twitch. "Few people can surprise me. But you, honey, are a bag full of surprises."

"Just keeping you on your toes," I retort lightly. Amusement reflects in his eyes as a big hand palms the back of my head, pulling me closer.

"Come here. You look like you need a hug." I go into his arms willingly. There is just something about hugs that always makes you feel better. It's like its own form of communication, letting the other person know they matter. I can feel my spirits lifting already.

He pulls away, holding me by the arms. "Okay, honey, let's get you loaded up, then in a bath ASAP." He sends me a wink, letting go and turning around for some bags. When he turns back around, there is a roguish smirk covering his face.

I laugh. "Don't be wasting all that charm on me, Zee," I say, gesturing at him. Zee looks down at his body, then back up at me, confused. Zee is extremely good looking, with the whole surfer look going on, blonde hair, and blue eyes that always glimmer with mischief when he smiles. He is becoming a good friend, and I need one of those more than anything.

"What charm?" he asks innocently.

"Oh, don't give me that, either. You know how hot you are, but you're not my type."

He barks out a sharp laugh and slaps a hand over his heart, trying to look wounded. "Honey, I'm everyone's type."

I shake my head at his antics, grabbing Astraea's backpack and two of the four suitcases before wheeling them to the door.

"You aren't scared to be staying on pack land, staying at the alpha's house, are you? I thought I'd have to drag you kicking and screaming."

"I'm more scared of my own kind than I am of yours, Zee," I admit truthfully. His look is full of sympathy as he gives me a curt nod.

"Hey, I've been wondering what happened to those hunters you took from my shop last week?" I ask as we make our way down the stairs.

"Oh, them. We couldn't get anything out of them, so we brought in a contact to erase their memories and sent them on the next bus to Vancouver."

I stop walking and blink at him. "What? Who can erase memories?"

"A high level vampire, of course," he says, like it's the only obvious answer.

The forty minute drive from my apartment to the pack lands was so beautiful I couldn't tear my eyes from the scenery. It was one reason I chose the Portland area to begin with. I love the hills, mountains, ocean, lakes, the greenery. As we pass a turnoff for a lumber yard I notice Lukas' name under the sign. I turn to face the front.

"You run the lumberyard?"

"I actually own the lumberyard, and a garage on this side of Portland. I also help my pack with purchasing their own businesses. If they need it, that is," Lukas replies reluctantly, squeezing the steering wheel tighter.

"Like Blue?" I question, ignoring his bad mood. Isn't my fault that car came barreling down the road for me earlier.

"Yes," is Lukas's curt reply. Yep, he's still pissed at me.

Good to know.

I'm not sure why he's so angry with me though. If I'm such a burden, why offer protection in the first place? It isn't my fault I have some crazy order after me. I don't know what I did to warrant their pursual. I will find out though, and keep my secret at the same time.

My phone dings with an incoming message, and I glance down.

**Suzy:** Sorry, I'm in class. Is something wrong?

I frown down at the phone. I didn't imagine that call. I know I spoke to Suzy. Confused, I type out a quick reply, saying we will talk soon.

We turn down a gravel road, and my attention is back out the window. A large two-story colonial-style home comes into view. It is beautiful. With a wraparound porch, the building itself is painted white with a featured front door in a dark oak wood, and with a sweeping staircase that leads up to it. I can just make out a building to the side which must be a shed. Further down the hill, I can see at least a dozen smaller houses fairly spaced apart, so each has some semblance of privacy. There's another large barn type building down there as well, maybe a common area. My eyes draw back to the massive two-story house we've stopped in front of.

My lips part in surprise. "This is your house?" I whisper, unable to keep the wonder out of my voice. My fingers touch the window as I stare at the house. I am probably drooling. This is, like, my dream home. Niamh and I once drew up plans for the house we planned to live in one day. The resemblance is scary.

My door opens and Zee smiles down at me. "Welcome to your new home, honey," he says with a bow.

I laugh at his absurdity and step out of the car. "Temporary accommodation, don't you mean?" I correct him.

"Sure," he says, turning for the trunk. I spin to grab Astraea only to see that Lukas already has her in his arms and is walking around the car to meet me. Grabbing my hand, he gives it a quick squeeze. "I'm sorry," is all he says, and I just nod, scared that if I open my mouth, I'll say something to ruin this truce and piss him off again.

We are just heading up the stairs when we hear yelling from the houses down the hill. We all whirl around and see a young woman waving her arms. I look around, confused.

Who is she waving and yelling at?

Not a second later, two small wolves run from the side of the house, coming directly for us. My heart threatens to fly out of my chest, and my magic automatically flares in my hands. Lukas puts a hand to my shoulder and squeezes firmly, but not painfully.

"It's okay. They won't hurt you," he murmurs between us. I look up at him, his soft smile reassuring me. Holding my breath, I turn back just in time as the two wolves reach us, running in circles around my legs, yipping happily. It is at this moment that I realize these wolves are smaller than most, and let the tension in my body ease.

"I'm so sorry. They saw you and just wouldn'," the young woman apologizes as she reaches us, brushing her thick brown corkscrew curls back from her face.

Frowning, I look down at the wolves rubbing along my legs and reach down, running my fingers through their coats. Both are a chocolate brown, and so soft I can't help the small laugh that escapes me. I am touching a goddamn wolf.

"It's alright, Kyra. It was to be expected," Lukas says, reassuring the woman everything was fine. Astraea wants to get down and see the wolves, so Lukas places her at his feet. The two wolves come over, sniffing her, then start barking and nudging her. I stiffen, ready to grab her, but Lukas merely shushes the wolves.

Then both start changing. I recognize them immediately as the two children I helped escape from the hunters. They must be brothers, because they look identical, each with brown hair and warm brown eyes.

The woman, Kyra, having moved closer, grabs my hand. "I cannot thank you enough for what you did for my boys. To think those hunters would have got them." She shudders. It occurs to me that this must be their mother. I can see the resemblance. They all have the same brown hair and eyes, but her hair has the most beautiful corkscrew curls, and her skin is just a bit darker.

"I did what anyone would have done," I reply, feeling a blush come to my face.

"No. No, they wouldn't. They would have saved themselves," Kyra argues, staring at me. She lets go of my hand and takes a step back.

"She is right," Lukas agrees, moving to stand next to me. His arm brushes mine, making butterflies take flight in my belly.

Trying to ignore the presence beside me, I glance over at Zee, who is sitting on the stairs behind Astraea and the boys, watching everything. When he notices my gaze, he winks.

Rolling my eyes at him, I look back to Kyra. "I could never let the hunters take them or anyone else. What would that make me if I just stood by? You have to help those who are unable to help themselves. I've spent most of my life helping others. It comes naturally to me."

Thoughts of Niamh and all those people outside watching our house burn flash through my mind. No one tried to help us that night.

Kyra nods. I can see she wants to say more, but she stops herself when Lukas clears his throat.

I turn to the boys, and introduce myself cheerfully, "Hi, I'm Nesrin."

Shyly, they look at each other and slowly approach. I try my best to hide my amusement, because not two minutes ago they were running circles around me. They stop a foot from me, and the one who is a bit taller smiles. "Hi. I'm, um, Noah, and this is my little brother, Liam. I'm seven, and he's five."

"Five and a half," Liam corrects his brother, pushing him. Oh my gosh, these boys are cute.

"Well, it's nice to officially meet you. This is Astraea," I tell them with a big smile. Both boys flash me a huge grin.

"Thank you for helping us, Miss Witch," Liam says with an adorable grin that shows off his two dimples.

"Liam!" Kyra shrieks, giving me an apologetic smile. I let out a laugh that I feel down to my bones, and with tears in my eyes, I hold my hands out to the boys, who don't hesitate to take them, which makes me feel really damn good.

"It was my pleasure. I'm always here if you need me," I assure them with a smile.

"Your hair is real pretty," Noah says before reaching out and lightly touching the mass of waves.

"Thank you."

Astraea, wanting to be part of this moment, moves up to my side and ducks under my arm. I squeeze the boy's hands and let go, holding Astraea tight against me.

"Well, I best get these two inside and settled in. Thanks for getting everything ready, Kyra," Lukas says, picking up my bags and turning to make his way inside. I smile at Kyra and the boys, giving them a wave as I head inside.

# CHAPTER SIXTEEN

T he house is enormous. A beautiful masterpiece. Dark wooden floors run the length of the foyer, to the foot of the stairs and into the spacious living area. The kitchen is located along the back of the house and is a dream, and probably the same size as my apartment. All the rooms had tall windows that gave the perfect view of the valley with a river running through it. The staircase that leads from the foyer to the upstairs bedrooms is a masterpiece in itself, with a hand-carved banister that has patterns of vines running along it.

Astraea and I basically have an entire floor to ourselves. There are four enormous bedrooms on the second floor. We will share one, and Lukas occupies another down the hall. I still can't believe I agreed to this, but I'm not stupid enough to put Astraea at risk. It doesn't hurt that I am in love with our bathroom, which does indeed have a claw-foot bathtub. Throwing my phone on the bed, I bend down to pick up a toy Astraea left on the floor. It appears Lukas has a soft spot for my girl and bought her a few housewarming presents. He has really gone above and beyond to make us feel welcome.

Making my way over the bed, I look down at the pile of clothes there. At the thought of unpacking, I groan, tipping my head back and staring up at the ceiling. There are much worse things I could be doing, but what I really need to do is get dressed and head downstairs. I scratch my head, contemplating what to wear. As I run my hand through my hair, my fingers get caught on a knot.

"Damn it," I curse, dropping my hand.

After going through my clothes, I settle on black jeans and an oversized gray sweater and my favorite pair of black suede ankle boots. My hands make quick work of tying my hair up in a messy bun, which is made difficult by how long it has gotten. Something tugs at my chest and I peer over my shoulder at the suitcase laying in the corner. I left the necklace Grace gave me in there. Should I put it on? I have this feeling deep in my gut that as soon as I put that necklace on, things will change. And I'm not sure I'm ready for that.

My phone dings with another incoming message, and I glance over at the screen. Suzy again. We've been messaging back and forth all morning. When I asked about her calling me, she swore she never did, that she had been in class all morning. Which is where she is now. I can't help but laugh at the message.

**Suzy:** He is such a jackass!

That girl has no filter. I shake my head as I make my way downstairs, running my hand along the smooth wood. When I reach the bottom, I veer left towards the kitchen. It smells amazing, and right on cue, my stomach growls. As I come into the kitchen, Astraea's laughter rings out. Surprised at the sound, I trip over my feet, catching myself on the door frame. Tears sting my eyes like they always tend to do when she makes a noise. I look up to see Lukas flipping pancakes high in the air and catching them again in the pan, and Astraea sitting on the bench next to him, clapping and laughing.

A pang of jealousy hits me square in the chest. You're being ridiculous, Nesrin. Nevertheless, I tip my head back as tears block my throat, my hand moving up to rub the pain that's building in my chest. It will take a while to get used to hearing her laughter again.

Lukas must have heard me, because he looks over his shoulder, giving me a blinding smile, which falters as he notices the expression on my face. He twists, turning the stove off, and comes towards me, stopping when he realizes Astraea is on the bench. He plucks her up, then makes his way to me, concern reflecting in his eyes.

My throat tightens. "Good morning, you two."

I try to clear the emotion swelling in my voice as my eyes rove over the two of them. Lukas is in dark jeans and a long sleeve white henley that stretches over his broad shoulders and chest. I can just make out the tattoos through the thin material. His choice of clothes does nothing to hide his amazing physique. Lukas is six feet of perfection with a face that could captivate anyone. Strong jaw with a hint of stubble, soft lips, emerald eyes that glow when his emotions are high, and . . . nope. No more. He is off limits to me. No matter how much my heart races when he's near, or how safe I feel with him. Goddess, I am as bad as a schoolgirl with a crush.

"Morning," Lukas says, coming to a stop in front of me. I startle as his hand drifts up to wipe a stray tear from my cheek.

*'Mommy?'* Astraea's voice echoes in my head. My knees wobble and I almost collapse. My eyes squeeze shut, and I take a shaky breath. She called me Mommy. This is the second time she has spoken to me, and she called me Mommy. I open my eyes and look into her blue eyes, so innocent and full of love, my walls crumble. This I would not . . . *could* not deny her.

"Come here, my sweet girl," I whisper.

This little girl is the most emotionally intuitive person I know. It's almost as if she can read my mind sometimes, which is scary to consider. She insisted on picking out her clothes today and was currently wearing a white jumper with colored polka-dots, a pair of cute pink leggings and sparkly gray rain boots. She looks adorable, and my heart melts a little more. I feel Lukas grab my hand, squeezing tightly, and I squeeze back, grateful for his silent comfort. Then I reach over and lift Astraea from his arms, needing to hold her close to me. Lukas is looking at me with a mixture of concern and confusion. Not that I blame him. *I'm sure he thinks I'm crazy.* He takes a step closer to the both of us, and wraps an arm around my waist, pulling me into him, the other reaching up to stroke Astra's face.

"I don't think you're crazy," he murmurs.

Embarrassment heats my face, and my head hits his chest as I breathe in slowly. Astraea uttered no words out loud, and I can't seem to keep mine quiet. Lukas doesn't know why I am such a mess. And that one word, *Mommy,* has just torn my heart to shreds. I need to tell him the truth, and soon. I open my mouth when the back door swings open, my words stalling on my tongue. Zee strolls in, followed by a young man I recognize as Gabe and a woman named Alex who is less than impressed with Astraea and me being here. I recognize her as the blonde who was standing with Lukas outside the front of my bookstore the day of the fire.

On my first day, Lukas took the time to introduce me to everyone. Gabe is of Asian descent with long black hair which, from what I've seen, he usually keeps pulled back. Today, it is in a half up, half down style which really suits him. His dark almond-shaped eyes hold too many questions, but he carries himself with confidence. Alex is aggravatingly stunning with her bouncing blonde hair and brown doe eyes, but her personality is crap, for lack of a better word. I take a step back, letting Lukas's arm drop, but not before they all notice how close we were all standing. Zee smirks, and the other two shifters frown in my direction. I have absolutely no idea what I should do. As comfortable as I am around Lukas and Zee, around the other shifters, I feel completely out of place, so I stand here awkwardly in the doorway, holding Astraea tightly, like she can save me from this unfortunate situation.

"What's cookin' good lookin'?" Zee says, approaching us with an easy smile and a wink. I roll my eyes, grateful for the icebreaker.

"Really, Zee?" I chuckle and scratch my head.

Zee's hand goes to his stomach, rubbing it as he drawls, "Honey, I'm hungry, and you're hot. So yeah, what's cooking?"

I let out a laugh, rolling my eyes again in his direction. I really do like Zee. He has a way of putting me at ease. And if I've learned anything these last couple of days, it's that shifters eat a lot. Waving him off, I clarify, "Don't look at me. Lukas and Astra are running the show today. I think it's pancakes."

"Really? What you cooking pumpkin?" Zee asks, plucking Astraea from my arms. Reaching up, she squishes his cheeks together. The scene is so damn cute I can't help but laugh. She is finding comfort with her wolf side, I'm sure of it. I don't know of any other hybrids, or how much of her is a shifter, which is something I really need to talk to Lukas about. As I come out of my thoughts, I peer around and realize two things: Lukas is watching me closely, and Alex is glaring daggers at me.

Okay then, someone needs her morning coffee. And so do I. It is far too early to be dealing with snotty shifters.

"Coffee, anyone?" I ask, turning for the machine in the corner. Lukas has the best coffee machine set up along the far wall in his massive kitchen.

"Sure," says Zee, still goofing around with Astraea.

"Definitely," Lukas agrees, coming up behind me to reach over my head for a cup, his arm brushing my hair slightly, his body heat soaking into my back. My body stiffens, and I attempt to keep my breathing even, doing my very best to keep from leaning back into his chest like I really want to do.

Alex's voice rises over everyone. "I'd love one, Lukas. You know how I like it," she adds, her voice all sugary, batting her false eyelashes. A flash of annoyance rolls through me, envy burning in my chest at what she is implying. I hate that I feel this way. I have no right. Alex is a suitable mate for Lukas. I am not. And, now I'm thinking about mates. Just great.

"Nesrin and I will get everyone a drink. So everyone else can sit down, dig in, and enjoy the pancakes," Lukas's deep voice rumbles behind me, sending butterflies scattering through my stomach. Ugh. Why can I not control my reaction to this man?

We get to work quietly, and all the while I can feel the heat from Alex's stare from Alex burning into my back. I try my best to ignore it, but the challenge is there. My magic is itching at my palms to be let out, to show her exactly who she is messing with. Just one little zap.

"Are you okay?" Lukas whispers, leaning down slightly, nodding towards my glowing hands.

Shit! When did that start?

Nodding, I take a deep breath, trying to center my emotions before I do something I might regret . . . or, more likely, really enjoy. Depends how you look at it. Suddenly, something hits me in the back of the head and a blueberry skims my cheek, falling onto the bench in front of me.

What the . . . I spin around to find Astraea and Zee pointing at each other. I scrunch my mouth up to keep from smiling. "Seriously, you two?"

Astraea has never thrown food, she loves it too much for that, but then again, she has never laughed, either. Another berry hits me, pulling me out of my head. I glance up at the two of them now throwing berries at each other. I look at Lukas, who has a big grin on his face while he watches his beta have a food fight with a toddler. Lukas catches me looking at him and flashes me a grin with dimples.

*Holy crap . . . I think I fell pregnant.*

The intensity in his eyes kicks up a notch, as if he heard me. His stormy green eyes drop to my parted lips, and my breath catches. Something palpable passes between us in that moment. I imagine what it would be like to have those lips on mine, his hands gliding over my naked body. I bite my lip and turn away, but when I hear his soft chuckle and risk a peek, his expression is knowing.

Damn shifters and their super senses. I flush with embarrassment and another berry hits me.

Lukas bumps my arm, "What can you do?" he questions, unfazed.

*Create a shield. That's what I can do.* I do not want berries in my coffee. With a few murmured words and a flourish of my hand, a shield erects in front of us. As I turn back to the counter, I hear Zee say to Astraea, "Astra, you think I can fit this whole pancake in my mouth?"

I turn, glancing at her. She is nodding excitedly. I shake my head because those pancakes are huge. Like, the size of my *face*, huge.

"Zee don't do it," I beg, but I see the twinkle in his eye, the wolfish grin. The challenge has been made. He is going to do it. "You're a hazard, you know that, right? You'll just end up choking," I groan.

"More like a coward. Do two," Gabe taunts. I swing my wide eyes to him. Gabe shrugs. These guys are constantly egging each other on.

"Twenty bucks says he can't do it," Lukas pipes in, grinning at me.

"You're on," Zee says, picking up one of the massive pancakes, sending a wink my way.

"You guys are the worst. I can't watch this," I say, turning to leave the room, taking my coffee with me. I make it up the stairs as cheers go up and I can hear Lukas grumbling about losing twenty bucks.

Well, looks like Zee has a big mouth, after all.

Later that morning, after all the mess has been cleaned up, Astraea and I decide to take a walk around the pack lands. The property is enormous, so we won't be going too far, just down to the river behind the house. On our way out the door, I let Zee know where we're going. I don't know where Lukas disappeared to after breakfast, and I don't care that he left with Alex. Nope. Not at all.

Astraea's face, at least, is full of excitement. She is in love with the wide-open space, not that I can blame her. It's truly beautiful here, with green rolling hills, a river, and the woods. It is going to be hard moving back to our small apartment after staying here. She looks at me and points down to the river, pulling on my hand to go faster.

"Okay. Okay." I chuckle, speeding up my steps. We make our way to the water's edge, and Astraea explores along the shore. I stick close by and take a seat on a grassy patch. Closing my eyes, I tilt my head back to soak in the sun. I hear Astraea's little giggle and smile to myself. Then I hear a tinkling sound, almost like music. I pop my eyes open, looking down at the river, and there, perched on the rock next to her, is the familiar sprite. She looks over at me, her bright violet eyes sparkling, and gives me a small smile that I can't help but return. Astraea bends and picks up a pebble, turns it over in her hands, smiling, and places it on top of a large rock, before bending back down to grab another. The sprite hovers close to her, helping her collect the smooth rocks. I'm happy Astraea has found a new friend, even if it's in the form of a sprite. I lay back, closing my eyes again, enjoying the sunshine, when a shadow falls over me, and everything goes still and quiet.

I hold in my groan because I know who this is without opening my eyes.

"You need to leave," Alex's voice whips through the air. I slowly open my eyes, blinking up at her. I can sense the hostility rolling off her. She is stating her place, setting a challenge.

I tilt my head, considering her. She is incredibly attractive in a girl next door kind of way, with long honey blonde hair and a curvy body. Eyes, no doubt, follow her anywhere she goes. I'm sure she has many admirers and is used to getting exactly what she wants. Though, her deep brown eyes, which are currently narrowed at me, have a slightly crazed look to them. I really do not want to get on the bad side of a wolf, and this one has anger radiating from her every pore. Admittedly, I'm confused by her open hostility towards me. It seems more personal than me just being a witch in her territory. I told Lukas not everyone was going to accept me, that they won't take a witch being on pack lands, but he assured me it would be fine. I decide to play it straight, no games. She knows why I'm here, knows the threat Astraea and I are facing.

"I can't at the moment, which I'm sure you know. Lukas is—"

Alex lets out a long growl, cutting off my words. "Not yours."

I roll my eyes. "I know that. Lukas is—"

"Don't say his name. You need to find somewhere else to go." Her gaze sweeps over me, and her nose wrinkles in disgust, making me want to lift my arm to see if I smell that bad.

"Lukas wants us here, so what you want doesn't matter, now does it?" I reply, standing up, needing to be on a level playing field with this crazy wolf.

She steps forward, sneering in my face. "He is just too honorable to kick you out."

I don't bother to tell her he's the one who invited us here. Alex grabs my arm in a painful grip, and I look down at her hand then back up, raising an eyebrow at her incredulously. "You are nothing but a fragile human. A *witch*. He will never want you." She spits the words at me, and I can't deny the twinge of hurt in my heart.

Magic builds in my chest, reacting instinctively to the threat, and the fierce need to release that magic, to show her just how fragile I am, overwhelms me. "Let go, now," I warn.

"I don't think you're getting my message, Nesrin," she snarls and tightens her grip, sending a sharp pain shooting up my arm and shoulder. My other hand strikes out on instinct, zapping her with just enough magic to get her off of me. She jumps back, letting my arm go, glaring at me. Unfortunately for her, I recently discovered that I can electrify my magic to create a shock. The first time I did it was the night Lukas startled me in the woods when the sprite had taken me to Merve.

"What was that?" she demands, irate. Well, guess what? I'm not exactly thrilled with her, either.

I shake out my arm to relieve the pain she caused, then glance at Astraea, who is watching the exchange silently, the sprite sitting on her shoulder offering comfort.

Looking back at Alex, I tell her, "This needs to stop. Now."

"I won't stop until you're gone." She makes to lunge for me, but my magic rips from my hand, wrapping around her and sending

175

her flying across the river. A loud splash sounds from a distance, and I don't even try to suppress my chuckle. *Take that!*

"Nesrin!" Lukas's voice echoes. I spin around to see him and Zee jogging over. Both look from me to Alex, who is climbing to the shore, soaked and yelling at me from the other side of the river. I can't help the satisfied grin that took over my face. Serves her right.

"Do I want to know what happened?" Lukas inquires, frowning over at Alex, who is stomping into the forest.

I shrug. "She wanted to push. I pushed back. My push just happened to go a lot further." Then I walk over to Astraea and pick her up, smiling at the sprite in thanks before turning back to the two men. Before I make another step towards them, Zee snatches Astraea from me and lifts her above his head, making her squeal in laughter. It amazes me how accepting these people are of her, and they don't even know her heritage yet.

"I'll have a word to her," Lukas says, turning me to face him. I look up at him, ready to argue that I can look after myself, but the second I make eye contact, all thoughts flee my mind.

*Goddess, does he have to be so handsome?*

A smug grin spreads across Lukas's face, and Zee bursts out in laughter, snapping me out of my daze. The tinkling from the sprite confirms for me that, as usual, that out loud.

Dammit. I really have a problem keeping my thoughts to myself. My face heats, and I turn, stalking off towards the house. Their laughter follows me all the way up the hill.

# CHAPTER SEVENTEEN

Whatam I thinking? I have to be crazy. Lukas is going to kill me when he finds out . . . Well, if he finds out. Ugh. Who am I kidding? He's totally going to find out.

Lukas told me not to leave the safety of the pack lands, especially not alone, but I've been cooped up there all week, avoiding Lukas and the incredibly inconvenient feelings he brings. If I'm being honest with myself, I have to admit to being afraid of how he made me feel, and those feelings only seem to be getting stronger the more time we spend together. There will never be any future for us. It seems I have to constantly remind myself of this. He is an alpha, and I am a witch. It is forbidden. Though, thanks to the shifters' heightened senses, I am fairly sure everyone knew how I felt about their alpha. My cheeks heat from embarrassment. I am a mess. My current living situation with the shifters is definitely a challenge. Constantly trying to keep my feelings and emotions locked away is exhausting. Especially since my mouth never seems to be rebelling against me, spewing my most inappropriate thoughts at every turn.

When I got a message earlier from one of my clients, a troll family who needed help, I jumped at the chance to bail for a while. The troll's wife is pregnant and is experiencing complications. I couldn't very well just say no when they needed me. The family is under a glamor spell, of course, but they still can't see a human doctor. The risk of being discovered is too high.

Without the glamor, trolls are not very nice-looking creatures. Their thin wiry frames and gray skin look extremely creepy, not to mention their razor-sharp teeth and fathomless black eyes. Initially, I ran into the husband when he was trying to find medicine for his wife, and he told me then of their situation. That was three months ago, and I've since become quite attached to the welfare of the family.

I pull up at a stop sign, tapping away on the steering wheel as I glance up and down the street. It feels weird being on my own for the first time in over a week. I've had a permanent shadow almost everywhere I've gone. Sure, I could have asked Zee, or even Gabe to come with me, and I probably should have. But I need a break from everyone. Especially that bitch Alex and her constant glaring. Since I threw her across the river, she has kept her distance for the most part. Whether that's due to my having bested her or fear of what Lukas would say, I don't know. Although, just this morning, she got bold and tripped me over as I walked past her with the laundry. Clean clothes scattered everywhere. The whole load ended up covered in dirt. As I walked the laundry back in to be washed again, I admittedly amused myself by thoughts of her flying into the dirt.

Of course, Zee knows what her problem with me is and loves to tease me about it every chance he gets. I'm pretty sure I know, as well. There is no way she doesn't know how I feel about Lukas.

Zee's answer to my question about why she was being such a raging bitch still brings a smile to my face. *First of all, she is a bitch, and nothing will change that. Second, she thinks she has a shot with Lukas. You threaten that.* That second part didn't have me smiling though. Instead, it filled me with a jealousy like none I've ever felt before. It was green and ugly and had no place in my life. I am not that person. She and Lukas would look perfect together, and she is a shifter. She would make a perfect mate for him. I want very much to claw her eyes out.

Argh. I hate myself.

I park my car around the corner from where I need to be, not wanting to park too close to my client's residence. I want to keep things discreet. It's safer that way—for them and for me. The neighborhood is in a fairly pleasant part of Portland. Gigantic trees line the street, creating a beautiful canopy over the road. It isn't raining tonight, but the air is crisp. I shove my hands in my jacket pockets, wishing I brought a scarf and gloves. I am one street away, so I speed up my steps. Lost in my thoughts, I round the corner and come to an abrupt halt. Leaning against the iron fence up ahead are Marcus and his sister.

Fuck, is this a trap? Have they done something to the trolls?

"So nice of you to rush to the aid of a family of trolls, Nesrin," Marcus says sarcastically, pushing off the fence and taking several steps forward. I clench my fists at my sides, angry at myself for being distracted, and angry at Marcus for pulling this shit in the first place.

"If you've hurt any of them, Marcus," I threaten, flexing my fingers around my dagger at my thigh. Two against one isn't great, but it's doable.

"You'll do what, Nesrin?" he taunts as he looks over at his sister who is still leaning against the fence, smirking.

Anger whips through me, making my skin feel tight. I will my heartbeat to slow as I carefully reach my other hand into my back pocket for my phone. I am worried about the trolls. The young family doesn't deserve to get mixed up in this mess of mine.

"What have you done, Marcus? If you've touched any of them," I warn, my fingers brushing against my phone. *Come on.* As discreetly as possible, I grip it, pulling it from my pocket as slowly as I can manage. I let out a breath, keeping the phone behind my back as I focus on Marcus.

"You're in no position to make threats." He tsks, taking another step toward me. At my growl, Marcus sneers. "Don't worry, no harm has come to them. Yet," he adds, then turns to his sister. "Anna, if Nesrin doesn't come quietly, go in there and kill them all."

Shock rolls through me at his words, spoken so coldly. Who is this man? Marcus has been incessant, yes, but never cold or cruel. An anger I have never known before sweeps through me like wildfire. My magic builds in my chest, power thrumming just under the surface, begging to be released. But a sudden chill spreads over me, giving me pause. My body trembles violently, my knees growing weak. Something is different. Something is wrong, but I can't place it.

Internal warnings are now blaring in my head. Screaming at me to turn and run, while I still can. Marcus says something else, but I can barely hear over the blood rushing through my ears. My scalp tightens painfully, the prickling sensation making me want to scream. My brain is urging me to leave, to get as far away as possible. Turning, I see four more witches behind me. I take in their menacing posture, sizing them up. Shit.

With shaky fingers, I unlock my phone and try to remember the right spot to press for recall. I faintly hear the phone ring as I whirl back around to face Marcus and Anna. Both wear a smug look on their faces. Oh, how I want to wipe that look off.

My body stiffens when a sweet sugary voice answers the phone. "Hi, you've reached Lukas' phone." I growl again. Why is Alex answering Lukas's phone? Jealousy fills my veins, and I struggle to temper my rising anger.

Discreetly, I slip the phone into the sleeve of my jacket. I bring my hand to my face, pretending to brush some hair away, "Alex, I need Lukas, now!" I hiss into my sleeve.

"Sorry he can't come to the phone right now. He is shower-ing." The smugness in her voice is clear. I feel sick to my stomach at the thought of the two of them together.

Marcus looks at me and smirks. "Something wrong, Nesrin?"

I move toward them, a growl slipping from my mouth. My steps falter when my scalp tightens further, something scraping painfully along my mental shields, sending goosebumps scatter-ing over me.

I cock my head, eyes narrowing, searching. Trying to find a way to block whoever is trying to get into my mind. Claws are being dragged down my mental shields in a slow, precise manner. Suddenly, blinding pain steals my breath as it spears through my head. I stumble forward, a scream slipping past my lips as a sharp pain explodes in my head, followed by a flash of light. My vision blurs as I peer up at Marcus in shock, tears scorching tracks down my face. The phone tumbles from my fingers as I reach up, gripping the sides of my head with both hands. There is so much pain I'm gasping for breath as I fall to the ground on my knees. Pain shoots up my legs at the impact and I lurch forward, curling into a ball on the ground, my fingers digging into my scalp. Through the tears, I see only boots coming toward me as Marcus approaches, then nothing as the world gives way to darkness. Absolute darkness.

I'm floating. I feel weightless as I bask in this sensation. Then I remember what happened. Panic races through me, my feet hitting the ground softly. A white mist seems to swirl around my ankles. Where am I? All I see is endless white. It seems to stretch on forever. I turn in a full circle, and suddenly she is standing there, just as I remember. My gasp is an echo around us.

"Mom?" My voice is hoarse. I have to be dreaming or . . . "Wait, am I dead?"

"You're not dead," Mom assures me with a gentle smile. God, I've missed her so much. She looks just as I remember. Her long blonde hair up in a messy bun, her amber eyes, just like mine, staring back at me. Niamh and I were a perfect mix of our mother.

"If I'm not dead, then where am I?" I croak out, looking around for no more than a second, too afraid that if I look away, my mom will disappear.

"This is your dream state, Nesrin. I brought you here to me, but it's not important right now. You must listen to me. We have very little time, and I have to show you something. Something very important. It's time you knew the truth." Her face is full of love and . . . there's regret there as well that has me alert. I'm still confused about how she is able to reach me here, but that will have to wait.

"What is it, Mom?" I'm getting nervous, even more so than before. As she grabs my hand, I half expect hers to go straight through mine, but it's solid as our hands clasp, and I let out a sigh of relief at the touch. It's warm and comforting, just like a mother's touch is supposed to be.

"I will show you first, then I will explain," she says. Then, slowly, the vast nothingness becomes a swirling tornado of mist around us as we find ourselves standing in a small single story log cabin. It's night, and the space is dark, so I can only just make out my surroundings. There's one large room with a small kitchen to my left, a fireplace and chairs behind me. Along the opposite wall stands a bed and wardrobe. To my right, I can make out two figures standing at the window near the front door, looking out through the glass. There are shouts from outside but, unable to make out what they're saying, I take several steps closer to the couple at the window and peer past them into the darkness. Witches and mages surround the cabin. They are all chanting, casting some magic spell. I can see the threads of their magic floating in the air, their arms raised to the sky. But an unmistakably dark energy swirls amongst the magic they are casting.

*What the hell? What are they doing?*

The couple turn to each other, and I get a good look at them. I inhale a sharp breath, looking over at my mother. It's me. Well, it looks a lot like me, but this woman is taller and softer looking.

The couple are gripping each other tightly by the arms. Suddenly, the man reaches up, cupping the woman's face.

"Blanchette, my love. I am sorry it is ending now, this way. Meeting you, falling in love with you, was the best goddamn thing to happen to me. I wish we had more time together. I'm sorry that we won't get to grow old and raise our daughter to be a strong, fierce woman like her mother. I love you with all my heart now and forever in this life and the next," he whispers, his voice cracking at the end. He leans down, kissing her slow and sweet. Pulling back to rest his forehead on hers, he whispers, "I regret nothing, my red-cloaked goddess. I was blessed to get this time with you." The woman, Blanchette, is crying softly, holding on to his wrists where his hands held her face. I wish I could see his face, but it's too dark to get a good look.

"I love you, too. I was a fool not to listen when you said we should leave, that they wouldn't understand. My mother said the same, but I chose to ignore it, and now look at what I've done. I've sealed our deaths. I'm so sorry, Leo," she cries. They embrace, falling to their knees, Blanchette sobbing.

My stomach drops like a ball of lead. A lump forms in my throat, and I struggle to swallow. They are saying their goodbyes. I look around for the daughter but see nothing. The only thing that stands out is the bright red cloak hanging on the door. Suddenly, fire lights up the room, quickly rushing up all the walls, faster than any normal fire should. This is hitting too close to home. I can't stand it. Is this what Niamh and Hunter went through? If so, I cannot bear to watch in silence.

"Get up!" I scream, moving toward them. They can at least try to get out. Why are they giving up?

"Get up! Get up! Get up! Fight!" I scream, but they can't hear me.

I run to the window and look outside. The coven is still there, but this time I see what I didn't notice before. They have placed a containment spell over the house they've trapped the couple in, condemning them to die a fiery death. A sob rips free from my chest as rage burns my throat. There is nothing I can do for these people. I am completely useless, just like I was that night almost a year ago.

"Please get up," I beg, my voice cracking under the pressure in my chest.

My mom appears next to the couple who are locked in an embrace on the floor, their knees touching, arms wrapped around each other, holding on as tight as they can. She looks down at them, sorrow and grief written all over her face. Then everything goes black for a moment, and I am back in the complete vast whiteness, tears still streaming down my face. My mother stands a few feet away, tears lining her own cheeks. I drop to the ground, my legs unable to keep me up any longer.

"What was that? Who was that?" My voice sounds strange to my own ears. I feel their death as if it were my own. I know deep down who I just saw, but I need to hear it from my mother.

"That was the start of our family being hunted. Blanchette and Leopold are our ancestors. She was the first witch in our bloodline, and her death set the groundwork for the rest who followed. Her story is tragic, like so many of us. We were cursed and hunted for what we are, the changes we sought out. They forced us to hide who we were at every turn. We had no one we could trust."

I peer up at my mother. "What? What do you mean?"

"It was rumored that Blanchette was a direct descendant of the goddess Althaea." At the name, my heart lurches. Grace hinted as much. "Blanchette had chosen to become a mortal when she fell in love with a shifter. It erased her from the history books as a lesser deity. Joining her mate here on the mortal plane. When she chose this path, Althaea blessed her with her power of healing, and Hecate blessed her with magic and witchery, making Blanchette effectively a witch in the mortal world. Being a witch was already dangerous, especially one in love with a wolf shifter. But it didn't stop her from wanting to be with her true soul mate.

"Unfortunately, Blanchette caught the eye of another before she left Greece. A fellow traveler, an ambitious mage who wanted her for himself, but when Blanchette revealed her true mate as a wolf shifter, this mage was furious. He went on a personal crusade to make sure she paid in blood for humiliating him. He didn't like being made a fool. Plus, the penalty for a witch having any sort of relationship with a shifter was forbidden. So, he had the blessing of the council to punish her.

"Witches at the time were meant to lure and hunt the wolves, not fall in love with them. So, branded the traitor in a red cloak, they cast her out. Those witches we saw thought they were burning a traitor and a wolf along with their abomination of a baby daughter, but as you saw, the daughter was not there.

"From what I learned, Blanchette asked her best friend Addy to take her daughter until the danger had passed. After the fire, Addy ran. She fled Germany to Wales, where she disappeared from the history records and raised Alisa as her own. That is where they stayed until, once again, they were discovered. Eventually, Alisa's grandchildren ended up fleeing to Ireland. You know of the history—of our fleeing through Europe—but it wasn't just the witch hunters we were running from, it was our own kind. Our family has been in hiding for centuries, but they always seem to catch up to us. Your grandparents' deaths had your father and me running from Ireland to hide, but this time in America."

I sit there unmoving on the ground, frozen to the spot as mist swirls around me. I'm not sure if I've so much as taken a breath since my mom started talking. We are descendants of a goddess and a wolf shifter. I feel too much, but at the same time, I am numb. If this is true, that means that I'm the same as Astraea, and I've been smart in cloaking both of us this whole time. How could my parents not tell me I am a hybrid? As hybrids, we are a mixture of two creatures, a combination that shouldn't exist. The council does not tolerate us, or any other mix breeds. There is an execution order for any who are identified. No wonder our family has long been hunted.

"Being hybrids means our bloodline carries a certain gene that makes us compatible mates for shifters. Some of us have been able to shift forms in the past, but not all of us. We have all had the gift of magic, and it's only the girls in our bloodline that mate with the wolves. Mixed with the blood of a deity, we are a rare class of witches. Born of gods, demigods, and wolves. We are more than any hybrid. We are legacies, Nesrin."

I think I'm in shock. This is not real. "Legacy?" I choke out.

She nods, kneeling in front of me, sympathy lining her eyes. Gripping my hands in hers, she continues, "There's more. I'm not sure if you know this already, but wolf shifters are a type of shape-shifting fae who can transform into a wolf at will. These fae take on the characteristics of their chosen animal. Unlike werewolves, they have control over their ability to transform and use their wide range of senses and powers," she regards me before continuing.

"Fae?" I ask.

"Yes. Shifters are fae."

"Really?" I laugh hoarsely. The Puca is a shape-shifting fae. The trolls are fae. The sprites, too. But the shifters . . . I never thought they could be. Though, I suppose it makes sense. Their magic has to come from somewhere.

"This is very real, Nesrin. Althaea understood the dangers awaiting her daughter and didn't let her go without a chance to defend herself. She gave Blanchette magic to carry through to this world. With her powers of light and healing, along with the uncanny ability to communicate on some level with any creature, she became known as the witch with the red hood, a healer for magical and supernatural beings. The red cloak was a beacon, a symbol that represents power and courage. She became a champion to many. It's quite funny that, to humans, she became known as Little Red Riding Hood."

That minor fact has me thinking of Niamh. As kids, we used to pretend we were Little Red Riding Hood because the grimoire mentions the red cloak. There is a verse in there that has always drawn my attention. *Audemus jura nostra defendere.* It's Latin, and translates to *we dare to defend our rights.* It then continues on to say, *love is an invisible string that draws two hearts to each other regardless of the hardships they will face.* This has to be talking about our bloodline's journey to be with the ones we love and the trials we would face to be together.

"Althaea had the help of her best friend, Hecate, to make a pendant. One that would carry the bloodline's ancient power. It offered protection and would unlock the hidden magic, pure magic. You already carry so many of her traits, Nesrin. Even without the pendant, you are strong. You are destined for greatness, to right the wrongs committed so long ago. To bridge the gap between witches and other supernatural creatures. You are the first since Blanchette to be blessed with Althaea's powers of true light and healing magic. Your ability to see magic in its raw form, I believe, is from your fae heritage."

My body locks up in disbelief. What the actual fuck . . .

"I don't know what to say, Mom. A legacy? That's a lot of information to process. Why was this never mentioned when we were younger? Why hide it? Why hide any of it?" I push to my feet, pacing back and forth, shaking my hands in front of me. "Why?" I demand, turning to her.

A look of remorse flashes across her face. "We didn't prepare you girls, and I will forever regret that."

"Did they kill you and Dad? Niamh? Is that why she didn't make it out, but that doesn't make sense? Astraea and I made it out?" I remember the blast of magic that shattered the windows. Could that have been Niamh sacrificing herself to give us a chance to get out?

It feels as if I am crumbling under all this information. We descend from a goddess. We are all hybrids . . . Our bloodline has been hunted and killed for centuries because of some mage who didn't get the girl. Fuck.

"Yes, it was the covens who were responsible for our deaths, but not all of those involved in the covens are guilty. Most don't realize what's happening or why. They are just following orders. It's the Order of Tartarus, a secret branch inside of the council, who is controlling certain members of the covens. They go by Tartarus because they are sending these so-called wicked souls into the depths of Tartarus. After all, you know Tartarus was not only a primordial force, but also a place. A deep abyss far below Hades, where the most sinful were sent after death to suffer and be punished for their misdeeds. Crimes they are accusing us of, but as you can see, I am not in the depths of Tartarus. We have nothing to atone for." She sighs, looking as if she carries the weight of the world on her shoulders, so different from the carefree mother I remember.

My heart is hammering almost painfully in my chest at what she is saying, the implications.

Something is bothering me . . . Well, a lot is bothering me at the moment, but this one thing stands out. "How did Astraea and I escape the fire?" I ask, eyeing my mother to see her reaction.

Her face remains neutral. "When Niamh was trapped, she realized she wouldn't make it and accumulated her magic so that when she left this world, she would release it, causing the burst of magic strong enough to break the containment spell, and giving you a chance to escape." My heart breaks all over to know my sister knew she was going to die.

Another thought occurs to me. "Niamh . . . she and Hunter . . . they were mates, weren't they?"

My mother bows her head. "Yes, they were."

"Hunter was a shifter. We knew it was forbidden, but we kept it between us. They never married officially, they kept their love a secret. No one knew. At least I don't think they did. Niamh mentioned a run in with a coven member weeks before her death," I say, my mind whirling with the idea of my sister being murdered.

"Niamh didn't recognize the dangers. Your father and I didn't have a chance to explain things to you girls yet. Like I said, I regret that now—that we waited too long. The Order of Tartarus wants our bloodline erased. I fear their motivation is increasing. It seems like it's become about more than it was when it started."

"You should have warned us. You left us unprepared when you and Dad died. We were *sixteen*. We had to hide what we were while surviving in a foster home." My voice breaks, and I suck in a deep breath.

"I'm sorry. I should never have left you girls that night. I never should have involved your father."

"It changes nothing!" I yell, chest heaving. I scrub my hands over my face before continuing in a softer voice, "You had to go. I understand what it's like, the need to help others. Dad loved you. He never would have let you go alone."

Her head hangs, and a slither of guilt worms its way into my chest. I have never raised my voice toward my mom before. My parents never said anything about covens or the witch's council, just that we had to stay away. Looking at my family's history now, with what I now know about all that the covens have done, I know that it can never be forgiven. I sense something bitter and burning, rolling through my body.

My emotions are all over the place, as is my mind. Bloodline, goddess, hybrid, council . . . the Order? What next? Unicorns, pots of gold, and fucking dragons? Unease slides through me. This is so much more information than I am equipped to handle. I feel like I'm going to pass out, which is funny because I'm pretty sure I'm already passed out.

"I can't change how things turned out, but you carry the very blood that ran through Blanchette. You are her descendant, Nesrin. You are a descendant of a goddess and a wolf. Both run through your veins and Astraea's. I want you to remember you are strong. Stronger than you think. You have the heart of a goddess, but the soul of a wolf. You are fierce and strong. Do not forget it, my daughter."

Frustrated, I run a shaky hand through my hair, my fingers catching on the tangled mess.

"I'm not so sure." My voice comes out in a half laugh. As I stare into my mom's eyes, I sense a surge of hysteria inside of me. A sick, twisted feeling rises in my stomach. I sure don't feel strong or fierce right now.

She steps closer, grabbing my face in both her hands. "Believe in yourself. The hard times, the pain, these are tough lessons. They build who you are and how you will act in times of adversity. Today, they'll be your strength and your awareness. I'm so proud of you. You're everything I ever dreamed of and more, Nesrin. You have grown into such an amazing woman. Just remember, the Order of Tartarus is old—ancient—and does *not* like their power being challenged. Though not everyone in the covens or councils are guilty, those involved will not stop until Blanchette's bloodline is erased. When you wake up, you must not give in to them. You must survive, escape, and keep my granddaughter safe." My mother looks worried, and my own stomach rolls as I suddenly remember what is waiting for me when I wake up.

I open my mouth, then shut it again. Suddenly overcome by the sensation that I've been dumped in an icy lake, I swallow a gasp. My body starts to burn and prickle all over. Pain takes over my limbs and I start panicking. I jerk my head up, meeting my mother's gaze.

"They are trying to wake you," she explains with a sad smile. "All bets are off now, Nesrin. Do what you must to ensure you survive. You are Astraea's only hope."

"Wait," I call out, reaching for her, but she is fading. "Mom!"

"One more thing. It's important. Find your sister," Mom adds quickly, worry lining her face. I take a moment to absorb her words.

"Niamh?" I reply dumbly.

Seriously, what is she talking about?

She shakes her head. "No, Leila." At my confused expression, she continues, but the pain radiating through me is growing stronger, making it harder to stay focused. I grit my teeth, pushing the pain down. I don't know how much longer I can hold on.

Tears line her eyes. "We didn't know . . . I'm so sorry . . . fire . . . fled straight away . . . Leila . . . Grace . . . shadow walker." She isn't making sense, her words fading and distorted. It's like a bad radio connection—I can only catch a few words through the pain tormenting my body.

What did Grace have to do with this? Shadow walker? Leila? I have another sister?

Before I can ask any more questions, she fades, the whiteness slowly swirling to darkness. I gasp again as I seize up with pain and jolt back to consciousness, eyes flying open with shock.

# CHAPTER EIGHTEEN

I jerk awake with a heaving breath, water spluttering out of my mouth, my chest icy and constricted.

"There she is," Anna snickers from above me. It takes me a moment to recover from the shock before I realize where I am currently sitting. They've filled the bathtub I'm in with water and ice. I look up at her, my teeth chattering and my body trembling uncontrollably.

"You might just be more trouble than you're worth." The smirk on her face has my rage building to new levels. How can she treat someone so cruelly? I truly cannot understand it.

My fury warms me as I glare up at her. "Forgive me for the inconvenience, then," I bite back.

A dark figure I didn't notice before steps forward from the other side of the tub, drawing my attention, and I startle as I stare up at him. Despite the fact that I'm already freezing, his deep voice chills me to the bones.

"Nesrin. So good to finally meet you. You're a hard one to get an audience with. I'm the high priest of this coven." His voice drips with contempt. I want to scratch his black eyes out.

I glare at him, determined not to show an ounce of fear. "Yeah, and I'm Little Red Riding Hood," I mock, dismissing him. Looking around the bathroom, my teeth knock together as I make sure nothing else lurks in the shadows.

"You will not speak unless I say so," his voice booms through the small room, demanding my obedience.

Well, tough shit.

"S-s-sorry, I'm a little p-p-p-preoccupied at the m-m-moment." The words come out stuttered, the cold getting the better of me. Shaking violently, I brace my trembling arms on the edge of the tub to get up. He moves quicker than I would have expected of the high priest, and I'm pushed back down under the icy water with barely enough time to take a breath. Once again fully submerged, I try to push myself back up, but bony fingers dig into my muscles, holding me under. My lungs scream for air as I thrash and kick out to no avail. I let out a drowned scream of pain or frustration. I'm not sure which. There is online emptiness when I try to call on my magic. My energy is sapped, my limbs numb from the cold. Just when I'm positive I won't last much longer, my lungs burning for air, the hands let go. Using as much energy as I can muster, I surge up out of the water and throw myself out of the bath as fast as I can. I land hard on the floor, jarring my shoulder with the impact, then open my mouth, gasping and coughing in effort to get some precious air into my burning lungs. There was no way I was staying in that tub to let it happen again. I can't bring myself to feel badly about the colossal mess I have made on their pristine tiled floor.

*Fuck them.*

As I roll over, my gaze collides with Marcus looking down at me with a frown. "Fuck. You," I bite out between gulps of air. His nostrils flare slightly as he stares down at me. Then he turns his eyes up to the man who held me under.

"Father, I thought we were going to talk to her, not torture her," Marcus growls, clenching his fists at his side, aggravation clear in his tone.

I burst out laughing rather manically, tears leaking from my eyes. I can't stop. I'm sure I look crazy, but shit, they are one crazy fucking family. A sharp pain in my side steals my breath, and it takes a moment to realize someone has kicked me. I curl into a ball, wrapping my arms around myself, trying once again to force air into my lungs. "Father, stop." Marcus steps in front of me, blocking me from the next kick that would surely have broken something.

I hear a loud, exaggerated huff. "Get her into the chair in the other room," barks the high priest, his voice ringing with authority.

Marcus hauls me to my feet before swinging me up to cradle me in his arms. I want to protest, but can't find the energy. There is no way I'll be walking anywhere right now, no matter how much I might want to. I take at least a small amount of pleasure in the fact that I'm soaking Marcus's nice clothes. Petty, I know. But he deserves far worse. They all do. Marcus carries me into the next room, where I am deposited onto a tall wingback chair sitting in the center of the room, one of two chairs sitting before the fireplace, my body melting into the cushions as the heat soaks into me. Marcus turns, disappearing back into the bathroom and reappearing a moment later with a towel. He passes it to me without making eye contact, the muscle in his jaw ticking.

Thank the goddess for small miracles.

I look around the small room as I wrap the towel around my shoulders. The walls are paneled with dark wood, and high bookshelves line the wall at one end of the room. There is a tall window behind a large ancient-looking oak desk. Books and papers cover every inch of the worn wooden surface. Somehow, I don't think this is the high priest's office.

As I take in my surroundings, I also do my best to assess my own condition. Am I missing anything? Are my mental shields intact? Have they done anything to me while I was unconscious? Other than trying to freeze me to death, that is. I move and wriggle all my body parts from fingers to toes. Nope, all good. My mental shields seem to be undamaged and strong. I feel myself relax a bit.

My magic, on the other hand, appears to be gone—cut off somehow. I take notice of the cuff around my wrist. This is new. The silver band seems to hum along my skin, and I wonder if this is what's keeping me from accessing my magic. I needed it online, to give me an edge to know what they were up to. Seeing magic came in handy. Apart from that, I think I'm okay. Sore, but okay. For now.

Anna moves, drawing my attention as she stands at the fireplace directly in front of me. The high priest—Marcus's *father*—takes the other chair to my left, while Marcus remains standing next to my chair on my right side. He must be staying close to keep me from doing anything stupid.

"I see you admiring the elven cuff on your wrist," the high priest says arrogantly, nodding to my lap where my hands are clasped. "Forged by the elves themselves to bind anyone's magic who wears it. It cannot be removed without the key, so don't bother trying. It's made of the strongest of metals and spells. Not even *you* can break it."

The confusion must have shown on my face, because he sneers at me, and I want nothing more than to wipe that expression off his face. It's funny, because I'm not usually a violent person, but lately I've been pushed too much and my patience for idiots is wearing thin.

"Can you or can you not unravel any spell? Can you not see magic in its purest form? Well, I suppose you can't right now, but I know what you are."

My heart jumps in my chest, thumping hard against my sternum. I do my best to show no outward reaction, keeping my face neutral as I stare back at him. I really need to pay attention. Especially with whoever—or whatever—was able to spear straight through my mental shields before.

*Wait.*

"The trolls– Are they okay? You didn't hurt them, did you?" The words are rushed as I spin in my seat to face Marcus. At his look of surprise, I gather he thought I would have forgotten about the family of trolls.

Looking past me, he focuses on the fire. "They are fine. We got what we came for," Marcus replies firmly. The reflection of the fire flickers in his black eyes, making him seem otherworldly.

"I'd think you would be more worried about your own well-being at this point," Anna sneers from the fireplace, and I stiffen at her tone that promises more pain to come.

"You, Nesrin, are a traitor to your kind. You have been found guilty of treason. We have brought you here to hand you over to the Order of Tartarus for the sins that you and your family have long committed," the high priest tells me, the air of disdain thickening around him. I rear back from the shock of his words. So much for not giving anything away.

Moving to the edge of the seat, I stare the high priest dead in the eye. "You don't know what you're talking about, *sir*." I drag out the last word. "They have lied to you. My family is guilty of nothing," I say, turning to Marcus, to the one person in this room I feel might listen.

"Your family has conspired with the wolves—the shifters—to take over the council, breeding with them like whores," the high priest shouts, drawing my attention back to him, spittle flying from his mouth along with his vulgar words. There's no sense trying to reason with a madman, but I can't help but try.

"Lies–" I start, but am quickly cut off as the man rambles on.

"I think not. Are you or are you not currently *living with* the pacific northwest alpha?" the high priest jeers, raising his eyebrow as if to dare me to deny it.

My heart thunders in my chest, fear and anger swirling inside of me, a storm of emotions. "The council has misled you. I don't know why, but I just want to live in peace. To stop being hunted." The high priest scoffs, and I know now that there is no point trying to persuade him otherwise. He has already decided my guilt. Whoever is pulling his strings has convinced him, without a doubt. Has the Order managed to convince our entire kind of the validity of such a flawed argument? Is he one of them?

"You are murdering your own kind, and with what proof of our sins?" My voice is rough from the exertion required to hold down my emotions.

"You are living with the shifters!" he roars. "What more proof do I need?"

I jump out of my chair, lunging forward, my hands aiming for his neck, only to have Marcus grab me around the waist, holding me back.

"What the council has done is unforgivable! You are the traitors. You have murdered generations of my family, and for what? Because we have wolves' blood running through our veins? Because we are hybrids? Or simply because some old man couldn't get the girl?" I scream, my voice hoarse with emotion. Marcus's arms tighten around my waist for a moment before he lets me go, and I stumble forward a step. I gaze up, my eyes connecting with the cold eyes of the high priest. He wraps his fingers around my throat, squeezing painfully as he shoves me back into the chair. The look of fury and hatred burning in his coal-black eyes has my blood running cold. Panic shoots through me when I can't suck in a breath, and spots begin dancing along the outside of my vision.

"You'll get what you deserve," he spits at me, each word emphasized as he brings his face within an inch of mine. He squeezes harder, to the point I think the bones in my neck will be crushed. My body grows heavy, my struggles weakening. My eyes move to Marcus, begging for help.

The last thing I see is Marcus reaching for his father, pleading with him, "Father, stop!" before the darkness pulls me under once more.

# CHAPTER NINETEEN

I wake to find myself lying on a single mattress on the floor of a tiny, darkened bedroom. There is only one door and one window. I slowly sit up, taking a deep breath. When I let it out, my breath puffs white in front of me. It's freezing in this room, and they haven't given me any bedding. A mattress, that's it. I suppose I should be grateful I have something soft to sit on. I rub my hands over my face and groan. Stupid, stupid, stupid. I can't believe I got myself into this mess.

But I will not give up. There has to be a way out of here. I stand on shaky legs, making my way over to the window, and peer out into the darkness. My heart deflates as my forehead rests against the cool glass.

"Damn it," I mutter, gripping the window frame . . . wishing I could rip it from the wall. The windows have been nailed shut, and even if they could be opened, I am very high up.

I turn to look at the door, wiping my hands on my jeans. Option number two it is.

Unease ripples through me as I make my way to the door. With a shaky hand, I reach out to try the door handle. My heart stalls in my chest when it clicks. It's unlocked. I stand in shock for a moment, letting it sink in that I'm not imagining this. I never thought it would be unlocked, but I will not waste this opportunity. Holding my breath, I turn the handle all the way and slowly pull the door open. A loud creak echoes around me. My heart races, pounding against my chest as I squeeze my eyes shut. I hold still, gripping the door so tightly my fingers ache. Pausing, I listen, but hear nothing. No pounding feet coming to stop me. I open the door the rest of the way and let out the breath I've been holding on to.

Inching out into the hallway, I look both ways, trying to decide which way to go. A door opens to the left and I freeze as Marcus steps out into the hall. Looking my way, his black eyes narrow as he frowns at me. I turn to run, but Marcus is already there, grabbing my arm.

"It's okay, I won't hurt you. It's this way, Nesrin," he says in a hushed tone, pulling me to the left down the hall. I don't know what to think, so I follow, hoping that my chance of getting out is higher with Marcus.

We round the corner and make it down a set of stairs without running into anyone. At this stage, I can't handle the tension, my body trembling with nerves. I'm wound tighter than a jack-in-the-box. I'm too young to have a heart attack, but I feel like I'm close to it at this point. As we move through the foyer, I feel something brush against my mental shields, then a tingling sensation works its way over my mind. I shake it off, knowing that I desperately need to get out of here. Marcus still has a hold of my arm, tugging me along. We make it to the front door of the mansion without running into anyone. He reaches for the handle, pulling it open, and my heart trips over itself.

Standing on the doorstep is Lukas.

Paralyzed by shock, it takes me a moment before I pull free of Marcus's grip and run to Lukas. His outstretched arms catch me, wrapping around my back, squeezing me gently. Marcus clears his throat behind me, and Lukas releases me. I turn back around to thank Marcus.

"Before you leave, Nesrin, are there any more of you out there? Any family we should know about?" Marcus inquires.

I stare at him, confused. Just as I'm about to answer, my mother's voice rings loud through my head, '*Do not give in, Nesrin. Tell them nothing. Survive.*'

I look up at Marcus, and that tingling, creeping sensation moves through my mind again. Shaking my head, I turn and find Lukas gone. My scalp prickles and I whip my head back to Marcus as his coal-black eyes bore into me. Waiting.

What the hell? I spin around in a circle and see nothing but darkness. "What do you want from me?" I whisper, my body trembling.

"Tell me if there are others," he repeats more forcefully. I tilt my head, narrowing my eyes at him. Something is different. He knows about Astraea, but he hasn't mentioned her at all. Something is off, not right about all this.

"There is no one else," I drawl. No way anyone would know I have another sister out there somewhere. I didn't even know until now. It hurts to think about her. I need to save my energy for escaping right now. There will be time to reflect on it when I am out of this house of horrors.

"Lies," Marcus growls, stalking forward. I back up, but suddenly he is there, his face barely a breath from my own, eyes piercing mine. "Tell me now."

"There is no one else," I say again, hostility creeping into my voice, this time straightening up to my full height. I will not cower to him or anyone else. I look around again and see nothing but darkness. No Lukas, no house, just the two of us. Something definitely isn't right.

Marcus pulls my attention back to him. I don't have time to react before he slaps me across the face. I'm stunned, my cheek burning and throbbing from the hit, but I refuse to touch it. I won't give him the satisfaction. My eyes light up with rage as I stare at Marcus. The hatred burning in his eyes makes little sense to me. Marcus, even with all our differences, has never looked at me like this. In my bones, I know this can't be Marcus.

"You're not Marcus," I say out loud, needing to voice it. Needing to see the reaction.

But Marcus simply stares back at me, his expression turning blank, bored. Then Marcus begins to change as he morphs into someone else, his body wavering as he transforms before my eyes.

"You're right, I'm not. My son is weak. He has turned soft, especially where you're concerned." The high priest is now standing in front of me, an arrogant look on his face.

He clicks his fingers, and the darkness falls away. Suddenly, I'm back, sitting in that chair in front of the fire, but now there is another person in the room with us. This time, Marcus is nowhere to be seen. I look at the newcomer and frown. There is something familiar about her, but I can't place it. She is standing in the shadows of the far wall with a black hooded cloak masking most of her face, but her long red hair peeks out from the hood.

I can tell she is watching me closely. It almost seems like she is waiting for something.

Heat sweeps up my neck in anger and frustration—mostly at them, but also at myself. I thought I'd come close to escaping. I believed their tricks. Tears burned the back of my throat, but I will die before I let him see them fall.

"I see you've noticed our guest. Nesrin, meet Emerson. She has a special ability. You just experienced it. She is very talented. Entering one's mind and altering their perceptions can come in handy, make you constantly second guess what's real and what's not. The council was kind enough to send her to me. We will get the answers we want from you, Nesrin, one way or another. Then you will get what you deserve," he added with disdain.

I shiver at the darkness lurking in his eyes. Unable to look at him any longer, I turn back to Emerson. I've never met someone who can enter one's mind before. They are extremely rare, gifted individuals. I've heard of them, of course. My mother told Niamh and I stories of the witches capable of manipulating the mind, creating illusions and hallucinations so real you can hear, touch, smell, or taste things that aren't there. She called them phantom casters. I never thought I'd meet one, though. My family has been removed from the witching community for as long as I can remember. Sure, we would see other witches and mages around, but that was it. I feel as if I'm playing a game I don't understand or know the rules to. Emerson pulls her hood back and steps toward me. She is beautiful with thick, long, wavy red hair, forest green eyes, and porcelain skin with no marks or imperfections. There is a kindness behind her eyes, and the look she gives me almost seems like regret. My stomach bottoms out as Emerson stands in front of me and looks over at the high priest, who gives her a nod.

Then his eyes meet mine, a cruel, twisted smile taking over his face. I want to tear his throat out. The thought flashes through my mind at lightning speed, surprising even myself. I lift my chin, bracing myself as I sit taller. This is all the defiance I can manage at the moment. I will fight, they won't get anything from me. I bury the sob that rises in my throat in anticipation of what is sure to come. Emerson shoots me a look of approval. She wants me to fight.

Give them nothing. Survive. Astraea. Survive. Lukas. Survive. I chant over and over as blackness takes over.

My mind is no longer my own. It doesn't matter to Emerson how strong my mental shields are. She can slip through them like a hot knife in butter.

# CHAPTER TWENTY

"How is the wine?"

I glance over at Marcus and smile. The feel of the sun kissing my skin and warming me is wonderful.

"Delicious. Great choice," I reply, taking a small sip from my glass. We're sitting on a picnic blanket overlooking a large lake. The sunshine sparkles as it reflects off the water. It looks almost magical, like the sun is sending messages in morse code. Birds are singing the most amazing sounds, and I close my eyes to fully take in their song. Chatter brings my attention from the sun's warmth and the birds. I open my eyes to Marcus and Anna, who are seated beside me, pouring wine into some glasses.

"This was such a good idea," Anna says, looking over at me with a bright smile on her face. She has been my best friend for as long as I can remember. Always dragging me into mischief at any chance she gets.

"Yes, it really was. I needed this, a day to relax with my two best friends." The words taste sour in my mouth. I frown down at the blanket, trying to place the feeling swirling inside of me. Uncertainty?

"Don't you wish your family were here, Nesrin?" Anna asks, throwing her long black hair over her shoulder.

*My family?*

"I have no family," I reply, confused at why they would bring up my family. They know my family is dead.

"Don't be silly. Of course you do. Where are they these days?" Marcus jokes, nudging my shoulder before popping a grape into his mouth. The movement seems rehearsed, the words too easy. I try to think back to my last conversation with either of them, but my mind keeps coming up blank. *That's odd.*

An image flashes through my mind, of me lying on cold pavement, gripping my head and screaming in pain as both of them watch unfazed by my state.

I furrow my eyebrows as I stare at my two companions and then at our surroundings. I can just make out a slight hum of magic in the air, and now that I've noticed it, everything comes rushing back. *Emerson.*

This must be an illusion. That's why it doesn't feel right. Just like that, it's as if someone has flicked a switch. My mind is clear again and I can breathe easier. As the room comes back into view, I can see the shock on the high priest's face. It's nice to see him thrown off kilter for once. His shock morphs into rage. He stalks forward, hitting me across the face so hard I fall to the floor, tasting blood.

He leans down, his hand wrapping around my wrist, the touch bone cold. "You think you're so clever," he sneers, right before he twists.

I hear the crack before any pain registers. I whimper, trying to hold back the scream that's lodged in my throat. He shouldn't have been able to break my wrist that easily. His face turns ugly as we stare at each other. I somehow manage to keep my face blank as I cradle my arm to my chest.

He turns to the man guarding the door. "Take her to her room. She is not to be fed. I want her weak and begging." With that, he storms out, Emerson following behind him, casting me a quick look over her shoulder, a slight frown marring her perfect face. I see something flash in her eyes. Trepidation, maybe? Perhaps fear? But at what or for whom? Her or me?

Heartache, anger, and vengeance are a constant companion as I sit in this room trying not to let everything drag me down into a pit of despair. After all that has been revealed, my emotions are at an all-time high. My family is descended from a goddess and wolves. We have been hunted and murdered for centuries simply for who we've loved. I keep thinking about why Althaea didn't step in, save her daughter from execution. The gods rarely get involved with this world and the matters of mortals, but her *daughter?*

The resemblance between Blanchette and I is uncanny and a little unnerving. Blanchette surely knew then as well as I do now that relationships between races are forbidden and punishable by death. Maybe she wanted to change things, make a stand, show everyone it was okay to love whomever you wanted. My thoughts turn to Lukas. I feel deeply for him, and if anything were to happen to him, it would tear me apart. This injustice has gone on long enough. Something has to change. I have done my best to keep Astraea hidden, cloaked from other witches and magical creatures, but even I know that can't last forever.

So far, the coven and the Order of Tartarus only know about me. Astraea and Leila are safe for now. I need to get out of here. I need to speak to Grace and see what she knows about my sister. A sister I don't even remember. How is that even possible?

My tummy chooses precisely this moment to grumble loudly, and I place my hand over it. I'm not sure how long I have been here. I don't recall eating anything. They refill my water bottle whenever I drift off, but never offer me any food. Goddess, I am starving.

My mind drifts to Emerson. I'm afraid that everything I see will be a trick of the mind. I don't know what I can trust anymore. I've never come across anyone with the ability to enter another's mind and alter perceptions to create an elaborate illusion. Getting into their mind and creating a world that is so real they don't even know any different.

But I will not let them break me. I am determined to get out of here and end this. It may be in my nature to heal, not hurt. I may be kind, peaceful, and caring. But when it comes to protecting my family, my friends, and my heart, nothing will stop me. I will do whatever it takes to keep them safe. The high priest may think of me as weak and powerless, but he has yet to notice the wolf hiding behind my eyes. Now I know the truth. That I have wolves' blood running through my veins. I feel stronger, more powerful. The need to protect those I love is overwhelming. I now know what Grace was alluding to with her cryptic words the last time we spoke. She knows I am a hybrid as well. Knows about my family, and has never said anything. Anger burns my chest at the things she omitted. Squeezing my eyes shut, I lower my head, resting it on my knees as I hug them to my chest.

An explosion rocks the entire house, ripping me from my musing. I jump to my feet, rushing over to the barred window that overlooks the back of the enormous property, but can't see anything from here. The explosion must have come from the front of the house. Another explosion rattles the window.

*What the fuck was that?*

I really don't enjoy being trapped in here. I frantically look around my sparse room, hoping to find something I can use to protect myself, even though I know there is nothing here.

I jolt as the bedroom door flies open, ricocheting off the wall. Marcus storms in. The look of rage on his face has me backing up until I'm pressed against the cold window. Without my magic, I'm useless. I've tried to break the elven cuff off my wrist but failed. It won't budge. My now dried, bloody fingertips throbbed at the memories. But I will fight with every last breath, magic or no magic. I'm not completely helpless.

Marcus closes the gap between us, wrapping his fingers around my wrist—the one that isn't broken—then drags me toward the door. I dig my heels in, refusing to move. I want to push past him and run, but I know if I do he will be on me in a second.

Doubt fills my mind and trepidation twists my insides. *How do I know this is real?*

"Quick, we need to hurry. I will get you to the ground floor and then I want you to run, okay?" His onyx eyes burn into mine with an intensity I've never seen from him before.

I pull my arm from his grip and take a step back. "Why are you helping me?"

I am tired, hungry, in pain, and absolutely *over* being manipulated. I don't even know if I can trust my own mind. Having been subjected to countless illusions at this point, not to mention deliberately starved, I have no concept of how much time has passed.

"Don't always trust what you see, Nesrin. Even salt looks like sugar," Marcus replies, his expression guarded, his eyes searching mine.

"No shit," I mutter. Gazing back at him, I try studying him, studying the moment. This feels real, he feels real.

"I want to trust you."

"Then trust me," he replies easily.

I stare at him for a long moment then give him a slight nod. Marcus relaxes somewhat, wasting no time as he grabs my hand, pulling me out of the room again.

"I don't agree with my family about any of this. I knew something was off, but I went along with it, anyway. You need to get somewhere safe. I will hold them off as long as I can," he rushes the words as we make our way toward the stairs at a clipped pace. "I never told them about your baby. They don't know, I swear. I always had my doubts about their motives, and these last few days prove I was right. I just wish things could have been different. That you and I could . . . " he shakes his head. "Doesn't matter now."

I keep my broken wrist protectively against my chest as we race down the stairs, taking them two at a time. As we get to the landing, two mages are coming down the hall. They see me and stalk forward, but Marcus steps in front of me, turning only long enough to nod toward the unbarred window behind me. My eyes widen as I spin back to look at him, but he's already making his way toward the mages.

He wants me to jump out the window? *Are you shitting me?*

I stand frozen to the spot, shock and anger swelling in my chest. We are two floors up. I am *not* jumping. Just as I'm preparing to turn and make a run for the stairs, another blast shakes the house. The men curse, stumbling on their feet, but their sights remain set on me. Marcus spins and his eyes lock with mine, softening for a moment as he reaches up to tug on some of my hair.

"Run," he urges, pushing me toward the window, before he turns to face them again.

*Window it is.* Spinning on my heels, I make a run for it. Yelling sounds from all around and the pounding of footsteps draws closer. I had to go now. Quickly glancing over my shoulder, I notice that one of the mages is quietly gathering a large amount of magic while the other is distracting Marcus. I know the spell is going to be nasty, even with this elven cuff binding my powers, I can tell. Marcus will not have time to deflect it while engaged in battle with the other mage. Panic seizes me and I spin, darting for Marcus as they unleash the spell. I collide hard with him, knocking us both over, and the spell misses us, hitting instead the other mage, taking the man down. A horrified scream tears from his throat and I cringe at the sound. I look over and regret it immediately, bile rising in my throat at the sight before me. The mage's skin has blistered and is oozing purulent liquid. The mage stills, his glazed-over eyes staring wide eyed at the ceiling. I cover my mouth with my hand and look at Marcus. That could have been him.

He drags me up to my feet and nods his thanks. The mage who cast that nasty spell is staring at me in shock and confusion. He looks over at his fellow coven member lying dead on the ground and visibly swallows.

"How the hell did you move that fast?" he asks, looking back at me.

"I have no idea what you're on about," I reply, before Marcus is pushing me toward the broken window, never taking his eyes off the mage. He backs up with me, keeping me covered the whole time. I reach the window and peer out. There is a path below, and gardens. It's a long drop from the second floor and it's going to hurt like hell. Pushing the broken window open so I don't cut myself on glass, I lift one leg over at a time so I'm sitting on the ledge. Deep breaths. You can do this. I chant to myself. Here goes nothing.

I push myself off the ledge before I can change my mind. A scream escapes my mouth and I'm hitting the ground a moment later, my bones protesting as I land heavy on my feet and roll across the pavement. Another scream tears from my throat as pain shoots up my leg. Clothing and skin rip as I roll a few times over the path. My broken arm throbs unbearably, the pain almost making me blackout.

Wow, this was a bad idea. I come to a halt when my head slams hard against the rocks bordering the beautiful gardens.

*Shit, that hurt.* I lay there a moment, trying to draw in a breath and taking stock of my body. Rolling over, I push up to my hands and knees, the world spinning around me. I'm going to puke. I try to stand, feeling nausea roll through me more violently. I push my tangled mess of hair off my face and try to focus on a point in my surroundings. I need to find the edge of the property.

However, my vision has other ideas. *How hard did I hit my head?* Everything is blurry, spots are dancing across my vision, which is really fucking distracting. I reach up, touching my forehead, and see blood coating my fingers. My insides roll again. Without warning, the wind suddenly whips around me, the cold shocking my system into moving. My hair is lashing around my face, making it even harder for me to see, but I blindly run in the direction I think the wall is. Oddly, I feel like the wind is pushing me in this direction.

Raindrops start falling heavily around me and I shiver forcefully from the cold that encases my body, making my movements become sluggish. The wind is going straight through my clothes, the bitter cold seeping into me. My muscles scream in protest as I hunch over, another round of dizziness hitting me hard.

"Nesrin!" Lukas's voice rings out across the yard. I spin around, searching, my vision blurring again and I'm blinking frantically, trying to clear it. I rub the back of my hand over my eyes and see more blood. My *blood* is blurring my vision. Just great. I can just imagine how hard it's going to be to get this blood out of my hair. Looking around, I can't see anyone. I must be hearing things. There's no way Lukas is here. Wherever here is.

Shaking off my disappointment, I start jogging in what I think is the direction of the property border. Pain is shooting like lighting up my leg, making me bite down hard on my lip. Finally reaching the edge of the property, I come across a stone wall. Curling over, I take a few deep breaths, trying to center myself. Exhaustion threatens to drag me down, but I refuse to let it. Looking both ways, I pick a direction. Placing my hand against the cool stone of the wall, I run, hoping to come across an opening. I find a tree instead that looks easy enough to climb to get over.

"Nesrin!" My name floats on the air again.

Confused, I whirl around, my hair whipping across my face, the wet slap of it sticking to my skin. I really hope this isn't Emerson getting in my head again. Seeing nothing, I climb the tree as fast as I can. The adrenaline that courses through my veins helps to push the pain from my mind. Pulling myself to the top of the wall, I look down. A moan falls from my throat. I could cry. It's a fair drop to the ground on the other side, and with my leg like it is, this will be painful. If I slowly lower myself over the other side while holding on to the edge, that might lessen the impact on my foot. Footsteps sound behind me and panic sets in. I can't wait any longer. After sitting down on the wall, I turn onto my stomach and inch my legs down the other side of the wall. Lowering myself, I take a deep breath before I let go.

I land hard on my feet and stumble backward, crying out in pain as my legs give out from under me.

Some escape. I can't even move. The pain radiating through my body is stealing my consciousness. Black dots swamp my vision once again and I lie there on my back, unable to move. Rain hits my face as I close my eyes. *I'm just going to take a nap.*

There's a soft nudge to my cheek. Lying there, I open my eyes to see a dark shape above me. I gasp, but the shape nudges me again, and I make out a set of luminous golden eyes. It nickers at me. The Puca. I reach up and stroke his cheek.

"Hey," I mumble, "I found myself in a bit of a pickle."

Another whine and nudge, as if he's telling me to move.

"I would if I could, but I don't think I can," I explain. The Puca backs up and I let my eyes drift close.

Suddenly, I'm lifted into the air.

"I've got you, sweetheart," Lukas promises. I'm weightless for a moment, then cradled against his warm, solid chest. This can't be an illusion, because he smells like Lukas. Like sandalwood and rain. Like home. I snuggle in closer to his chest, soaking up his warmth and strength, and that familiar scent.

"You came for me?" I murmur, leaning my head on his shoulder, willing my body to relax. Even if it isn't real, I'm going to soak in the comfort of Lukas, the safety of his arms, if only for a short while.

"Of course I did," Lukas whispers into my hair, and it feels like he places a soft kiss on my head.

I close my eyes and breathe in the smell that is Lukas. It is him. I am safe. "I'm glad you're here," I whisper, and my head throbs again, stealing my breath.

"Me, too," Lukas replies, and I feel him move, causing pain to flare again behind my eyes.

Gripping my head, I groan, "My head hurts."

"You've got a nasty cut on your head, honey, that's probably why," Zee says from somewhere behind me.

"Probably a concussion," someone else suggests. Merve? Is that Merve? My head spins as I try to look around, the wind picking up again with an unnatural breeze.

"We need to get out of here. Now," another voice chimes in. I think it's Gabe. "Declan is bringing the car around."

I hear yelling coming from the other side of the wall, followed by the pounding of feet. Out of instinct, I try moving from Lukas's arms, but he only grips me tighter. "Hold on, sweetheart." Lukas takes off running, every part of me protesting at the move-

217

ment. Next thing I know, I'm in a car, the soft hum of the engine lulling me to sleep.

"Nesrin, wake up. You can't go to sleep. You need to stay awake until I have Asena, look you over." Lukas sounds worried, but I am so warm and cozy bundled in his arms. I just want to close my eyes and rest.

So, I do. I let darkness carry me off and the last thing I hear is Lukas's furious growl, "I'll kill them all for what they've done to her."

# CHAPTER TWENTY ONE

L ukas has me wrapped in his arms, hoisting me from the car, as I wake. Half-heartedly, I protest, arguing something along the lines of, "I can walk." Of course, I really don't think I can walk, even if I wanted to. My whole body feels like it's been hit by a truck.

Lukas grumbles under his breath, and continues on as if I didn't speak. My head feels heavy, so I rest it back on his chest, wanting nothing more than to go back to sleep. His powerful arms tighten around me, pulling me from thoughts of sleep, as he carries me into the house, making for the sofa in front of the fireplace. The warmth of the crackling fire instantly soaks into me, relaxing my exhausted body further. Lukas takes a seat on the sofa with me still on his lap. I tilt my head back and peer up at him, raising my eyebrow in question.

"I'm not ready to let you go yet. I need to make sure you're okay," Lukas admits gruffly, and my heart melts. Lifting my hand to his stubbled jaw, I run my hand over it, enjoying the sensation of his prickly hairs scraping against my palm.

"I like this look," I breathe, giving him a small smile. His eyes soften as he looks down at me.

"Shaving was the last thing on my mind, so I'm glad you like it," he quips as we stare at each other, and the world around us falls silent. There is no one else but us.

A cough interrupts our moment and I turn as much as Lukas will allow me. A young woman with long brown hair stands to the side, watching us.

"You must be Nesrin," she says in a quiet voice. The brightness in her soft blue eyes, striking against her brown skin, speaks to a level of kindness that is rare to find. The warmth of her smile makes me feel like we've been friends forever. I know in my gut I'm going to like her.

"Yes, that's me." I give a little wave and hear a huffed laugh come from behind Lukas. Zee. I fight back my own laugh at the sound.

"I'm Asena. I'm the doctor in the pack. I want to thank you for what you did for the two shifters caught by that nasty hex." The compliment makes me blush.

"It was no problem," I reply.

Beaming, Asena asks, "I would like to check you over, if that's okay?"

"Yes. I usually heal pretty fast, though sometimes not fast enough."

"Okay, then. Lukas, can you put her down on the couch so I can look at her?" Asena asks, giving Lukas a wary glance. Confused, I tilt my head up at Lukas and see him glaring at her. I reach up and tap his cheek softly to get his attention. *He can't expect her to look over my injuries while he's holding me, right?*

Lukas looks down at me, a frown on his perfect face. "I can, and she will."

*Shit.* "That was supposed to stay in my head. Why does this keep happening to me?" I groan, covering my face with my hands, wincing at the pain there. Zee barks out a laugh and I can't suppress the smile that forms behind my hands because I really missed his laugh.

"Shut it, Zee," Asena snaps.

I raise my head, dropping my hands, and stare at her, my mouth hanging open.

"What? You've been through hell, and he's annoying. Plus, it's not cool to laugh at you right now, even if you are being cute," Asena states, shrugging a shoulder.

I blink up at her. Cute? Me? I'm not cute.

Asena turns to look at Lukas and huffs, placing her hands on her hips. "Now, are you going to let me do my job?"

Lukas lets out a low, menacing growl, but relents. Standing with me cradled in his arms, he turns, gently placing me on the sofa, then leans down, getting so close we are nose to nose. "You need me, just call. I won't be far." He leans in even closer and inhales, his nose brushing along the sensitive skin of my neck, sending goosebumps scattering over my body. I bite my lip to silence my gasp as he places a soft kiss on my jaw.

Lukas stands, making his way to the door where I assume Zee is waiting. I flush with embarrassment, knowing that, apart from my ice bath, I haven't showered in . . . huh . . . I don't actually know how many days.

"Thank god," Asena huffs, coming over and sitting down next to me. "Now, let's look at this cut on your head. It seems to have stopped bleeding and won't require stitches, which is a bonus. I can just clean it and use the butterfly stitches, but it will probably be tender for a while. You may also have a concussion, so we will need to monitor you," she informs me, all this while poking and prodding at my head. I try my best to hold still, wincing occasionally as she works.

A thought pops into my mind. "Was Merve with Lukas tonight? I thought I heard him, but that could have been this bump to my head," I admit, pointing to my head as if she doesn't know where it is, and quickly drop my hand.

"Yes, I believe the satyr was with them, along with that sprite that has attached herself to Astra in your absence," Asena says, finishing up cleaning the cut on my head.

I let out a relieved breath and ponder all the weirdness of the last few weeks. I have a banshee following my family around because of some promise made to my grandparents. There's a sprite and a satyr who are like family. A missing sister whom I really am eager to find as soon as possible. Though, I don't even know where to start on that. Then there's the coven, the witch's council, and a secret order who are actively hunting us. And, of course, I can't forget about the shifters and . . . whatever is happening between Lukas and me.

Without a doubt, it's time to come clean with Lukas about Astraea and myself. He deserves to know the truth, no matter how much I'm dreading the conversation. I just hope he doesn't reject us after learning the truth. I don't think he would. My mother and Grace have both said that Lukas can be trusted, and deep down, I know I can trust him with anything. It's time to take a leap of faith. As I've found out the hard way time and again, life is extremely unpredictable. Not a whole lot is in our control, as much as we like to think differently. But at the end of the day, we choose who to have in our lives, and as long as we are with the right people, we can handle anything that's thrown our way. I choose this. I have to believe Lukas won't turn us away.

Asena kneels in front of me, taking my shoes and socks off. Slowly, she prods and feels up both of my legs. Frowning, she says, "You have a badly sprained ankle. You're incredibly lucky it's not broken. I'm going to need to ice it for at least twenty minutes tonight, and then I will wrap it. You'll need to stay off it for a week."

"Thanks," I whisper, suddenly not feeling all that lucky at the moment. Yes, I escaped, I survived, but everything else is a mess.

"You've been holding that arm close to your chest since you got here. Is it broken?" she inquires, nodding to my arm.

"I think so."

Asena gently grips my elbow and rests my arm on the side of the sofa. The corners of her mouth turn down as she slowly glides her fingers along the ulna bone and then the radius. When she reaches my wrist, I let out a hiss of pain, and her eyes dart to mine. "It's definitely broken. The radius bone has separated from the scaphoid. I can strap it as tight as I can without causing you too much discomfort."

"Great." I look down at my other wrist and a sense of dread washes over me as I remember the elven cuff. I turn my wrist over, as if studying the bracelet more than I already have might show me how to get it off. Noticing, Asena gestures to it.

"What's with the chunky cuff? Doesn't seem like something you'd wear. I could be wrong, though. Wouldn't be the first time." She shrugs and the look on her face tells me she doesn't believe that for a minute.

A huff falls from my lips and I sigh. "You're not wrong. I need to get it off. I'm just not sure how. It needs a key." A feeling of hopelessness courses through me, souring my mood. I have so much to sort out in my head, I don't know where to start.

"Lukas will figure it out. He would do anything for you," Asena assures me, continuing to wrap up my wrist like she hasn't just said in no uncertain terms that the alpha would take care of a witch. As if that's no big thing. And yet, somehow this statement doesn't strike me as false.

"Are all the wolves so accepting of a witch being here?" I ask, quirking an eyebrow at her openness.

"Well, I'm not a wolf, for starters. And when you are important to the alpha, you're important to us all," Asena replies, smirking at me with amusement in her dark brown eyes.

"Wait, you're not a wolf? What are you?" I'm just going to pretend I didn't hear the bit about me being *important to the alpha* for a moment.

Laughing, Asena stands, patting my shoulder. "I'm a lynx, a drifter that has found my home here, and I'm not the only one. There are a few other shifters here who aren't wolves." With a wink, she turns and starts to pack up her supplies, leaving me to gape at her back.

"Like what? What kind of shifters?" I ask, unable to stop myself.

Asena looks over her shoulder at me and smirks. "There is a family of badgers."

Badgers? Living amongst the wolves? My eyes widen as my mouth drops open, and Asena laughs at my reaction as she turns back to her task. How did I not know this? Probably because I've never asked. I've always just assumed they were all wolves.

"We also have cougars and a couple of bears," she finishes. Turning around, she leans back on the table, crossing her arms.

Adjusting to get more comfortable on the sofa, I ask, "And you are all loyal to Lukas?"

"Yes. He took us in and gave us a home when no one else would. As you know, Lukas doesn't follow normal pack ruling," she responds, her expression now completely serious. I nod absently as my mind goes over this new information. There is so much more to Lukas than I could have ever imagined, and each new facet that is revealed just makes me fall for him that much harder.

Once Asena was finished, she left to get some food for me. I didn't even realize how hungry I was until she asked. Laying back on the couch and closing my eyes, a noise draws my attention to the door as a tiny form runs like a flash through the room, startling me. Suddenly, Astraea is there in front of me, lunging into my arms. I catch her, wrapping my arms tightly around her, and breathing in her scent. My heart warms instantly at having her in my arms.

"Wow, sweet girl! You've gotten fast. I missed you so much. I thought you'd be sleeping," I say, squeezing her to me. Something soft lands on my shoulder. Lifting my head, I look over and see the sprite standing there, smiling at me. "I need a name for you. I know Fae don't give out their names, but I need to call you something," I whisper.

"Astraea calls me Nissa," she replies softly, a small blush reddening her cheeks.

"Thank you for watching over Astra for me." I smile at her before my brain connects with what she said, and I ask, "Wait, Astra talks to you?"

"It was my pleasure, and we talk telepathically," Nissa explains, giving me a small nod before sitting on my shoulder and crossing her legs. Her actions surprise me, and warmth fills my chest. Sprites aren't typically very trusting of others, and for Nissa to be so at ease with us speaks volumes.

I glance down at my niece, who hasn't moved from her spot buried in my arms, and smile. "You truly are a special gift, sweet girl," I whisper into her hair, the smell of strawberries soothing my soul.

"That she is," Lukas replies from where he waits by the door.

I look over as he pushes off the door frame, coming toward us, rubbing at his stubble as he walks. He looks exhausted. A pang of guilt goes through me at the realization of all they've gone through on my behalf. Lukas sits next to me on the couch, close enough to wrap his arm around my shoulder, pulling me into him. Guessing his movements, Nissa flies to the arm of the chair as he sits. Astraea raises her head slightly to peer over at him.

"Hey, my little star," he says to her, running his hand over her head, and my heart . . . It melts. I want to cry at the tenderness in his voice.

Goddess, I hope what I say doesn't change anything. That he will still accept Astraea in all her wonder. Even if he doesn't accept me, she is all that matters.

Threading my fingers through Astraea's hair, I try to arrange my thoughts. Goddess, I hope I don't regret this.

"I need to tell you something," we say in unison.

My gaze catches his, and though we both smile, it's strained. He seems to be just as nervous as I am. What on earth could be making the alpha nervous?

Asena chooses this exact moment to walk in with food, drawing my attention away from Lukas. "Oh, that smells amazing," I moan. The smell makes my mouth water instantly, and I am completely focused on the food. I sit upright, looking down at Astraea and then back to the food. I really don't want to let her go, but I am starving. As if reading my thoughts, she decides for me and moves onto Lukas's lap. Asena hands over a bowl of chicken soup and fresh bread. I devour it all, forgetting about everything else happening at the moment. When I'm finished, I look up to see four sets of eyes looking at me. All seem worried and surprised. A blush works its way across my face.

"Sorry, I was starving. They didn't give me any food while I was there. Wait, how long was I there?" I query, looking between each of them.

Asena's eyes widen in shock, and Nissa titters angrily from her spot on the back of the sofa. Looking at Lukas is a mistake. The fury in his eyes makes my gut clench. The tension is palpable as it rolls off him in waves, pulsing between us.

"You don't have to apologize for eating," he snaps, shaking his head, causing some of his hair to fall and rest on his cheek. Worry lines marr his forehead, and I want to reach up and smooth them away. I am tired and emotionally drained, my thoughts weighing me down.

Breaking the silence that has descended, Lukas clears his throat. "You were gone for four days, Nesrin." Lukas' eyes flash yellow.

Reaching out my hand, the trembling betraying how I feel in this moment, I cover his hand with mine, squeezing. "I'm okay now, Lukas, thanks to you." I swallow hard around the lump forming in my throat.

"I'm so mad at you," Lukas admits harshly. I'm sure if Astraea wasn't on his lap, he'd be pacing about the room in agitation. "I was furious when I realized you'd left, and all I could think about was what would happen to you if the coven got to you." I felt him sigh. "All I want is to keep you safe."

My chest squeezed at the pain in his voice. "I'm sorry I left like I did. Yes, I know it was stupid, irresponsible, but I've spent most of my life taking care of myself and others. I have had no one to worry about me in a long time."

"That changes," he growls, flashing me a look. A thrill goes through me at the promise that those words, that look, hold.

"I'm sorry, Lukas, I am. But I had to go. The trolls needed me. I realize now it was a trap, but I *had* to go," I plead, hoping he will be able to understand my need to help others.

"I understand that, but you didn't have to sneak off. I would have come with you. Or Zee. Even Gabe would have gone. You were reckless, and it almost got you killed," Lukas growls, raising the tiny hairs on my arms.

Oh yeah, he's pissed. I can feel my anger rising in challenge, letting my guilt slip away. Before I can respond, Asena clucks her tongue. "Seems to me she did just fine, Lukas." Shit, I forgot we weren't alone.

His growl sends a wave of power through the room. Asena just turns, stalking out, muttering under her breath about dumb men. A smirk pulls at my lips. I really like her.

Suddenly, Grace is in the doorway, Merve right behind her. "Grace," I stammer. What is she doing here? "Oh, Nesrin. I'm so glad you're okay. I was so worried. Never scare me like that again, you hear me?!"

I chuckle and hold my arms out for her as she reaches me and bends for a hug. Grace pulls back, taking a hold of my face, turning it side to side.

"I'm fine, Grace. I promise."

I hear Lukas's answering huff and glance over at him, raising my eyebrow. "I'm fine."

"Happy to have you back, Ness." Merve's voice sounds from behind Grace, and I smile at the satyr. Grace steps back and Merve reaches out, wrapping an arm around her shoulders. I do my best to hide my surprise. "I'm going to take Grace home, give you a chance to rest. But we will be back tomorrow, Ness," Merve says, attempting to give me a stern look.

He fails, and I try not to smile. "Okay."

There are a good many questions I need to ask Grace, but that can wait for now. I need to clear the air with Lukas first. Once the others have gone, I turn back to Lukas. I grabbed his hand, squeezing hard. By the slight flare in his eyes, I can tell the move surprised him. "Lukas, I'm sorry, okay? But nothing I say is going to change what happened. What's done is done."

"I know that. I was just so damn . . . " he trails off, pulling his hand away, and rubbing it over his face. "This isn't what I wanted to talk to you about." Blowing out a breath, he looks out the window.

I look over to Astra, who is still sitting on Lukas's lap, and Nissa, who's on the back of the couch now, both looking back and forth between Lukas and me, worry contorting their little faces.

"Nissa, could you take Astra to get cleaned up for bed? We will be up in a minute. I need to talk to Lukas alone." I run my hand through Astraea's hair then down her face, "Can you give me a minute to talk to Lukas?" I ask her. She moves over to hug me once more, then she is off, racing out of the room with Nissa flying after her.

Turning back to Lukas, I take a deep breath. Before I can speak, his mouth covers mine, his fingers burying themselves into my hair, holding me to him. All thoughts flee my mind at the feel of his lips on mine, so soft as they move over mine in earnest. My insides dip and tumble, a delicious warmth spreading through my body. Lukas is kissing me. And man, can he kiss. I lean into him, wanting more.

All too soon, Lukas pulls back slowly, letting his finger trail down my face to my shoulders as he sits back, giving me space while he studies me with his deep, intense eyes. Dragging a hand over his head, he lets out a long-suffering sigh, and I feel the urge to giggle, but I'm too mesmerized by the way he is messing his hair up.

"This is not going how I planned," he breathes, standing up.

I tilt my face up to watch him. "Seems like it's going fine to me," I reply, my voice husky. Luke chuckles, walking to the window, but as he turns around I can't deny the obvious stress written on his face. I hate seeing him like this.

"Okay, you go," I say when he doesn't continue. My heart speeds up with his silence, and I grip my hands in my lap. Lukas paces again. I wait patiently as the minutes pass.

"Lukas, just tell me," I blurt, unable to watch the pacing any longer.

Then he turns those emerald eyes to lock on me once more, and I startle at the anger in them. Then he blinks—a long blink, the kind of blink that is leading to something. I brace myself as he speaks. "I understand, I do. But if you ever do something so reckless again . . . " He angrily slashes a hand through the air in front of him.

Anger burns my cheeks. "*What? Whoa. Whoa.*" I cut him off. A moment ago he was kissing me, and now he's telling me off?

He holds up his hand to silence me. "It was fucking stupid to go off alone. Like I said, I understand why you left, but . . . "

"Lukas, I'm fine. The trolls are fine. Everything is okay now." But my words do nothing to dispel his anger. He just stares at me with a look that makes the tiny hairs on my neck stand up. *Shit, he is really pissed at me.*

"If something happened to you, *I would not be okay.* Astraea would not be okay. *We would never be okay,*" he hisses.

Guilt pricks at my chest and I run my teeth over my bottom lip. "I'm fine," I argue.

He snorts, shaking his head. "You are practically starved, have cuts and bruises all over you, a mild concussion, a broken wrist, and a sprained ankle. How is that *fine?*"

Okay, he's got me there. But everything worked out . . . kind of. Lukas lets out a long breath, his hand running through his hair.

"That first night at the park, when I followed you to your car, you intrigued me. I thought to myself, who is this crazy ass woman, this witch who had the balls to enter my territory unannounced? For days, I couldn't get you out of my mind. I didn't know a thing about you, but my instincts told me you were someone important, someone I couldn't forget. Even before I realized what you were to me, I was drawn to you. When I first heard your voice, everything fell into place inside me. It was like a calm had settled over my heart and soul. My entire world became brighter, something different when I was around you." I don't dare move a muscle while he speaks. The change in topic, the naked emotions that fill his eyes, have my breath catching.

Lukas moves, dropping to his knees on the floor in front of me, one of his large, warm hands coming up to stroke my cheek. I'm startled by the movement, and by how gently he has a hold of me. Without hesitation, I open my knees to allow him to move closer. His eyes search mine like he is looking for the answers to all of his questions. I'm captivated by the storm raging behind those green eyes. When he speaks, his voice is deep with emotion but unwavering.

"The night I stayed at your apartment and held you all night, I realized why I needed to be around you all the time. My need to protect you above anyone else." Lukas takes a deep breath, letting it out slowly, his eyes never leaving mine as he stares with a deep intensity that has my stomach doing somersaults.

"What are you talking about, Lukas?" I ask hoarsely, afraid to hope. Afraid to dream that maybe this man might feel for me a fraction of what I feel for him. What I have refused to let myself think about, for fear it would break me. I'm not sure when it happened, or when it even started. All I know is that right here, right now, I am falling in love with this man.

"You are my mate, Nesrin." My heart begins to race and I hold my breath as he continues, "And I'm scared as hell to want this, to want you, but I refuse to give this up. You make me want to move mountains and brave the worst storms. I will fight for you, fight for us."

My heart thuds painfully in my chest. I am utterly speechless. My brain is short circuiting on one word. Mate. He wants me. Has chosen me—a witch—as his mate. I sit back, breaking his gentle hold on my neck. Green eyes burn into mine, his hands dropping to my thighs, squeezing them as he whispers softly as if trying not to startle me.

"Nesrin, I am falling in love with you. I want to start a life with you, with Astraea. You are so strong, loyal, and you protect those who can't defend themselves. A true luna. I was drawn to you because we are mates, but I love you for just being you, and the thought of almost losing you . . . " he trails off, gathering his thoughts before he continues, "I'd have destroyed them all, laid waste to the coven and all they stand for." His hands reach up, framing my face, as he flashes me a devastatingly handsome smile. One that makes me swoon inside, my heart beginning to race anew.

"I know this would be hard for you, so I held off telling you until things with the coven eased, but things aren't easing. I couldn't wait any longer. We are meant to be together, Nesrin. You and my little star are meant to be here with me." Lukas is closely gauging my reaction and, to be honest, I am gauging my reaction as well. It's part of why I have yet to utter a word, not that I could form a coherent thought anyway. I mean, it certainly explains a few things, like the pull I get in my chest when I see him, how I'm drawn to him like some magnetic force. Everything about Lukas elicits a chemical reaction from me. Just earlier, I thought he smelled like home, for goodness sake.

But the image of Blanchette and her mate's last moments flash through my mind, and I know I have to tell him the truth about who I am, who Astraea is. We will have no future if I build our relationship on secrets and lies. He has to know the risks of loving me, what it will mean for him. Although I have a feeling it won't matter either way. He already knows I'm a witch. Our relationship is forbidden.

"Please say something."

I close my eyes at the hope and fear in his voice. I blurt out the first thing that pops into my head.

"Are you sure?"

Opening my eyes again, I search his swirling emerald irises, finding a flicker of what I think might be hope, but it disappears too quickly for me to know for sure. A small smile tugs at the corners of his mouth and the warmth from it spreads through my body. A primal need to take what is mine comes over me, but I hold it down.

"Yes, sweetheart. We are mates," he answers, as if those three words hold all the answers in the universe.

A laugh bursts out of me—a totally inappropriate response—as the tension washes away. I open my eyes, smiling at this handsome man in front of me, still on his knees. With both hands, I reach up and take hold of his face, my fingers lightly stroking his cheeks.

"I'm falling in love with you, too," I whisper against his lips.

I didn't realize how tense he was until just then, that moment of acceptance. He sags forward, wrapping his arms around my waist as he buries his head in my lap. The gesture is so simple, so innocent, it has my heart melting. I run my fingers through his dark strands of hair and smile. After several moments like this, he still hasn't moved.

"Are you alright?" I ask.

His muffled "Yes" is barely audible over the sound of my thumping heart.

Laughing softly, I skim my hands over his hair and grip his cheeks, tilting his face up at me. The fire in his eyes has my pulse skyrocketing. He straightens and draws back slightly until his eyes are level with mine. God, they are so beautiful. The deep green with flecks of glowing yellow are captivating.

"I thought you'd fight it. Fight me," he admits quietly.

"What? Why would you think that?"

"Witches and shifters are forbidden to have intimate relationships. It's been that way forever."

Okay, now I am annoyed. "And?" I question.

"I thought that would maybe put a damper on how you felt about being my mate."

Frowning, I sit back. "It doesn't."

Lukas is silent for a long moment, as if contemplating what he wants to say. "Others don't understand the true nature of mates and the mating bond. It can scare them. They . . . You . . . " He takes a deep breath before continuing, "You can reject it."

My eyes widen and, dumbfounded, I ask, "You thought I'd reject you?"

"I did," he confesses, not taking his gaze from mine. I don't even think he's blinked since we made eye contact.

Despite my own fears, it hurts knowing that he would think that of me, that I'd reject him so quickly. Surely, he has to have noticed my growing feelings for him. I am not that good at hiding them. Okay, who am I kidding? I am terrible at keeping them hidden. This strong, protective alpha has been terrified that I would reject him and our mating bond. Little does he know, since the conversation with my mother, since learning about my family, I have been hoping with everything I am that he would be my mate. I want so much to show him what it's like to be loved by a Carson witch, that we love hard and fierce. That I will protect him as much as he will protect me. He is my alpha.

Wait. Shit. Alpha. That means. Oh no.

"I can hear your heartbeat, sweetheart. Why is it suddenly beating so fast?"

"You're an alpha," I blurt out.

"Last I checked," he chuckles lightly.

Without thinking, I throw a punch at his arm. He looks down to where I struck him, then back up at me, amusement shining in his eyes. "What was that for?"

"Don't be annoying. If you're the alpha and we are mates, that would make me . . . " I trail off, wanting him to finish for me.

"The pack's luna."

At those words, my stomach tumbles. Okay, that definitely makes me nervous.

Being mated to Lukas, that I am fine with, more than fine with, but the pack's luna? I blow out a long breath, glancing at the window. When I turn back, Lukas has a worried expression on his face.

My stomach knots. "Would they . . . I mean, *will* they accept me?" I whisper, afraid of the answer.

Lukas moves faster than I thought possible, his massive hands on either side of my face, his fingers sinking into my hair. "That is nothing you need to worry about," he assures me, his voice soft yet filled with power as his breath skates over my lips. If we were to move even an inch, our lips would touch.

I close my eyes and rest my forehead against his, chuckling as I point out, "It kind of is, Lukas."

"Nesrin, most will welcome you. Okay, yes, some may need convincing, but I have faith in you," he does his best to convince me, closing that last inch between us and brushing his lips over mine. I shudder at the contact, desperate for more, but I know I need to confess my secrets before anything else.

"Lukas . . . Before we go any further, I need to tell you something. Things that might change how you feel about me."

"Nothing will change how I feel about you, sweetheart," he vows, pulling back and taking a seat next to me on the sofa again. I turn to face him, bending my good leg up onto the seat between us. Lukas mirrors my position, his face alert even though his body seems relaxed.

Running my fingers through my messy hair, I mutter, "We'll see," under my breath. Okay, now it's my turn to hesitate and stumble over my words.

*Shit, I'm nowhere near ready for this.*

Lukas leans forward, pressing his lips to mine, and I melt into the touch. When he draws back, he whispers, "Just tell me, sweetheart."

Ignoring how my stomach flips when he calls me that, I squeeze my eyes shut and blurt out the words, "Astraea isn't my daughter." After a moment, I peek one eye open to see Lukas's eyes wide.

"Okay . . . Not what I thought you'd say." He draws out each word as if he's stalling until he can figure out how to respond. "I mean, I noticed you don't share the same coloring, but I just assumed she looked more like her father. With how you two are together . . . Never would have thought it." He shrugs a shoulder.

"She is my sister Niamh's daughter," I explain, then take a deep breath. "When she and her husband, Hunter, were murdered last year, I became Astraea's legal guardian. She is mine in every way that counts." I rush through the last bit because it's true, and I want him to know that. Everything I do is to keep that little girl safe. None of the pack has even realized what she is, what I am, thanks to my cloaking spell.

Before he can speak, I calmly add, "There's more."

He gives me a small smile, shaking his head. "There always is."

"Hunter, Astraea's father, he was a wolf shifter." I don't look away from Lukas as the information sinks in. The gold swirls through his green irises as a myriad of emotions pass over his face too quickly for me to read. I swallow around the lump forming in my throat. "Astra is a hybrid, Lukas. She and I are being hunted by the Order of Tartarus, a secret group of witches hidden within the covens and the council. My grandfather and father were also shifters. The gene runs in my bloodline, wolf's blood runs through my veins." I take a breath and hold it, waiting.

Green eyes glow brightly, the yellow rimming them. "You've got shifter blood?" he questions, his voice deceptively calm.

"Y-Yes." I clear my throat. Do I tell him about my mother's visit? Argh, I am really not prepared for this.

Lukas is studying me, a frown on his handsome face. After a brief pause, he asks, "Why have I not sensed it before?"

I scrub my hands over my face. "Umm . . . Well, you see, I put a cloaking spell on us." I cringe as I peek at Lukas through my fingers. He is still staring at me, that frown firmly stuck in place. I hate that I put it there.

I drop my hands, a sigh falling from my lips. "Also, I'm fairly sure Astra can mind speak. Is that something wolves can do?"

"It is usually only the alpha and luna that can mind speak between pack members. Others in the pack cannot mind speak with each other unless they are mates."

"Oh," I reply dumbly. "There's one more thing. Well, actually, two things," I say, wincing as Lukas stiffens next to me. He reaches for a glass of water on the coffee table. Taking a sip, he motions for me to continue.

"I'm . . . Well . . . I'm a descendant of a goddess."

Lukas chokes on his water. "A witch, a shifter, and a *goddess?*" His tone is incredulous.

"Weird, I know. It's a long story, and I can fill you in on all the details tomorrow. How did I not realize that shifters are fae?"

"You didn't know?"

I shake my head, and the corner of his mouth lifts, clearly glad that he's not the only one to have missed key information. "We don't really class ourselves as fae. Even though we are technically shape-shifting fae."

"Why did I not know this?" I muse, rubbing my eyes and chewing on my bottom lip, before looking back at him.

His eyes darken slightly, wholly focused on the lip held between my teeth, and my stomach does a flip. Before I lose my nerve, I hold up my finger. "One last thing, I swear."

Lukas lets out a hoarse laugh, then clears his throat. Shifting closer, he waits, and I am absolutely awed by how well this conversation is going. Still, I need to say this last part.

"I also have a sister who I need to find. During my stay at the coven, I learned about her. I didn't even know I had another sister." I wring my hands together, hoping like hell that Lukas is okay with all of this.

Finally, after what seems like forever, Lukas moves, shaking his head. He blows out a deep breath. "That's a lot to take in, sweetheart."

That last word, *sweetheart*, allows my muscles to relax. That's got to be a good sign. Right?

"I'm sorry I kept this from you, but I had to make sure it was safe here. It's odd, but I have trusted you from the beginning.

I just wasn't sure if my instincts were right. I was raised to be careful, to not trust anyone."

Lukas raises his hand to brush the hair from where it has fallen over my face. "I understand why you didn't tell me. I'm also happy to hear you trust me," he tells me gently, and the corner of my mouth ticks up. "We will figure this out together, all of it. This Order cannot have either of you. You're mine, freckles," Lukas growls, and a delicious shiver skates over my body at his possessive words.

My eyebrow quirks up as I lean back a bit, fighting a losing battle to hide my reaction. "Oh, is that right? And freckles?"

"Yes. I will protect you and Astraea. Both of you are my entire world. Tomorrow, after you've rested, we can revisit . . . all of that, because there's a lot there we need to cover. And, you have the cutest dusting of freckles on your nose. I have to admit that I'm dying to know if they're anywhere else on your body." His fingers reach up softly to graze over my nose and cheeks, then run down my neck and across my collarbone.

I draw in a sharp breath at the touch, and my eyes widen at his words. I try my best to breathe, but he has stolen the air from my lungs. My pulse kicks up a notch as my attention narrows on his lips. All I want to do is kiss him, soak in his scent. I move closer to him and sensing my need, he envelops me in his powerful arms, drawing me up into his lap and holding me close.

I let out a sigh and rest my head on his shoulder. "Okay, but I want to get one thing straight. I will protect you as well. We are in this together, Lukas," I whisper, and he presses a kiss to my head before resting his chin there.

"I'm still pissed at you," he says tenderly.

"I know."

Closing my eyes, I feel him take a deep breath. "They could have killed you." The words are barely audible, the pain and fear he felt evident in his tone.

"I know," I repeat. My mind drifts to my escape and how badly I was hurt. If Lukas and the others hadn't shown up, I would have been dragged back there, and this time Marcus wouldn't have been able to help me.

"Thank you, Lukas," I whisper, needing him to understand how grateful I am that he came for me. That I am important enough to him that he would risk a fight with the coven.

"For what?"

Before answering, I pull back just enough to stare into his eyes and then I kiss him softly, just barely a touch. "For caring," I whisper against his lips.

Lukas stands up, taking me with him, my legs wrapping around his hips. I slide my arm around his neck, my fingers threading through his thick hair at the back of his head.

"You can put me down, you know."

His eyes roam over my face, as if he is memorizing every detail. "I know."

I laugh when he makes no move to release me. "Please, can you put me down?"

Lukas seems ready to argue, but I unwrap my legs, letting them dangle. Ever so slowly, he lowers me down until my feet reach the floor. He keeps a firm hold on me until I'm steady on my feet. When I am standing, he releases my waist, then brings his arms up to take my face in his hands. He rests his forehead on mine and I reach up to grip his wrists, pushing up on my tiptoes. A slight pain flares in my foot, but I push it aside. The moment our lips touch, a rush of desire curls in my lower belly. This man is built for pleasure. I'm sure of it. My hands move from his wrists to his broad shoulders. My arm is throbbing intensely from being moved about, but I need to touch him more than I need air. His muscled arms cocoon me against his chest as he presses his lips firmly to mine, lifting me off my feet completely. Lips that were so gentle and soft moments ago are now kissing me with a passion I've never felt before. But then Lukas pulls back and I groan. He looks down at me, the lust and desire burning in his eyes knocking the wind out of me. He closes his eyes briefly, taking several deep breaths, and I follow his lead, hoping to slow my heartbeat. Then, slowly and softly, he pecks my lips two, three, four more times, sending butterflies scattering inside me.

Squeezing my waist where he has a firm grip, he lowers me down again, my feet landing gently on the ground. He keeps me close, our bodies pressed together so there is absolutely no space between us. Lukas nuzzles my neck, pushing my hair over my shoulder and running his hand down my back. I blush at the hardness I feel pressed against my lower belly. I can't help my body's reaction as I rock my hips against his.

Lukas groans into my neck. "You're making this really hard, freckles."

I tip my head to the side, further exposing my neck to him. "I can tell." A laugh bubbles out of me, and Lukas pulls away from my neck, his eyes, lit with amusement, meeting mine.

"I meant to take it slow," he growls, nipping at my bottom lip.

I smile against his mouth. "I know."

Lukas pulls back reluctantly. His eyes lock with mine, and my breath catches at the raw longing in them.

"Kiss me again," I whisper. I don't think I'll ever get enough of this man. His green eyes ignite just before his mouth claims mine with a fierce tenderness that has my toes curling, my soul crying out to his. Something deep in my chest aches for him, craves him. My good hand slides into his hair, pulling him closer as his lips possess mine. My knees buckle, and I sway slightly on my feet, the intensity between us leaving me feeling almost intoxicated.

Noticing my state, Lukas gives me one last kiss before he steps back, putting more space between us. "It's been a long day, and don't you even try to deny your exhaustion. I think you should get some rest and spend some time with our little star. She was so worried about you." He takes a deep breath before continuing, "But Nesrin, I don't want to put us off any longer. Witch, shifter, goddess, my mate and luna—I love every part of you. We belong together. I will do everything in my power to prove it to you every day," he vows, not breaking eye contact.

Utter exhaustion blankets me, weighing me down even as moisture rims my eyes, and I whisper the only response my brain can manage, "Okay."

Letting go of my pride, I allow Lukas to help me up the stairs to my room. Well, it's not like I could do it on my own, anyway. Astraea is already waiting, tucked under the covers, her tiny face barely visible.

Moving to sit on the bed, I stop as Lukas's arms band around me, dragging me back into his chest. "I'm so fucking relieved you're back, Freckles," he breathes into my hair, then kisses the top of my head. Closing my eyes, I relax in his embrace, running my good hand up his forearm. He places one more kiss to my head before helping me settle into the bed. I really need a shower, but I think I need Astraea more. The shower can wait.

I wake tangled in the sheets, sweat coating my body, making hair stick to my face. The bed is empty next to me, giving me time to compose myself. Pushing the covers off me, I sit on the edge of the bed, breathing in short, sharp pants, feeling as if I ran a marathon, instead of just trying to get in a little sleep. I lean forward, resting my elbows on my knees and my head in my hands as I stare down at the floor.

I'm not in that room. I escaped. I am at Lukas's. I am safe.

I've greatly underestimated the power of dreams, of my nightmares. When I was a kid, and I woke from a nightmare in the middle of the night, I had Niamh and my parents there. I could climb into bed with them and let their body heat chase away the icy feeling of dread that the nightmares brought up. I was comforted then by the knowledge that the dreams weren't real. It was merely in my mind. But the thing is, what happens inside your head is just as dangerous as any outside threat. The monsters lurking in my mind, in those dark corners, are the most dangerous of all. They are simply my own demons, made up of my greatest fears and regrets, and my worst memories.

The fire. Niamh. My parents.

All those things you'd rather not think about, those things you push to the back of your mind, pretend don't exist, and hope like hell they will disappear. But who are we kidding? Ignoring them doesn't make them go away. No matter how deep you think you've buried them, they will always claw their way back to the surface, bringing as much pain as they possibly can. Our subconscious doesn't let us forget. It never will. When we are at our most vulnerable, they show their ugly faces. When you can't push them away or fight them off, that's when the demons make themselves known.

A sharp pain shoots through my foot and I grit my teeth, breathing heavily through a clenched jaw. I can't believe I forgot about my sprained ankle. Using the furniture, I hop my way to the bathroom and turn on the shower. I step under the hot water, putting my good hand on the wall. I stand under the spray, letting the water run over my head and face, washing away the lingering sense of unease and dread.

# CHAPTER TWENTY TWO

"Argh, this sucks," I moan, dropping my head to the counter of the kitchen bar. I've been stuck inside for three days, and still, my ankle is too tender to walk on without help. I can put a little weight on it, but not enough to walk properly. Not to mention, my phone was lost when I was kidnapped, so I haven't even been able to call Suzy to let her know I was okay. Merve and Grace stopped by the day after they rescued me, together giving me an hour-long lecture, and made me promise to never run off and get myself caught again. Up to that point, I had never seen Merve angry before, but that day, I'm pretty sure he stomped one of his hooves at me. I felt like a little girl who had broken her father's trust. When I woke up this morning, I was alone once again, and as before, I showered and slowly made my way downstairs. The house was quiet, but I found Lukas and Astraea asleep on the sofa in the front room with a slow-burning fire going. Lukas, dressed in sleep pants and a well-worn gray henley, was stretched out across the sofa with Astraea nestled into his chest, one of his arms curled around her, holding her in place.

It was the sweetest thing I've seen in a long time, and tears filled my eyes as I watched them. I wish I could have gotten a photo. Instead, I did the next best thing, standing there longer than I care to admit, just burning the memory into my mind.

Although our time together has been limited, Lukas has made sure that I know he cares by leaving me handwritten notes around the house. Most of them stuck to the coffee machine, which he has obviously figured out is my favorite part of the house. I have woken the last couple of days to the sweet smell of flowers that he has left on my pillow. I love the gestures and the stolen moments throughout the day, but I miss him. From what I understand, there's some urgent pack business he has to deal with that has been keeping him busy.

Unfortunately, between my injuries and how busy everyone has been, I have grown bored, grumpy, and more than a little petty at this point. So when Zee comes strolling into the kitchen with a smirk pulling at his mouth, my first reaction is to growl in warning. Laughing, he sits down next to me with a massive grin on his pretty face.

"Pity party, is it?" Zee asks, flicking my nose. I try to swat his hand away, but he dodges, laughing at me.

"Don't poke the bear, Zee. You won't like what happens," I grumble. Being cooped up is not my thing. I am fully craving the outside world. I miss my magic. Being cut off from it has been a whole other form of torture. But we still haven't been able to get this stupid elven cuff off my damn wrist, and it is driving me crazy. I need it off, and soon. My skin is crawling with my pent up energy, and I've been constantly on edge, just waiting for the other shoe to drop. Wondering when I'll wake back in that frigid room to find that this whole thing is another illusion, courtesy of

Emerson. So, yeah, I am more than a little cranky and unsettled, which means everyone has been, for the most part, steering clear.

Zee lets loose a laugh, his blue eyes twinkling in the light. He looks so delightfully carefree. I try my best to keep the smile tugging at my lips from forming. Heaven forbid I let the man know he amuses me.

"Goddess, please give me patience," I murmur, and Zee's eyes sparkle with amusement.

"Don't you mean give me strength?" Zee says, popping a strawberry in his mouth. That was *my* strawberry from *my* plate, dammit. I narrow my eyes at him.

"No, I said what I said. If she gave me strength, Zee, I'd be strangling you right now for laughing at me and stealing my food. So, unless you're here to take me out of this house or get this damn cuff off me, go away," I snap, dropping my head to the bar again, regretting the words instantly. I don't really want him to leave. Everyone has been so busy with whatever pack business is going on that I've barely spoken to anyone.

Though, Kyra did stop by yesterday with the boys. I've really come to love that little family, at least those I've met. Her husband, Sander, has been visiting family in Canada, and will be back next week. While we spoke, she told me that Lukas sent Alex to one of the other pack housings, just outside of Portland, in Cascade Rocks. Apparently, she caused quite a scene when Lukas returned with me after my escape and subsequent rescue. I can just imagine the shit show it will be when she hears that Lukas and I are mates.

Bringing me out of my musings, Zee taps the top of my head. "Well, you're in luck. We have a pack visiting for a few days. They arrived this morning. Lukas has asked me to bring you and Astraea out to the feast we're having in the clearing."

I lift my head, almost jumping out of my chair. "Really!?" I can't believe how excited that sounded. Ugh. I am so lame.

Understanding shines in Zee's eyes as he replies with a small smile, "Yes, really."

Having heard her name, Astraea comes running into the kitchen. Seeing Zee, she lets out a squeal and practically flies into his arms. Zee doesn't miss a beat, catching her with ease and swinging her up and over his head while Astraea holds her arms out wide like wings. Bursting into laughter, I admire the two of them. They are true partners in crime.

"Alright, little one." Zee lowers Astraea to the ground, then looks to me, holding out his arm for me to take. "Let's go."

I slowly stand, using him to steady myself as we move toward the door, Astraea hot on our heels and Nissa following behind. Zee glances down at me, giving me a brief smile.

"I really like this dress on you. I know Lukas will."

I look down at my white maxi dress. The material is light and airy, flowing beautifully down to my ankles. Buttons run from the deep plunging neckline all the way down the front to the ground, but I've left them from the mid-thigh down to form a split. The long, flowing angel sleeves make me feel like a goddess. My face warms at the unexpected compliment. I hope he's right.

As we walk out the door, Zee grabs for something resting up against the outside wall of the house, then proudly holds it out to me. A laugh erupts from me as I reach out to take it from him. "Is that for me?"

"Yep! I thought you might like one for now, but with your mood, I didn't think bringing a weapon inside would be wise." He smirks down at me, and I lightly punch his arm.

"Thanks, Zee," I say and really mean it.

We make our way across the yard, waving at Gabe as he walks past. He gives me a quick nod before continuing. I can't remember ever having seen him so anxious before. The tension is rolling off him in waves.

"Zee, who is this pack, exactly?"

"Just a pack from Pennsylvania that Lukas has been trying to negotiate an agreement with for a while," Zee replies, seemingly unfazed.

Pennsylvania. My heart speeds up slightly. But Pennsylvania doesn't mean Pittsburgh, so I'm sure it's okay. There's nothing to worry about. Still, I can feel the nerves overshadowing my previous excitement at finally getting out of the house.

It occurs to me as we walk that I don't know who we're meeting, and last time I checked, not a lot of wolves tolerate witches. Maybe this is a bad idea. I would hate to put Lukas in a position where he might have to choose to defend me over something he has been working toward with the packs.

Zee, obviously having heard my heart rate pick up, looks down at me and reaches out to wrap his hand around my upper arm, pulling me to a stop. His expression is full of concern and understanding as he assures me, "You'll be safe, honey. We won't let anything happen to you. If Lukas even thought you'd be in any danger, he wouldn't have you here."

"I know. Sometimes I can't help the nerves." I squeeze his hand as much as my splint will allow. Asena bandaged my wrist up tightly enough that, while I can move my arm freely, I can't hold anything or move my fingers, not without a sharp pain taking over.

"You sure? I can take you back to the house." His eyes search mine.

I shake my head. "No, I am going crazy in there."

"Onward we go, then."

As we approach the large gathering, Astraea takes hold of my hand, and I look down at her with a reassuring smile of my own. There is a soft fluttering by my ear, followed by the warm, gentle weight of Nissa perching on my shoulder, holding onto a lock of my hair for balance. My heart swells as I realize that we're all comforting each other. Nissa has so easily become part of our family. Her uncompromising insistence of sticking by Astraea has cemented her place here with us.

We turn our focus back to the gathering just as Lukas spots us approaching, and breaks free from the group, strolling over. I barely suppress a moan of delight as I take in his form walking toward me in the clearing. Those dark jeans look fantastic as his legs saunter forward. The sleeves of his gray button-up shirt are rolled up to his elbows, putting his muscular forearms on display, and I marvel at how defined the muscles are, knowing how gently they embrace me. My gaze travels to his face, a smirk pulling at his lips, and a flush works its way across my cheeks. Lukas winks, and for anyone else, that might seem corny, but, oh, can he pull it off. The simple motion sends butterflies scattering through my stomach.

Astraea lets go of my hand and runs for Lukas, leaping the last few feet in the air, and Lukas catches her, tossing her up in the air in one fluid motion. She lets loose the most magnificent laugh I've ever heard, and joy surges through me as I realize I will never get enough of hearing it or seeing these two together.

"You're drooling," Zee whispers in my ear, smirking at me, and I hear Nissa giggle before she takes off toward the two of them.

I shoot Zee a glare. "Whatever," I reply lamely. Because he is right, I am practically drooling.

"Nesrin?"

I startle at the voice. A voice I thought I would never hear again. Looking past Lukas, I see what looks like a tall viking approaching. He is even bigger than I remember.

Zee's body stiffens beside me as I take a moment to respond.

"Finan?" I finally manage to get out. It feels like my heart is in my throat. I can't believe he's here. In Portland. The corner of his mouth goes up and the next thing I know I'm being scooped up in his massive arms into a bear hug. My shock is so complete that I don't move at first, just letting my arms dangle, then slowly I lift them to wrap around him, hugging him back. My cheek rests on his shoulder, and I smile to myself. I only knew Finan a short time before I left Philadelphia, but he had become a good friend when I needed one the most. Awareness suddenly washes over me as the air thickens with tension, and I note that everything has gone dead quiet. A loud, inhuman growl vibrates through the air, making the hairs on my body stand on end. This can't be good.

I pull back to search for the source of the sound, my eyes widening in surprise as I find Zee restraining Lukas, and I gasp at the look on Lukas's face. He is literally vibrating with the change. The anger pulsing in the air is stifling. I have never seen him like this. I push at Finan's arms, hoping he gets the hint to put me down. Thank the goddess, he does. But, because nothing can just be that simple, as he sets me down, he pushes me behind him and out of my mate's sight, sensing a threat.

I groan, tipping my head back. Worst. Idea. Ever.

I hear scuffling and growling. Moving to the side, I see Zee is trying to speak to Lukas. Finan, the giant oaf, moves to block me again, and this time Lukas loses it. Shifting into his huge black wolf, he knocks Zee to the side as he stalks forward. Gabe, who was running over to help, draws to a halt. I quickly step toward Lukas so he can see that I'm okay. All else has fled my mind. My only focus right now is Lukas. I have never seen him this out of control. Behind him, I spot Astraea and Nissa, both looking very worried. I take another step and pain flares in my foot, causing me to stop and breathe through the pain.

"Lukas, it's okay," I say between breaths as I try to get his attention, but his focus is on my friend.

"Nesrin, stay behind me," Finan growls, trying to step in front of me again, followed by Lukas snapping his teeth as he growls. I may not be able to access my magic, but I can still sense the two shifters' power rolling off them in waves, and the others can as well.

"My mate will not hurt me, Finan," I snap back. He spins to face me, his eyes widening in shock.

"Your mate?" he chokes out, the expression on his face so comical that I'd probably laugh if the situation wasn't so serious.

"Surprise! Yes, my mate. Now, can everyone calm the hell down?" I yell in exasperation, wanting to stomp my foot like a child, but thankfully remember that my ankle is still tender.

Astraea chooses that moment to tug on Lukas's fur, and as he looks down at her, he deflates instantly, all the anger draining away as he nudges her with his head. Shifting back, Lukas runs his hand over Astraea's hair, his head jerks back suddenly and shock lines his face. All at once, he is scooping her up into his arms and burying his face in her hair, and I have this sneaky suspicion she just spoke to him. He seems to take a few deep breaths and when he lifts his head again, he looks calmer.

Lukas prowls over to me, his stride purposeful. His powerful arm slides around my waist, tugging me into his warm chest, and I wrap an arm around his middle, giving a comforting squeeze. My mate's warm breath skates over my neck, sending a shiver through me as he whispers in my ear, "You look stunning in this dress, and adorable when you're flustered." It's as if nothing happened. Like he didn't almost attack Finan for touching me. I give him an exasperated look and turn back to Finan, who is staring at the three of us like we are aliens.

"What the hell, Nesrin? Any more magical folk going to show up to be your BFFs?" Zee asks in irritation, taking a deep breath of his own. I look over and give him the finger. I love him, but does he always have to be a smart ass? Seeing that he's on edge from the near disaster, I decide to keep my mouth shut. This time.

"So, this is where you disappeared to? Portland?" Finan asks, running a hand through his blonde hair. It has definitely gotten longer since I last saw him, reaching down to his mid-back now, a few small braids on either side of his head. His blue eyes are just as pale as I remember, almost silver in color. He's always reminded me of a Viking warrior, with the way he looks and carries himself.

"Yes, I've been here almost a year now," I reply. When I left Pittsburgh, I didn't tell anyone where I was going. I simply packed up and left in the dead of night, my gut telling me to run and tell no one. I was able to cover my scent enough with magic that I couldn't be tracked and I had already placed a cloaking spell over us the night Niamh and Hunter died. A cloaking spell I still had in place. Just because I told Lukas about Astraea and I, it didn't mean I felt safe enough to take down my spells.

"Astraea has grown," Finan comments, looking at her with affection. The last time he saw her, she was only eight months old. I feel Lukas tense under my arm, and Astraea must notice as well, because she puts a hand on his cheek and pats him as if trying to reassure him it's going to be okay.

"Yes, she has. Faster than I'd like," I reply. Truth is, Astraea is developing faster than I expected for a nearly two-year-old child. Finan knows about Niamh and Hunter, but he doesn't know about Astraea being theirs. If he did, he would have demanded that I stayed. Everyone just assumed Astraea was mine, and I never corrected them. It felt like the safest option at the time. He helped me with the funeral and in the weeks after their deaths, when I was a zombie healing from my own injuries. Finan was Hunter's best friend, and he felt their loss just as much as I did.

"Nesrin, we need to talk," Finan says, his eyes pleading with me. He casts a quick look at Lukas, who growls in response. Finan raises his hands. "Just talk," he swears.

Rolling my eyes, I shuffle in front of Lukas, leaning back into his chest. I can understand that he's struggling and feels threatened by Finan, but there is nothing to worry about. I am falling for him and only him.

"Of course. Can you give me a second?"

Without waiting for a reply, I pull out of Lukas's embrace and turn to face him. Just as I'm readying to speak, Nissa lands on my shoulder, leaning in to whisper in my ear so only I can hear, though I'm sure Lukas could hear if he wanted to.

"You and Astraea have become the most important things in his life. He will do what he thinks is necessary to protect you both. He is responding as a mate would." And with her wisdom imparted, she flies away toward the river, leaving me to frown at her.

Lukas is watching me with a guarded expression on his face. I know I need to step gently, that wolves are possessive by nature, especially with their mates, and process things differently. Lukas was an alpha as well, so he has more to prove, more at stake. But damn it, I am not in the mood. These last two weeks have been hell, and I have finally been able to get out of that house just to end up in the middle of a pissing contest.

"Lukas, he is not an ex-boyfriend, so can you please just relax?" The frown on his face only deepens with my words. Okay, maybe that wasn't so tactful.

But he remains silent. Concern starts to creep in, and I shift uncomfortably on my feet, feeling anxious. What is he thinking?

"Look, he was Hunter's best friend, and he helped me after the fire. Okay? There's nothing to worry about. I promise," I whisper to him softly, reaching up to stroke his growing beard. "You know I care about you, right?"

He smiles, and sunshine breaks out. I am struck dumb for a moment, soaking in his smile. Astraea claps her hands, clearly happy he is now smiling as well. His hand reaches up, cupping my face, his thumb moving over my cheek, before leaning in and placing a soft kiss on my lips. "What was that for?" I ask breathlessly. Not that I'm complaining.

Before he can reply, shouting comes from behind me. "Is that her? I want to see them now! Get out of my way, Roan!" a woman yells.

I spin quickly on my bad ankle and yelp in pain. Lukas quickly sweeps an arm around me, holding me up against him. The woman could be Finan's twin, with her long blonde hair and pale blue eyes. But I'm more than a little confused. *Is she talking about me? Why is she so eager to see me?*

Finan storms over to her and speaks to her in a low voice. She stops trying to push past him and sends him a glare before turning to storm away. Puzzled, I look up at Lukas, and I'm just about to ask who she is when he beats me to it.

"That was Finan's sister, Kate. Seems Finan has been keeping some things a secret, but I will let him explain it to you." Taking a deep breath, he continues, "I'm sorry. It is hard for me to let him near you. I'm really trying, but all my instincts are telling me to keep you away from him, that you're mine. Things will settle down when we are mated, but for now, he and I are both unmated, and he is alpha. Both make him a threat to me," Lukas says roughly.

"Or you could get worse," Zee pipes in from behind me.

Lukas growls again, glaring at his second. Ignoring Zee, I tilt Lukas's face down to me. "I am yours, Lukas. Nothing will change that. Why don't you come with us to talk?" I offer, grabbing his hand and giving him a small smile.

Lukas shifts Astraea in his arms and pulls me closer. "Like I'd let you go alone. We're in this together, remember?"

My heart rate picks up as his lips claim mine in a soft kiss. Lukas pulls back and I follow, wanting more. When I open my eyes, he's smirking down at me.

I scowl at him. "Not fair."

When Lukas grins, I feel a weight lifting from my shoulders, even though his expression is still guarded. I didn't realize how desperately I needed to see his beautiful smile. My whole body warms at the sight. *I have never felt this content ever.*

"Me either," he says, pressing his lips to my hair. "Come on. We can talk in the house away from prying ears," he adds, turning us toward the house and letting the others follow.

We all make our way into the main living room, as the large room is large enough for meetings of this size. Lukas helps me over to one of the two large sofas, and Zee takes his place behind us. I twist around in my seat to look at him in question, but his arms are crossed over his chest and feet slightly apart, eyes scanning the others in the room when he sees me watching him. Sending me a quick wink, he continues to survey the room. Okay then, he must be in protect-the-alpha mode. I don't think we need him to stand guard at our back, but if that's what he wants to do, fine.

I notice Gabe making his way into the room and frown. Why all the people? Gabe takes a spot next to Zee, face stoic as he looks around, his sharp eyes not missing a thing. In this stance, if he had a sword strapped to his back, he would resemble the samurai warriors of old. I giggle at the thought of Gabe running around with a katana and shifting. I wonder how it would work. Would he still be holding the sword? Lukas looks at me in question and I shrug, adjusting Astraea on my lap. She is staring with an odd expression at Finan, who is sitting across from us on the other large couch. Next to him sits a man who was introduced to me as Roan.

He's a stocky red-headed man with kind blue eyes. And when I say stocky, I mean he is *built*. He is broad, and his body is corded with muscles on top of muscles. Lukas and Zee are pretty big, but this guy is humongous.

"So . . . " I break through the silence, wondering why no one has spoken yet.

"Alpha, I think we–" Roan starts and I feel myself jerk forward.

"Wait, you're the alpha?" I cut in, shocked that I never picked up on that.

"Yes, Nesrin. I'm the alpha. I run the pack in Pittsburgh," Finan smiles softly. "And Hunter was my brother, not my best friend." He lets out a long sigh at my stunned look. Running both his hands over his face, he continues, "I'm sorry I lied to you. Not sure why I didn't tell you the truth straight away, but I made a mess of things. I should have told you that night that Hunter was my brother. That we were family." He looks at Astraea thoughtfully and I tense. "She is Hunter's, isn't she?"

My pulse speeds up. "Yes," I whisper, feeling like the ground is crumbling beneath my feet.

"I found a photo in his room. It was of him, your sister, and Astraea."

I nod, unable to speak.

"My sister has been so angry that I let you get away, especially with Astraea," Finan says, then cringes because that last part didn't sound particularly good. I know he meant nothing by it, but really, let me get away? With Astraea . . .

I'm sitting rigid in my seat, emotions building. He lied to me before. Did Niamh know who his family was? Are they only here to take Astraea from me? I will not let them take her. She is mine.

I don't realize I'm trembling until Lukas squeezes my hand, drawing my attention. I look over at him and he gives me a reassuring smile.

"Relax, Freckles. I won't let anything happen to either of you," he whispers, and I nod, taking a deep breath.

"That didn't come out right," Finan says softly, his eyes pleading with me to understand. Finan should be happy that I don't have any magic at the moment, because it would absolutely react to the threat he poses. And not in a nice way.

I don't respond.

"It's okay, sweetheart. No one is taking our little star away. Isn't that right, Finan?" Lukas growls the last part.

Taking a deep breath and then another, I get myself under control and face Finan again.

"I don't want to take Astraea from you, Nesrin. That came out wrong. We just want a chance to be part of her life. And yours, of course. We were hoping if we found you, we could take you both home with us. However, I see that is not an option anymore," Finan finishes quickly at the growls erupting from both Lukas and Zee. My chest warms at their reactions.

But . . . Astraea has more family out there. She has an uncle and an aunt who want to know her. I look down at her adorable little face, set into an expression of concern, and smile at her. I guess she's worried because tears are lining my eyes, causing them to sting.

"*Mommy?*" Her voice echoes through my mind and a sob breaks free, so many emotions flooding through me that I can't make out what each of them is.

Lukas pulls us to him, whispering words I can't begin to understand at the moment. When I pull back, I wipe at my face, looking down at Astraea. Why does she never speak out loud? I look over to Finan. He has a sad look on his face, elbows braced on his knees, watching us. I wonder if he thinks I will deny him this chance to know his niece, deny her a chance to know her family.

I would never do that.

"Maybe if I hadn't lied to you, you never would have left, but it worked out for the best. I can see that now. This was how it was supposed to happen. Kate would like to meet you both. Ever since she found out about Astraea, she has been on a mission to find her niece. She was very close to Hunter, and we both knew he had been seeing someone. We just didn't know who, or how serious it was until the fire. It broke our hearts that he never told us about any of you. After the fire, at first like everyone else, I thought she was your daughter, but I saw the resemblance of my brother there, and your sister Niamh from some photos I found in the house. By then, you'd already gone." Finan's throat bobs. I understand his pain. He lost a brother, and I lost my sister. But we have Astraea, a piece of both of them.

"I would love it if you would get to know Astra while you're here," I say around the lump in my throat. I stand up, holding her, and amble over to him, wincing at the pressure on my ankle. Finan rises swiftly, eager to meet me halfway. He brushes his hands over his jeans, and I smile reassuringly at him. He is nervous. A big powerful alpha nervous of a little girl.

"Finan, I'd like to officially introduce you to Astraea Nora Carson, your niece."

Finan sucks in a sharp breath that seems painful. "Hi Astra, I'm your Uncle Fin." His deep voice sounds rough and uneven.

In the background I faintly hear Zee whisper to Lukas, "I thought her last name was Locke?" Lukas murmurs something back that I can't quite make out. Lukas knows of my name change, and why I did it.

Watching Finan, I can see he is fighting his emotions, and when Astraea puts her arms out for him to take her, a tear slips free, falling down his cheek. Reaching for her, he lifts her from my arms, not bothering to wipe the tear away. It makes me like him even more to know he has no qualms about anyone seeing how emotional he is in a moment like this.

Astraea doesn't miss a beat as she wraps those tiny arms around his neck and hugs her uncle tightly. Finan looks up at me, and I give him a watery smile, squeezing his arm before moving back to my seat with Lukas.

A knock sounds at the door, and Zee walks over to pull the door open. The blonde from earlier, Kate, comes rushing in, stopping short at the vision of Finan and Astraea. Tears fill her eyes immediately as she slowly walks over to them and places her hand on Finan's back. Finan looks down at his sister and grins.

"Kate, this is Astraea Nora Carson, your niece," he says softly, turning Astraea slightly so she can see her aunt.

"They put mom's name as her middle name," Kate gasps, and I'm just as shocked because I've never known where her middle name came from.

"She looks just like him," Kate cries.

Finan reaches for her, pulling her in for a hug as she sobs into his chest, and Astraea doesn't hesitate to put her arm around Kate's head in an awkward hug, which tugs at my heart.

But Kate breaks away, half laughing, half crying as she holds her arms out for a proper hug, whispering, "Hi, Astraea." Astraea goes right to her and snuggles straight in.

I can't look away from the happy trio. Seeing them together now, all three with the same shade of blonde hair and striking blue eyes, it's easy to see the resemblance between them.

The tears are freely streaming down my face. At this point, I don't bother trying to stop them. Lukas wipes my cheeks with his hand as I look over at him, his bright green eyes full of affection. I am damn lucky to have him by my side. I lean in to give him a peck on the cheek, but before I can pull away, he grabs my face with both his hands to capture my lips. Desire blooms in my belly just as I hear Zee clear his throat. Pulling back, I can feel my cheeks heat, and I press the backs of my hands to my cheeks to cool them down.

Finan steps closer to Kate and turns her toward us. "Kate, this is Nesrin Carson"

Kate's blue eyes are red with tears as she meets my gaze, her smile hesitant as she walks over, Astraea still in her arms. "I'm so happy we found you two. Thank you for taking care of her and keeping her safe. I didn't think this was ever going to happen, that we would get this chance."

"Of course. I'm glad Astra has family out there. I know she will love having you around," I say, trying to stand so I'm not looking up at them. Lukas helps me up and stands firmly by my side, his finger linking with mine.

"We look forward to getting to know everyone. This means a lot more visits between packs, with Astraea being a part of both now," Lukas says, smiling down at me. I get lost in his eyes for a moment until a startled gasp breaks my gaze when Kate registers what Lukas said. I jerk my head back to her, a frown pulling at my face as I take in her reaction.

Kate's eyes are wide, her mouth hanging open. Then it changes to a scowl as she looks between us. "You're coming home with us. Right? Finan?" she asks, turning to look at her brother. Finan cringes and looks to me apologetically, then back to his sister.

"Kate, Nesrin is Lukas's mate. She and Astraea will remain here with the pacific north pack," Finan declares this firmly but softly, like he knows how much this will hurt his sister.

"But we just found her," Kate protests, holding Astraea tighter. Lukas steps forward to take her if he needs to, and Kate takes a step back, looking frantic. I understand that look. I felt it myself in the days after the fire, like any minute Astraea would be taken from me. It's why I ran.

"I will do everything in my power to make sure you see your niece often. I won't keep her away from you," I promise, lifting my hands to cover my chest, hoping she will realize I mean every word.

"But you're just a witch. How can you be mates with an alpha? That makes no sense? You can't be. You're a witch," she blurts.

I stiffen as I try not to feel the sting of her words, but it's like a dagger to the heart. Is that all I'll ever be to everyone? Just a witch?

The muscle in Lukas's jaw ticks in annoyance. "I assure you it is possible, Kate," he growls, wrapping his arm protectively around my waist. He doesn't like what came out of her mouth any more than I do. "There is much we need to talk about. Things you will need to know," Lukas adds sternly, his alpha powers leaking through into his words, saturating the room. I can see Finan,

Kate, and Roan stiffen in response to the power, the warning and threat in it.

I square my shoulders as I stare at them. "Niamh and Hunter were mates." The room falls completely silent at my declaration. At their shocked looks, I continue, "They chose to keep it a secret. I'm not sure if they ever completed the mating bond."

"They would have completed it, or they wouldn't have been able to conceive Astraea," Finan replied. Astraea looks at each of us, confusion twisting her sweet face. She tries to reach for Lukas as Kate takes another step back, shaking her head, her blonde hair flying around. Denial is written all over her face.

She doesn't believe us.

Lukas and I both growl in unison. We don't want trouble, but if she hurts Astraea or tries to take her, all bets are off. Roan steps forward, as does Zee.

"Kate!" Finan's voice booms, his own alpha power rolling through the room now. We all stiffen, but Kate's shoulders deflate and she shuffles forward to hand Astraea to Lukas. Before she can let go, Astraea leans in, kissing her cheek. Kate looks startled, but quickly kisses her back. I exhale in tentative relief as everyone once again takes a seat. As Kate moves to sit beside Finan, however, her posture is tense, and she looks uncomfortable.

Lukas fills the others in on everything that has happened, with me adding details when I need to. It's . . . a lot for everyone to take in. When I get to the parts about my sister Leila and Grace, Zee's expression turns irate. He is obviously not a happy camper. I can feel his anger from where I'm sitting, and if I can feel it, I know others can as well.

But what's wrong? What part of the story has brought on this reaction? He is refusing to look at me as I try to catch his eye. I rack my brain, trying to understand why he's taking the news of my family history so hard. I'm fully focused on Zee now, because, seriously, he is freaking me out. His handsome face is set, hard as stone. Finally, he turns to me, his clear blue eyes locking on mine.

"You have a sister named Leila?" he growls, clenching his fists at his side. I frown, confusion swirling through me because he sounds furious about this revelation. Zee is usually so easy-going. Nothing ruffles his feathers. But right now, he is on edge. I have no clue as to why, but I can *see* the tremble in his body. He is doing his best to keep himself composed, but one little thing will set him off.

"Yes, from what my mother said. Why?" I reply dumbly, staring back into those fierce blue eyes, hoping to understand why he's being like this. I mean, I'm the one with the lost sister. The sister I didn't know existed a few days ago. I had a reason to be bent out of shape. But Zee?

He just stares back at me for a moment, seeming to search my face. Then, turning abruptly, he stomps from the room, slamming the door shut behind him. I look at Lukas in uncertainty.

"What just happened?"

"I actually don't know. I will talk to him." Lukas looks just as perplexed as I do, his gaze still on the door his best friend and beta just stormed through.

After that, we wrap it up for the day so we can get on with the feast and mingle with the rest of the two packs.

"I can't believe you're a hybrid—I mean a legacy." Finan's words are filled with something like wonder as we file out of the house with the others, Lukas helping me keep the weight off my foot. The mood is light, even joyful, until I see a car driving down the gravel road toward the house.

*Dammit. Now what?*

# CHAPTER TWENTY THREE

A black escalade similar to the one that almost hit me outside Blue's pulls to a stop at least twenty yards away, instead of driving up to the house. We are all standing at the bottom of the steps, waiting. I look around and see Lukas, Finan, Roan, Gabe, Kate, and Astraea all staring at the car.

Nobody makes a move to exit the car and I can feel the energy around me building. The wolves were uneasy. I can feel the tension rolling off them. Lukas turns, handing Astraea off to Kate and motioning to her to go back inside, and I let out a sigh of relief. The last thing I want is Astraea in the middle of a fight. I flash a reassuring smile at her as they head inside, receiving a smile and wave back. I spot Nissa a second later, her golden dress sparkling in the sunlight as she follows the pair into the house. Astraea will be safe, Nissa and Kate will make sure of it. Surprisingly, I trust that sprite with her safety and wellbeing.

Turning back to face the car, something else near the house catches my eye. Zee is storming around the side of the porch, heading directly for us, the look of absolute wrath on his face making me want to take a step back. I have never seen his look so furious before. He stops, taking his position on my left side. Finan is on my right, and Lukas has now taken up the spot in front. I frown at the car, but whoever is inside makes no move to get out. Gabe and Roan are behind us, and Asena appears from nowhere, coming to stand next to Zee. The shifters are showing a united front, and I seem to have been put in the middle. I feel a pang of uselessness because I don't usually need protecting. It's just this damn elven cuff.

Lukas reaches behind him, blindly grabbing for my hand, and I reach out, taking it. "You aren't useless, sweetheart, far from it," Lukas assures me, and even as warmth fills my chest at his sweet words, shock rolls through me, because this time, I know for a fact that I didn't speak out loud. I stand there dumbfounded as his fingers squeeze mine once before letting go.

Suddenly, the driver's side door flies open, revealing Marcus. He steps out, stumbling a little, and I gasp, bringing my hands to cover my mouth at the condition he is in. His face is a mask of bruises, his left eye swollen shut, and he holds his midsection as he takes slow, measured steps.

Lukas takes a step toward Marcus, fury rolling off him in waves as he snarls, "What are you doing here, mage?"

Marcus hesitates, then scans the group, his one good eye settling on me in desperation. I move forward a step, feeling a twinge in my ankle, but I do my best to ignore it, coming to stand at Lukas's side. I place my hand on his arm, both to steady myself and to calm him.

"Marcus? What happened? Why are you here?" I ask, surprised at how steady my voice is. I can feel the energy of the others at our backs, ready and waiting for anything. They all have mine and my mate's backs, but in the end, Lukas and I will do anything to protect them. Not that I think Marcus poses much of a threat. Looking at him, he can hardly stand.

"I came to give you this." His voice is hoarse, barely above a whisper. It's not lost on me that he's skipped over my question about what happened, but I can guess. Marcus reaches into his pocket, pulling out a small metal-looking disk and holding it out to me.

I frown, taking a step forward, but Lukas halts me with an arm across my chest.

"What is it you want, Mage?" Lukas bites out, tension rippling through his body. His arm is trembling with the effort it is taking to maintain control. Today has been a highly emotional day for everyone. Adding this to the mix might just push Lukas over the edge.

"Nothing," is the quick reply. Marcus isn't stupid. Anyone can see the rage written on Lukas's face. And Marcus is definitely aware of how unpredictable shifters can become during times of stress.

"What is it, Marcus?" I ask, pointing at the object he was holding in his hands.

"It's the key." He shrugs, tossing it at me. It only just makes the distance, but I catch it and stare down at the shiny object. Frowning, I flip it over in my hands.

"Key for what?" I inquire, looking back up at him.

"The elven cuff."

Hope fills my chest, but I purse my lips in confusion. This looks nothing like a key. But the elves had always been tricky with their objects. They were incredibly smart creatures and forged a lot of weapons and magical objects.

"You will need your magic for what's coming," he adds cryptically.

A knot forms in my throat. "Really? Why? What's coming, Marcus?" I force out the question, annoyed by his vague responses.

"What they are doing is wrong. I'm not the only one who thinks so either. It seems there is some corruption in the council, and it's leaking into the covens." He explains, his voice hardening.

"Tell me something I don't know," I mutter, looking down to study the object once more and turning it over in my hand. There appear to be elven runes etched into the smooth flat surface on one side.

"There will be a war, or at the very least a fight," he rises to my challenge.

My head whips up to meet his gaze. "What?" I croak, not sure I heard him correctly. A war?

"They will come for you. There are a few of us who have taken a stand against my father and those he is following. When the time comes, we will fight."

Lukas loses the struggle with his temper, lunging forward, and is on Marcus before I can blink. He has Marcus by the shirt as I rush over, pain shooting up my leg.

"Lukas!" I snap, pushing his arm down, but he refuses to let go. "Let him go."

Lukas's eyes are filled with fire—and not the good kind—as he glares at me before slowly looking back at Marcus. "He almost got you killed," he grinds out through his tightly clenched jaw.

"He also saved my life, Lukas," I reply sharply.

But he doesn't respond to me, his focus wholly on Marcus. "And whose side will you be on, mage?" Lukas demands, getting up in Marcus's face. Even though I don't want to admit it, I swallow at the hostility coming from Lukas.

"I will be on Nesrin's side." Marcus looks at me with regret in his eyes. "I'm sorry for everything, Nesrin. If I could change what happened, I would. I thought they were just trying to scare you into joining the coven. I didn't know . . . " he trails off as he takes in the look on my face.

I cross my arms and let out a huff, shooting him an incredulous look. He may not have known they planned to torture and kill me, but he did know they were up to no good. That the high priest's obsession with me isn't normal.

I breathe deeply, battling the emotions welling up inside of me. "I know. But Marcus, you had to have known something was off. That it wasn't normal behavior." I believe he's sorry, that he didn't mean for this to happen. Marcus has risked a lot to help me, and given the condition he's in now, that fact didn't go unnoticed. Even now, coming onto pack lands and giving me this key, he is taking another risk knowing full well what he's walking into.

"I'm sorry."

"I forgive you, but I will not forget."

"I will prove myself to you."

"Not good enough. You hurt my mate!" Lukas snarls, every word more forceful than the last, as he pushes him backward. Marcus stumbles, just getting his feet under him before Lukas continues, "My mate accepts your apology, so I'll give you this one chance. But hurt her again and I will kill you." The threat is accompanied with a burst of power that prickles my scalp and tightens my skin.

Marcus pales and looks to me for confirmation. He must read something in my expression, because his face falls. Then it's as if a mask is put in place, after closing his good eye tight for a moment, he looks back at me with understanding and acceptance. He takes a step back toward his car. "I will be in touch. When the time comes, we will have to join forces. You don't stand a chance without us."

"Don't be so sure, mage!"

"Don't go into this with an ego, alpha. You'll get your *mate* killed," Marcus fires back, and my heart starts pounding like the hooves of a runaway horse.

Lukas shifts in a heartbeat, and before I can react, he's charging Marcus. I spin around, looking at Zee and the others, hoping they will intervene, but they just stand with their arms crossed, watching.

"Help!" I shriek at them.

Zee just shakes his head. Gabe and Asena refuse to meet my gaze. *Argh! Bloody wolves.*

I spin back around to see my mate's formidable black wolf form stalking around Marcus, his enormous paws making no sound as he circles his prey. Marcus has a shield around him. My eyes widen in shock at the magic he uses. It's a nasty shield, one that will hurt any person who touches it. I understand an angry mate sometimes can't be reasoned with, but seriously?

"No, Lukas, don't!" I warn, moving toward the two as he lunges forward, bouncing off the shield. He's sent flying through the air, sparks grazing his fur as he slides across the gravel. Growls erupt behind me, but I put my hand up to silence them. They wouldn't help me before, so they can't help now.

Lukas stumbles to his paws, shaking off the effects of the spell. I nod at Marcus, motioning to the car. He should go while he still can. Marcus hesitates before turning and making his way to the car. Getting in, he casts me one last look before closing the door, leaving in a cloud of dust.

It's only now that I realize I was able to see the magic of Marcus's shield, and turn my eyes downward. The cuff is gone. Looking around, I spot it on the ground a few feet away from me. Dismissing my relief at being rid of the cuff, I turn and make my way to Lukas who is pacing back and forth, watching the Escalade as it drives off. Though I'm cautious in my approach, it is impossible not to admire him.

I'll never get over seeing Lukas in wolf form. He is gorgeous. The wolf before me is gigantic, his thick fur black as midnight. As I approach, his head lifts so his yellow eyes are level with mine. I try to calm myself down, not wanting him to think I fear him in this form. Reaching a hand out, I run it over his chest. I can feel the power under his fur, his muscles coiled with tension. I glide my hand up and slowly bring it up to his face. Lukas stills, and it seems like he is holding his breath, those luminous eyes watching my every move. My fingers slide between his ears and back down his neck and he nuzzles in close, almost knocking me over with the force of it. I wrap my arms around his neck and nuzzle him back, enjoying the feel of his fur against my skin.

"I'm okay, Lukas. When you're calm, we can talk more about Marcus and hi–" Lukas's snarl of protest cuts me off, and I can't help but roll my eyes.

"Change back so we can talk. Please," I murmur, stepping away from him as I put my hands on my hips, pushing aside the pain from my injuries.

Lukas shifts, and I wince at the cuts all over him. That spell was nasty alright. Even his clothes are singed. Though, it still amazes me how their clothes are able to stay intact when they shift. And to see that they are even affected even though they can't be seen is mind boggling. Without words, I grab his hand, pulling him past everyone else, refusing to meet their gazes. I am beyond pissed at all of them right now.

# CHAPTER TWENTY FOUR

I look over at Lukas, guilt churning in my stomach. He got hurt because of me. Lukas sits on the end of the bed, his elbows resting on his knees. Even though he's looking at the floor, I can see the frown pulling at his lips. I move in front of him, wanting to clean the cut across his eyebrow. It looks deep, and I can't stand seeing him injured. The anger drains from his expression as he looks up at me and the cloth in my hand.

"May I?" It comes out as a whisper. For some reason, my voice has stopped working properly, and a whisper is all I can manage.

Lukas nods, sitting up and opening his legs to allow me to move closer. He lightly grips the back of my legs, pulling me in, and I try—and fail—to calm my racing heart.

Reaching up and gently wiping away the blood, I can see he's already healing. Wanting to boost the process, I open up my magic. Slowly, I run my finger along the edge of the cut. A soft glow appears as I trace the cut, sealing it up as I go.

*Good as new.* I smile to myself. It feels so good to have my magic back. Being cut off from it was like I was missing an arm. Joy fills me at the feel of the magic humming under my skin and the warmth it creates in my chest. My eyes roam Lukas's face and, when our gazes meet, I see the heat burning in his eyes as they observe me with an intensity I want at once both to explore and hide from. The slight yellow glow around the edge of the green is captivating. My heart knocks wildly against my ribs in a code I can't decipher. Lukas brings his hands to encompass my waist and pulls me down to sit on his lap, my knees resting on the bed, my hands holding his shoulders.

His hands move up to cup my face. "Thank you," he says gently, bringing our faces closer together, his lips lightly brushing mine. The kiss is soft, tender, making me sigh into his mouth. I feel his lips pull into a grin at the sound, and relax more fully on his lap. One of his hands skims down my back, the other lightly cupping my neck.

Breaking the kiss, he opens his eyes and looks at me. "He has feelings for you." His voice is rough, like it hurts him to speak the words. His hand reaches to twirl some of my hair around his finger as confusion rolls through me. Who? After that kiss, I'm not thinking about anyone else but my mate.

"Marcus?" I question.

Green eyes flare at the name and his body goes tense. This beautiful, handsome, amazing man is jealous. I try to keep my face neutral. I really do. But a smile breaks free anyway, excitement setting my body alight at the realization.

Shaking my head at my reaction, I tilt my chin so I can meet his eyes, murmuring softly, "Lukas, I don't want him. I want you."

His eyes flare even more intensely. "He fucking took you away from me," he snarls, and I startle at the words and the anger behind them, the sound coming from deep in his chest.

"Yes, unwillingly. And I came back to *you*."

His reply is swift. "If he hurts you again, I will kill him." Butterflies take flight in my stomach and heat courses through my body at his promise.

I roll my eyes, sighing in exasperation, because I'm not a hundred percent sure if I'm more bothered by his reaction or mine. Reaching up, I run my fingers over his brow and down his stubbled cheek. His eyes drift closed at the touch.

"You can't kill everyone who hurts me, Lukas."

His eyes flash open, fire lighting them. "The fuck I can't!" he swears.

Grasping the back of my neck firmly, but gently, he makes a low rumbling sound in his throat before he starts again, "You are mine, Nesrin. I will take care of you, whether you like it or not."

Then his mouth claims mine in a demanding kiss, this one full of desperation and desire. His hands run down my body and he grips my waist, pulling me even closer against his warm, massive body. We both moan in unison at the feel of our bodies against one another.

He nips my bottom lip then moves his head, trailing his nose along my jaw, down the column of my neck, sucking on my pulse before moving down to the swell of my breast. My breath is coming out rapidly as his hands slide up my ribs, gently cupping the underside of my breasts. His mouth finds mine again and I lean into the kiss, a shiver racking my body. My hips have a mind of their own, rocking against his erection.

Pulling back, he slips his shirt off and tosses it aside. I hesitate only a second, then reach for the buttons on my dress, undoing enough that I can slip it off my shoulders. It falls in a pile around my waist, the cool air caressing my exposed breasts. Lukas reaches up, taking the clip from my hair, and auburn curls tumble around my bare shoulders.

"You are so beautiful, Nesrin," he breathes against my mouth, his eyes capturing mine. "Your eyes are honey and whiskey swirling in cut glass. They have me completely mesmerized." His hand runs through my hair, tipping my head back, and baring my throat to him. Leaning forward, his lips brush along my jaw. "You're everything I've ever wanted. There is nothing I wouldn't do for you. Please say you want this."

Tipping my head back down to meet his gaze, I stare into his eyes, finding them filled with hope. I think I might just love this man. He has made a home in my heart. I don't know how it happened or when, but he is there.

Smiling, I lean into him, kissing him slow and soft, and when the kiss is done, I pull away enough to look into his emerald eyes. "I want this more than anything in the world," I whisper, wrapping my arms around his neck and grinding down on him to prove it to him.

Eyelids falling closed, Lukas grits his teeth, biting back a groan. All at once, he stands with me still in his arms, spins us around, and places me down on the bed. I stare up into his eyes as he pulls my dress off and slides my panties down my legs. He moves up my body, taking his time as he explores every dip and crease along the way. It feels like forever before his lips find mine again, my body trembling with need. I grab his hair, sinking my fingers into the dark, thick strands to pull him closer, loving the feeling of his weight pressing down on me.

Moving down, his tongue flicks over my nipple before his mouth covers my breast, nipping and teasing me into a frenzy. Suddenly, Lukas stands, stripping off his pants in seconds, then he moves back over me, my legs opening to let him in. He nudges my entrance and I grip his arms in anticipation, body trembling as I wrap my legs around his waist. His mouth claims mine again, this time with more urgency.

"Are you sure you want this?" Lukas asks, pulling back slightly, his voice strained. "Cause if we go any further, it'll be absolute torture to stop, but I will if that's what you want."

"Of course, I'm sure. Please, Lukas." At this point, I am not above begging. I need him now.

Lukas doesn't make me wait, though. With a sound that resembles a feral growl, he pushes in with one hard thrust, stealing the breath from my lungs. He holds still for a moment so I can adjust around him, then he pulls out slowly. I arch my back as he pushes forward, filling me again, stretching me to the edge of pain and pleasure. Lukas sets a hard pace, slamming into me over and over. His hand moves to the back of my head, his fingers threading through my hair, pulling my head back so he can suck and lick his way up my neck, making me shudder and convulse around him.

Panting, we move together, sweat coating our bodies as the friction we create is building more and more. This is a claiming. This isn't soft or sweet, this is fast and desperate.

"Yes . . . " I breathe, pushing my chest to his, savoring the contact of our bare skin against each other. I can feel the tension in my body winding tighter, my muscles clamping down around him as he drives in harder and faster. Lukas adjusts his angle, hooking my leg over his shoulder, sending waves of pleasure through me as he slams deeper into me. I can't hold back any longer. A gasp falls from my lips as I break apart, trembling in pure ecstasy. "Lukas," his name is a breathless whisper, a plea as my body floats on a wave of pleasure.

I can sense that he is close, his strokes getting rougher, more uneven. I run my nails down his back, and lean up to clamp my mouth on his neck, biting down hard. His body trembles before going taut. He lets out a long, sexy groan that has me following him over the edge again, before he collapses on top of me, and I bring my arms up and around his neck, basking in the weight of him pressing me into the mattress. Lukas lifts up on his elbows, taking his weight off me and I want to protest, but he looks down at me, pushing the sweaty hair from my face. He kisses me gently before rolling off of me onto his side, then pulls me to his chest.

As we lie together, content, I realize my wrist is no longer throbbing with pain, nor is my ankle. Perhaps my magic is dulling the pain. I'm not going to question it right now. Instead, I snuggle closer to Lukas, letting his scent wrap around me, knowing that, eventually, we will have to make our way down to the welcome feast.

# CHAPTER TWENTY FIVE

As we make our way to the feast a couple hours later, I am finding it difficult to contain my shock and confusion at how all of my injuries have healed. I can't begin to explain how or why it happened. I've never been able to heal myself before. Perhaps the shifter genes in me have finally awoken with me being around so many shifters? Do certain genes only unlock once you've acknowledged that part of your heritage? At this point, it's hard to imagine that anything else could surprise me. So much has happened in the last five weeks, it's hard to keep up with it all.

The feast is well underway when we crest the hill. The sheer number of shifters in the clearing is staggering. A huge bonfire has been lit and large logs have been placed in a circle around it, leaving enough space for those who are dancing. I spot Zee and Gabe standing over by one of the logs, talking with two younger boys. A warmth soaks into my lower back where Lukas has placed his hand.

He leans down, whispering in my ear, "Want to find our little star, then get some food?"

I turn my head, looking up at him. His face is so close our noses almost touch, sending my pulse into overdrive and butterflies scattering in my stomach.

"Yes," I murmur, my voice barely above a whisper, "That would be nice. I'm starving."

His eyes grow dark, a frown marring his handsome face as he pulls back and straightens up.

"What?" I ask, confused by his sudden change in mood.

Lukas shakes his head and starts guiding me forward. "I just hate that they didn't feed you," he grunts.

I stop walking, making him stop with me. "Lukas, I'm fine. I'm here now. That's all that matters."

Emerald eyes search mine. "I know, I just want to-" He hums, cutting off his words as he looks away. His jaw is clenched, and I can't quite tell if it's in effort to stop himself from talking or in anger.

"What?"

"I want to do very violent things when I think about you being taken, what they did to you. I want to tear them into pieces for the shit they pulled."

When he finishes, I rock up onto my toes and give him a small peck on the cheek. "I know you do. I like it," I say, giving him a wink.

Lukas huffs out a laugh, and a lightness fills my chest at the sight of his smile. Turning back toward the gathering of shifters, my eyes find Zee's. His face is a mask of pure mischief as he gives me a knowing smirk. I feel my face heat. Unable to help myself, I poke out my tongue. Then I send my magic drifting toward him, the magic weaving around the others as it moves along the ground, then swiping his legs out from under him. My laughter has me doubled over, excitement flashing through me at the look on Zee's face as he falls. I am *ecstatic* to have my magic back.

"You two are like children," Lukas chuckles. Straightening up, I wipe the tears off my face and smile up at him, feeling lighter than I had in months.

"He started it." I shrug. To be honest, I'm mostly just happy to see Zee smiling again. I need to find out what had happened earlier that turned him into Oscar the Grouch.

Lukas just shakes his head, strands of dark hair falling onto his forehead as a light laugh bubbles out of him. "Come on, it's time for food."

Steering me toward the table lined with food, the heat of his body brushes along my side comfortingly. His hand pressed into my lower back, the warmth from his palm seeps through my clothes, covering my skin in goosebumps.

"What do you feel like?" he whispers in my ear. Delicious shivers race down my neck at his warm breath, making it difficult for me to respond. Lukas smirks at my reaction and pulls back, giving me space.

I spot Astraea playing with Liam and Noah on the grass by the tables, the boys' shaggy brown hair flopping over their foreheads as they turn, following the blonde head of curls that runs our way. Kyra is standing off to the side, watching the three of them, and as she notices us, she flashes me a cheeky smile and waves. Returning the gesture, I feel Lukas's arm go around my waist and a gentle kiss placed on my head. I close my eyes at the tenderness I feel in that one move. When I open my eyes, Kyra is grinning widely, shaking her head, her corkscrew curls falling around her face. Warmth rises to my cheeks.

"*Mommy!*" Astraea's voice floats through my head. I grin down at her as she slams into my legs.

"Hey, sweet girl," I say, lifting her into my arms. "Are you having fun?"

She nods her head, brushing the strands from her face, then leans in, giving me a kiss before wriggling like a worm to get back down. I let out a small laugh and place her on the ground, and within seconds, she is racing back to the boys.

"Kyra will watch her for us," Lukas's words tickle my ear as he turns me toward the food. My mouth waters at the sight of hot roast beef sandwiches. I could eat at least two of those. Lukas piles up two plates and I point at the sandwiches. He shoots me a grin that does funny things to my insides and puts two sandwiches on each plate. The smile stretching across my face is so huge it likely looks dopey, but I am so damn happy right now. Even with all this crap hanging over my head, somehow my mood is unshakably good.

Lukas leans in closer to my ear. "Good sex will do that to you." He shoots me a wink. My mouth drops open but no response follows. I'm lost for words. Heat blooms all over my face again, traveling down my neck. If he wasn't carrying my food, I would punch him.

"Did you read my mind?" I accuse, placing my hands on my hips, waiting. Without answering, Lukas turns and makes his way toward one of the tables. I quickly follow. "Hey, are you going to answer me? Because I'm pretty sure you did this earlier when Marcus showed up."

I'm not mad, just curious. Plus, it would be handy to know if I need to shield my thoughts. Lukas places the plates on the table and turns to me. He steps right into my body, his hands gripping my waist. "I can't read your mind, Nesrin. I can pick up some feelings from you, but that is because they are loud like you're shouting them at me, and I only get bits of them. When we mate, we will be able to communicate telepathically, I think. With you being a legacy, it may be different."

"Huh. Okay." My stomach chooses this moment to growl loudly, and Lukas spins, pulling a chair out for me.

Frowning, I take a seat, something still bothering me. "Will you be able to read my mind or thoughts when we mate, then?"

"When we complete the mating bond, we will communicate telepathically and read each other's feelings, but not thoughts unless we wish to share them."

A wave of relief sweeps over me and I slump in my chair. "Okay, that's a relief, then."

Lukas flashes me a wicked grin and takes a seat next to me, pouring us each some water. "Scared of what I might find out?"

"No."

"Good, because you voice most things without thought anyway," Lukas chuckles, and I give him a smirk. It's true, my thoughts do sometimes get voiced unintentionally. I'm working on it, but I just don't even realize anything has been said out loud until it's too late. Lukas hands me a fork and picks up his water.

"Thanks, stud muffin," I say with an exaggerated wink. Lukas's eyes widen as he chokes on his water. Laughing, I hand him a napkin.

"Stud muffin?" he questions, looking at me funny. I shrug. "You don't like it? Shame." I tap my chin. "Hmmm, how about sugar?"

His lips twitch and his eyes go squinty, like he is trying really hard not to laugh.

"No? Hmmm, me neither. Okay, I'll have to think about it more. Baby? Boo?" I wrinkle my nose. Definitely not. This time, Lukas bursts out laughing, a deep belly laugh that has me smiling and watching him in awe. He has also drawn the looks of others. When his eyes meet mine again, there is humor reflecting back at me. His hands reach up, cupping my cheeks as he leans in and gently takes my lips with his. I sigh into his mouth and feel his lips turn up at the side again.

"You can call me whatever you want, sweetheart. As long as you call me yours, I'm happy," he whispers, and my heart . . . it melts. This man has been a total surprise. A good surprise. Never in a million years would I have thought I'd get someone so wonderful.

"Okay," I whisper against his lips. "Babe." I pull back with a smirk, picking up my sandwich. His small chuckle wrapped around me like a calm, caressing breeze.

I flick my gaze toward where Finan and Kate are standing talking with Gabe and another man I'm not familiar with. Probably someone from Finan's pack. We have a lot of shifters here with two packs occupying the pack lands, while Lukas and Finan negotiate an alliance. Finan looks my way and excuses himself then heads toward us. I do my best to push down my unease. There are very few things I've regretted in my life, but how I handled leaving Pittsburgh is one of them. I never should have left without at least saying goodbye. But if I had, he probably would have convinced me to stay, and I just couldn't. Since moving to Portland, I feel like a part of me has found its place, like this is where I'm supposed to be.

Glancing sidelong at Lukas, I wonder if it was him that drew me here. No. Maybe. I don't know. My magic has gotten stronger, more stable since settling in Portland. That was before I met Lukas. I've always been good with my magic, but it comes with a lot less effort these days, less drawing from the elements and more from my core, like I am its source. I have a lot to learn about who and what I am. A legacy, a mortal child who is a descendant of a god. It's crazy. I've always known the gods are real. But to be a descendant of one, to have the healing abilities of Althaea. It doesn't feel like any of this could be real.

Finan reaches our table and nods at the chair in front of me. "May I?" he asks, bringing me from my thoughts.

"Of course," I mumble around my food, sending a sheepish grin his way.

Taking a seat, Finan chuckles softly. "Hungry?"

"Bery Hmmbhy," I manage to get out. Not very ladylike, but meh, I don't care. Finan has seen me at my worst and still cared for me. I watch, intrigued, as Lukas takes food from his plate and adds it to mine. Finan's eyes spark with amusement as he watches us. "It's so good to see you again."

My stomach flips and I swallow my mouthful of food. "I'm sorry I left the way I did, Finan. I wasn't thinking clearly. The only thought that came to my mind when I got spooked was Astraea's safety."

He nods stiffly and reaches up, rubbing the back of his neck. "I understand, Nesrin. You don't need to explain. There's nothing to forgive. I shouldn't have lied to you. If I hadn't, maybe you would have come to me for the protection you needed." He flashes me an affable grin, and my shoulders relax. I didn't even realize I've been holding myself so tense.

Lukas's eyes move from Finan and back to me. I lean into him slightly, soaking in his warmth and smile at Finan. He looks so much like Hunter it makes my chest ache. How did I never notice the resemblance before? In all fairness, I wasn't in my right mind when I met Finan, the grief of losing my sister having completely overwhelmed me.

I reach over, resting my hand on top of his. "Well, we are both off the hook, then. Fresh start?"

Finan's eyes soften, and he lets out a breath he's been holding. "Sounds good. Fresh start."

Lukas leans over, kissing me on the head. "I'm going to get some more drinks."

"Okay." My eyes trail after him as he walks off.

Finan leans back in his chair, crossing his massive arms over his chest. "It's good to see you happy."

My voice refuses to work for several seconds before I manage a simple "Thanks."

"I hear you are a talented healer, even before the whole goddess powers you'll inherit,"

I raise my eyebrows. "Random, but yes, I've been steadily improving over the last few months."

"How much do you charge for the healings?"

"I don't, not the healing anyway. For spells, charms, etc, sure, a small fee to cover materials, but never the healing. I couldn't take from someone who needed help when the magic of healing doesn't cost a thing."

Pride shines in his eyes, making my heart swell. "That's honorable, Nesrin. Not at all in line with the covens and council rules. Nothing is free when it comes to witches and mages. A price must always be paid."

I shrug. "Why? It's not like it cost me anything. And the council has everything wrong," I reply. I reach for my drink as someone bumps into the table, sending it tumbling over.

"Shit, sorry. Oh, it's just you." The voice turns cold, chilling me to the bone. I tilt my head back, studying the man standing next to the table. He looks familiar, but for the life of me, I can't place him. His face hardens as he steps closer.

"Why are you still here, witch? You don't belong here. A witch on our lands is not right," he growls low, leaning his hands on the table in an attempt to seem threatening. I don't say a word. I just watch him carefully, my face a mask of indifference. He sneers like he has won whatever game he thinks we are playing.

"That's what I thought," he says. Pushing off the table, he goes to walk away, and I realize I should keep my mouth shut, but it's never been my strong suit.

"You know, just because I was silent doesn't mean I agree with you. It just means your level of idiocy rendered me speechless for a moment. So, to answer your question, I belong here just as much as you do." I grin, and by the widening of his eyes, I can tell it's not what he was expecting.

Recognition slams into me as he moves closer. He was at the house when I healed those shifters who were hexed. The shifter that didn't trust me. He thought I hurt Lukas, and if Zee didn't stop him, he would have hurt me. What was his name? Ryan!

"I'm not going anywhere, Ryan."

Enraged, he stands taller, looming over me. "That's what you think, witch," he snarls, but before he or I can say another word, Finan is out of his seat pushing Ryan back, his fist bunched in Ryan's shirt. Having realized who was pushing him away, Ryan backs down, his cold brown eyes glaring back at me.

Finan's massive form is almost double the size of Ryan's as he leans in closer. "That is enough. You don't speak to her like that. Ever. Understand?" Finan's voice is quiet and deceptively calm. My skin pricks with awareness, nerves taking flight in my stomach as it occurs to me that, at some point, I stood up.

"Yes, alpha," Ryan growls. Finan lets go of his shirt, turning back to me, a look of thunder on his face. I shrug my shoulders, cringing because I baited him, and we both know it.

"What's it to you, anyway? This isn't your pack," Ryan sneers.

My breath catches in my throat, and I freeze. Finan stops walking and, ever so slowly, turns back toward Ryan. I squirm in my seat, part of me starting to feel a little sorry for Ryan and his big mouth. Before Finan can continue, Lukas is there, grabbing Ryan by the throat. With a swift sweep of his legs, he takes Ryan to the ground, pinning him there. Shocked by my mate's sudden appearance, I jolt back a step, bumping into the table. Lukas tightens his grip on Ryan's throat, snarling in his face.

"Not only did you disrespect a visiting alpha, but you also disrespected my mate." Lukas's eyes flash yellow before he slowly stands up, towering over Ryan. His power thrums in the air, daring anyone to challenge him.

I see and feel the pack around me go quiet and turn, watching their alpha cautiously. "That witch, as you call her, will be your luna. You will show her the respect she deserves." His voice seems to carry over the gathering, and embarrassment and shock roll through me.

Some gasps sound around those gathered, and murmurs start to move through them. It takes all I have to keep my eyes focused on Lukas. Magic hums along my skin, setting my nerves on fire, a knee jerk reaction to my fight-or-flight response to the situation.

Ryan slowly rises to his feet, his eyes down and neck bared.

"I want you to apologize," Lukas commands, his voice deceptively calm.

Ryan's head jerks up to Lukas, surprise on his face. Then he nods, turning to Finan. "I apologize, alpha."

"Now Nesrin."

Ryan's eyes flare with anger. "What?"

"Apologize to Nesrin," Lukas repeats, clenching his jaw.

Turning to me, Ryan's eyes are full of resentment. "I regret my actions tonight, Nesrin." My name on his lips is a curse, like saying my name causes him pain. Lukas takes a step toward him, and he quickly continues, "I apologize." His voice is hard, angry.

I bite back my comment of *sure he is*. This public display has cost him enough. Ryan turns and storms off into the night and I let out a breath, the tension leaving my body. No one speaks or moves for a long moment.

After a few minutes, Lukas makes his way over to me. I cross my arms in front of me, tipping my head back to keep eye contact. "You totally could have warned me, you know. That you were going to out me like that. As the luna." I sound like a pouting child, I hate it.

Lukas stops in front of me, fury still evident in his eyes, and I peer down. His fingers slide under my chin, tilting my head back up to meet his gaze. "You never need to hide from me. Don't submit and look away. I want that fire, Nesrin. You are my mate, my equal."

My breath hitches just as his mouth claims mine in a demanding kiss, his soft lips moving over mine. Sagging in his hold, I grip his arms tightly, unable to help the soft moan that escapes my mouth. All thoughts flee my mind at that moment. A throat clears behind me, startling me. I pull back, realizing everyone has been silently watching us.

Zee moves closer. "Lukas, man, you just dropped a bomb on everyone and now you're going to make out in front of them?"

I attempt to move from Lukas's grip, but he only tightens his hold on me. Nuzzling his face into my neck, he pushes my hair aside. His nose follows the column of my neck and then across my collarbone, as he tugs the neck of my sweater aside, placing a tender kiss on my shoulder. Is he seeing how strong my self-control is? Because I'm not sure I have any where he's concerned. I look at Zee for help and the ass just laughs at me, his damn blue eyes twinkling in the firelight.

"Lukas, we need to socialize and see what Astraea's doing," I note, in an effort to push him away. It doesn't work.

"I know, freckles," is his muffled response from my neck. With a long-suffering sigh, he pulls back and looks down at me. "You smell amazing."

Laughter bubbles up as I push at his chest. "Okay, thanks." I pat his arm and turn around to see everyone has gone back to partying. Finan has moved back over to where Kate is sitting with Asena and Gabe. Only Zee remains standing in front of us, his head tilted as he studies me. "What?" I ask self-consciously, twisting my hair in my fingers.

Shaking his head, he mutters, "Nothing."

"Sure. Nothing." I squint my eyes at him, sarcasm in full force.

Peering past Zee, someone comes into focus and my smile is automatic. "Blue!!" I exclaim.

"Nessy, honey! Here you are! I've missed your beautiful face in my shop."

I throw my arms around the old man. "I've missed you, too! And your coffee and muffins." We laugh and pull back.

"How's my boy?" Blue asks, looking at Zee, and my eyes widen. My boy?

"I'm good, Dad. Same as this morning," Zee replies, watching my reaction with amusement.

"Dad?" I choke.

Lukas chuckles, "You should see your face right now."

I gape at the two of them. "Why didn't you tell me Blue was your dad?"

Zee shrugs. "You didn't ask. Plus, we all took bets to see how long it would take you to figure out."

I gape at him. "What?" I stare at each of them and they all look thoroughly amused. I cross my arms, looking back at Zee. "Well, who won?"

"No one, actually. Dad just gave it away. I had two weeks."

I turned to Lukas. "And you?"

"Three weeks." He shrugs, giving me a small grin.

"Really?" I reply in mock outrage.

"You didn't seem to realize I was a shifter, so it's not too hard to assume you wouldn't notice a family resemblance." Blue laughed warmly.

I'm lost for words, but now that I know, the resemblance is uncanny. How did I miss it? We chat for a bit before I excuse myself. My social battery is running low, and I definitely need a moment alone. Making my way down to the river, everyone I pass casts me nervous glances and gives me a wide berth. Slipping off my shoes, I step into the cool water as I stare up at the darkening sky. Out here, away from the city, the stars are especially bright. I love it. The sound of the river drowns out the noise of the gathering behind me. I love the water, the way it moves, the feeling of it lapping around my ankles and flowing over my feet. Everything about it is calming.

I hear approaching footsteps. Turning my head, I see it's Zee. He stops next to me, putting his hands in his pockets, and stares out over the river. Neither of us says a word, the silence comforting.

"Don't feel bad about it," Zee says into the night.

Confused, I look over at him. "About what?"

"Ryan. He's an idiot and his being sent away was the best thing for everyone. He knew better."

"Sent away? He was just here."

"Lukas put you under his protection the minute you made it out of Forest Park the first night you crossed paths. Ryan understood that and he ignored it."

My body jolted in surprise. "He did what? Why?" *Is he serious?*

"Very serious. He saw something in you. Maybe how much trouble you'd get into." I punch him in the arm and shake my hand. Shit, that hurt me more than him.

Zee rubs his arm dramatically. "Ouch."

Rolling my eyes, I face toward the river again. "He didn't have to do that," I reply quietly.

"He did it to warn away anyone who might want to hurt you. Shifters work better when we have orders, someone to follow.

That's why we have an alpha. We need to be kept in line to survive."

I can't believe Lukas has been on my side since the beginning, and I didn't know. My silent champion. An alpha's order is very hard to go against, and most wouldn't dare try it anyway. Except for maybe Alex and Ryan, who are both now taking a sabbatical.

"Why didn't anyone tell me?"

Zee looks down at me. "Are you seriously asking?"

I put my hands on my hips. "Yes."

"Because he ordered us not to. And because you would have hated the idea. Every part of him was screaming to throw you over his shoulder and take you to safety. He found his mate, and she was in danger. There is a reason he is an alpha. He would protect you at any cost, but he had to change his approach. If he didn't, you would have hated him or run. So, he did what he could, and it was a silent claim. You and Astraea were under his protection."

I nod absently. He's right. If I knew a month ago, I would have fought against it. If he tried to drag me here, even with good intentions, it would not have ended well.

Gathering my courage, I voice the question I've wanted to ask all night. "Would you take me to see the trolls tonight?"

His incredulous gaze turns to me. "Tell me you're joking, right? Like that didn't just come out of your mouth right now." His mouth tightens in displeasure.

I can't help my eyeroll. "Oh, come on Zee, you're overreacting."

"Am I? You are under Lukas's protection. That means not leading you into danger, honey. Lukas may grant me clemency because he knows how headstrong you are, and the fight I'd be up against, but I won't risk it, won't risk you."

I scowl at him. "Now you're just being dramatic."

Letting out a huff, Zee shakes his head at me, knowing I will not win this battle.

It's time to change the subject. I nudge Zee with my shoulder. Of course, he doesn't move an inch. "What happened earlier, at the house? You got angry. What did I say that caused that?"

His muscles tense, even as his focus stays on the dark lake in front of us. He is quiet for so long I don't think he's going to answer me, but then Zee looks down at me and smiles. It's a small smile, one that doesn't quite reach his eyes or make his dimple show.

"It was nothing." He turned back to look out over the river.

"That wasn't nothing Zee."

"It was just a lot to absorb, Nesrin. I got angry."

"Yeah. Just, you seemed furious at the part where I have a sister."

Shaking his head, he reaches into his pocket and pulls out the elven key, holding it out for me. This must be his way of ending the conversation, and I guess that's alright. I understand better than anyone, you can't force people to open up. I reach out my hand and take it from him, the key seeming cool in my palm. Turning it over in my hands, I try to understand the markings etched into it. I really wish I could translate it. I wonder if I can find someone who can speak Elvish. The magical community is huge, and I have helped quite a few out since moving here. Perhaps one of them would help point me in the right direction.

I see Lukas walking our way and slip the key into the back pocket of my jeans, smiling up at Zee. "Thanks. Never know when I might need it again."

Zee scoffs, "Hopefully never."

My mate's arms slide around my waist. "Damn straight." His voice comes out deep and gruff, hating the idea I might need this again in the future.

Astraea runs over and presses her face into my legs. "Hi, sweet girl. Are you tired?" I run my fingers through her hair.

Staring up with her beautiful blue eyes, she shakes her head, curls flying everywhere. *"Mommy?"*

I swallow the golf ball sized lump in my throat before answering, *"Yes."* I'm still struggling to get used to her using that particular word for me. Every night before bed, I sing *That's an Irish Lullaby* and tell her a story about her mother from our childhood. I will always do my best to make sure she knows her mother, knows how wonderful and loved she was.

*"Pretty lights?"* Some nights, when we have trouble sleeping, I weave the magic across the ceiling of our room to look like the aurora borealis. It's similar to the way I see magic work, like I can share that part of myself with her.

*"Should we show them?"* I ask, the entire conversation just between us, taking place in our minds.

Astraea nods eagerly, and I bend down to pick her up. Perched on my hip, she wraps her arms around my neck, nuzzling her head into my shoulder. I quickly glance at Lukas before closing my eyes and muttering the incantation under my breath, pushing my magic outward.

"Flame of Fire, Spark of Light, bring those here the brief gift of my second sight. Light the sky with all your wonder. Make it bold, make it bright, make it spectacular."

I hear a collective gasp ring out over the entire pack. Opening my eyes, I see the darkened sky alight with hues of greens, blues, purples, and pinks, the bright dancing lights changing colors as they move through the sky. The river becomes what looks like a magical arena, the reflections of the lights giving the illusion of neverending colors. The scene is truly breathtaking. Lukas looks over at me in shocked amazement.

"This is how you see magic?" His voice is filled with awe.

Before I can speak, Zee turns, wrapping me and Astraea in a hug. Lukas growls in warning at him, but Zee just ignores him, his body shaking with laughter. Drawing back, his eyes are shining brightly as he tugs on my hair playfully. "This is amazing."

My chest warms at his genuine happiness and praise.

I rest my head on Astraea's. "Good idea, sweet girl."

"Truly amazing," Asena agrees, coming up behind Zee. Reaching up, he wraps his arm around her shoulders, pulling her into his side. Asena wraps her arm around his waist, and they smile at each other. I turn, arching an eyebrow at Lukas in question.

Leaning into me, he whispers softly, "Leave it be."

Though I am beyond curious to know if they are seeing each other, or if this is just a casual thing, or friends with benefits, I push the urge to pester them for details down. It, too, can wait till tomorrow.

People are laughing and dancing under the lights weaving through the sky. It fills me with a happiness I haven't felt in a long time. Nissa and several other sprites dance across the water, and my heart leaps with joy watching them.

Much later into the night, close to 10 p.m., Lukas, Astraea, and I are seated near the fire. Holding up my new phone Lukas gifted me earlier in the day, I'm trying my best to get a good photo of the three of us. I tilt it sideways and frown. It doesn't matter which way I angle it, the light from the fire and lanterns is making us look weird. I let out a huff and just take the blasted shot, and it isn't lost on me that Lukas is silently laughing at my attempts.

"This lighting does nothing for us," I pout, showing him the photos on my phone.

"Well, I don't know about you, but I look amazing," he teases, a lazy grin on his face.

Jerk. I reach over, punching his arm. "I can't believe you just said that." I laugh.

A loud, sharp whistle sounds, followed by two more, which has Lukas lurching to his feet, all signs of humor fading.

"What is it?" I stand, keeping hold of Astraea just in case.

"We have a visitor."

I glance to where Lukas is facing, and sure enough, a small white hatchback is gunning it down the gravel driveway, dust flying up behind it. Who the hell can that be? The car skids to a stop at the top of the hill near the house, the front driver side door swings open, and a furious, disheveled girl steps out. She pushes her purple hair from her face as her wild blue eyes fly around the gathering of people and land on me.

"Nesrin!" she shouts frantically.

"Suzy?"

"Oh my god!" she cries and runs toward me.

Gabe goes to intercept her, but Lukas holds up a hand. He must tell everyone to stand down because everyone takes a big step back.

Next thing I know, Suzy clashes with me, and I let out a "oomph" as I take the impact of her hug. Though I'm still holding Astraea, I manage to get my arm around her as she squeezes me.

"Suzy! How did you find me?"

Pulling back, she glares at me before punching me in the arm.

"Ouch! What was that for?" I ask, putting Astraea on the ground.

Placing her hands on her hips, Suzy has the teenage glare spot on. "I haven't seen you for two weeks, haven't spoken with you in eight days. I didn't know if this one"—she flings her arm toward Lukas—"had kidnapped you, or killed you and buried the body somewhere."

"Me? Really?" Lukas is clearly amused by the dramatics.

"Yes!" Suzy's hands fly into the air, and as my eyes follow them, I notice that her purple hair isn't in her usual stylish, messy bun. Instead, it's down and just plain messy. "I was *worried* when I heard nothing from you. After the fire and everything, I just . . . I was worried."

Shame washes through me as I realize how long I've put off going to see her. True, I did lose my phone and her number with it, but I could have gotten someone to pass on a message.

"I've been a terrible friend," I admit.

Suzy lets out a huff and crosses her arms, a sweet pout on her face. "Yes, you have."

"I'm sorry, Suzy. I lost my phone, but that's no excuse."

With a huff, she looks sideways before turning her face back to me. "You're forgiven."

"You never said. But how did you find me?"

"Oh. I, umm, went by the store and there was this man there poking around. Very handsome, by the way. Like most of the people you hang around with these days. Like, do you have any ordinary looking people around?"

Shaking my head, I laugh. "What man? What was his name?"

"I don't know. He just told me I could find you here, and that you were in trouble."

I frown and peer at Lukas, who is now watching my friend closely. His deep voice is deadly calm when he speaks. "What did he look like?"

Startled, Suzy flicks her gaze to him, her sass coming out in full force. "Bossy much?" When Lukas doesn't reply, she huffs and rolls her eyes. "Well, he was tall, dark, and handsome."

I try pressing my lips together to stop the smile from spreading, but fail.

Lukas's brow furrows. "Anything else?" he asks patiently.

Suzy goes starry-eyed as she replies, "Blue eyes, well dressed, and dreamy accent."

Lukas nods and leans over, kissing my cheek. "I'm going to talk to the others and send someone over to your store. See if they can smell out who's been poking around," he whispers in my ear before strolling away. Zee and Gabe follow close behind, and Finan joins them as they make their way up to the house.

Suzy watches them leave before turning back to me with wide eyes. A squeal escapes her lips as she bounds over. "Oh my god! I told you to get his number. He likes you and he is *so hot.*"

I laugh, pulling her in for another hug, mostly to hide the blush now covering my face. At this point, everyone has gotten back to the party, barely paying us any attention, but now, with a human around, things will have to stay as normal as possible. Just as the thoughts go through my mind, Astraea lets out a playful squeal and runs from Noah and Liam, who are in their wolf cub forms. Suzy's grip on me tightens, her nails digging into my arms. "Nesrin. Are those wolves?"

"Ahh . . . yes. Yes, they are. Astraea is fine." I turn Suzy around and walk her up toward the house. She tries to turn, looking for the pups, but I pull her along behind me.

"Did Astra make a noise?" she asks, startled.

"Yes. She's been opening up a bit more. Come on, let's go to the house and talk," I suggest, dragging Suzy up to the house. When we enter, I seat her at the kitchen table, brew two coffees, then begin to explain the non-magical version of why I'm here.

Suzy's breath catches and she stares at me, her blue eyes wide with shock.

"Are you okay?" I wave my hand in front of her face.

Blinking, she opens and closes her mouth several times. "You're telling me some cult is after you, so you're in hiding here with Mr. Tall Dark and Mysterious!?"

"What's with the descriptions?" Amused, a laugh bursts out of my throat.

"This isn't funny!" she shrieks, jumping to her feet.

I try to smother my laughter, knowing full well that Suzy is just worried about me. "I know."

"Why aren't you more worried?"

"I am. I've just had longer to absorb it," I explain gently, hoping to calm her before she brings everyone running.

"Well, this is crazy. You need to go to the police," she argues, biting her nail.

"No."

"They set your bookstore on FIRE!!"

Letting out a deep breath, I stand and make my way over to her. My hands rest on her shoulders and gently squeeze. "I will handle it. I'm safe. Astra is safe. I promise."

Suzy lets out an incredulous huff, pulling me into a hug. "I'm just worried, Nesrin."

"I know you are, but I'm fine. Astraea is fine."

"You promise?"

"Promise."

Suzy blows out a long breath and steps back. "Okay. Well, you need to promise me you will keep in touch."

"Yes, mom." I chuckle.

Suzy rolls her eyes and shakes her head at me. "Whatever. I'm just glad you're okay and happy."

When I see the glint of humor in her eyes, I can't help but return her grin. "I am happy."

"Like, how happy?" Suzy asks, waggling her eyebrows and holding her hands apart to indicate length. I burst out laughing at her absurdities.

"I'm not telling you that!"

"Aww . . . " she pouts.

After Suzy has calmed down, she leaves with strict instructions to keep in touch. But I don't head back to the bonfire. Later that night, after Astra has returned home, we curl up in bed together and drift off to sleep with the sound of chattering down the hill, surrounded by Lukas's comforting scent.

# CHAPTER TWENTY SIX

Kyra and I are by the riverbank the next morning, soaking in some sunshine. The warmth is finally returning, the chill in the air lessening. Last night was the best night I've had in a long time. With the exception of Ryan, the others were remarkably welcoming, all things considered. Especially after my magical display over the river. Thanks to the behavior of the majority, witches have unfortunately earned a bad rap, but I'm not only a witch, I'm a legacy and part shifter. Lukas has promised the pack will be made aware of that fact when the time is right, but for now he wants them to get used to the idea of me being around. But I can't deny how much I want them to accept me as a member of the pack without the knowledge of my heritage swaying them. I want to prove to them that I am worthy of being part of the pack.

I drop to my butt on the grass, and a thought occurs to me. Witches have a slightly longer life span than humans, but I have no idea how long shifters live for. I can't believe it never occurred to me to ask Hunter, or even Finan, before. Especially with Astraea to think about.

"Hey, Kyra. How long do wolf shifters usually live for? Are all shifters the same?"

"Lukas hasn't spoken about this with you?" she questions, raising her eyebrows in surprise.

"Umm, no. Why?"

"Well, things will change for you after you complete the mating bond," she replies slowly.

My eyebrows furrow, shielding my eyes from the sun as I gaze up at her. "Change how?"

She looks uncertain. "Maybe you should ask Lukas."

"I'm asking you."

Kyra lets out a long sigh and sits down next to me on the grass as we watch the children play in the water. Nissa and two other sprites are racing around them, playing. Nissa is wearing a beautiful shimmering white gown today. She looks like a star shooting around the surface of the water.

"Shifters have a longer lifespan than most. Once we turn eighteen, our aging begins to slow." She twirls some of her hair between her fingers.

"How slow?"

"Most of us live for around two hundred years, some up to four hundred. But we are not immortal. We can be killed, as you very well know."

My head whirls around to gawk at her, speechless. What the hell? Two to four hundred years?! Witches can live a little longer than humans, not enough to be noticed. But two to four centuries is a seriously long time. And am I different because I have shifter blood in me? What about my goddess blood? Does that make any difference in my life span? There aren't any older relatives to even ask. Their lives were stolen from them. My chest pulses with anger and sadness at the thought of what happened to them.

"But when you mate with Lukas, it will slow your aging process down as well. It will match his," Kyra rushes to add, seeing my internal panic setting in. She doesn't know about me being a legacy yet. I want to tell her, but how will she take it?

My mouth opens and closes. Wheezing out a small laugh, I fall onto my back, looking at the sky. "Wow, okay," I mutter, mostly to myself.

Kyra laughs at my reaction, her ponytail of corkscrew curls bouncing with the motion. Reaching over, she grabs my arm, shaking me a little. "Nothing too different. You'll just live longer, and with great company, of course." She winks down at me.

A smile tugs at my lips. "Yeah, I just never imagined I'd live that long, much less that I'd find my place in this world."

She bumps her shoulder against mine. "Yes, well, no offense, but I never thought we would have witches living with us, either." A simple smile on her face, telling me she means no insult.

Bumping my shoulder into hers on my way up, I say softly, "None taken. I'm so relieved you all have been so accepting of Astraea and I."

"Well, not everyone. Alex and Ryan were . . . not very welcoming." An annoyed expression flashes across her face as she plucks a wildflower from the grass then rubs the petals gently between her fingers.

"Yeah, everyone except those two." I turn to watch Astraea playing in the water and smile. She is so happy here.

A flash of movement on the other side of the river catches my attention. But as my eyes shift toward the movement, they find nothing but a mass of shadows among the trees. Weird. As I watch, the shadows move, and a barely visible figure forms amongst them before slowly disappearing, fading into the woods. Frowning, a memory tugs at my mind, but I can't grasp it. It's like water trickling through my fingers.

Standing, I brush the grass from my jeans and look down at Kyra, her eyebrow raised in question.

"Do you mind watching Astraea? I need to head into town. I have to see Grace." It's time to get some answers. I've rested enough.

Of course, Lukas refuses to let me run off into town alone, so here we are driving to see Grace—me, Lukas, Zee, and Asena all piled into the car.

"So, who are we going to see exactly?" she asks before applying a layer of lip gloss that seems to make her dark skin glow.

"A close friend of the family," I answer, Lukas and Zee both chuckling from the front seat. Asena's eyes dart around between the three of us.

"What? What am I missing?" Asena's curious eyes turn back to me, waiting.

I puff out a deep breath, because this could go one of two ways. Either she loses it like I did and freaks out, or she could be totally cool, calm, and collected. "Grace is a banshee," I blurt out.

Asena's pale blue eyes widen comically. "A what now?"

"You heard right," Lukas remarks from the driver's seat. Looking up, I catch his gaze in the mirror. He sends me a wink before looking back to the road, and butterflies swarm my belly. I hope that feeling never goes away.

Clearing my throat, I run my hands up and down my legs. "A banshee." There was no answer when I tried to call before we left. I am beyond nervous. I haven't seen Grace or heard from her in a week.

Climbing the stairs to her apartment, I'm shocked to see her door hanging off its hinges. Immediately, Lukas and Zee take the lead. I roll my eyes, trying not to be offended as I summon my magic, letting it seep in from around me and draw from the well deep in my chest. Muttering under my breath, I send out a seeker spell. A wave of magic drifts from me into the apartment to detect any presence there. Nothing. Grace isn't here.

"Who could have done this?" Asena whispers from close behind me, making me jump. My whole concentration having been on weaving the spell, I forgot she was right behind me.

"The coven?" I guess, slowly approaching the door. Lukas and Zee enter the apartment, pushing past the broken door. The alpha bends to pick something up, then turns, holding up a dagger in his hand. A burning sun with two swords crossed over it is clearly visible on the dagger. The symbol of–

"Hunters," Lukas finishes my thoughts. A shiver works its way through my body. Hunters? What would they want with Grace? Dread fills me at the thought of Grace at the mercy of those monsters.

Grabbing the dagger from him, my fingers turn it over, studying it. "But why?"

"I don't know, but I know someone who will," Lukas turns, sniffing the air. I raise an eyebrow at him. "Uhh, what are you doing?" Wolves have a very acute sense of smell that they use to detect other animals or creatures more than a mile away. If Lukas can pick up Grace's scent, maybe he can track her.

"There were two hunters here. They tried to take Grace, but . . ." he trails off, then turns on his heels, walking out the door and into the hall.

Confused, I follow close behind. "But?" I prompt.

Ignoring me, Lukas turns and looks at Zee, who has come to a stop behind me. "Zee, who else do you smell?"

I turn around to face Zee, "What's going on?" I am getting anxious now.

He discreetly sniffs the air. Suddenly, a thunderous expression crosses his face. "Stephan," his voice is furious.

I turn back to Lukas as Asena joins us. "Who is Stephan?" we ask in unison, then glance at each other, both of us frustrated with the lack of communication right now.

Lukas's eyes meet mine, hesitation evident in his gaze. "Stephan is a vampire, an old one. He's our contact when we need something. He was also the person your friend Suzy ran into at your bookstore."

Vampire? "Like when you wiped the memories from those hunters last month?"

"Yes."

"Why would he be poking around my store? And why would he be here, at Grace's?" I can't shake the lingering sense of disquiet.

311

Lukas runs a hand over his head, dragging his dark hair off his face. "I don't know, but I want to find out. He may not have been here for Grace. He may have been here for other reasons."

\*\*\*

My gaze lifts to the old church in front of us. "Are you sure the vampire is in there?" A vampire living in an old abandoned church seems odd. Glancing to my left at the creepy cemetery spread out over the property, a shiver runs up my spine. That seems more likely. This whole place is creepy as hell.

We all climb the steps together. My hands rub against my jeans, trying to rid themselves of the sweat gathering in my palms. Lukas glances over at me, and for a moment, his eyes ensnare me. Noticing that his mouth is moving, I blink, shaking my head.

"Sorry, what?"

His expression softens. "I said, are you sure I can't convince you to wait in the car?"

I snort. "Not a chance." This will be my first time meeting a vampire, and I won't miss this chance. Yes, my hands are sweating, and my heart is pounding, but if Grace is in there, then that is where I have to go.

As we approach the door, Lukas steps forward and knocks twice before moving back to my side, brushing his arm against my shoulder. His touch brings with it a sense of relief, no matter how subtle the contact. The double doors in front of us swing open, revealing . . . no one. Just a dark, empty space.

Asena meets my gaze and her eyes widen, her expression suggesting she's fairly unsettled. Seems I'm not the only one a little freaked out.

Taking a deep breath, the two of us follow Lukas and Zee inside as the door shuts behind us, sealing us inside the huge dark church. My eyes are slow to adjust to the dim room, my mouth dropping open in wonder at the interior. It's beautiful. Totally not what I was expecting at all.

The pews have been removed to make a giant open room and the dark wooden floors are polished. Plush rugs in an assortment of colors are scattered artfully about the space with luxury armchairs atop them. Some along the wall are surrounded by thick curtains for privacy. Red and black seems to be the primary theme, with gold splashed in here and there. The space is lit with old fashioned black and gold sconces mounted along each wall. A massive chandelier hangs in the center of the high ceiling. Though it isn't lit at the moment, I bet it is a spectacular sight.

Sheer silk fabric hangs from the ceiling, possibly for aerial dancers. There is an enormous bar that takes up the entire back wall opposite us, where the altar would once have been. This place is gorgeous and totally opposite to the creepiness from the cold exterior. Inside is warm, inviting, sensual.

I quietly follow the others, taking in all the details around me. I don't realize they've stopped until I run into Zee's back. "Shit. Sorry," I mutter, moving around him to see why we've stopped.

Relief flows through me. "Grace?"

I make my way forward when Lukas's arm shoots out across my chest, stopping me. I glance over and frown at him, but he doesn't look at me. He keeps his eyes straight ahead, a soft yellow glow lighting the outer rims.

Turning in her chair, Grace looks at me, her eyes slightly dazed. "Nesrin, my girl. You're early."

Frowning, I push Lukas's arm down and step closer. "Early? What are you talking about? What are you doing here? Is everything okay?" I cast a quick peek at her companion and force my eyes away, looking back to Grace.

Grace looks confused. "Nothing is wrong. I've been enjoying a nice cup of tea with this gentleman while we waited for you. He told me you'd come." Her eyes move from me back to the young dark-haired man sitting across from her. A look of affection drifts over her face as confusion rolls through me. Why is she being weird and calm? Does she not know what he is?

My attention is drawn to the man as he unfolds himself from the chair. He is tall and looks to be in his late twenties. He's well dressed in dark gray pants and a white shirt, the sleeves rolled up to his elbows, showing off toned forearms. The shirt does nothing to hide his lean but defined physique. There is mischief in his blue eyes and a grin tugging at his full lips. This vampire is dangerous, a pure predator. I can sense the energy and power coming from him. It makes my skin tingle with awareness.

"White doesn't seem like a very good color choice for a vampire." My own eyes widen. Shit. I definitely said that out loud.

Zee chuckles, casting me an amused look. I can feel Lukas's eyes boring into the side of my head. I look over at him, apology in my eyes, only to find amusement in his.

"Sorry," I whisper anyway, with a small shrug.

"No need for apologies. You are right, black hides blood better. Good thing I'm not a messy eater." Stephan's grin is pure sin as he tilts his head forward slightly, his brown hair falling into his eyes.

"Well, good for you," Zee says dryly, coming to stand next to me.

Staring at Stephan, my vision narrows. All I can see is him, those hypnotic blue eyes. I sway on my feet, lightheaded, and take a step forward, feeling myself being pulled toward him. The predatory glint in his eyes sets my nerves on edge and I struggle to breathe. Without taking his eyes off me, he addresses Lukas, "Lukas, what can I do for you today?"

Lukas steps in front of me, blocking me from Stephen's view, and I sag with relief, drawing in a deep breath, my hand rubbing at my chest. *What was that?*

Lukas's voice is hard when he says, "We are here for Grace."

"Who? Grace? This Grace?" is Stephan's arrogant response. He knows who we came for.

Lukas crosses his arms as I move to stand beside him again, refusing to cower behind him. "Don't play games, Stephan," Lukas growls.

"Why would I play games?" the vampire chuckles.

"Because you're a dick," Zee mutters, and I can't hide the small smile that pulls at my lips. Asena's eyes flare in warning, but Zee merely shrugs. "What? It's true."

Looking back to Grace, who's just sitting there sipping her tea, I realize she has been silent this whole time. It clicks. She's been glamored. Anger burns through my veins, and I bite my bottom lip to keep from saying something that might worsen the situation. Suddenly realizing that Lukas and Stephan have been talking, I try to catch up on their conversation.

"I locked those hunters up," Stephan finishes, and I can't stop the shock that rolls through me.

"Where?" Lukas demands, clenching his jaw, his eyes as cold as chips of ice.

"My dungeons, they will be a great source of entertainment for my guests tonight."

He can't be serious. But the gleam in his eyes says he is, and that he dares us to challenge him. I take a step forward, flexing my fingers. "You can't do that. Other hunters will come looking for them. You'll put a target on everyone here!" I exclaim.

"Are you offering yourself up instead?" His voice once again takes on that sugary tone.

"No. I–"

"I thought as much, but you would be a delicious treat," Stephan purrs then dashes forward, standing inches away from me, in less time than it takes me to blink.

Sucking in a stunned breath, I will my heart to slow. Having never seen or dealt with vampires before, I did not know they could move that fast.

The others all let loose a growl, Lukas's voice barely human as he warns, "Back it up, Stephan."

Stroking my face, Stephan's eyes remain locked on mine. "I could make her forget you, you know. Your bond. You'd be nothing to her."

He flicks a quick look at Lukas before looking back to me, drawing me in with those intense, hypnotic eyes. I let my magic coat every part of me like armor just as I begin to sense his magic looking for entrance to my mind, trying to sweep me into the glamor, to bend to his will. At every turn, I block it. A smirk pulls at my lips, my hand slowly removing the dagger from the waistband at my back. Quicker than any of them expected, I have the dagger pressed against Stephan's throat, blood beading along the blade as his skin starts burning. Not taking my eyes from his, I push up onto my toes and lean in closer, whispering in his ear.

"You couldn't even if you tried."

Stephan is immobile, his eerie blue eyes blinking slowly as he appraises me, a grimace pulling at his lips. Silver has a unique effect upon vampires when it touches their skin. Not only does it burn like a bitch, but it also has a paralyzing effect, making it so a vampire cannot pull the silver off themselves. It's the same as when humans become paralyzed by electrical currents.

"Huh. Quick little thing, aren't you? Does your mate know you carry a silver dagger laced with iron?" Stephan grits out, his jaw clenching.

Lukas doesn't miss a beat. "Her mate knows she would never harm him."

"What about your pack, though? Are they safe? Would she harm them?" If he's looking to divide us, he will fail. I know not everyone in the pack trusts me, but I will do what I can to earn their trust.

"I'd never harm them," I snarl. "Now, release Grace from your glamor."

"I don't think you should be making demands." Stephan's eyes flicker to Grace. Following his gaze, my breath catches. Grace has a knife pressed against her throat. A white haze takes over my vision. My free hand stretches out toward Grace and I mutter a few words. The knife rips free from Grace's hand and sails through the air toward me. I catch it and throw it toward Lukas, where it lodges in another vampire's leg. The vampire falls to his knees, a loud screech coming from him. Lukas, Zee, and Asena spin around, not realizing someone was coming up behind them as they were focused fully on me. Their shocked faces turn back to me as my vision clears.

I look back to Stephan, his blue eyes shining with . . . pride? No, that can't be right.

"Release your glamor," I repeat in a calm voice I'm proud of. Stephan nods and I hear Grace gasp. I sigh in relief and take a step back from Stephan, pulling the dagger away from his neck. "Thank you."

Stephan raises an eyebrow at that, rubbing his neck. The cut is already healed now that the silver isn't touching it.

"Let's go." Lukas gently grabs my arm, turning me toward him. His eyes are ringed in yellow. Without thinking, I reach up and stroke his face. Bending, he quickly sweeps me up in a brief kiss.

Turning back to Stephan, who's standing there casually, hands in pockets and a serene smile on his face. "Pleasure as always, Lukas." He rocks back on his heels as he speaks.

Lukas ignores him and pulls me toward the doors. I peer back and see Zee and Asena helping Grace along.

"Are we just going to let him keep the hunters?" I mutter under my breath, unsure how good vampire hearing is.

"Yes."

Shock rolls through me. "Really?"

"We got what we came for, Nesrin." He nods to Grace.

I'm not happy, but I suppose there isn't much else we can do. The hunters don't deserve my sympathy, and they don't have it. But there is still the worry that others might come looking for them.

"Wait!" I dig my heels in, spinning back to face Stephan, "Why were you poking around my bookstore? What were you looking for?"

Stephan's eyes flash a deep magenta and then return to a startling blue. If I blinked, I would have missed it.

"A rose sauvage," he answers in French. At least, I think it's French.

I scowl. "Okay. I don't know what that means." Obviously, I don't speak French. "Why were you at the apartment?"

"J'ai senti la rose sauvage," he replies, assessing me with a twinkle in his eye and a smirk on his face. I growl, taking a step closer.

"What the hell are you on about?" I snap, feeling Lukas press up against my back.

"He's showing off," Zee says, smirking. "Thinks all the ladies love a French man."

Stephan's gaze turns bland as he swings his head in Zee's direction. "Think what you want, boy."

Zee smiles as he walks backward out the door, arms held wide. "I do, but thanks for the permission, old man."

I don't get to see Stephan's response because Lukas grabs my hand and tugs me out to the car, and I am more than frustrated by the lack of answers I have been getting lately.

We all pile into the car and head back toward the apartments.

"Wait. Where are we going?" I ask Zee who is now driving, joined by Asena in the front.

"They are taking me home," Grace replies, with a determined look on her face, I don't agree with her decision, but it's ultimately her choice to make. I give her a terse nod and look out the window, biting down on my thumbnail.

We help her inside, Zee and Asena deciding to head to Little Bites while Grace and I have a talk, Lukas insisting to stay with us and fix the door. But I think it's more for his peace of mind, knowing I was safe.

"Are you sure you're okay?" I ask, resting my hand atop hers as we take our seats at the table.

"Yes, Ness, thanks to you. I'm fine, just a bit worn out." She rubs her temples. "Being glamored is strangely draining." I walk over to the sink, fill up a glass of water and hand it to her. She looks up at me gratefully, her face looking haggard and pale.

I frown as anger swamps my body. "How did you end up with Stephan, Grace?"

She lets out a breath, pushing aside her exhaustion to answer me. "Some hunters showed up at my door. I tried closing it, but they forced their way inside. I did my best to fight them off, and made a run for it. That's when I bumped into Stephan in the hall, and he handled the Hunters. Stephan and I know each other and, honestly, I'm shocked he would glamor me. I have the impression he did it to see what you would do. He was provoking you."

Provoking me? More like testing my patience. "Why?"

"Vampires are mostly just old and bored, and they like playing games for entertainment. It could be anyone's guess what he wished to learn."

I frown as I think about the encounter with Stephan. I suppose he had plenty of opportunities to hurt or even kill us. But he worked alongside Lukas against the hunters, so they aren't enemies, more like business partners.

"Why aren't you wearing the necklace I gave you?" Grace demands. My eyes dart to hers, surprised by the hardness in her voice.

"I wasn't ready to put it on yet."

"That necklace will *help* you, Nesrin. It will not do you any harm. You need to wear it."

Stubbornness flows through my body, setting my jaw. "Why are you pushing this?"

"It's your destiny," she snaps.

I'm shocked silent for a moment, something close to hurt festering in my chest. Grace has never snapped at me before.

"What is? What is my destiny, Grace? Tell me because *I don't know.*"

She groans, rubbing her temples again. "I . . . can't say. I've been bound." A chill skates down my spine. Who would bind another to silence?

"What? By whom?"

Looking defeated, she cradles her face in her hands. "I can't say."

My anger at the constant lack of information gets the better of me, and I slam my hands on the table, making her jump. "What about my sister?" I demand. "Can you tell me about her?"

Grace's eyes widen in shock. She shakes her head.

"You know her, don't you?" I push. "Don't lie to me, Grace."

She stands, looking left and right. She reminds me of a cornered animal right now, nervous and scared. But scared of what? "What aren't you telling me, Grace? And why?"

"I would tell you everything if I could, but I cannot. I'm sorry, Nesrin."

I push out of my chair and start pacing. Flexing my fingers, the magic warms my body and hands in reaction to my emotions. I need to take a breath and calm the fuck down.

"Look, Nesrin, I'm sorry I can't be of more help. But until the person who has bound me releases me, or you discover the truth on your own, there is nothing I can reveal to you, except to say that what you seek hides in the shadows."

I frown, considering her words. More riddles and twisted phrases. Shadow walker is what my mother called Leila. Could she be the shadow I keep thinking I'm seeing? It would make sense, but why not make herself known?

"I don't like it, Grace. All the riddles and lies. I trust you, but you need to give me more."

Her face drops and she comes to stand in front of me, taking hold of my hands. "Follow your gut. Remember, diamonds form under pressure. We crush grapes to make the richest wine, and seeds grow smothered in complete darkness. Nothing is as it seems, and no matter what happens, you fight tooth and nail, and you claw your way back to the surface. I believe in you."

My shoulders slump, shame washing through me. I can't be mad at her. She has been bound to silence, and that's a spell even I can't undo. I let go of her hands and pace the small kitchen.

"Okay, Grace. I'll drop it for now," I relent, twisting around to face her. She sags with relief and runs a shaky hand through her long gray hair. "Are you sure you won't come with us? There is plenty of room."

Grace shakes her head and glances at Lukas, who has made his way over, finished replacing her front door. "I will be fine here. Plus, Merve said he would come and stay," she adds, standing taller.

"Okay, well, let me at least put a ward on your apartment," I offer, my thoughts plagued by the curse that has darkened my life. I swallow back the fear of losing Astraea or Grace the way I've lost everyone else. Grace probably would be okay without my wards, but it isn't a risk I am willing to take. I'm not leaving without placing them, and I think Grace can see as much in my eyes because she smiles softly and grabs my hands in hers.

"Okay," she whispers softly. "Thank you, Ness."

When I've finished with the wards, I turn to Grace. "I guess I should get out of here. Leave you to get some rest."

I give her a warm smile then make my way to the door where Lukas is waiting patiently for me. Grace follows behind me on silent feet, but when I reach for the door, I hesitate, looking back at her over my shoulder.

"Take care, Grace. Call me if you need me."

She smiles softly. "Same to you, Nesrin."

One last look and Lukas and I are out in the hall, the door quietly clicking shut behind us. His intense eyes drink me in as I approach, and I feel the butterflies take flight. It's always the same response when he looks at me.

# CHAPTER TWENTY SEVEN

A little past midnight, Lukas and I are sitting together on the back deck, soaking in the cool night air and thinking back to what ended up as a really great evening. I'm really growing to love being around the pack. It's true that some still keep their distance, but on the whole the pack has welcomed me with open arms since learning of my place with Lukas. He reaches over, threading our fingers together and stands, pulling me up with him and leading me back to the house. A small smile tugs at my lips. Even with all the shit going on, I am happy. So unbelievably happy. And so is Astraea. A laugh threatens to erupt out of me as I think about all the mischief she got up to with Nissa tonight. The little sprite is turning into quite the bad influence on my innocent little niece, but I can't deny how much Astra is flourishing here with her pack of shifters and sprites and me. Nissa took her to bed hours ago. I sigh as it occurs to me how quickly her second birthday is approaching. I can't believe it.

Lukas opens the back door, holding it open for me. I duck under his arm, slipping inside, then let out a shriek as he swings me up in the air and throws me over his shoulder. His arm is wrapped tightly around my knees, keeping me in place.

"Lukas, what on earth are you doing?" I laugh, pushing off his back.

"Carrying you," he states matter of factly.

I roll my eyes, laughing. "I can see that. Put me down."

"No."

"May I ask why?"

"Because I like you in my arms."

"Well, technically I'm over your shoulder, you caveman." I poke him in the ribs.

"Behave," he chuckles, smacking my ass. I jolt, letting out a squeal. Then melt into him as he rubs away the sting. My view isn't much to complain about as he makes his way up the stairs to our room.

I can't keep the big grin off my face as we step inside the room. He slowly brings me over his shoulder and lets me slide down his body so there is no space between us. Our eyes stay glued to each other as his hands move from my hips up my body at a slow pace, like he has all the time in the world.

A small gasp escapes me as his hands skim up my ribs, brushing the side of my breasts, then move up to hold my face as we stare at each other. The only sound in the room is our breathing. His green eyes glow brightly and the shadows in the room play off the angles of his face. It's beautiful. He is so gorgeous.

Lukas leans down, lips brushing mine, causing my heart to jump and an insistent throb between my legs to grow, one that doesn't want to be ignored. I nip at his bottom lip, capturing it between my teeth. Letting out a growl, he grabs me behind the legs, spinning and tipping me onto the bed in a move so fast I have no time to react before his warm body is covering mine. Slowly, we strip each other's clothes off, exploring every inch of skin. When he sucks on the skin where my inner thigh meets my pelvis, I jerk off the bed. Liking this response, Lukas moves to the other side, repeating the action and sucking harder. A loud moan escapes me this time.

"Lukas, please, I need you now," I beg, grabbing his arms to pull him to me, but he resists.

"I'm not done, sweetheart. I need to taste you, have you withering under my tongue," he says with a wicked grin. My stomach dips at his tone. Bending his head, he presses his tongue to my core, giving me a long, slow torturous lick then sucking my sweet bundle of nerves hard. I jolt and my legs tremble as I cry out at the pleasure he was creating. A few more passes of his tongue and I am indeed a withering mess. Kissing his way up my body, Lukas settles his hard body over mine, nudging my entrance with his cock. My hands explore the dips and swells of his ripped chest as I lift my legs, wrapping them around his waist, desperate to feel him inside of me, to have him buried so deep we become one.

Slowly, Lukas inches inside of me, the feeling as he slowly stretches me is torturous bliss. When he is fully inside me, we both moan as one at the feeling of being joined. Lukas keeps a slow, steady, agonizing pace, working me into a frenzy. Needing more, I try to roll us over. Lukas reads my thoughts and, gripping my ass, he rolls us so I'm on top. I sit up, taking him deeper, and my stomach tightens, making my inner walls tremble. Lukas clenches his jaw, the muscle in his arms and neck tense with restraint.

"Lukas . . . " I breathe, then gasp at the feeling of him filling me.

I lift my hips until only the tip of him is inside me, then slam down hard. A sexy groan falls from Lukas's mouth as he grips my hips, guiding me up, and then pulling me back down hard, grinding me against his pelvis. I can't help but cry out at the sensations he is creating.

I can feel my climax growing, winding me higher, and falter in my movements as the waves of pleasure begin to take over. Lukas suddenly flips us back over, dragging me under him and plunging back in. I let out a startled cry, which he swallows with his mouth. Our kiss becomes deeper, more desperate. Both his hands slip under my back, one moving up to cup the back of my neck, the other over my shoulder in a firm hold. I feel possessed, cherished, consumed. I love it.

I lift my hips to meet his and feel an uncontrollable tremble take over my body. My toes curl and I slide my foot up Lukas's calf to his ass, digging my heel in. His head lifts from my neck, green eyes glowing brightly as they lock with mine. I raise a hand and run it through his thick wavy hair, tugging on the strands.

"Mark me. Make me yours, Lukas," I whisper. His eyes glow impossibly brighter, the flecks of yellow mixing in with the vibrant green.

"Are you sure? There's no going back if we do this," he pants, his eyes searching mine.

"I'm sure, Lukas. I love you. That will never change. I want forever with you," I moan into his mouth. I have never been so sure of anything in my life. My fingers tighten their grip on his hair, moving his face to my neck, and his breath skates over my neck, making my body break out in a new type of awareness. Lukas lets out a groan that almost has me climaxing just from the sound alone.

"Nesrin."

That's all he says before he starts pounding into me faster, harder, sweat making our bodies slick. I meet him thrust for thrust, friction building in my core. Dragging my nails down his back the rumble from his chest is felt in my own as he growls his approval. Bending his head to the junction between my neck and shoulder, his mouth brushes over the sensitive spot, sending a flood of goosebumps all over my body. I felt his canines lengthen and scrape the skin of my neck. I moan, tightening my legs around his waist, grabbing his head as I pull him closer. With a snarl, Lukas bites down, piercing the soft skin, a sharp pain stealing my breath for only a second before an invisible string tugs from the bite to my core. Crying out in pleasure, I splinter into a million pieces. It feels as if I am floating, even though I can feel the weight of Lukas on top of me, pinning me to the mattress, and suddenly I can feel the first tingle of magic wash through me. Forcing my eyes open, I see the room filled with a kaleidoscope of colors so bright they dance off our bodies. Lukas's head lifts, and he cups the back of my head, guiding it to his neck, his movements desperate.

"Bite me, Nesrin. Now," he pants. Blood beads along the cut he has already made on his neck. When did he do that?

I don't hesitate as I lean forward, grabbing his shoulders, and placing my mouth over the cut. My magic builds in me, filling me to the brim as I suck on his neck. The warmth of his blood filling my mouth, a moan rumbling in my throat. I expected his blood to taste metallic and bitter, but it is an explosion of flavors on my tongue, reminding me somehow of chocolate. Lukas shudders above me, my magic bursting from my body as I push it into the bite, wanting to mark him as he has me. Another orgasm washes over me, and through it, I faintly hear my mate's deep and guttural growl, "Mine," as his own pleasure takes over, his movements slowing. I let go of his neck and fall back onto the bed, Lukas's body covering mine as we both struggle to catch our breath. Opening my eyes, I find the room still alight in colors. Magic is floating around the room like specks of dust, as if it burst from us. Finally, Lukas lifts onto his forearms and looks down at me, a tender expression on his face.

"I love you, Nesrin." He brushes the sweaty hair from my face. His gaze locks on mine, holding me still as his fingers continue to brush through my hair at a slow pace, his eyes dropping back to my mouth.

"I love you, too, Lukas," I whisper, emotions clogging my throat as I pull him back to me, hugging him tightly. No words can describe how I feel. I can sense our bond being forged and hold onto him with what strength I have left. Lukas shifts to the side, pulling me against his body and curls around me, my back to his front. I let out a sigh, my eyes feeling heavy, and let sleep pull me under.

I wake up before the sun has fully risen and look over my shoulder at Lukas. He looks so young in his sleep, his dark hair is falling over his forehead in soft waves. I slowly turn over and trace my fingers over his face, down his jaw and neck to my mark on his shoulder. A small gasp leaves my mouth in amazement. I've never seen anything like it. The cut has fully healed but in its place is a pattern of shimmering colors that looks almost alive, moving under his skin in intricate whorls. There is a pale raised mark like a tattoo in the shape of a paw print. I trace my fingers idly over the swirling pattern. It blends in nicely with his other tattoos. I hope Lukas doesn't mind having a mark, because I'm not sure I can remove it. In my daze, I don't notice Lukas is awake until he lifts a hand to cup my face, and I raise my eyes to his, startled. He leans forward, kissing me softly, teasingly. I open to him, and within seconds, Lukas has me pinned to the mattress possessively as he settles between my thighs.

All he does is kiss me, working me into a flurry of need. I try to pull him closer, needing to feel all of him. Instead, he rolls us over to put me on top, straddling him, and I rock back and forth over him before lifting up and gripping his cock to guide him into me, then slowly lower myself. As he stretches me, I tip my head back, moaning as the sparks of pleasure zap through my body, making all my nerves stand on end. I let out a breath at how deep he reaches, how he fills me, and start moving slowly, teasing him. Lukas's hands clench the sheets by his hips, his body tensing. At his low feral growl, a scattering of goosebumps races over my body, my nipples hardening and my core clenching. His emerald eyes glow, sparks of yellow flashing through them.

Reaching up, he grabs my breasts, running his thumbs over the nipples, and my skin tightens, my breasts feel heavy as my chest rises and falls with my rapid breaths. Suddenly Lukas's restraint snaps. Both his hands grip my butt cheeks, squeezing, then lifting me up and down to take him deeper and harder with each stroke. His fingers dig into my hips as he moves me over him. Pure bliss cascading through my body, I topple forward, my hands falling to his chest, and I let him take control as he pounds deeper and harder into me. Pleasure flows through my body in wave after wave of sheer pleasure.

Lukas lifts his head to take a nipple into his mouth, sucking hard, and I shatter, the orgasm rippling through me in waves as I cry out, trembling, and collapse on top of him. Lukas rolls us over, gripping my waist as he flips me onto my stomach, drawing my hips up before slamming back into me. The new angle and force of his thrust sends another orgasm ripping through me. I bury my face in the sheets as a scream of ecstasy tears from my throat. Lukas moves inside me, his rhythm fast and hard. I moan into the sheets. His pace is relentless. It doesn't take long for him to find his own release. He falls forward, flattening us to the bed, his hips still moving, slowing, drawing his cock in and out of me. He pushes all the way in and stays there. After a few heartbeats, he rolls to the side, wrapping an arm around me and pulling my back against his chest. Moving my hair to the side, he finds his mark and leans over to admire it, then kisses my neck and shoulder.

"Mine," he says, kissing the mark, and a shiver runs down my spine. We lie together for a few moments, trying to catch our breaths.

"Good morning." I giggle as he rolls away from me. I miss his touch already.

Lukas chuckles, standing from the bed. I roll onto my back as he grabs my ankle and drags me to the end of the bed, lifting me over his shoulder.

"What are you doing?" I laugh as he carries me to the adjoining bathroom.

"Taking a shower," Lukas replies, and excitement washes through me. I can't wait to see his face when he sees the mark. I also can't wait to explore his body slowly in the shower, washing every muscle and dip.

After the shower, I take some time to admire my mark in the mirror. It's identical to Lukas's. Looking up to my face, I study my reflection. The girl staring back at me is happy. Her eyes seem brighter, her skin flushed and has a healthy glow. For the first time in a long time, I really believe I can be happy.

I look over at Lukas in the mirror as he pulls on his jeans. *How did I get so lucky?* Lukas's eyes meet mine in the mirror, surprise on his face.

"What?"

'*You mean how did I get so lucky?*' Lukas replies. My mouth falls open. I was watching him. He didn't say those words out loud.

"No fucking way," I stammer, spinning around so fast I almost lose my balance. A huge grin breaks out across Lukas's face as he stalks over to me, leaving his jeans unbuttoned. *Damn, that's distracting.*

Cupping my face, he bends, taking my mouth with his in a scorching kiss, his lips moving over mine, slow and sensual.

'*I love you,*' sounds in my head.

"Oh my goddess, we can mind speak!" I shriek in excitement. Lukas pulls back, chuckling.

"Looks like it, sweetheart." This time, he says it out loud.

"This is so awesome." I'm giddy with excitement, almost bouncing on my feet. Then I feel an emotion that isn't mine, a slight feeling of pride and amusement that only adds to my own. I concentrate on those feelings, and I find a single glowing thread, one that flows straight from me to Lukas. Surprised, I look up at him. "I can feel you, your emotions, your happiness."

"I can feel you, too, sweetheart, I wasn't sure if you would get these parts of the bond. I didn't want to tell you and then you be disappointed if it didn't happen."

"I understand." I reach up, running my fingers lightly over his mark. "Do you like it?" I ask quietly. His fingers grip my chin, lifting my face up to his. He bends, taking my mouth with his again, and when he pulls back, his eyes are bright. The way he looks at me, the warmth in those green eyes, it washes over me like a shot of whisky. The corner of his mouth lifts and I can feel his love through the bond.

"I love it."

# CHAPTER TWENTY EIGHT

Z ee is seated across from me at the table in the kitchen later in the morning. Everyone else is out doing goodness knows what, yet, somehow, I got stuck here learning how to communicate telepathically with the wolves of the pack, despite not having officially been made luna yet. Lukas is planning to announce it to the pack tonight. But for now, he wants me to practice my connection to communicate telepathically, and thinking he would be too much of a distraction, Lukas disappeared with Astraea and left the task to Zee.

The mating bond is extremely strong, and thankfully we share the abilities other mated partners enjoy, even though I'm only part shifter. I love being able to sense him physically and mentally.

Zee watches me, a frown marring his face, which is rare. He's always smiling.

"What?" I ask, running a hand through my hair. I can't believe how soft it is today, and no tangles. Usually, my wavy hair tangles so easily.

"You're not even trying," he accuses, snapping me from thoughts about my hair. I mentally chastise myself. Focus.

"Yes, I am," I fire back weakly. We both know the truth.

Rolling his eyes, which is totally unlike him, he waves his hand in front of us, motioning for me to continue. We've been at this for over an hour, and I can't do it. I can't concentrate. I lower my head, hiding my face with my hair. Drawing a deep breath through what feels like a constricted chest, I try again to reach out to Zee with my mind.

After a minute or two, Zee taps the table. "Nothing?"

Shaking my head, I close my eyes and try to relax. I sense Zee leaning forward, trying to get a look at my face. Ignoring him, I focus on finding that mental link. Blackness greets me. *Dammit, why can't I do this?*

Tears sting my eyes and I throw my hands in the air. "I can't do it."

Zee's hand lands on my forearm and squeezes gently. "I'm sorry, I was pushing you. You'll get there, honey. I have faith in you."

"I'm useless. I can't be your luna if I can't communicate with you when you're in wolf form." I sound whiny, but I can't help it. There's a lot to prove. The pack has to see me as worthy of this role.

"It's okay. This is new to you, Nesrin. We don't expect you to get it straight away."

A deep feeling of failure rises inside of me, a dull ache forming behind my eyes. I rarely get headaches anymore. As a teenager, I suffered from them often. Sometimes they would last for days, bringing me double vision and nausea. Another throb forming at the base of my neck, I tilt my head from side to side, hoping to relieve it, but all that does is make my head spin. I groan before huffing out a deep breath and resting my head on the cool table.

"Argh. I think I need food," I mumble into the table.

Zee pokes at my head. I slowly raise my eyes, glaring at him. "What?"

"You seem different," he says, studying me like I'm a puzzle. Frowning, I shake my head, which I immediately regret. Nausea swamps my stomach and a sharp pain shoots through my temples. I let my head drop back to the table. Definitely need some food.

I move to stand, using my arms to help force myself up, but Zee quickly moves to my side, grabbing my shoulders and turning me to face him.

"Zee," I complain.

Ignoring me, he leans in close, bringing his nose almost to mine. I startle, trying to pull back. His big blue eyes widen, a slight glow flickering through them.

"What the heck, Zee?" The sudden movement so close to my face has me swaying. "Whoa. Back it up, Zee." Bringing my hands up, I push at his chest. He steps back, but keeps a hold of my shoulders, which I'm thankful for. I don't appear to be very steady on my own.

Zee's eyes move to my neck. His fingers brushing over my mating mark, and I sway again. Reaching up, I break his hold to rub my temples.

"He marked you!" It's a statement, not a question. I frown, bringing my hair over my neck to cover up my mark.

"Yes? We completed the mating bond last night." A blush heats my face and neck, and I roll my eyes at my embarrassment. I'm not a teenager anymore. Why am I still blushing about these things? One side of Zee's lips tips up as he stares at me.

"Lukas didn't tell me. Congratulations, honey." Zee pulls me into a hug, sounding relieved at the news, but my head is pounding too much to analyze it.

"Thanks?" I say from where my face is crushed against his chest.

Zee chuckles and pulls back. "Now it makes sense that Lukas left with Finan this morning and asked me to do this with you."

I scrunch up my nose. "It does?"

"Yes. Newly mated couples have a hard time not rolling around in the sheets every chance they get." Zee laughs, and the smirk he directs my way has my cheeks burning. Damn it.

My fingers idly move through my hair. "Oh. Well. This is awkward. Will everyone be able to tell?"

His lips twitch, and I can tell he wants to laugh. "It's not awkward. It's natural, Nesrin. And yes, everyone will scent it on the both of you. I'm actually annoyed I didn't pick up on it straight away."

I groan and cover my face. How am I supposed to go get lunch now? The pounding starts up again in my head and I have a suspicion it's stress related. I feel Zee's hands wrap around my wrists as he pulls my hands from my face. His eyes have softened, but there is still amusement there.

"Don't tell me the brave legacy is scared to face a few shifters to get some lunch because they will know she had sex with their alpha? Nesrin, they all expected this to happen. They all respect you and that won't change. The only one who feels awkward about this is you. I have to say, it's refreshing and cute watching you get all flustered, when most women would brag and strut about. But you're different. You're brave, strong, and independent. Stand up and show everyone who you are, prove you'll be a good luna."

His words resonate with me. I am strong. I've endured more than most and come out on the other side. I have finally found where I belong, and I shouldn't feel uncomfortable about that. My spine straightens. He's right. I am a legacy. Their alpha chose me as their luna. I have nothing to be embarrassed about. Tonight, they will all find out what I am and swear me in as their luna.

Zee holds out his arm for me, eyes shining with pride. "Shall we?"

Taking a deep breath and squaring my shoulders, I loop my arm in Zee's. He nudges me with his elbow when I still don't answer.

"Yes. Take me to food, please." I laugh.

When we approach the communal area, it's already packed, everyone milling around getting their lunch. The smells that drift our way make my mouth water. I open my mouth to ask Zee about the mark when a sudden silence falls around us. Looking up, I realize everyone is staring at us. And by us, I mean me.

"Well, this is awkward," Zee chuckles under his breath, leaning closer to me. I elbow him in the ribs, earning a small grunt for my efforts. The shithead is teasing me.

"Thanks for pointing that out for me, Zee."

Gabe wanders over, a curious look on his face. He has his hair tied back today, and he's wearing loose-fitting pants and a shirt. I really want to know more about him. He's the first shifter I've met of Asian origin.

"Hey guys, what's happening?" he greets, coming to a stop in front of us.

"Not much," I reply, bouncing on my toes as I look around, noticing that everyone has gone back to what they were doing, though some still cast me quick looks before turning away again.

Gabe tilts his head, studying me. I squirm under his gaze, then his eyes widen and dart to Zee's. "Is she?"

Zee nods. "Yes, they completed the mating bond."

"Zee!" I exclaim, hitting his arm. My self-consciousness makes me shift around on my feet. I look at Gabe and give him an awkward smile and shrug.

"What? Everyone knows, and if they don't, they will. You have a glow. And you smell of Lukas. Like, worse than before. I can't believe it took me an hour to notice it," Zee explains.

"What are you talking about? I don't smell, and I'm certainly not glowing."

"When you mate, the male marks you and his magic infuses with yours, causing a glow. It will fade, but for now you're glowing with Lukas's magic and his scent is clinging to you more than usual. It will let every shifter know you are his," Gabe says with a shrug. My mind catches on one thing.

"The male infuses their magic, marking the female?" I ask, my voice going a little squeaky.

"Yes," Gabe confirms as we make our way to a table to sit.

I bite my nail as I mull over this new information. "What if the female marks the male as well?"

"I haven't heard of that happening. Customarily, it's the male who does the marking to show everyone she is taken."

My eyes flare in annoyance. "That's sexist!" I snap. At this point, my head is threatening to crack open with its insistent pounding, making my temper shorter than usual.

"But I don't see why she couldn't," Zee says, pulling a chair out for me and I take it, smiling at him. He has always been such a gentleman.

Turning back to Gabe, I see him frowning. "What?" I ask.

Gabe squints his eyes and groans. "You marked the alpha, didn't you?"

I open my mouth and close it again, unsure how to answer.

"Of course, she did." Zee ruffles my hair before turning and making his way over to the food tables. Having been left here, I'll get whatever he decides.

I glance back at Gabe and shrug. "I mean, yeah . . . I think that's what I did."

He smiles at me, the smile transforming his face from handsome to stunning. He nods his head as if coming to some conclusion. "Well, good for you, Nesrin. It's never been done before, not that I'm aware of anyway, but congratulations."

I press my lips together to keep my grin at bay. "Thanks."

As Gabe takes the seat across from me, my tongue is practically burning with questions about his history. Asena has already confirmed that different species of shifter live here and are part of the pacific northwest pack, but I'm dying to know what Gabe is.

"Can I ask you something?" I blurt.

"You're my luna now. You can ask me anything."

"Not officially," I point out.

Gabe simply shrugs. "Semantics."

The word luna echoes through my head, the pounding in my temples increasing to new levels. I grit my teeth, and I wince as a throbbing starts in my jaw. Gabe watches me, concern lining his eyes.

"Sorry, I have a headache. I wanted to know what kind of shifter you are?"

Gabe gives me a cheeky smile. "You really been holding onto that question for weeks, haven't you?" he teases.

Zee is suddenly there, dropping two plates on the table. My mouth instantly waters at the sight of roast meat and vegetables. "Thanks, Zee." I flash him a smile before turning back to Gabe. "I have."

"Well, some people get uncomfortable when I reveal what I am."

I notice Zee stiffen next to me, his fork raised halfway to his mouth. "I don't think now is the right time, Gabe," Zee says, a growl edging his words.

I turn slightly in my seat to face Zee, eyeing him. "I want to know."

"Not yet," Zee argues, which only makes me want to know more. It's like they don't know me at all. Turning to Gabe, I motion for him to continue. He hesitates, glancing at Zee.

"I will tell you, but I need you to know I would never ever hurt you, Nesrin."

Okay, shit. Now I'm getting nervous. "Just tell me."

"I'm a kitsune." At my silence, Gabe continues, "Hunters caught my parents not long after we moved here from Japan. I was eight, and they sacrificed themselves, giving me a chance to get away. I would have died, alone in the woods, that young. But Lukas found me, saved me, gave me shelter, a home. I will forever be in his debt."

My heart sinks for him. He lost his parents so young, and to hunters. I've never met a kitsune shifter before. I know they're rare, and usually only found across Japan. To have one so far away from home is odd.

Kitsunes are identical to wild foxes, only larger. In human form, the kitsune are known for being very attractive, which explains Gabe's good looks. I tried to recall what I know about them, but everything I learned was from myths about them. I know they are extremely intelligent and some hold elemental gifts. They always keep their promises, repay any debts, and are loyal to a fault. A kitsune's power varies and not all inherit all the gifts, but what are they? Oh yeah, their magic lies in their charm abilities, illusions, possession, and mind manipulation.

I bolt upright, my chair tumbling over behind me, and my hand goes for the dagger I keep strapped to my thigh, my fingers brushing the hilt. Gabe's eyes track the movement, and panic flares in my chest at the thought of someone tampering with my mind again.

"Easy there, honey. Gabe isn't like that," Zee assures me, standing up at my side. My eyes are glued to Gabe's, his deep brown almond eyes reflecting surprise. Then all I see is understanding as his eyes soften, and he gives me a small, sad smile. I will my heart to slow, but my body has other ideas. A white glow emits from my hands. I struggle to pull my magic back.

Zee grabs both my arms, turning me to face him, bending so he is at eye level with me. He reaches up, cupping one of my cheeks, voice low and reassuring. "It's okay to be wary, but Gabe is pack, our friend. He would never use his gifts on any of us. You can trust him, Nesrin."

My eyes widen at the word gift. I know Gabe is our friend, however I can't stop the panic building. The thought of Emerson's favorite form of torture runs rampant through my mind. I feel a warmth spreading in my chest, my fight-or-flight response kicking in. Closing my eyes, I sense Lukas. He can feel my panic and is worried. Through the warmth of the mating bond, he sends his love and support, and it soaks into my body like a hot cocoa on a snowy day, warm and comforting. I take a few deep breaths, which seems to help calm me down.

"Nesrin."

I blink at hearing my name and turn to look at Gabe. He is frowning at me, worry etched in his face. I attempt a half smile, one I know I don't even remotely pull off, unease still twisting my stomach.

"Are you okay?" he asks. I hate the edge of hurt in his voice, that I put it there.

I wave him off. "Yes, I'm fine. I'm sorry I reacted like that." But inside me is a maelstrom of emotions. Despite my unease, I take my seat again.

Lukas's comfort washes over me, drowning out all my fears. I can trust these people. They are my family now. Zee's palm lands on my back, giving me a little pat as he takes a seat. We all start eating and Gabe watches me silently. I can see he is regretting telling me now that my reaction hurt him in some way, and feel terrible about it, but I can't take it back now.

I reach over the table and cover his hand with mine. "I really am sorry for the way I reacted, Gabe. I trust you, I do. For a moment, I let my fears take over. I am glad you told me," I say in earnest.

Gabe is silent for a few heartbeats, then gives me a huge grin. "You're going to make a great luna." Then he stands and walks off. I watch him go, a small smile on my lips.

Zee and I decide to take a walk along the river to the forest. I ate so much I feel like laying down and going to sleep, but I really can use the fresh air. Astraea and Nissa are walking just in front of us, having decided to join, and smile as Astraea stops to pick flowers along the way. I bask in the serenity and fresh air, the smell of the trees and moss growing over fallen stumps tickling my senses, the sound of the river trickling around rocks washes away my headache and calms my frazzled nerves. Zee lightly bumps my shoulder, and I open my eyes, glancing over at him. He opens his mouth to speak, when a high-pitched shriek cuts through the air. My heart misses a beat as I search for the source. Whatever it was, it sounded distressed. Nissa flies circles around Astraea, tinkering loudly. Zee shifts in an instant, his enormous gray wolf backing us away from the forest. Nissa's eyes meet mine and she tilts her head toward the forest as if telling me to go. Another shriek echoes from the forest and I can't take the sound any longer. Danger or not, the creature needs help.

"Zee, guard Astra," I yell as I break into a run, heading for the forest. I hear Zee's rumbling growl. He is going to be angry, but I need to help. My feet pound against the ground as I run straight into the tree line, lifting my arm up to push through some of the denser parts. The terrified shriek comes again. This time, it's much closer. I vault over a few large boulders, the green moss soft under my touch. I sense Lukas before I see him. His black coat blends in well with the forest. I notice he has something cornered between some rocks. Two other wolves are with him, a white and gray wolf and a reddish brown one.

"Lukas," I shout as I jump down from the boulder, my feet landing gracefully on the dirt. Lukas swings his eyes my way and I suck in a breath at those luminous yellow orbs. The other two wolves turn toward me, but my eyes go past them to the terrified troll huddled against the rocks.

"Joseph?" I question. When the troll looks up, relief floods his face at the sight of me.

"Nesrin!" He moves to step forward and the white wolf growls loudly. He looks around at the wolves nervously, wringing his hands together. I rush toward the troll and Lukas steps in my way. Drawing to a stop, and glare at him. Lukas shifts, towering over me.

"Nesrin, go back to Zee."

"No. That is my friend and you've scared him half to death," I snap, pointing to the troll.

Lukas turns, looking back at Joseph. The two wolves shift and I recognize Finan and Roan.

"You've all scared him, and you need to apologize," I demand, my hands planted firmly on my hips.

"He trespassed on pack lands," Lukas counters calmly.

"He is a friend."

"He didn't tell us that."

"Well, have you looked in the mirror? You're terrifying!"

Lukas's eyes widen and he smirks. His look is predatory, and I shiver. Damn wolf!

I push past him and move to Joseph. I take his hands in mine and smile. "Is everything alright? How's Sophie?"

He looks behind me at Lukas. "Don't worry about them," I say gently. "How's Sophie?" His completely bottomless black eyes met mine, and he sags. "She is in terrible shape. I haven't been able to find you. I heard you were here, lying low. That the coven is after you."

I nod, my heart dropping at the thought that they needed me, and I've been hiding. "Okay. Let's go," I say and pull on his hands.

Lukas frowns. "Where are we going?"

"Joseph needs my help. We are going to his house."

"No, the coven knows you are helping him. They will have his house watched."

"We could bring them here," I suggest.

Lukas looks bewildered, like I've suggested something absolutely crazy, and maybe I have. But I am helping them.

Lukas seems to think about it before answering.

"I have an empty house. That should work. I'll send Gabe and Roan to collect the other troll." He looks at Joseph. "You should probably go with them."

Joseph nods and turns back to me. "Will we be safe?"

"Of course."

An hour and a half later, a truck speeds down our drive, skidding to a stop at the front of the house. Doors fly open and screaming is coming from the interior. Panicked, I race down the stairs to the car. Joseph's normal gray skin is as white as a ghost as he holds Sophie's hand in the backseat. Gabe moves around the car to help them out.

"She is in labor!" he shouts.

"It's too early, Nesrin. It's too early!" Sophie cries. Black tears track down her gray face as she sobs. Joseph's eyes plead with mine.

I look to Gabe. "Can you carry her inside?"

He nods, scooping up the young troll and gently carrying her toward the house. Lukas opens the door and looks down at me, his expression strained with worry. I'm worried, too. It is too early, and the chance of the baby surviving is slim. Taking a deep breath, I race up the stairs after Gabe, Joseph following right behind me. Lukas has placed pillows and a blanket down on the lounge room floor and helps Gabe settle her there. Joseph sits by his wife's head and strokes her face softly. I move between her legs and call upon my magic, grabbing Sophie's hand and letting my magic flow into her, calming her mind and helping her body relax.

"I need to check on the baby," I coo gently. She nods her head and rests it back against the pillows, her eyes focusing on her husband. I place both my hands on her stomach and feel for the baby. My heart drops. It's not moving, and its heartbeat is weak. I push my healing magic deeper, surrounding the baby in a casting of light.

*Please live. Please, please live,* I chant in my head.

Sophie cries out as another contraction hits. I take my hands from her stomach, lifting her dress to check the baby.

"It's time to push, Sophie. When I say, I need you to push."

"No. No. No. No. It's too early!" she wails, trying to sit up. I lean over her and gently push down on her shoulders, stopping her movement.

"Listen to me. I will do everything. And I mean *everything* in my power to save you and your baby. But I need you to push."

Her watery black eyes stare into mine. "Promise?" she chokes out.

"I promise."

"Okay," she whimpers.

I can see as the pain overtakes her again. "Push!" I command.

Her screams of pain echo through the house and I do my best to temper her pain, but I focus most of my energy on the baby. The front door opens, and Asena runs in, her face flushed. "What can I do?" she says, dropping down next to me.

My eyes are void of color, a white haze moving over my vision suddenly. "Take my place once the baby is out. I need you to take care of Sophie. Help her while I see to the baby."

Asena nods, taking Sophie's free hand. I'm proud of her for stepping up. Trolls are terrifying creatures to look at, but deep down they are soft and caring.

"One more push. You can do this," I prompt, giving her a nod.

The baby comes out on the next push, and I hold the tiny troll in my hands. I block out the noises around me and curl my hands around the small body, bringing it to my chest. I close my eyes, letting my magic seek out what it needs to fix. The warmth of my magic encases the baby troll, finding quickly what the problem was. The baby's heart is only half-formed. A sob tears from my chest at its fighting spirit, at how tired it is from struggling. I watch as my magic surrounds its heart. It pulses and flares. A glow of warmth surrounds the baby's tiny body and, when the light recedes, I hold my breath. The troll's tiny heart gives a loud thump, whole.

Tears fall down my face in rapid succession. Noises filter back in, and I hear Sophie sobbing uncontrollably. Her words are incoherent. Opening my eyes, I blink several times, trying to clear my vision of the white haze. Asena holds a distraught Sophie in her arms, and Joseph is sitting next to her with his head in his hands, his shoulders shaking as he cries silently. Suddenly the baby lets out a piercing wail and both parents' eyes snap up. Tears sting my eyes as I smile over at them.

"It's a girl."

# CHAPTER TWENTY NINE

I pad barefoot across the room to the window. There is a perfect view of the valley from here. The sheet from the bed is wrapped securely around me. I don't know how long I stand here staring out into the night, memories replaying over in my mind of my time with the coven. It has been a week since Lukas and I completed the mating bond, and I had officially been sworn in as luna of the pack. To my surprise, everyone was overjoyed by our union. I now have a thread that links me to each member of Lukas's pack. I can't mindspeak with anyone yet, but I've been training with Zee and Gabe a lot.

What's bothering me now is that we have heard nothing from the coven. No one has. It seems they've gone into hiding. Just thinking about them has my blood boiling, but I can't tell anyone about the feelings of vengeance that consume me. How the need for revenge is so strong it feels like wildfire running through my veins, ready to burn all those responsible for my family's heartache. For all the loss I've endured. They wouldn't understand, couldn't understand, so I keep that part of me hidden.

Even from Lukas. I bury it deep and cover it up, plastering a mask on my face and braving the next day.

I close my eyes and the high priest's sneering face fills my mind. *You'll get what you deserve*, he spat, his eyes full of a deep-seated hatred I can't understand. His eyes blink, and I startle at the memory, unable to comprehend what I'm seeing. His pupils changed, elongating into vertical slits, a membrane sliding across his eyes from inner corner to outer corner. I shake the memory from my mind and open my eyes. That can't be right. I would have noticed that at the time, surely. It's just my mind playing tricks on me. Still, unease ripples through me.

A shooting star catches my attention and I watch as it disappears as fast as it appeared, my mind drifting to Niamh. As kids, we spent a lot of time under the stars and moon with our mother. She taught us how to harness the moon's energy, how it called to us. The secrets of the moon, how it can help heal your mind, body, and spirit. It is one of the strongest energy sources that we can absorb, and so many people don't take full advantage of that because they simply don't know how. Every birthday, we stayed outside until we saw a shooting star while performing our rituals. Then we would each make a wish. On our last birthday together, I wished I would find my place in the world. And I did, I found it. I just found it without her.

A muscular arm slides around my waist, tugging me into a warm chest. I didn't even realize he was there. So lost in my own thoughts, I didn't hear his approach. I was also blocking our connection somewhat, so he wouldn't have to endure these terrible feelings. Lukas's voice murmurs in my ear, sending his hot breath skating over my neck, sending a wave of goosebumps to prickle across my skin. "What's wrong, sweetheart? I can hear you thinking from the other side of the room."

I lean back into his embrace, tilting my head to the side as he places a soft kiss on my neck, right on my mating mark. It sends a tingle through my body. His familiar scent of sandalwood and rain encases me, giving me the strength to tell him another truth.

"She would have been twenty-nine today," I whisper so softly, as I look over the valley lit only by the moon.

Lukas's arms spasm around me, pulling away slightly so he can turn me in his arms. "It's your birthday?" Hurt coats his words.

My heart is in my throat as I nod my head, unable to voice it. Tears rim my eyes, blurring my vision, and I hold my breath in hopes it would ward off the tears. Lukas's hand comes up and cups my face, swiping under my eye as a tear escapes.

"Why didn't you tell me?"

"You would . . . I couldn't . . . You would have wanted to celebrate." I feel one, two, three more tears escape and fall down my face. *Fuck, this hurts.*

"I would have done what you wanted, Nesrin," he says, shaking his head. I could feel his sadness and disappointment through the bond, which hurts more than it should. Stabbing me in the heart probably would hurt less than this.

I reach up, rubbing at my chest. "It's the first birthday without her, Lukas." More tears spill down my face. "In two days, it will be a full year since her death. Since I lost a part of my soul. Since Astraea lost her mother," I cry, and Lukas pulls me into his warm chest, wrapping his arms tightly around me. One hand cups the back of my head, holding me tenderly but firmly, like I might break apart in his arms if he doesn't hold me together.

"I told you we were in this together, Nesrin. You don't have to face any of this alone anymore."

"I know. I'm so sorry I didn't tell you." A sob explodes from my throat as pure agony slashes at my already shredded heart.

Lukas rests his head atop mine, heaving a sigh. "I know, sweetheart." His hands run up and down my back.

"I wanted to tell you." My body heaves as I try to breathe through the tears and pain. I think about those responsible for my twin's death, sadness giving way to anger in an instant. An anger so hot and fierce it's like wildfire as it races through my blood, demanding payback.

Lukas pulls back, holding me by the shoulders, his eyes darting back and forth between mine. "What was that?" he asks, frowning.

Wiping my face, I frown, confused. "What was what?"

"I felt the change in you just then. You went from grief to anger in a heartbeat. And not just any anger, hate-filled rage."

Sighing, I rest my head on his chest. "It's nothing." I know I'll have to tell him about my need for retribution, but I'm not sure how he'll take it. His fingers grip my chin, tilting my eyes up to his. Worry twists his handsome face. The moonlight shining through the window, casting shadows over his features, make them seem sharper. He shaved off his stubble growth today, leaving the outline of his strong jaw on display.

"Nesrin, I understand you're angry and upset with the coven and the Order. What they have done is despicable. Nothing excuses it. You don't have to hide that from me, trust me. Whatever you need, I will help you get it. I love you. I will fight for you."

"I trust you," I whisper softly into the space between us.

"Then don't hide from me. I'm your mate," he whispers fervently back, pushing the hair from my face. His fingers linger in my hair, and I wilt, the weight of this curse, this responsibility, dragging me down. I know I will drown at any minute. Astraea is relying on me to end this centuries old feud with the Order of Tartarus, so she can live her life without fear of execution. There is a lost sister for me to find. And I still haven't put that damn necklace on that is supposed to help me unlock some magical power.

"I'm not okay, Lukas. I'm broken. Why would you want someone who is broken?" I choke out, the words clogging my throat.

"I know you're not okay. And I don't care if parts of you are broken or damaged. Being perfect is not what this is about. It's about being you. It's you I love." He pulls me against him again, his grip on me so fierce, as if he were protecting me from my past, like he could shield me from it.

"I love you, too," I mumble into his chest, breathing in his soothing scent, it always manages to calm me. If only I could bottle it and take it with me wherever I go.

Lukas dips his head, claiming my lips in a kiss both deep and passionate, leaving me lightheaded and breathless. Hands softly holding my face, he pulls back too soon. He rests his forehead on mine, his eyes close for a moment before they open, and I am mesmerized by the intensity in them. His eyes shine with magic. A dark, alluring, beautiful magic.

"I would do anything for you, Nesrin. You know that. Just don't hide things from me. I see you." He bends down, still holding my face, so we are eye level with each other. "I see that behind the smile your heart is hurting, that you're trying so hard not to fall apart. No matter how broken you think you are, just remember I love you more than enough to put all your broken pieces back together." Love and support pour through the bond, sealing his words, searing them to my heart and soul.

My hands lift and I run my fingers through his hair, stretching onto my tiptoes as I pull his head down to meet mine. Our lips collide in a desperate, raw, and uninhibited kiss. His tongue sweeps into my mouth and I open for him. Growling, Lukas runs his hands down my body, cupping my butt and lifting me in the air, and I wrap my legs around his waist, losing the sheet in the process, as he walks over to the bed. He leans down, placing me in the middle of the bed, and hovers over me. Tenderly, he reaches up, lightly stroking the side of my face as he trails his hand down my neck over our mating mark. I gasp at the sensations the mark causes, heat pooling in my body, filling my veins with a fiery lust.

His hand continues down between my breasts, coming back up to cup one, lightly squeezing. Lukas keeps his eyes on mine as he leans down, flicking his tongue over my hardened nipple. I gasp as he swirls his tongue around the peak and then sucks it deep into his mouth. I lift my hips, seeking contact, my hands flying to his head, pulling his hair. Lukas's eyes turn wicked, a smirk pulling at his lips.

His other hand trails up my leg from my calf, past my knee, light feathery touches reaching the apex of my thigh, swiping a thumb over my center. I arch my back, pushing into his hand, wanting more. Needing more.

"Lukas . . . " I breathe. Letting go of his head, I reach down, just able to grip his massive erection in my hand. As I run my hand slowly from root to tip, Lukas's answering groan and the thrust of his hips send desire pooling in my belly.

I moan as his fingers enter me, sliding in and out of me slowly, heat washing over me in waves. Lukas keeps going, winding me higher and higher. My legs quiver and my breathing hitches as I near the edge. I want to draw him in closer and push him away at the same time. *When I come, I want him inside of me.*

"Don't worry, sweetheart. I will be. I will be buried so deep inside you, I will enjoy every tremble, every muscle clenching around my cock."

I moan into his mouth, his words almost pushing me over that edge. I'm hardly able to move my hand over his erection, the pleasure coursing through my veins overtaking all thought. Withdrawing his fingers, Lukas's eyes burn into mine as he brings them to his mouth. My eyes widen at his boldness and then his lips claim mine and the taste of myself on his lips drives me crazy. Lukas settles between my legs, pushing them wide as he leans down, sucking on my nipple before plunging in and filling me. His mouth captures my whimper as he devours me, his thrusts starting out slow and controlled. Lukas is holding back, but I don't want him to. I want all of it. Leaning up, I bite his neck where my mark shimmers beneath his skin. With an animalistic snarl, Lukas increases his pace. Grasping my hands, he pins them above my head, causing my back to arch. Savagely, he plunges into me. The only sounds in the room are those of our bodies slapping together and groans of pleasure.

My legs tremble around his waist. "Yes," I breathe, rocking my hips into his as pressure builds. Suddenly, stars explode behind my eyes as pleasure seizes my body. I hear Lukas's groan join mine, his body going taut above mine.

"Mine," Lukas's voice is deep and gruff. Primal. Shivers rush over my skin.

"Always," I answer, my voice sounding husky.

We move so Lukas is on his back, and he drags me up, so I'm laying with my head on his chest. I idly trace my finger over the swirl of tattoos along his side. "Thank you," I murmur, snuggling deeper into his arms.

He pokes me in the side and I jolt, hearing his soft chuckle. "Are you thanking me for sex?"

"No!" I shriek, lifting my head to look into his emerald eyes. "For being you. For piecing me back together." I lay my head back down, taking comfort in the rise and fall of his chest, in his scent as it wraps around me, his steady breathing and strong arms. I feel safe and cared for, both emotionally and physically, for the first time in a long time. Lukas is quiet for so long, I think he's gone back to sleep.

Then his hand moves up, stroking my hair softly. "Happy birthday, sweetheart."

I sigh deeply, snuggling closer, and let my eyes close, falling asleep to the sound of his heartbeat.

# CHAPTER THIRTY

"I can't believe I got to see a kelpie," Zee says, blowing out a breath. "That was just . . . Wow." He runs a hand through his blonde hair. I grin over at him as we make our way back through the forest. It's a long walk back to the car, and it's getting late.

Dealing with the injured kelpie took longer than I expected, and left me feeling drained, but the excitement of seeing my first kelpie gave me a bounce in my step. The creature is a magnificent water-spirit, taking on a white silvery coat. Its mane is long and lush, dripping with water. I can definitely see how these beautiful creatures are able to lure people to their deaths.

"I know, right?" I move a branch to the side so we can get past, and Zee smirks at me, shaking his head.

"Yeah, it was cool, honey. You have some talent for being able to help all these creatures. I hate to say it, but I was more than a little terrified, but mostly in awe." He nudges me gently with his elbow as he walks past.

Zee and I have grown close this last month. He's like what I'd want an older brother to be. Zee is protective, my cheerleader, and constantly does his best to get on my nerves. I love how simple things are between us, and honestly, I would be lost without him. I open my mouth to tease him about being a scaredy cat when a sudden hush falls over the forest, everything going unnaturally still. Zee and I share a look and automatically turn to put our backs together, scanning the trees. The sun has almost set, casting everything in shadow. The forest was darkening quickly, and unlike Zee, I can't see in the dark. I do my best to keep my breathing steady and will my heart to slow down.

Two figures appear in the distance, far enough away that I can't make out any details, the shadows cast by the trees hiding them from view. Zee must notice my body stiffening because he spins around, eyes landing on the two figures. He lets loose a long, low growl, pushing me behind him.

"Nesrin, run!" he snarls.

My anger at his request is swift. "No. Not happening, Zee!" I snap. My magic hums along my skin in warning. This can't be good. I will my magic to the surface, bracing myself, ready for anything. Without warning, Zee shifts, changing into his wolf form faster than I have ever seen.

I suck in a breath, having forgotten just how big shifters are when in their wolf forms, his head level with mine, his gray coat rippling with tension. Zee's lips peel back in a viscous snarl as he takes place in front of me.

Lightning strikes nearby, causing me to jump as thunder rumbles overhead. A sense of dread drifts over me, like a soft icy breeze, sending a shudder running through me.

*Where the hell did this storm come from?*

Another bolt of lightning lights up the sky. Then, Zee is off running toward the pair before I'm able to process what's happening, his massive form covering the ground between us and them quickly. My heart races as I watch him draw nearer.

My magic wavers and blinks out as something hard hits the back of my head. I gasp, falling forward, my knees scraping the ground. My hands land in the dirt, and I clench my fists as a wave of dizziness strikes. Blinking away the pain, I reach up, touching my head. My fingers come away bloody, and I cringe at the sight. *Shit, that hurts.*

The pounding pain that radiates through my skull intensifies as I push to my feet, looking around. Has it gotten darker? I can't see Zee anymore. I can't see anyone.

*What hit me?*

"Zee," I scream, my voice coming out hoarse. Where did he go?

Up ahead, I hear snarls and growls. My first few steps are a struggle as I make my way toward the noise. A loud yelp has my heart dropping to my stomach. I pick up the pace, barreling through the underbrush.

*Zee . . .*

I push into an enormous clearing, jerking to a stop as I notice all the purple flowers. There are hundreds of them. On the far side, I see an enormous wolf struggling to get to his feet. Blood coats his gray fur from multiple wounds. Zee freezes when he notices me, his eyes full of pain. He's in awful shape. My healing magic pushes to the surface in response to the severity of his injuries. *What the hell happened?*

"Zee," I whisper, then I started running over to him. A loud roar shakes the trees and lightning hits the ground somewhere close by. I skid to a stop, paralyzed with fear, as a dark shape falls from the trees behind Zee. Landing on its hind legs with a grace I wouldn't have expected, its large front talons dig into the earth as they settle. Massive leathery wings sweep wide before tucking in at its side. Stretching its neck forward, it lets out a roar of fury. The long tail whips back and forth in agitation.

I can't believe my eyes. My mouth drops open in surprised shock and terror. It is a dragon.

A fucking *dragon* in Portland. I can't stop the scream that comes from my throat as it moves toward Zee. Letting go of my magic, I reach out my arms, and within an instant, it surrounds Zee, encasing him in a protective bubble. I add an extra layer, so nothing—not even a fucking dragon—can get to him.

The dragon slams into the shield with such force it shakes the ground. Roaring in fury at not being able to reach Zee, it begins clawing with all its might at the shield. Sparks of magic flare from the shield, burning the dragon, but it keeps up its attack, undeterred.

Zee spins to me, realizing what I've done.

*'Run, run now, Nesrin.'* His voice echoes in my head.

I stand here, shocked, for half a second. We have never been able to mindspeak before, as much as we've tried over the last few weeks. I just couldn't do it.

*'Nesrin, please run.'*

Anger and frustration rush to the surface, but my fear for Zee is overwhelming. I shake my head vehemently. *'Zee.'*

Zee's wolf seems to stand taller as he stares back at me. *'I will be fine. You need to go.'* His request is gentle, as if trying to convince a child it would all be okay.

But I am having none of that. I will not leave him. He knows deep down I would never leave him behind. That isn't who I am. I just need a plan. Taking a step back, I move to edge my way around under the cover of the trees. Stumbling on a branch, I falter a step before gaining my balance. My head snaps up as I freeze in place. Startling golden eyes stare back at me. It tilts its head in a slow, predatory way, sizing me up. I try to swallow over the fear clogging my throat.

The creature is truly impressive. If I wasn't so terrified, I would take the time to memorize every detail, but right now it is staring right at me, its remarkable size roughly that of a school bus from nose to tip of the tail, which is whipping back and forth in agitation. Its front legs push off the shield that surrounds Zee and land gracefully on the ground.

The leathery scaled body shimmers, but from here I'm unable to fully make out the colors. Spikes run down the length of its back, starting from the top of its head and ending at the tips of its tail. They look to be joined or webbed, like a wave down its back. The webbed spikes around the head flare as it watches me. I wonder what it's thinking. I have next to no knowledge of dragons. None have been seen in centuries, and most think them to be extinct or in a deep slumber.

The dragon steps away from Zee toward me. Swearing under my breath, I call forth my light. I wonder if it now recognizes me as an easier game. From what I *have* learned about dragons, they are incredibly intelligent, ruthless creatures. Its massive wings unfold, spreading wide, it launches into the air and takes flight, the wings blocking out the sky as it flies toward me. I can just make out Zee's snarls and growls over the blood rushing in my ears. I dive under the claws that are outstretched and hit the ground hard, rolling back to my feet, spinning around as not to lose sight of the dragon.

I stand speechless, watching it. The creature is as beautiful and utterly terrifying up close, as it is far away. I can make out the color of its scales now. They are a shimmering kaleidoscope of blues, purples, and greens, but it's the giant iron cuff around its clawed back leg that draws my attention. I squint, the cuff looking awfully familiar, like the one that was stuck around my wrist for a week.

I glance around, looking for the two figures that we saw earlier, now positive this dragon isn't alone. I notice Zee scratching at my shield, trying to get out, but I need him safe. His eyes meet mine, frantic.

*'Nesrin, let me out now.'*

I shake my head at him. As bad as I feel, I will not lose Zee. He's like a brother to me.

Twisting around in a slow circle, I try to see where the dragon went, and barely have time to dive to the side as it swoops down for me. Wind from its massive wings blowing my hair over my face, pain shoots through my hands on impact as dirt and rocks dig into my skin. Raising on my hands, I curse myself. I need to keep my head in the game. Glancing up, I roll over just as it swoops down again, claws outstretched. I lift my arm to cover my face and a shield bursts to life in the space between us. The dragon pulls back when it meets resistance. My pulse thunders in my ears as I watch the dragon fly overhead.

My breathing is labored, mostly from the adrenaline pumping through my body. Climbing back up to my feet, I glance up, my eyes connecting with shimmering golden ones. The dragon gives a short huff before it dives for me again. This time, I feint left and then dive right, blasting the creature's underbelly with a defensive spell. The roar that follows shakes the ground, making me stumble as the creature spins quicker than I thought possible, blowing a heavy, misty fog around me.

Shit. I can't see a thing. I turn in a slow circle, trying to hear over the ringing in my ears and my pounding heartbeat. Zee's howl cuts through the air, making my heart trip over itself. The mist makes it hard for me to see a foot in front of me, so it's not a shock I don't see the dragon lunge for me again, until it's too late. I grit my teeth and lurch to the side, throwing out a ball of light meant to shock the dragon, only not quick enough. Its claws rip into my thigh, tearing clothes, skin, and muscle. I scream in agony as I fall, looking down at my leg as the pain takes over my body.

My scream tapers off, and I'm left dragging in deep breaths through clenched teeth, warm blood flowing quickly down my leg. Zee's snarl draws my attention and I look up, my vision blurred with tears. A warmth rushes over me, filling my entire body, a burst of love being sent down the mating bond. *'We're coming, sweetheart. Hold on!'*

*Lukas!* He's close. I blink away the tears, noticing that the mist is gone. My eyes move over to Zee. He slams his body against the barrier over and over, and I know he, too, can sense his pack getting nearer. His agitation is clear as the shield around him wavers slightly from my weakened state.

The ground shakes as the dragon comes to land in front of me, drawing my attention back to it. I blink several times, trying to clear the haze that has taken over my vision. Two figures step out from the trees and come to stand next to the dragon.

*These bitches. I want to tear them to shreds!!*

*'Let me out and I will gladly do it for you,'* Zee replies to my thought, and I gasp at the ferocity thundering in his voice. I reach down and try to stop the bleeding. The warm flow of blood oozes through my fingers, nausea churning my stomach.

"The last of the infamous red cloaks. I'm disappointed you weren't much of a challenge. I thought wolf's blood ran through your veins?" sneers the older witch. The younger witch takes a step forward. She looks a lot like Marcus, and I wonder if she's a family member. Where hatred shines in the older witch's steel-gray eyes, only sympathy looks back at her from the younger witch.

My expression is blank. I don't want her sympathy. I am proud of my bloodline and there is no way I'd give away Astraea or Leila. They will get nothing from me. As far as they're concerned, I am the last one left.

"Nothing to say?" she continues, annoyed I haven't taken the bait. The dragon's eyes burn into mine as I look past them to the elven cuff around its ankle and wonder how long they've had it trapped, kept prisoner for them to use. I slowly move one of my hands from my wounded leg and feel for the metal disc in my jeans pocket. When my finger brushes along its outline, I sigh, relief rushing through me.

The younger female version of Marcus finally speaks, "You're bleeding a lot. We should go now." It comes out clipped, annoyed, but the concern in her eyes can't be hidden.

A snarl rumbles up my throat. "I'm not going anywhere."

Zee's echoing snarl fills the air in agreement. The older witch throws her head back and laughs. The sound grates on my nerves, making me wince. "You don't have much of a choice," she says with a pointed look at my mangled leg.

*'Freckles, you with me? Nesrin?'* Lukas's voice fills my head, concern so wild and intense fills the link, verging on panic.

"You are in no shape to fight us, Nesrin," the other says, the wind around us picking up. So, she's the witch responsible for the weather changes. Her eyes seem to say, be smart about this. I wonder if she's the one who helped guide me from the mansion when I escaped.

I keep my voice as steady as I can, doing my best to block out the painful throbbing in my leg. "I won't go with you," I repeat.

The older witch's gray eyes harden. "We know that mate of yours is on his way. Stalling will only kill him and the others loyal to him." My heart rate picks up at those words, but I keep my face blank.

"If you don't come willingly, the dragon will rip the pack to shreds. In your condition, you cannot shield them all for long," the younger witch says, lightning cracking at her words, making me flinch.

"It will be a massacre. Is that what you want? To watch them all die trying to save you?" By the sly look on her face, she realizes she has me.

I know I don't have a choice. I would gladly sacrifice myself to save the pack. They are my family. A family I didn't realize I needed. They would take care of Astraea. She would have Lukas, Zee, Finan, and Kate. The witches still have no idea Astraea is a hybrid. I wonder if they even know about legacies. I am drowning in so many emotions and so much pain, I can barely focus. If I am to make a deal, it needs to be now. The gashes in my thigh are deep. I have to finish this fast before I lose consciousness.

Clearing my throat, I stare up at them. "If I leave with you willingly, I have your word no harm will come to the pack?" I ask, looking at the younger witch.

*'Nesrin! No!'* Zee snarls, his wolf form pacing the shield in frustration. *'You are ours, and we will protect you. It's an honor to protect our luna.'*

I block out his words and the anguish they bring.

"You have our word. If you come and face your end, we will leave the pack alone," the younger witch replies. Relief flows through me, but I need more.

"I want the sealed promise, a magical contract," I demand, raising my bloody hand toward them, not able to hide the tremor.

The older witch sneers at me, "You just wish to waste time."

I can still hear Zee snarling and barking at me, his body banging against the shield. I know he won't give up, just as I know that it will only get him killed. No. I will not let that happen. Looking over at him, I see him shift into his human form, his body shaking in rage. Blood runs down his body as he limps back and forth, watching me with a fierce look in his eyes. Air catches in my throat as I stare at him, and my shield flickers again. I have to complete this before Zee realizes my magic is failing.

"No. I don't. But I need assurances." My consciousness is wavering as I look at the two witches. My body is growing heavy. I need this done now. Black spots are dancing across my vision, threatening to drag me into oblivion. The young witch steps forward quickly, pulling a small dagger out from her robe and cutting her palm. I sigh in relief as she grabs my hand and we both say our parts, the promise sealed. I make sure it is an unbreakable promise that no member of the pack will be targeted, hunted, or killed by any witch, coven, or order with ill intent. The witch's eyes find mine, and I can see that she knows I'm taking this too far, being too specific with my wording, but she says nothing, only nodding, sealing the promise with blood and magic.

*'Nesrin, hold on. We're almost there. Don't you give up, you hear me!'* Lukas's voice echoes in my mind with desperation. Tears well in my eyes, making them burn. He'll be too late. I turn to Zee, our eyes connecting. He sees what I'm planning. Shaking his head, he starts banging against the shield with both fists.

"Nesrin, don't you dare!" he bellows, fury lining his eyes as tears fall down my face.

*'You fight, you hear me? They are almost here,'* he said into my mind. My whole body shakes violently, but I manage to lift my hand to my mouth, blowing him a kiss.

*'It's okay, Zee. I have to do this. It's the only way. I'm not afraid. Take care of them for me. I love you, Zee. You are the brother I never had, but always wished I did.'*

His bellow of outrage sends a crack through my heart.

*'I have to do this.'*

"No. Don't even fucking think about it, Nesrin. You will not die as some sacrifice!"

Closing my eyes against the pain, I turn my thoughts inward, to Lukas, finding that link between us.

*'Lukas, I need you to listen to me. There was no other way. I'm so sorry. I know I promised you forever, but I have to break that promise. The witches have made a deal with me. They can't hurt the pack, including Astra. I made sure of it. I want you to know I love you so much. I am so grateful fate brought us together. Take care of our bright star. Give her a kiss and hug from me, and tell her I'm sorry. I'm so, so sorry.'* I choke on a sob, my chest heaving. Goddess, this hurts physically and emotionally. It feels as if I'm being torn in half.

The sudden disbelief and violent fury that shoots through the bond is suffocating. His anger and fear presses in from all sides as if he knows I'm giving up. My skin prickles with all his emotions, and I have to do the next thing, or I'll never survive.

'*Nesrin—*'

I quickly shut off the link, blocking out his voice, his emotions. I can't bear hearing him plead with me, because I know if I did I would give in, and I won't be that selfish. I won't risk the pack. Looking back at the witches, I give them a nod, ready. The older witch's lips twist into a knowing smile, which sends alarm bells racing through my head. The dragon moves on a silent command, stepping forward, its claws wrapping around me surprisingly gentle as it lifts me off the ground. My leg throbs, sending hot burning pain through my body, blood gushing from the wound. I can't suppress the scream that is ripped from my throat as blackness swarms my vision.

I feel the moment my shield around Zee drops. His savage howl fills the air, stabbing at my already bleeding heart. But the dragon is airborne in seconds. I manage to turn my head, looking down at Zee. He is on the closest witch, the old one, a moment later, ripping into her flesh, tearing into her neck so fast and lethally I am stunned by the brutality of it. Lucky for her, the younger witch has already disappeared, taking the storm with her. Zee howls again, this time full of sorrow and regret as he tries to follow, but is slowed down by his injuries.

A wave of darkness sweeps over me, making me sag in the dragon's grasp. Blinking, I look up, seeing the stars twinkling in the darkened sky. A huffing sound draws my attention to the dragon who's bending its head to look at me, massive golden eyes burning with what looks like concern. Its eyes flash to my leg and it lets out a sound of distress, like seeing me injured upsets it. Confusion rolls through me. Why would this beast be concerned about me? Dizziness swamps me and blackness closes in on my vision, my body going limp in the dragon's sharp talons.

# CHAPTER THIRTY ONE

# Lukas

I walk in the back door of the house, spotting Astraea first. She is sitting at the kitchen table with Kate, crayons scattered everywhere, coloring in her new book. Walking over to her, I lean down and give her a kiss on the head, mumbling in her hair, "Hi, my little star."

Looking up at me, she sends me a bright smile that catches my breath. This kid could capture the heart of even the most hardened man. I would do anything for her, and my mate, I adore them both. Finan turns from the stove and whatever he is cooking smells great. I look around for Zee and Nesrin. Frowning, I turn back to Finan. "Zee and Nesrin aren't back yet?"

Finan looks at me, shaking his head, "I haven't heard from them." Moving to the fridge, he grabs two beers, passing one to me. I give him a nod in thanks. They should be back soon. I can't wait to wrap my arms around Nesrin, to take in her unique scent of rose, jasmine, and lily, with a hint of coffee. There is nothing else like it. And a whole day apart has me on edge. I can feel an ominous energy in the air. Taking a long swig of my beer, I turn, leaning against the counter. I watch Astra and Kate and look around for the sprite. Weird, she isn't here. I wonder if she finally got sick of hanging with the wolves.

Terror, panic, and pain blasts my body through the mating bond, making me stumble. It happens so quickly I don't have time to prepare myself for the onslaught. The beer falls from my hands, smashing to the floor as I struggle for breath, the feelings and emotions swamping me, taking over all my senses. I can hear Kate and Finan yelling at me, but can't make out the words over the blood rushing in my ears. I'm having trouble controlling the fury burning through my veins at the thought of someone hurting my mate. *Where are they?*

My body is trembling with barely restrained rage, but finding my voice, I growl, "Nesrin. She's in trouble. We need to find her. Now!"

Finan looks stunned for a moment, then he's moving for the door. Kate jumps up to follow her brother, but I need her here with Astraea.

"Stop!" I roar into the room, the windows shaking. Finan casts a quick look at me, but I shake my head.

Not wasting another moment, he bursts out the door, getting out his phone and barking orders into it. Astraea's wide eyes are fixed on me.

*'Mommy?'* she echoes in my head. I stalk over to her and lift her into my arms, squeezing her tight.

Dropping a kiss on her forehead, I murmur. "I'll be back." Before I pass her over to Kate, whose eyes mirror the panic in Astraea's.

I point at her. "Don't leave the house. Protect her with your life," I order, fury making my words harsh and clipped.

On my way out the door, I pull my phone out of my pocket and call Merve. I have already sent orders to the pack to get ready to head out, my muscles rippling under my skin, readying for the shift. Merve picks up on the second ring. "Hello, Lukas. What–"

Wasting no time, I cut him off, barking, "Nesrin's in trouble. Get to the house," before hanging up. Kate can fill him in when he gets here. My mate needs me.

Shifting into my wolf, I launch into a run, my bond guiding me toward my mate. Finan's white wolf joins me to my left. Along with Roan's red wolf, Gabe's fox, Asena's lynx, and a dozen others. It's time to find my mate and beta.

Nesrin's emotions are barreling through the bond, making me frantic. I put on a burst of speed as I try again to get through to Zee. The link with my beta is muffled. This has never happened before and it's making me even more nervous. But at least I know he is alive. Suddenly, excruciating pain radiates down the bond. It increases tenfold and my steps falter. Finan is there at my side, keeping me steady, urging me on. I'm grateful for his presence. His loyalty to Nesrin has been unfaltering. My mind is trying to process Nesrin's pain. She has been hurt . . . badly. Focusing on the link, I send my strength, unconditional love, and support down the bond to her, believing like hell it will help her, at least until I can get there.

*"We're coming, sweetheart. Hold on."* I can feel her desperation bleeding down the bond, as well as defiance and misery. We have to be getting close now. My heart thumps wildly in my chest, my vision laser focused on my surroundings as I run faster than I ever have toward my life, my universe.

I reach out for Zee again, tugging on that thread that links him to me. I can sense him now, and he is injured badly. His fury and pain mingle, rippling down the pack bond. I howl as loud as I can. *'Zee?'*

Zee's voice finally fills my head. *'Lukas, they are going to take her. I can't. I can't stop them.'*

*Shit.*

*'Freckles, you with me? Nesrin?'* I demand, needing her to answer me. I know she must be able to hear me because I can sense her down the bond, her pain, her fear, her acceptance. A snarl works its way up my throat, a feral need so wild and intense fills my body. My mate needs me, and I am going to fucking destroy those responsible for hurting her.

*'Nesrin, hold on. We're almost there. Don't you give up. You hear me?'*

For the first time tonight, Nesrin's sweet voice fills my mind. *'Lukas, I need you to listen to me. There was no other way. I'm so sorry. I know I promised you forever, but I have to break that promise. The witches have made a deal with me. They can't hurt the pack, including Astra. I made sure of it. I want you to know I love you so much. I am so grateful fate brought us together. Take care of our bright star. Give her a kiss and hug from me and tell her I'm sorry. I'm so, so sorry.'*

My heart goes wild. She has given up. Does she think we won't make it? *'Nesrin—'* The connection goes silent. Like she's blocked the bond somehow. I didn't even realize that was possible. Raising my head, I howl my anguish to the sky, my pack following, their cries carrying on the wind. Terror seizes my heart in its deathly grip, ripping it from my chest and tossing it aside.

Suddenly, Zee's howl sounds from further ahead. We are so close. I answer with my own, letting them know we're here. We burst into a large clearing. I spot Zee limping in the opposite direction, head tilted up at the sky, another howl ripping from his throat. Keeping my pace, I pass a bloody lump on the ground, a witch by the looks of what remains. Zee left little of her to identify. I reach him, following his line of sight. Shock and fear quake through my body as I see an enormous creature—a fucking dragon—flying away with my mate in its claws. I start after them, but there isn't a damn thing I can do about it. My heart feels as if it's being torn from my chest.

# CHAPTER THIRTY TWO

I wake up on a cold, hard stone floor, lying on my stomach like I've been dragged in here and dumped. Keeping as quiet as possible, I take stock of my body. Everything aches fiercely. My leg is throbbing and tender, but it's the hollow space in my chest that hurts the most, and that was my own doing. The emptiness from blocking my bond with Lukas hurts. That chasm echoes pain and loneliness. I'm not sure what exactly they have in store for me, and I will not allow him to feel my pain. He won't suffer with me. I refuse to put him through that.*'That's all I ask of you, daughter of light,'* she replies, bowing to me.

Blinking a few times to clear my vision, I lift my head, listening for any noise, any indication that I'm not alone. I hear a scraping noise like a chain being dragged across the stone floor and tilt my head back further, trying to get a look behind me. I slap my hand over my mouth to muffle the scream that builds in my throat. A soft whimper escapes me, and I try to control my building panic. My heart is racing, and I can feel adrenaline flooding my system, causing my body to tremble uncontrollably. I shuffle around slightly to get a better glimpse of the dragon on the other side of the dungeon, and that's what I'm in, a dungeon.

Stone walls rise around me, the ceiling high and arched—it would have to be to house a dragon. There are no windows or bars, just a large double wooden door to my right. Shuffling, I attempt to move, but a blinding pain radiates from my leg. I gasp, pulling in a sharp breath, then letting it out slowly. I can feel the bandages around my thigh. They patched me up, but made no attempt to heal the wound. Assholes.

Moving my hand away from my mouth, my eye catches on the metal around my wrist. They've put another elven cuff on me. My heart leaps with hope as I lean to the side so I can reach into the back pocket of my torn jeans. Smiling, I pull out the small circular disc. *Idiots forgot to check my pockets.*

I wave it over the cuff, and it falls uselessly to the ground. At the clang of metal on the stone floor, my eyes snap up. Only, I can no longer see where the dragon is. Pushing up onto my hands and knees, I ignore the searing pain moving through my thigh. Then I feel it. I close my eyes in relief as my magic moves through me. It instantly starts warming my body as it gently creeps back in, like sinking into a warm bath. I groan, opening my eyes. Looking down at my hands, I wiggle my fingers and smile. I already feel better just having my magic back. It almost seems like it's wrapping me up in a protective embrace.

The sensation of being watched prickles the back of my neck and I slowly lift my head. A pair of golden eyes glow as they watch me from the darkened corner of the dungeon. We stare for what seems like an eternity, my heart thumping frantically before the dragon blinks those enormous eyes.

*'How is your leg?'* a feminine voice asks in my mind. I fall back on my butt, my eyes wide as I stare at the majestic creature. It takes a few steps forward out of the dark, golden eyes burning into mine. I feel the heat from those eyes like a physical touch.

I find it hard to swallow, my throat tight. "Did– Did you just speak to me?" I squeak out loud.

The dragon bows its head slightly, letting out a huff that sounds an awful lot like a laugh.

*'Yes, daughter of light. I can speak with you.'* The dragon's voice is regal and enchanting, nothing like what I would have expected at all. I'm totally speechless. I realize after a moment that my eyes are wide and my mouth is hanging open, but I can think of nothing to say.

Taking pity on me, the dragon lies down, stretching her long body out, her tail sweeping across the floor to rest at her side. *'Your leg, how is it?'* she asks again.

I blink several times, as if I'm coming out of a trance. "Oh, um . . ."

I look down at the blood-soaked bandage and frown, moving my leg carefully to find there is no pain anymore. "What on earth?" I mutter as I reach for the bandage, unwinding it. No surprise, my jeans are ruined. Also, I will probably have a nasty scar, but that's the least of my problems right now. The last of the bandage falls away and I gasp, reaching for my leg, running my fingers over where the wound should be. There is nothing there but three faint pink lines marring my thigh.

"How?" I whisper to myself, confusion jumbling my thoughts. I've never healed this quickly before. I peer up at the dragon, who is regarding me with open curiosity. Those large golden eyes give one slow blink, and I squirm under the intense gaze.

*'Once your magic was restored, it began healing you. It seems your powers are developing, even without the key to unlock them fully.'*

My voice was barely above a whisper, my mind whirling. "I've never healed myself before," I say mostly to myself. I was so focused on the dragon before, I didn't even realize that I've healed myself. My gaze shoots to hers. "What do you mean my powers are developing? What key?"

*'The necklace Althaea and Hecate made. It will unlock the magic that is still dormant inside of you.'*

The necklace. I completely forgot about it. I haven't even taken it from my suitcase yet, knowing that once I accept my fate and put it on, things would change. That's something I'm not prepared for. Not yet.

I lock eyes with the dragon. She really is magnificent. "What's your name?" I blurt, my cheeks heating at my abruptness.

She swishes her tail and huffs again. Which I'm now ninety percent sure is her way of laughing at me. *'My name is Kaida.'*

Kaida looks at me. Her golden reptilian eyes blink long and slow, a second eyelid sliding across her eye from the outer corner. The way she's staring at me is creeping me out, and though I try not to fidget under her intense gaze, it's still unnerving.

*'And to answer your other question, Nesrin, you are a legacy. A descendant of a goddess. Your powers are bound to grow, are they not?'*

I mean, my mother told me we're legacies. That I will most likely develop powers and gifts beyond what I have now.

*'You are from Leopold's and Blanchette's bloodlines. Together, they created something new, a generation of hybrids. Also, there's your father.'*

How does she know all of this? Wait . . . my father? Before I can ask either of those questions, she continues.

*'Althaea has gifted you with her powers. The gifts your parents had sealed at birth to keep you safe and hidden. The time has come to unlock them. Althaea, as you know, is a goddess of light. You are light and hope to all those around you, those who wish for change.'*

Disbelief and confusion roll through me, making me feel sick. I rub my hand over my forehead as my mind runs over everything that has happened.

*'You know what I say is true. You've known for a long time there was more to your gifts. That the magic inside of you was different.'*

I avert my gaze. She's right. I've known for a long time that I'm different, that my magic is different. There's something locked away, something just out of reach. Something I've never been sure I want.

*'The goddess fell into despair and disappeared after her daughter was killed and her granddaughter lost. Althaea swore revenge on those responsible and declared an heir would be granted her gifts to seek justice. Only, it was up to the Fates to decide who this heir would be. That is one of the reasons why your family is still being hunted. They have been waiting for the heir to reappear.'*

"Why couldn't she seek justice? Why me?"

*'The gods cannot act against each other. That is why you were chosen. The Fates have forbidden any interference from the gods.'*

I blink several times, letting that sink in. "I don't understand."

Kaida's large reptilian eyes flash, sending a shiver down my spine. Her massive tail swings back and forth with impatience.

*'Your birth awoke her. She sensed you and the magic you hold deep within your core. When Althaea and Hecate helped Blanchette escape Olympus, she was running from someone. That place is full of lies and deceit, and only the strong survive. Blanchette was too kind to live that life. Jealousy and envy started this whole mess. You see, Blanchette*

*didn't just capture the eye of some mage. No, before she chose her path in the mortal world, she also caught the eye of a god. One who doesn't enjoy being refused. One who thinks they should get anything they want, no matter the cost to those around them. One so merciless that she had no choice but to run. One her mother wanted her far away from, so she and Hecate plotted to get her daughter out of Greece.'*

I'm about to ask who this god was and how she knew so much about my family history, so much about Althaea, when the doors to our stone dungeon burst open. My head swivels that way as six large men walk in, each dressed for combat, guns strapped to their chests. They take up place at either side of the door. The high priest, Marcus's father, walks in, an air of arrogance surrounding him.

Anger bubbles up inside of me at the sight of him. I wonder if this is all the protection he has. It's unlikely. He probably has more people inside and outside the grounds. I have to assume there are more armed guards and coven members here. I take in the guards. Though they didn't seem to be magical, I could be wrong. It can be hard to tell. Could he have hired these men? Could they be human? These are the things I need to know if I'm going to make it out of here, which I am. Because if I stay, I will die, and I'm not ready for that. Even though I said goodbye, I haven't given up hope just yet.

The priest's black, soulless eyes search back and forth between Kaida and me. "Enjoying yourself?" his patronizing voice says, grating against my ears. I clench my jaw, keeping my gaze averted, and notice the young witch from earlier trailing a few feet behind him. Her gaze is pointed at the floor as she shuffles nervously on her feet, like this is the last place she wants to be. I can sense her distrust and unease from here.

"I see you've met my dragon. Beautiful, isn't she? Too bad about the other. He was fearsome. Truly something to behold."

Disgust and fury are vying for first place inside me. I do my best to push my magic down. I can't let them notice I've taken off my cuff. Not enjoying being ignored, the high priest storms over to me, gripping my chin painfully as he turns my face toward him. I glare daggers at him as he puts his face in mine. "You think you can look at me like that? Like you're better than me?" he spits.

I tear my face from his grip and lean forward. "I know I'm better than you," I seethe. The sting to my face is sudden and unexpected. I never even saw him move. My cheek burns, but I refuse to touch it. I will not give him the satisfaction of getting a reaction from me. I just continue to glare back at him, clenching my jaw shut to keep from saying something else.

"You're still looking at me like you're better than me."

"How am I responsible for what my face does when you are around me? That sounds like a you problem!" I snarl back.

His eyes flare in shock and then fury as another hit lands on my face. I lift my head, tasting blood. Gathering it in my mouth, I spit it at his feet and grin up at him, knowing my eyes have a crazed, feral look. I take a deep breath, reining in my emotions. If I let my temper get the better of me, it won't do me any favors. I need to stay calm and clear-headed if I want to have any chance of getting out of here alive.

My mind goes to Lukas and, not for the first time, I wonder how he's doing, if he's okay. I want so badly to rip the lid off the block I've put on our bond, to open that link up, but I can't, not yet. The young witch clears her throat, ending my stare off with the high priest. Straightening, he takes a step back.

"You're a hard woman to kill, Ms. Carson. If I wasn't aware of your crimes, I would think the gods were on your side." His face has gone blank, but I can see the hatred burning in his eyes. Still, I cannot fully understand it. I have done nothing to this man.

"Seems maybe you *should* think they are." I shrug, making sure to keep my wrist hidden. Keeping my magic contained is difficult though, as it's always reacted instinctively to danger.

*'Don't give them anything, Nesrin. Be smart.'* Kaida's voice echoes through my head, and I try not to outwardly react.

"Thanks to our new ally, we were able to ambush you. You should thank him, because we were going to storm your house if we failed."

I don't utter a word, as he lets those words sink in. Movement by the door catches my attention. Rolling my shoulders back, I let my eyes move from the high priest to take in the figure standing there, hands in his pockets. I do my best not to let the shock show on my face as I glare at Ryan.

"Why?" I seethe, pity for this man like acid in my stomach.

"You've bewitched my alpha. I had to do something," he snaps back.

"So, you joined the coven? The people you hate so much?"

"No. I just gave them the information they needed to get you. To keep my pack safe, I did what the others wouldn't."

I want to wipe that sneer off his smug face. So many emotions are blazing through me. I can't believe one of the pack would do this. Betray Lukas and me, especially Lukas, after all he has done for them. Sweat beads my forehead at the effort it takes to contain my magic. It wants nothing more than to lash out at those around me right now.

"Enough chit chat," the high priest says, cutting off my thoughts. "My niece, Claudia, told me of your deal. I don't approve, but what's done is done. It's only you I wanted, anyway. You will be executed at midnight tonight. Watching you burn will be so sweet," he gloats.

My stomach drops as my pulse kicks up. So soon. I thought they would have their fun with me again, giving me a chance to come up with an escape. I glance at the young witch—Claudia. Her dark gaze is on her uncle. Not only does she not seem thrilled to be here, she actually looks at him with disgust. Good.

"I won't give you the chance to escape again, so you will stay here with my dragon under guard until it's time."

He speaks as if we were talking about some bad weather, not my murder. I bite down on the inside of my cheek to stop myself from speaking. What's the point? The metallic coppery taste of my blood spreads throughout my mouth.

The high priest raises an eyebrow mockingly. "Nothing to say. No? Maybe you will think of some ultimate last words when the witching hour is upon us."

With that, the high priest and his entourage turn and leave. Claudia turns to follow but glances back at me, a sadness in her eyes. When the doors shut, my whole body sags. I stumble to the wall and slide down, landing softly, pulling my knees to my chest. This is it. I'm going to die tonight if I can't come up with a plan. I'm not ready to die, I only just found Lukas, and I have Astraea. She has a whole life ahead of her, one I would miss out on.

My stomach clenches and my chest caves in. I'm on an emotional rollercoaster, one I can't get off. My eyes burn as they fill with tears, blinking rapidly as they fall down my face. Tipping my head back against the cold stone wall, I close my eyes, taking deep breaths. Crying won't fix this. I need a plan.

Kaida moves closer and lies in front of me. *'What are you thinking about?'* Her voice is gentle, almost soothing.

I force a small smile. "Nothing. Tell me about how you came to be here."

*'My mate and I were captured many centuries ago. The council had found us sleeping dormant in a cave in the Swiss Alps. While we slept, they put us in Elven chains and under an enchantment. Ever since, we have been slaves. We have no power to defend ourselves and no freedom, bound and chained in all ways.'*

"Where is your mate now?"

*'When we thought we might become parents, my mate Tarien died trying to free us. He refused to rest until our baby was free.'*

"That's the reason he died, to get you and your baby out?"

Kaida nods her massive head, looking away, her bright golden eyes alight with a mixture of sadness and hatred. I slowly stand and make my way over to her, reaching my hand out.

"May I?" I ask, and her head swings back to stare at me. I know she won't hurt me now, not unless they make her.

She bends her head down in silent consent, and I move closer, running my hand over her head, then lean forward, resting my forehead against hers. Holding onto her surprisingly soft scales, I hug her, my heart bleeding for this poor, magnificent creature that has lost so much.

"I'm so sorry for everything you have suffered at the hands of these monsters, Kaida," I murmur before pulling back, keeping my hand on her. Her eyes are closed, and when she opens them, I'm shocked by the tenderness in them.

*'They tried to break me. They nearly succeeded. They thought they broke my spirit, but they were wrong. My spirit is strong, and I have more than that. I have claws, wings, and magic. And something worth fighting for.'* She growls fervently, and the words resonate deeply with me.

Reaching into my pocket, I pull out the disk as I move to her hind leg and wave it over her cuff. It clangs uselessly to the ground, along with the chain attached to it. Kaida rises to her full height as I pocket the disk. I run my eyes over her and sense more than see the enchantment. I cast my magic out, and it covers her body completely. Then, there's a flash of light. When the light dies down a moment later, I see flecks of the enchantment that was keeping her a servant to the council floating broken in the air around us.

Kaida shakes her body as if to shake off cobwebs, her wings spreading wide and her shimmering scales flaring in ripples of metallic shades of green, blue, and purple. There is a glow beneath her scales that wasn't there before. This is the power of the dragon. A free dragon.

*'Thank you, daughter of light.'*

Something inside of me clicks into place at those words, a rightness.

*'Tell me of your mate.'*

I smile, picturing Lukas. The sparkle in his emerald eyes as he looks down at me. The way his dark hair falls over his face, the sense of belonging I get when I'm around him.

"Lukas, he is like no one else in the world. When I'm with him, it's like we are two halves made whole. He is sweet, strong, and he accepted me and all this mess that comes with having me as a mate. I would do anything for him, sacrifice anything for those I love." Goddess, I miss him so much. My heart physically aches. I love that man with every fiber of my being.

*'Which is why you're here.'* It's a statement, not a question, but I nod anyway. I walk back over to the stone wall and rest my back against it, sliding down until I'm seated again. I miss his warmth, his smiles. He is by far the best hugger I've met. The way he holds me was like he's afraid I'll be taken away from him at any moment. Guilt churns in my stomach. I know he must be going crazy right now, blaming himself, and want nothing more than to open the bond back up and connect with him. But I can't bring myself to do it. Until I am free, I can't risk it. I will protect Astraea and Lukas at any cost, so if it has to end with me dying, so be it.

I hope Zee doesn't blame himself, but deep down I know he will. I've made a royal mess of everything. What am I going to do?

I didn't realize I spoke out loud until Kaida replies, *'You're going to fight like hell until you can't fight anymore. That's what you're going to do.'*

My head snaps up and I stare at her. "I will, but I need to figure a way out of here first."

*'I will help you escape, but I need you to do something for me.'*

"Anything," I swear.

Turning back to the darkened corner, she disappears into the shadows. Nerves take flight and my stomach tumbles a bit, and I rest my head on my legs, trying to calm my racing thoughts. Whatever she wants of me, I will do it. She has suffered so much already. I hear Kaida coming back and lift my head, my eyes going straight to her front talons, where she holds a turquoise egg about the size of a football, and I slowly stand on shaky legs.

She holds the egg out to me and I hesitate before reaching out, taking the brightly colored egg gently in my hands. It's heavy for its size.

"This is your baby?" I whisper in awe. I assumed the baby dragonling died along with her mate. Running my hand over it in a soft caress, I look up at Kaida, her golden eyes observing me closely.

*'This is my dragonling. I will help you escape, but I want you to take him with you and watch over him. Give him shelter and protection. He must not live the life I have. I will not see him enslaved by these monsters. I entrust you with my kin, Nesrin Carson.'*

My mouth goes dry. I remain silent for a moment, in shock, thinking I've surely heard her wrong. "Why can't we all go? Escape together?"

*'The council will hunt me down. They will not stop until I'm back under their control. But they don't know about him, and I want to keep it that way. I will hold them off while you escape.'*

A bolt of panic hits me, causing my body to lock up. My mouth opens, then closes. What am I supposed to say? I don't like this plan. Deep down, I know Kaida won't go back under their control, which means she isn't planning on coming out alive. I study the egg in my hands and whisper, "Promise me, if there is a chance for you to escape, you'll take it."

*'I can't make that promise. I don't plan to survive,'* she says, voicing what I feared. *'You are stronger than you think, Nesrin. Others follow you because you are brave and loyal, you protect them, you respect them. You give them something to fight for.'* Her voice is strong and final.

She's standing so close now, waiting until I look into her eyes before she speaks again. *'You do what you have to do to survive and keep those important to you safe. That is what I'm doing. That's what you must do.'*

Tears well in my eyes. I don't want to leave her behind, but realize this is my best chance at escape, so I clear my throat, trying to get rid of the lump lodged there. "Okay . . . Okay, I'll get your baby out of here. I promise to always protect him. He will be part of my family. This I swear." I raise my fist over my heart.

# CHAPTER THIRTY THREE

The dungeon door swings open, startling me, and my body goes tense, fighting to keep my breathing under control. I grip Kaida's egg tighter, concealing it as I turn my head to see who's there.

A hooded figure stands shadowed in the doorway. Slowly, they lift their arms and pull the hood back. To say I am surprised would be an understatement. Emerson doesn't say a word, just motions for me to follow her.

I hesitate to follow, but do I really have a choice right now? She raises an eyebrow at me, waiting for me to make my decision. As I take a step toward her, a look of relief flitters across her face so quickly I'm not sure I saw it. I hope I don't regret this.

*'Go now, Nesrin,'* Kaida urges, nudging me forward with her snout. I glance over my shoulder at her, guilt stirring inside of me.

"Hurry," Emerson whispers harshly, a fire burning behind her eyes.

I nod and move quickly toward her, holding the giant-sized dragon egg under my arm protectively. I cast one last glance at Kaida, who bows her head.

*'Go, child.'*

"Good luck," I whisper before I'm out the door, following Emerson down the corridor. Her pace is swift as she leads me away from my prison cell, from Kaida. Emerson's long black cloak is billowing behind her. She is moving so fast, I struggle not to fall behind. We pass so many doors I lose count and have no way of finding my way back if I need to. Up ahead, I become aware of approaching voices. We both freeze. I hold my breath, listening. The voices are coming closer. Emerson curses under her breath and spins, pushing me into a doorway. Covering my mouth with one hand, she lifts her other, bringing her finger to her lips in the silent *Shhh* sign.

Nodding, I close my eyes and try to slow my breathing, which is coming out in rough pants from trying to keep up and the adrenaline pumping through me. I do not know how she thinks they will not see us standing in this small alcove, but I know she has powers beyond what is normal. Right now, I am trusting her. I hear the voices moving closer. My thundering heartbeat is sure to give us away. The two voices are right behind Emerson now, and both of us hold our breath.

I open my eyes, a muffled gasp escaping my mouth. Emerson's eyes flare in warning. All I see behind Emerson is blackness, shadows so thick I can't see through them. I've never put myself in a cloaking spell like this before. I can say it's quite unsettling. As the voices pass and start to fade away, Emerson pushes away from me, looking both ways down the corridor as the shadows melt away like they were never there to begin with.

"Come on." She grabs my hand in an iron grip, pulling me along behind her even faster than before. I have no choice but to be dragged behind, watching her black boots and quick steps as we go, but my mind keeps flittering back to Kaida. I hope she makes it out alive. That her distraction doesn't mean her death. I glance down at the dragon's egg in my arms, a pang of guilt sharp in my chest. Kaida trusts me to take care of her baby, and I refuse to let her down. Emotions swell up as I think about all that Kaida is sacrificing for me and for her baby.

We come to the end of the corridor and notice a set of stairs. I'm expecting to go up, but Emerson pulls me down. There is hardly any light to aid in our descent so I take my steps carefully. I don't need another sprain, or to break this precious cargo.

The bottom of the stairwell opens up into a long passageway that fades into darkness. There is no light down here, just endless darkness and cold, stale air. I summon a ball of light, so at least we will be able to make out what's in front of us. It appears a foot in front of Emerson, startling her. Her steps slow and she glances back at me. I shrug. "Light is my thing," I mutter.

Emerson hasn't spoken a word since we left the alcove. She hasn't even mentioned the dragon egg or looked twice at it. We walk in silence for what seems like forever. The only sound is our footfalls and breathing. I can make out an opening up ahead and hold my breath as we step into an enormous cavern that has a small canal running through it.

Emerson turns to me. "This is the way out. If you follow this, it will take you out on to the Columbia River."

I gape at her, then search for a boat or anything. "You want me to swim?" I adjust the dragon egg in my arms. It's getting heavy.

"Look, I didn't have time to organize a boat. You can swim, right?" she now looks concerned at the fact she didn't check before leading me all the way down here.

I roll my eyes, frustration making me act out. "Yes, of course I can swim." I spear her with a scowl, then sigh, "It will be fine. Thank you for all your help, Emerson."

She is helping me when she doesn't have to. I owe her. Reaching out, I squeeze her hand. She looks uncomfortable for a moment, then pulls me in for a hug, surprising me.

"Marcus will wait for you at the bridge. From there, he will take you to meet the pack." At the mention of the pack, my heart misses a beat. I want nothing more than to be back home.

A loud roar fills the air, causing the ground and walls around us to shake. Debris falls from the cavern's ceiling. Kaida has begun her diversion. Which means they have figured out I'm gone. That they will likely send people out looking for me soon.

Emerson brings my attention back to her. "You need to leave now. They will realize soon what is happening, and I cannot be missing when they do, or they will suspect me. I can do more damage from inside these walls than out there," she says, urging me toward the water.

I slip off my jacket, wrap it around Kaida's egg, then with Emerson's help, I tie it around my torso like a makeshift baby sling, freeing up my arms to swim. Carefully, I step down onto the lower embankment and then slowly slip into the water. When my upper body slips into the frigid water, my gasp echoes around us. My breath quickens at the cold temperature, and I send a prayer to Hecate that the dragon's egg will be okay, that I can make it to Marcus without either of us freezing to death.

"Be careful, Nesrin," Emerson calls out. I turn back to glance at her. She is standing at the mouth of the tunnel, hand gripping her cloak, her knuckles white. She looks like she is holding herself back from coming with me. Giving her a small smile, I nod, then push off the wall. The icy cold water splashes my face and I gasp as the freezing water moves around me. I push forward down the dark tunnel, concentrating on the light orb floating a foot in front of me. I drift slowly through the tunnel, taking short breaths. I'm trying not to hyperventilate at the thought of it being in deep, dark water that I can't see the bottom of. My imagination will run away with me soon enough, and I'm going to freak out. I do my best to keep my breathing slow and steady. My technique is a little rusty, but I'm somehow managing to make my way quietly down the tunnel. My muscles ache like I've been swimming for hours, when it's probably only been ten minutes. I blink when I notice a light up ahead, moonlight. Instantly, relief hits me. I let a huff of laughter escape me. I'm almost out of this tunnel. But just then, I feel something large brush against my legs.

I let out a rather loud squeak that echoes around me and down the tunnel. Treading water, I stop swimming and look around. I can't see anything, but that is no shock. It's so dark even my orb barely lights the way. The side of the tunnel shows no sign of somewhere to lift myself out of the water if I need to. A moment passes and the water remains calm. I shake off the unease slithering down my spine.

"Get a grip, Nesrin. It was just your imagination." I start swimming again, this time a little faster. I want out of this tunnel. My heart jumps into my throat as I feel another brush against my legs. Okay, I didn't imagine that. My heart is hammering against my ribs. I gather some magic and send it wafting out into the water, a seeking light of sorts. My magic finds something in the water up ahead and swirls around it like a beacon.

Dread seizes me, and I stop swimming. "SHIT!" I curse. I frantically look around for anything I might use to defend myself. Nothing. All I have is my magic, but with the water making me so cold, I'm not sure if I'd last long holding something off with my magic alone. The form makes its way toward me, my magic following it. I automatically swim backward until the wall meets my back, the frigid chill of the stone seeping into my body.

The shape rises slightly in the water, and my magic gathers, ready to fight. As the shape emerges out of the water, a beautiful, majestic creature takes its place. I suck in a sharp breath and choke on a mouthful of water. I stare, stunned, at the kelpie floating in front of me. Even in the minimal lighting, I recognize it as the same kelpie I helped only yesterday. It approaches slowly, bowing its head to me.

I'm sure I must be dreaming—that I'm back in my cage—because what the actual fuck is happening right now? The kelpie raises its head and looks at me, its bottomless black eyes staring into mine. Slowly, I raise my hand, holding it out in front. The kelpie, to my shock, moves forward until it nudges my hand with its nose. I run my hand up his head and through his ears, and to my surprise, he leans in closer so I can reach better. In the light coming from my orb, its silver coat is shimmering like diamonds as water runs off its body. The kelpie moves, motioning with its head for me to get on his back.

"What?" I ask, startled by the gesture. This is unheard of. Why would he offer me a ride?

The kelpie motions again, this time snorting as if to say, *We haven't got all day.* I swim closer but hesitate. I don't want to end up like all those people who have been lured to the depths to drown. The kelpie lets out an impatient snort and we eye each other for a moment. Sensing that this creature means me no harm, I take a leap of faith, moving to its side, and pull myself onto its back. Wrapping my hands in his remarkably silky white mane, I pull myself further up until I'm seated comfortably. As soon as he's satisfied that I'm secure, he shoots off for the exit.

Within a matter of seconds, we are bursting into the open air and moonlight. My hair is streaming behind me in ribbons, the wind snapping at my wet clothes. I'm absolutely freezing. My body trembles uncontrollably, my fingers aching from the tight hold they keep on the kelpie. I glance down, making sure that the dragon egg is still secure, and breathe a sigh of relief, knowing it's still tucked in tight.

Looking around, I try to make out where we are. My eyes are burning with tears from the icy wind, making it hard to see. I try blinking, but my sight remains blurry. Underneath me, the kelpie is slowing down, so I relax my hold on his mane. I can just make out land up ahead. That must be where we're heading. I twist around and look behind me to the small island in the Columbia River where I escaped from, and see faint spiderweb patterns in reddish blue. A cloaking spell surrounds it. I give myself a moment to mourn Kaida, the sacrifice she made for me and her hatchling. Tenderly, I run my hand over the egg. I hope I have what it takes to raise a dragon, because there is no way this dragon will be leaving my side. I owe it to Kaida to see this through, just like I owe it to Niamh to take care of Astraea. I will not fail either of them.

The kelpie heads for the riverbank, its strong muscles taut under its skin, water streaming on either side of us. I take a moment to admire and appreciate the beast, the way its coat shimmers in the moonlight. I'm so grateful he came to my rescue, because I'm not sure I would have made it otherwise. Especially with the dragon's egg weighing me down. I take a chance and stroke my hand down his powerful neck, then grin, hearing his pleased nicker. We make it to the riverbank and he stops just before the water's edge, keeping his hooves in the water. I pat his neck again and slide from his back, stumbling back a couple of steps as I will my legs to function. The kelpie turns, making its way further out into the river, water still running from its mane, its coat shimmering in the moonlight.

"Thank you," I call out.

The kelpie turns its head and looks at me with those huge dark eyes before bowing his head. Letting out a breath, I watch him disappear under the water. Now what? Scanning the area, I see nothing. I'm not sure where I've ended up, and Emerson said Marcus was waiting at the bridge. I scan my surroundings, looking down the river for a bridge. Nothing. Wherever I am, it's nowhere near civilization. There is a field of tall grass ahead of me and a forest beyond that. I stumble forward, willing my frozen limbs to cooperate. I walk briskly toward the forest, my gut telling me to go that way. My gait is not quite a walk, but not a jog either, the dragon egg bouncing awkwardly against me as I move. When I stumble across a small dirt track, I glance left, then right. Can I risk using the road? It's a small access road, so the chance of people from the Order coming across me is slim. Still, I'm unsure if I should follow the road. My gut is still urging me toward the forest, so I cut across the road and continue on through the tall grass, running my hands over the tops of the grass. I draw on the magic from the air around me, letting it drift around me like a caress, lifting the hair from my shoulders.

I know what I have to do next. It's time to reopen the connection to Lukas through the mating bond. I'm sure he will be pissed and worried, but I hope he'll understand why I did it. The only way I will be found is if Lukas can feel me. I take several deep breaths, then I rip off the block I put on the bond. Suddenly, I am flooded with feelings of grief, anger, guilt, worry. Swallowing down my guilt for causing my mate to suffer such pain, I send a pulse of affection down the bond and wait. But the wait isn't long, as I feel the moment Lukas realizes I'm here at the other end. The relief I sense from Lukas is instantaneous, then love radiates through the bond in droves, making me laugh out loud, tears falling freely down my face. We are still too far away from each other to communicate telepathically, but that's okay. This is enough for now.

Too many emotions are swirling inside of me, making my thought process extremely difficult, not to mention the cold is affecting my body. I don't think I've ever been this cold before. Just breathing is difficult.

The forest is dark. I don't want to risk my light orb giving me away, so I move slowly, picking my way through the trees and broken branches. The longer I walk, the warmer I get, and the more my vision adjusts to the dark. I can almost make out everything around me. The trees here are bigger, their branches twisting around each other, almost like a grove. I contemplate trying to climb one of them to rest, but my legs are far too fatigued. I would never make it up there.

I'm not sure how long I've been walking when I hear a noise up ahead. It's subtle, but enough to make me realize something is approaching me, stalking me. I stop between two trees, bracing my hands on the rough bark to steady myself. Feeling out of breath, I take a moment to rest, scanning the area.

A massive, dusty wolf with streaks of white through its fur steps out from behind a boulder. There is something familiar about the wolf, but I can't put my finger on it. It has to be a member of either Lukas's or Finan's pack for me to recognize it, so I relax slightly. The wolf lowers its head, showing me its deadly fangs as they glint in the moonlight. My heart trips over itself as the wolf lets out a long, low, hair-raising growl. I freeze to the spot. Doesn't it recognize me? I frown at the wolf, tilting my head to the side. Surely it knows what I am, right?

The wolf slowly approaches, head lowered, ears pinned back, a menacing growl rolling continuously from its mouth. My heart is racing and I am struggling to keep calm. I let out a shaky breath, keeping eye contact and backing away slowly. The wolf doesn't like this. Another louder, more menacing growl rumbles from its throat. There are at least a dozen feet between us when it breaks into a run. Unprepared, I duck, covering my head with my arms, only to have the wolf jump over me, dodging a blast of magic which splinters the tree in front of me. Shocked, I spin to catch the wolf circling a dark figure. Movement beyond them catches my attention, more figures moving toward us. The coven has been tracking me. *Shit.* There have to be fifteen or more of them spread out. How long have they been following me without me realizing it?

I feel Lukas's bond wash over me, love and desperation pouring through. He is close, thank the goddess. My attention never strays from the approaching group, but I don't recognize any of them. The closest mage has a sneer on his face.

"You are an abomination," he spits, looking at me with pure hatred.

Do they really think I care? The gray wolf snarls in warning, snapping its powerful jaws as the mage takes another step forward.

The mage's eyes flare, but not in fear like I was hoping. He starts chanting an incantation, the words barely above a whisper, but I understand them just as clearly as if he were standing next to me. Since my mating with Lukas, some of my wolf's traits have been coming through, merging with my witch side. Too bad they didn't alert me to the fact that I was being followed. With Kaida's egg still strapped to my body, I take a step forward, drawing on my magic and the surrounding elements faster than I ever have before. With my body filled to the brim with magic, I raise my hands and shove my magic toward the mage, knocking him off his feet, but not quickly enough. A ball of red energy races toward me. I manage to throw up a shield in time for the spell to bounce off.

My mysterious wolf has already taken down one mage and is now backing up to stand at my side. Its hackles are raised as it snarls, baring its long, savage teeth. We are severely outnumbered, but I am extremely grateful to have this wolf by my side. Then, a chorus of howls reach my ears, causing my heart to flutter wildly. *Lukas. He is close.*

I growl at the witches and mages, "I'd run while you still can." The wolf next to me growls in agreement, stamping a large paw on the ground.

"Not until you're wiped from this world and in the depths of Tartarus with the rest of your traitorous family."

"I see," I sigh, looking over my shoulder as over fifty wolves bound over the hill. Growls ripple from them, and a thrill races through me at the sound of my family approaching. I spot Lukas, and my heart soars at the sight of him, his impressive wolf form, his black coat gleaming in the moonlight, white fangs glistening as he bares his teeth in a snarl. He is as absolutely terrifying as he is magnificent. His eyes clash with mine and his massive form aims at me as he races down the hill.

*'Nesrin,'* he practically growls. A small shiver runs over me as his voice echoes through my head, and hot tears course down my cold face.

"Lukas," I croak.

A moment later, he's at my side, pushing up against the side of my body. I place my hand atop his back, sinking my fingers into the fur there. Turning back to the witches and mages, I feel a renewed sense of determination. My mate is here, my family, and we have turned the tables. Surely, they will leave now. They have to realize it will not end in their favor.

"You think these wolves will stop us? We have a powerful god on our side."

Lukas snarls and snaps at the converging coven. His wolves spread out around us. I tighten the jacket around my body to anchor the dragon egg.

"Yeah, yeah. I've heard the speech before," I mutter, rolling my eyes. I glance around at Lukas's pack, my pack, drawing strength and comfort from them, from the pack bond nestled close to my mating bond. They are all lending me their strength. My heart swells at the act.

Lukas places his massive form in front of me. *'When I say, I want you to turn and run. Gabe will lead you to safety.'*

*'No, I won't leave until this is done.'*

*'Nesrin, please. I can't risk you getting hurt. You need to leave. Please, go with Gabe.'* The anguish in his voice is my undoing. I owe Lukas this much. If I leave the fight, it goes against everything I stand for. I hate it. But I will do this for him. I glance down at the egg strapped across my chest, and Kaida.

*'Okay,'* I reply.

Even though he isn't facing me, I can see him visibly relax. I receive a nudge at the back of my legs and turn to see a cute but large fox behind me. Gabe.

"Are you even listening to me, you traitorous bitch?"

Snarls erupt around us, and the mage's eyes widen in response.

"I don't think they like their luna being called names, do you?" I reply.

"Luna?" the mage splutters in outrage, his face going red with anger. I can see them preparing to attack. The shifters also notice the change in the air and their muscles coil, ready to pounce. I glance around at my pack. Wolves, cougars, badgers, and bears. They have all come for me. The mysterious wolf who found me has now joined Gabe behind me.

*'Go!'* Lukas shouts. I spin on my heels, running and muttering an incantation of protection for those around me, to deflect the first attacks. I won't be able to stop all the magic coming their way, but if I can give them a head start, I will.

Gabe and my mystery wolf lead me up the hill. Growling in frustration as my feet keep slipping in the loose dirt, I grab hold of a tree branch to pull myself up. When I reach the top, I spin, taking in the chaos behind me. The coven battles with the shifters, and it's hard to determine who has the upper hand. I watch as Lukas's large black form lunges for a taller mage, sinking his teeth into the man's arm and jerking his head violently, ripping at the arm. Even from here, I think I can hear the sound of bones breaking and flesh tearing. The man howls in agony, trying to blast Lukas with a defensive spell, but Lukas is too quick. He darts around behind the mage, jumping on his back. The mage falls forward, his head smashing into the ground, hard.

Bending, I put my hands to the ground, closing my eyes. *'Nesrin, we have to go. I promised to get you out of here.'* Gabe's voice in my mind startles me. I wasn't expecting it, but sure enough, there is now a bright golden link between him and I.

"I just have to do this," I argue. I'm not sure it will work, but anything is worth a try.

Closing my eyes, I send my thoughts and pleas to the trees, asking for their aid. Suddenly, I hear the snapping of branches as screams erupt down the hill. My eyes fling open as tree roots rip from the ground, wrapping around witches and mages, sending them flying through the air.

Lukas's surprise and shock echo down the bond and his head swivels my way, our eyes locking. *'Go, sweetheart.'*

I nod, getting to my feet and running again.

*'That was fucking amazing,'* Gabe says, running right beside me.

"It was, wasn't it?"

My mystery wolf suddenly leaps, stunning me as it knocks me to the side. I stumble, narrowly missing a low-hanging tree branch, and spin to watch as the spell hits the gray wolf. A scream tears from my throat, a wave of magic tossing everyone a few feet backward. I watch, horrified, as fire erupts, engulfing the wolf in flames. Its steps falter, an agonizing howl of pain tearing from its throat. Then it collapses, withering on the forest floor.

Where did that mage come from? Gabe is standing in front of me, so I take the chance, working fast to deconstruct the spell that still has the wolf in flames. I struggle to regain control of my emotions as the flames go out and I can assess the damage.

From behind me, I hear something crashing through the trees. It sounds like . . . a horse. Spinning, I watch the Puca sprint toward me, racing past as it barrels into the group of mages who appeared behind me from nowhere. It knocks them over and tramples several of them, sending their screams ringing through the air. I block out the noise. It's them or me at this point. A blast of magic heads straight at me, and lifting my arm, I throw up a shield as I counter it, sending one of my own spells whirling back. I don't wait to see if it hits the mark, though I know it does by the screams that rise from behind me as I run for the gray wolf laying in a smoldering heap.

The snarling of wolves reaches my ears as Lukas and Finan break through the trees, jumping and landing atop the two mages that circle the Puca. Not a second later, what looks like two dozen other wolves descend on the rest of the coven, who are now severely outnumbered. I crawl over to the gray wolf on my hands and knees, and as I grow near, the wolf shifts into a girl. I stop short with a horrified gasp, my hands flying to cover my mouth. Oh my goddess.

"Alex?" I whisper, reaching to brush matted hair from her face.

Whimpering, she opens her eyes and stares at me, dazed, her expression filled with so much pain. "Why?" I ask, my throat tight with emotion. I am shocked she would risk her life for mine.

*'You are my luna. I will always protect you,'* she answers, pain lacing her words.

"But that's my job, to protect you," I sob, grabbing her hand and squeezing gently. I accept her pain and anguish as it washes over me, then turn, emptying what little I had in my stomach, the smell of burned flesh and fur hanging in the air. If those mages and witches weren't dead already, I'd kill them for this. Turning back, I grip the egg still strapped to my body and whisper an incantation to put her to sleep. We cannot move her in this state. As I prepare to heal her as best as I can, a hard blow lands on the back of my head. This really has to stop happening.

# CHAPTER THIRTY FOUR

## Lukas

Looking over, I spot Nesrin on the ground next to Alex, hovering over her. Her red hair is pulled back in a braid that is barely hanging on. Auburn hair frames her sweet, delicate face, her cheeks are flushed, and sweat dots her brow. There is mud caked all over her. She is beautiful. Absolutely stunning. I watch as she summons a ball of light, hurling it at a mage coming their way. It hits the mage in the chest with a sizzle, shocking him. Surprise flickers over his face before he falls to the ground, unconscious. Pride and lust shoot through me, and Nesrin's eyes find mine. Love shines in her eyes before she focuses back on Alex.

I can sense Alex's pain through the pack bond. In this state, she can't control what she's sharing. Then, Nesrin's feelings hit me like a steam train. Guilt, agony, and grief pour through the bond. I make my way over to her when a short, stocky, dark-haired mage jumps in front of me, a cruel grin on his ugly face. These guys don't stand a chance against a pack of angry shifters. Why they haven't run away screaming is beyond me. He lunges forward, striking out with a long dagger. A red haze of fury coats my vision, the animal side of me wanting blood as retribution for stealing my mate away from me. I am going to rip their throats out for all they have done, all they plan to do. I don't waste any time. Ducking under his arm, I pivot on all fours and lunge, going straight for his throat. The mage's eyes widen in shock at my sudden movement, my jaw locking on his neck, teeth piercing his skin, the tearing of skin and flesh echoing around me as his warm blood coats my mouth. Shaking him once, I hear the crack, and drop him to the ground. Looking around, I see there are only two mages left standing. Finan and Roan take them down swiftly, so I turn back to Nesrin and see her lying unconscious next to Alex. What the fuck happened? Fire ignites in my chest as I run to where they lie and see a mage only a few feet away pinned under Gabe, his teeth bared as he growls down in the mage's face.

*'He knocked her out,'* Gabe growls.

Snarling, I leap forward, Gabe swiftly moving out of my way as I loom over the mage. "I'm— I'm so-so–sorry," the mage stutters, tears streaming down his face, mixing with the blood splatter there. My jaws snap inches from his face. And I smell urine. Weak, pathetic man. I want nothing more than to end his miserable existence. But I can't kill in cold blood. It's not who I am. But one more scratch, one more mark on my mate, and I won't be responsible for my actions. I back away and turn to Nesrin. She and Alex both lie side by side, unconscious. We need to get them back to the farm to be looked over immediately.

I shift to my human form and reach my hand out to sweep the hair from Nesrin's face. She looks so beautiful and peaceful.

Leaning down, I place a soft kiss on her cheek, noticing the dark circles under her eyes. She has only been gone a day, but it has seemed like an eternity. My eyes go to the giant green egg strapped across her chest. I smile. Who or what has she rescued now?

Breaking me from my thoughts is a savage snarl and the sound of ripping flesh. I spin around to see Zee standing over the stocky mage, a dagger laying loosely in his hand, blood bubbling and gurgling from his mouth. My eyes go to Zee's. *'Thank you, brother.'*

Zee bows his head and sits back on his haunches, tilting his head. *'She okay?'*

I look back down at Nesrin, then to Alex. "I think Nesrin has just been knocked unconscious, but Alex . . . Alex is in bad shape. We need to get back to the farm as soon as possible."

"I've sent some others to retrieve the cars. We just need to get to the road," Zee says, shifting into his human form with me. I pick up Nesrin, careful of the large egg, and nod to Zee to grab Alex. It's not far to reach the road on foot. The sooner we can get back, the better. I need to make sure my mate is okay.

"Everyone remains on high alert. Spread out, I want to make sure we aren't followed," I command, and everyone scatters. "Finan, Gabe, Roan, and Asena stay with Zee and myself," I say looking to my closest friends. Staying in their animal forms, we quickly make our way north toward the road.

The ride back to the farm takes way too long, my mind playing over all that happened in the last twenty-four hours. I left Kate and Merve at the house with Astraea and the sprites. Grace was on her way there. She had Suzy with her, which I wasn't happy about, but apparently the teenager wouldn't take no for an answer. I had at least a dozen shifters guarding them. Last check in was ten minutes ago, and it was all quiet.

The tires crunch on the gravel as we turn down the road to my house and the rest of the pack lands. When we pull to a stop in front of the house, Zee jumps out to open the door for me. I cradle Nesrin's slight frame to my chest and step out of the car, her soft breaths blowing on my neck. Without saying a word, I nod to Zee and storm past everyone into the house and up the stairs to our room.

Gently, I lay Nesrin on our bed and move to untie the egg from her body. Looking around, I see a pile of pillows beside the bed and set the football-sized egg there. Nesrin's face is covered in dirt and blood, mingled and smudged all over, but there aren't any visible wounds. With a shaky hand, I reach down, running the tips of my fingers across her cheek before straightening up, heaving a deep sigh. I walk to the bathroom and wet a towel under the warm water, bringing it over to her, then wiping away all the blood and dirt until the cloth is too dirty to continue.

My eyes land on her mating mark and my heart rate speeds up. I almost lost my mate. I failed to keep her safe when I told her I would. Defeated. I feel defeated. I haven't slept or stopped moving since she was taken. If necessary, I was planning to burn the coven to the ground to find her again. They can't have her. She will not die as some fucking sacrifice. I will never allow it.

A bone-deep wariness comes over me, and with a huff, I turn, sitting on the floor, my back against the bed. I stretch my legs out in front of me, crossing them at the ankles, tipping my head back to rest on the bed. My eyes close as I try to rein in my emotions. The rage I felt when Nesrin was taken is still burning deep in my chest.

"Watching you get carried away like that, hearing you give up and then blocking the mate bond. It was the hardest thing I've ever endured. It nearly destroyed me," I whisper into the silence of the room. I feel a hand run over my head and I jerk up in surprise. My eyes connect with warm amber ones that cause my heart to speed up every time they land on me.

"It wasn't great for me either, Lukas," she whispers back in a soft, vulnerable voice I haven't heard from her before. I want nothing more than to sweep her into my arms, but I'm still mad at her for giving up, for sacrificing herself, and shutting me out.

"You think I don't know that?" I snap, shoving to my feet. I pace the room, running a hand over my head and stare back at Nesrin. Her face is stricken as she sits on the bed watching me. "I didn't know you could block the bond. It terrified me. Just . . . Please don't shut me out like that again. Promise me. Whatever it is, whatever comes next, we are in it together."

She drops her head, letting her hair cover her face. "I promise I won't do that again, Lukas. I just didn't want you to feel my fear, or death when it came." The words are so soft that if not for my enhanced hearing, I wouldn't have caught it.

Startled, I drop to the bed in front of her. "What the fuck, Nesrin!" I demand, weaving my fingers in her hair and gently tilting her face up to mine. My heart cracks open at the sight of tears streaming down her cheeks, and I decide I never want to see her cry again.

"I'm sorry," she cries, more tears falling from her beautiful eyes. *Fuck!*

"No. You have nothing to be sorry for. You did what you thought you had to. Just don't block our mate bond again. I need to know what you're going through, always." I move so quickly she's not expecting it. Within seconds, I have her flat on her back under me, my arms braced on either side of her head. Nesrin blinks in surprise. Her whiskey-colored eyes shine up at me, her auburn hair fanned out under her, mud clinging to the strands. She couldn't have looked more beautiful. I love this woman more than anything else in this world. I will cherish every moment and I will not waste a single second of the time we have together. That I promise.

She puts her palm on my cheek, drawing my attention back to her. "I'm okay, Lukas."

The moment she touches me, I breathe a sigh of relief. The way she says my name has my heart skipping a beat. Closing my eyes, I press my face firmly into her hand. I love the touch of her hand on my skin, her palm tickling my beard. I stretch out beside her, keeping her tight against me.

"Tell me what happened?" I mutter into her hair, pressing a soft kiss to her head.

Then she tells me the tale of the dragon Kaida and her egg, of Emerson helping her escape, how she was meant to meet up with Marcus, the kelpie aiding her, and up to when we found her in the woods. I swear I hold my breath the whole time. Rage runs hot through my veins like lava the more she speaks. I hold her as she trembles, as she relives everything again. When she tells me how they planned to burn her alive. I struggle to rein in my fury. I want to hunt them all down. But my rage isn't what she needs in this moment, so I keep it locked up, knowing she would still feel it simmering through our bond.

"Fuck. It's a miracle you made it out in one piece." I should have been there. She never should have been taken again.

"I know." Her response is soft, and it wobbles a bit. She was scared. She looked up at me, her amber eyes so bright, my breath catches. "You have to know, I wasn't giving up. I would fight for my life and everyone else's, as long as there is breath in my lungs."

I close my eyes at her words, soaking them in. "Marcus was supposed to meet you. He came here when you were taken. If it wasn't for Merve, I would have killed him on the spot, but he told me he had people on the inside. That they would get you out of there. I just had to wait for the signal. But shit went sideways. The island they kept you on was cloaked, then suddenly it wasn't and half of the building, an old convent, went up in flames. The explosion was enormous, the coven was scrambling to cloak everything. Marcus couldn't find you, and we weren't sure what had happened. I almost went crazy until you opened the mating bond back up." I stop talking and look over at her.

Tears trail down her face as she stares at the egg.

"What is it?"

"Kaida. She created the distraction. She sacrificed herself, giving us a head start. Does Marcus know if his people got out?"

"I don't know, sweetheart."

# CHAPTER THIRTY FIVE

A lex screams from the room beyond. Her cries of agony tear
through me, ripping pieces from my heart and stripping
me bare.

"Lukas, please let me see her. I can help," I beg. He has to know
I can heal her.

Shaking his head, Lukas looks at me, pure pain radiating from
those swirling green eyes. "Nesrin, I can't. I'm sorry, but she is
unstable. I won't risk it." He sounds so broken. I hate it.

"I'm going in, Lukas. You can come and help, keep me safe or
not, but I'm her luna and she saved me. I owe her."

Merve comes into the hallway, his face pale. He looks at Lukas.
"She *can* help, you know."

Lukas shakes his head as another gut-wrenching scream floats
through the air. I can't take it anymore. I dash for the door, Lukas
hot on my heels.

"Nesrin. No," he growls, trying to grab my arm, but I seem to
be quicker, dodging his hand by sheer luck.

I push into the room and gasp at the sight of Alex lying on the floor in the small room. Horrific burns cover most of her body. She's withering, shifting sporadically in and out of her wolf form. Her fur is matted and burned in patches, her skin red and angry, the sight turning my stomach. A growl of agony rips from her throat as she slashes out with her claws. Not at anyone, just in agony. The howl ends in a scream as she shifts back into her human form.

Only Lukas, Zee, and I are in the cramped room with Alex. She seems so small curled in on herself. Her blood-shot eyes rose to meet Lukas's. "Lukas, just kill me. I can't stand the pain. Please," Alex begs, her voice catching on a sob before ending in a howl as another involuntary shift overtakes her body.

Spinning to Lukas, my hands grip his shirt. "Lukas, we need to sedate her. I can help. I can," I say, pleading with him to let me try. Merve stands in the doorway, sympathy lining his features. His eyes meet mine and he nods, as if to say, *You can do it. I believe in you.*

"She is lucky to be alive after that attack," Zee says, frowning down at Alex. It's easy to see how much he's struggling with his own emotions.

"Lucky? *Lucky?*" Alex snarls. "This isn't lucky. This is torture. You should have let me die," she wails.

My heart breaks at her words, and fresh tears stream down my face. It seems like the walls are closing in on us. The utter despair we're all feeling is too much to handle. I could feel everything, emotions running so high in the room I can't tell whose feelings were whose. It is suffocating.

"Alex, I can help," I whisper, knowing she would hear me.

Shaking her head, she moans in pain. "Lukas, put me down." Brown eyes lift to us, pleading with Lukas. "Please. You know it's for the best."

Zee looks to Lukas, giving him a grim nod.

*No, no, no, no . . . I will try, I will heal her.* That's what I do. It's what I am good at. Alex saved me. Now I will save her.

Zee moves toward us and pulls Lukas away from me to talk near the door, leaving me standing in the middle of the room. I don't care what they're whispering about in hushed voices. All I care about right now is Alex. Magic hums along my skin as determination fills me. I catch them both off guard with a burst of magic, pushing both men out of the room and slamming the door behind them, sealing it off. There is pounding on the door, wood splintering under the force.

"Nesrin!" Lukas yells. "Let me in now!"

I hear Zee curse as Lukas slams his fists into the wood. I can just see him in my mind, pacing behind Lukas, his hand running through his hair in agitation. I tune them out, securing the door magically so they won't be able to break it down. Finding that link with Lukas, I send my love and strength through the bond. He knows I have to try. He needs to trust me right now. I can do this. I know I can. I shift my focus to Alex, my heart skittering as I lock eyes with her.

A feral, pained look washes over her face as she grits her teeth. "Nesrin, no. I can't control it."

"It's okay," I try to reassure her, raising my palms up.

Alex shakes her head. Scorched and matted hair stick to her scarred skin in clumps. "No. What if I hurt you?"

My heart breaks at the sound of fear in her voice. "You won't hurt me."

"You don't know that."

"Yes, I do." I approach slowly, letting my magic float out, a white light covering her body, calming her. I move down on to my hands and knees, crawling forward the last few feet, closing the space between us. Alex's eyes dart back and forth between mine nervously before casting one last glance at the door behind me.

"I'm going to help," I whisper. Alex shifts back into her wolf form, her eyes pleading with mine as she whimpers. I let my magic seep into her. She stiffens for a moment, then relaxes.

"Shh, it's okay. You will be okay, Alex." I reach out but hesitate. There is nowhere I can put my hands that isn't covered with burned flesh and matted fur. Shaking my head, I warm up my hands, gathering up what magic I need. I stare down into Alex's wolf eyes, focusing on her as I give her a reassuring nod. "I will fix this," I promise.

My palms tremble as I place them on her side, resting on top of her ribs. I let my magic flow freely into her. Seeking and mending her injuries. There are so many. Tears streak down my face as I'm hit with the full force of pain she's suffering. I focus on the more severe burns, healing those first, as her wolf cannot heal so many injuries at once.

Magic drains out of me at a rapid pace. I am growing fatigued, and fast, not giving myself time to fully recuperate, but Alex needs me. It can't wait. I require more magic. Suddenly, my chest warms, and through the mating bond, I feel Lukas's undying love and support wash over me, bringing more tears to my eyes.

"You can do it, sweetheart. Take what you need," his beautiful voice fills my head. I draw on his power through the mating bond, but I am having trouble maintaining the flow. The room suddenly goes dark around me. It must be the exhaustion getting to me. I grit my teeth, pushing more magic into Alex. Then the softest touch is felt on my shoulder, and magic blasts through me, fueling my healing abilities. *What the hell is that?*

Magic flows more easily, and I push more and more of it into healing Alex. I feel her body changing forms, shifting into her human body again. I open my eyes, seeing movement to my side. I turn and gasp. In the corner of the room is a mass of shadows, a form barely visible in the thick inky blackness. They seem to reach out and swirl around, mingling with my light.

Confused, I shake my head. I am tired. I have to be seeing things. Ignoring the shadows, I focus back on Alex. Her body is glowing in a pure white light, as is mine. The magic in my body recedes, settling deep in my chest as the light fades. My breathing evens out as relief blankets me. I feel as though I've weathered a cold and dangerous storm. My lungs struggle, fighting to expand with each breath.

My tears come swiftly as I look down to Alex, filling my chest at what I find. Only faint scarring remains, marring her skin in certain places, but she is otherwise whole and alive and no longer in pain. I did it. A wave of exhaustion has my head drooping. Everything seems so heavy. I slump down next to Alex, my hand reaching out to grab hers. I close my eyes, giving myself a moment of rest. Suddenly, there is a brush of cool fingers against my forehead. Forcing my eyes open, I barely register the shadowed figure leaning over me. I can't make out any features as I watch the shadows dissipate around me.

I hardly have enough energy left to unlock the bedroom door, but I let go of the spell holding it in place. The last thing I see is two sets of combat boots rushing into the room.

# CHAPTER THIRTY SIX

Spinning in a circle, I take in the endless field of white flowers that surround me as far as the eye can see. Thanks to my mother, I know a lot of flowers, plants, and herbs, and these are meadow foam flowers. Apparently, they only grew where the tears of gods fell. They have a unique cup-shaped white flower with a brilliant yellow center. The blooming fields look like a field of sea foam. It is beautiful. Up ahead, something sparkles in the moonlight, catching my eye. I make my way through the field of meadow foam, my fingers drifting over the blooms, taking in the soft petals and sweet aroma.

I look up, noticing the evening star has grown brighter, shimmering and sparkling overhead. A howl from a wolf drifts on the air, surrounding me, filling me with warmth and familiarity. I keep my eyes on the sky and watch as the evening star and moon merge with a flash of light so bright, I cover my eyes with my arm. When the light fades, I put my arm down as a figure walks toward me. Gasping, I watch her approach. She walks as if floating just above the ground, the ethereal glow surrounding her shimmering white, blue, and violet.

I realize what she is immediately. There is only one obvious guess. She is a goddess. Her long hair is like silk as it floats in golden brown hues around her body, skin so pale it's almost luminous. She wears a long blue and silver gown that hugs her waist and floats around her ankles. It has long, flowing sleeves with delicate lace around her wrists. She smiles and her bright blue eyes that are ringed with gold twinkle in delight.

"Nesrin," she says, her voice so soft it's almost musical. Surprising me, the goddess closes her eyes, bowing her head in greeting. My mouth snaps shut. I am utterly speechless. *I mean, what do you even say to a goddess?*

My stomach erupts in a flurry of butterflies, as I bow my head in return. When I look up, the goddess is standing close enough to touch. When did she move? "Do you know who I am?" her soft musical voice drifts over me, calming the nerves that are firing at rapid speed through my body.

"Althaea?" I guess.

A broad smile spreads across her face. "Do you realize who I am to you?"

I nod my head dumbly. Althaea reaches her hands out and cups my face tenderly. "You look so much like her, you know. You have her spirit as well. That gentle, loving, innocent soul, but also a fierce fighter." She smiles sadly, letting go of my face.

The cold air washes over my skin, and I miss the warmth of her touch. I think back on the vision my mother showed me of Blanchette. We could have been twins for all the similarities between us.

"Thank you?" I mumble, my chest warming at her words.

"You need to be ready to make some tough calls, Nesrin. The others you are up against will fight dirty. Their jealousy and greed got my daughter killed. They continue to hunt and kill her bloodline. It needs to stop. The Fates chose you. They accepted you to inherit my powers and end this. Finish what Blanchette couldn't. Unite all."

"How? I'm nowhere near as powerful as you think I am. I will fight, of course I will. They will not ruin what I have, what Astraea has. She will not lose anyone else."

"You will find a way. I have faith in you. You are strong, Nesrin."

"If I destroy the Order, will we be free? Will it stop?" I ask. Will Astraea be safe?

"Not all is as it seems. Look beyond the obvious. Destroying them will only get you so far. You need to go after the one whispering in the ear of your enemies. Cut the head off the snake. Once you have done that, getting the coven to fall into line will be easy with the help of your friends."

"Who is–" I start, but she cuts me off.

"I cannot intervene. The Fates won't allow it, this must play out. Even now, I'm pushing the boundaries by bringing you here, but I needed to see you. Your pendant, the one I gave to my daughter. It was used to seal your powers at birth to keep you hidden and safe, but Nesrin, now is the time to unlock them. You must accept your destiny, for all will be for nothing if you don't. It will protect you and help you channel your gifts. You have two powerful bloodlines running through your veins," Althaea is fading. I can see her shimmering body flickering. She glances down at herself, and regret washes over her features. "They have found us already," she sighs.

Dread has my pulse kicking up. "Who?"

"You must find your true light, Nesrin. Unlock your power." She reaches her hand out, gently placing it in the center of my chest.

"Wait!" I call out, my voice sounding odd, even to my own ears. I'm not ready for her to leave. I need more answers. Althaea smiles lovingly at me, lifting her hand to my face. I feel only a whisper of a touch as the goddess disappears, taking all the light with her. I am now standing in darkness. A darkness so heavy it feels suffocating. Precious seconds pass as the darkness gets heavier, like a thick blanket wrapped around me. I spin in a circle as my breathing hitches. How do I get out of here? I push forward and am surprised by how solid and thick the air appears around me. Darkness encases me, pushing in from all sides. As I struggle against the invisible force, I can sense its malicious intent wrapping around me. My lungs gasp for air, but none reaches that deep as my throat closes, constricting my breathing. My hand flies to my neck, clawing at nothing but air as I drop to my knees, fumbling in the dark. For what, I don't know. Something, anything to help fight off this entity, to defend myself from certain death.

Feeling absolutely useless, I try to call out, even though I know no one is here to help me. A croak leaves my throat as I fall, my body hitting the ground with a thump. I roll onto my back, moisture from the soft dewy meadow soaking through to my clothes. Suddenly, the world feels as if it's tipping and I flail about, searching for something to grasp onto before finally connecting with something solid.Slowly, I pull myself from the haze of the nightmare, my lungs greedily drawing deep breaths of fresh air. Feeling around, I realize I have fallen out of the bed. My entire

NATASHA MADDEN

body is also soaked in sweat, which is probably why my clothes felt damp in the meadow. Noises and footsteps filter in through the door, a hushed conversation reaching my ears. "Did you know she could do that?"

"No, I didn't. We know she's a legacy. That could account for many things, but she never mentioned this."

What on earth are they talking about? Are they talking about me? About healing Alex? They knew I could heal. Pushing up, I try to stand, my body trembling with the effort. I shake my head, dizziness making me falter slightly. The room is bright and the smells drifting through the air make me blink in surprise. I look down at my feet and, startled, I scramble back, hitting the wall with a hard thump. The door flies open, Lukas filling the doorway, Zee close behind. My frantic eyes dart between them and the snow-white paws I'm standing on. A whimper comes from my mouth. *'What's happening to me?'*

Lukas steps into the room, crouching down in front of me. "It's okay, sweetheart, calm down."

*'It's not alright!'* I scream as panic fills me, the sound coming out as a snarl, startling me further. I whimper again, dropping my head. An insistent whine rises in my throat, and I can do nothing to stop it. What is happening to me?

"Lukas, what's wrong with her?" Zee's voice is filled with worry.

Lukas's stormy green eyes swirl with emotion, reminding me of the ocean swells during a hurricane. Concern and respect flow through our bond, calming me to a certain extent.

"Nothing, Zee," he replies gruffly.

I drop to my belly and crawl over to Lukas, nuzzling his hand when I get close enough. Lukas runs his hand over my nose and

422

head, then down my neck. I close my eyes, enjoying his touch. *'What's happening to me?'* I ask again.

*'I don't know, sweetheart. Maybe your hybrid side was triggered because of the mating.'*

I peer up at him. *'Lukas, I'm scared. How do I change back?'* I am terrified. What if I'm stuck like this? What if . . . Can wolves have panic attacks?

His lips part slightly as understanding dawns in his eyes. Without taking his eyes off mine, Lukas murmurs to Zee, "Leave us."

Zee nods, walking to the door. He opens it and stops, looking back at me, his blue eyes luminous with overflowing emotions. "Thank you," he rasps before stepping out and closing it behind him.

I cock my head to the side in confusion but shake it off as Lukas sits cross-legged on the floor in front of me. "I will help you through the change. It will be painful, and for that I'm sorry, sweetheart. But it will get easier the more you do it."

*'What! I'm never doing this again.'* I tremble, a whine escaping my mouth, and Lukas smiles, running a hand over me again.

"I promise it won't hurt for long."

I huff and lay my head on his knee, staring up at him. *'I trust you.'*

"Don't give me those eyes. Those eyes will get you the world on a platter," Lukas chuckles, but there is hardly any joy in it.

*'I love you,'* I say, stretching up and nuzzling his face.

Lukas's hands sink into my fur, stroking my face. "I love you too, sweetheart. Are you ready?"

*'Yes. No. Yes. Maybe?'*

Understanding fills his eyes. "You'll be fine. I'm right here." His hand glides over my head and I nuzzle closer, taking a deep breath as Lukas smiles warily down at me.

"Okay, I want you to draw in your magic and concentrate on your human form. I will guide your magic with my own and help you with the shift."

Closing my eyes, I do as he says and pull in all the magic I can. Slowly, a tingling sensation takes over my body. My bones crack and sharp stabbing pain takes over all other thoughts as my bones break and reshape. I try my hardest to picture my body like Lukas said. But the pain . . . I scream out in agony as my body rebuilds itself. I feel like I'm going to black out from the pain.

*How do they keep doing this all the time?*

Lukas's voice is the first thing to break through my distress. His voice is strained, but his warm, powerful arms are wrapped around me tightly, rocking me. Us. His lips are against my cheek, his hot breath caressing my face. Thank the goddess, it's over. A violent tremble runs through me, and I let out a stuttered breath, relaxing more fully into Lukas's arms.

"I'm sorry," I whisper, my voice hoarse.

Pulling me even tighter against him, Lukas cradles me. Lovingly, gently, innocently. He kisses away my tears. I am so incredibly lucky to have found this man, this wolf. To have him claim me as his, take me and Astraea and all my problems on board without complaint. I find only love, warmth, and peace in his arms.

My life has changed so much in the last couple of months, it has been an absolute whirlwind. We need to stop the Order of Tartarus, and the only way to do that is to find out who is pulling the strings. Simple, right? Whatever happens, I will let my light guide me. I just hope the darkness doesn't drag me under.

Lukas adjusts his head, kissing my temple and whispering in my ear, "You are a beautiful wolf, your fur such a brilliant, striking white. You took my breath away."

My chest warms, and I snuggle closer, resting my head under his chin and closing my eyes. I let his scent, his arms, and the beat of his heart carry me away. I am tired, so damn tired.

# CHAPTER THIRTY SEVEN

I take in the sight of the valley before me, feeling the warmth of the sun on my skin and the sweet scent of wildflowers. With my foot dangling over the railing, I pull the other close, wrapping my arms around it. My mind flashes back to when I told Lukas about Ryan's betrayal the night before, how he played a part in my capture.

*He was furious, to say the least. So furious, he called a pack meeting. Ryan hasn't been seen since the night of my escape, so we figure he tucked tail and ran, but it's still important to discuss the matter with the rest of the pack. The air has such a deadly calm to it, and I find myself fidgeting in my seat, unsure about what will happen. Lukas paces at the front of the room, his eyes taking on a predator's glint as he looks over his pack. Everyone is silent, waiting to see what has their alpha so worked up. Lukas then told them about Ryan's betrayal, a wave of shock and disbelief floating through the room. A few cautious looks are thrown my way, but I ignore them. Then, he stops and looks at me, the hardness of his eyes softening as he speaks.*

"Nesrin has given you no reason not to trust her. None. To insult her or cause her harm is to insult me and cause me harm," he says coolly. "She is a goddess, a witch, a warrior, and she is more than capable of defending herself against any of you. But in this pack—as my mate, your luna—she shouldn't have to." All hints of the gentle, fair alpha are gone. His tone is as harsh as his expression. "Nesrin doesn't need us or me. If she wanted to, she could have fled and stayed out of reach of the coven, but I asked her to stay. I placed her in danger for my own selfish reasons, believing I could protect her."

I shoot to my feet, upset that he thinks any of this is his fault. "That's not true. I was always in danger, whether I stayed or left."

He tilts his head, his eyes meeting mine. "Isn't it? You were going to run. I asked you to stay. I promised to protect you."

'I failed,' is spoken into my mind, his feelings of failure drifting down the bond.

"No!" I counter fervently.

Lukas looks away and resumes his pacing, his voice even lower than before. "What Ryan did was unforgivable, and I expect anyone who sees him to report to me or Zee."

He stops pacing and faces the room. "If I hear anyone speak to Nesrin in any way that is disrespectful, or if any of you hurt her in any way. I will cast you from the pack." He pauses, his eyes moving over his pack. Not a single shifter moves. I'm not sure anyone, including myself, is even breathing at this point. "This is your warning. I opened this pack to all who needed a home. Don't take my generosity as weakness." And with that, he simply storms off, leaving me standing here, gaping at his back.

Kyra appears next to me from out of nowhere, whispering in my ear, "That was hot."

*I snap my mouth shut and make an unintelligible sound, because, well, it was hot. And he was right. I can defend myself against them, but I shouldn't have to.*

Blinking several times, I clear the memory from my mind. Gabe makes his way up the stairs leaning on the railing.

"What the hell is wrong with you today?" Gabe grumbles, leaning his back against the porch railing. It has been two weeks since they rescued me, and in that time, I've healed Alex, changed into a wolf, and met a goddess. More often than not, my mind has been occupied with the pendant, what it will mean to put it on. My whole life has been spent in hiding and learning my gifts in secret. Deep down, I feel like I've always known there was more. That I had something locked away inside, simmering just beneath the surface. Now I just need to find the guts to unleash it. Easier said than done, though. I am scared.

"Nothing," I shoot back from my spot, perched on the railing, my back against the post, hugging one knee to my chest, the other dangling over the edge.

"We all know that when a woman says nothing, it is definitely something," Zee says, coming out the front door, letting it bang shut behind him.

"Do you have to do that?" I snap, shooting him an irritated look.

Confusion flashes in his eyes as he takes me in carefully. "Do what?"

"Let the door bang shut." *Obviously.*

Zee's eyes widen in surprise.

Okay. Yes, I am in a bad mood. But for the life of me, I can't figure out why. I stare back out at the valley, taking in the cool afternoon breeze.

"Yep, something is definitely up," Gabe says, a smirk pulling at his lips. I could feel Zee's eyes boring into the side of my head, and I can't help the growl that crawls up my throat.

Looking back over at him, I widen my eyes. "What?" I snap again, guilt churning my stomach. My bad mood isn't their fault.

"Are you hungry?" he asks, drawing the words out cautiously.

Rolling my eyes, I look away. "No. Has it ever occurred to you that I might just be having a bad day?" I mutter.

"She is definitely hungry," Gabe whispers. My head swivels his way, and I glare at him.

"Totally hungry," Zee adds.

Flipping him off, I open my mouth to argue, but shut it. What's the point? Laughing, Zee reaches behind his back, pulls an apple from his back jeans pocket, and throws it at me.

I catch it and immediately toss it back. "I'd rather starve."

"Well, that's dramatic, even for you," Zee says, catching the apple and taking a bite. Gabe pushes off the railing and starts walking for the door.

"You just randomly carry apples around in your back pockets now?" he asks Zee.

"Yep," Zee's reply pops with the P. "Never know when you'll run into a hungry female."

A low growl rumbles up from my throat as I glare at the blonde shifter who clearly has a death wish.

Turning to me, Gabe's warm brown eyes soften. "What did you want to eat? I'll make it," he offers. My stomach rumbles loud enough I know they can hear it.

My face heats. "Nothing," I mumble back.

"Was it what Grace did to Suzy?" Zee asks gently. My head swivels his way, and I stare for a moment. I'm not happy Grace stole one of my sleeping potions and slipped it to Suzy to keep her from coming to the house that night. But I also know it would have been bad for Suzy to walk in on the chaos the night of my rescue. I am both upset and grateful for what Grace did. Gah, I hate mixed emotions. But no, that isn't what has me in knots. I've just had this bad feeling all day. Some impending doom shit, twisting my insides up.

I sense Lukas and turn my head toward the driveway. Sure enough, his new black Ford F150 is coming up the drive. I let out a breath I hadn't realized I had been holding at the sight of his return. I had been on edge all morning. Now that they're back safely, a weight lifts from my shoulders. Lukas and Astraea went to see Sophie, Joseph, and their baby girl, Rose. They moved back into their own house a few days ago. I opted to stay behind to watch over Kaida's egg. So much has been happening lately. as the car pulls to a stop. Lukas gets out and moves to unbuckle Astraea, turning to look at me as he does. His brows furrow, and I know he can feel my mood. Once out of the car, Astraea is off, running up the stairs. I jump down from my perch on the railing, bending down to catch her as she leaps into my arms. As often as she does it, I really feel this might be her favorite thing to do. I lift her up and bury my head in her hair, smelling her. She was only gone for a short while, but I missed her the whole time.

Pulling back, she pushes to get down and whispers in my head, 'Hungry?'

I tip my head back and laugh. "Not you as well," I say, tickling her tummy.

Laughing, she wriggles like a worm on a hook, and I set her down on her feet. Peering up, I watch Lukas make his way to the porch carrying six pizza boxes. How does he always know when to bring me pizza? Smirking, he holds them up higher. "Joe's had a buy two, get the third free today, so I thought I'd grab some."

Grinning, I make my way toward him, pushing up on my tiptoes to give him a peck on the cheek and grab the box on top. Then, turning, I sit down on the top step and open the lid. The smell of meat and cheese hits me and my stomach grumbles again. I waste no more time before I dig in.

I faintly hear Zee say, "I told you she was hungry," but pay him no mind.

Astraea takes a seat next to me with her own box and I cast her a smile as we eat. I'm on my fourth piece when I realize everyone has stopped talking. Looking up, I see three sets of eyes watching me, each with their own expressions. Lukas with concern, Zee curious, and Gabe thoughtful.

"What?" I mumble around a mouthful of pizza, just now noticing none of them has moved to eat.

It's Gabe who breaks the silence. "Maybe she is with pup," he says, shrugging. I swear, the only noise that can be heard is the crickets down by the river. No one moves or even breathes.

"I am not," I say, choking on my mouthful of pizza as I come out of my shock, and suddenly not feeling hungry at all. But each male is looking at me very carefully. "I'm not."

At that moment, I see Alex, Liam, and Noah walking toward the house. Astraea spots the boys at the same time and gets up, running for them. The three of them have become the best of friends and I'm so happy Astraea has some good kids around her. Astraea's blonde curls fly around her face as she looks back at me and points at the river, where they all love to play. Knowing the sprites will watch over them, I nod my head.

"Be careful!" I shout as they all run down the hill.

"We will," come three voices, one in my head.

"Hey, guys," Alex says, walking up to the bottom of the steps. "What's going on?" she asks, obviously sensing the tension in the air.

"Hi, Alex. Nothing's going on. Want some pizza?" I blurt out, holding up the box, glad for the interruption.

The streaks of pink and purple in her blonde pixie cut are vibrant in the sunlight. Her hair was burned too badly to salvage most of the length, so we opted to give her a makeover with a new cut and color that really suit her well. I am so happy to see her walking around and socializing after her ordeal. We have become close over the last week, which I honestly never thought would happen. She has changed in her time away. Alex proved that when she saved my life, almost giving hers up in the process. I'll never forget that. Even though she believes we're even, I owe her so much.

Zee and Gabe move over to the chairs, dropping the topic of babies, thank the goddess. I cannot be having a baby, not with the mess we're in. Do I want to have children with Lukas? Of course. But right now? No.

"How's the dragon egg going?" she asks, sitting next to me and taking a piece of pizza from the box.

I place the box down and glance over at the crate I take with me everywhere. "Nothing yet. I'm not sure when it'll hatch."

"I'm sure it will be soon. What are we going to do with a dragon?" she asks, munching on her pizza.

It's a good question, one I'm not sure I can answer just yet. I can easily cloak the dragon, but I can't cloak what it does. I don't understand the first thing about dragons.

"We will figure it out as we go," Lukas answers for me, coming over to take the spot behind me, and wraps me in his arms, pulling me back against his hard chest. I close my eyes, savoring the moment, surrounded by his warmth and scent.

"I'm leaving," Alex says so quietly I'm not sure I heard her at all.

Straightening up, I spin toward her. "What?!" I basically shout.

Cringing, she shrugs and looks down to the river where the kids are playing. "I was going to ask permission to leave with Finan's pack."

Confusion rolls through me, and I search for a reason why she would want to leave. I pull out of Lukas's embrace and turn to face her fully, my knees pressing against her thigh. "Why?"

"I-I- Well . . . you see, Roan," Alex stutters and then groans, dropping her head into her hands. She peeks at me and I feel my eyes widen as she blushes. I have never seen her blush before.

"Wait. Are you and Roan a thing now?" I ask, excitement bubbling up at the thought she could have found what she has been wanting for so long.

"Yes. He's my mate. We found out last night during the run," she replies, looking to the ground, trying to hide her face. I reach over, grabbing her shoulder and squeezing it gently, waiting for her to look at me. When she does, there are tears brimming her eyes, which, of course, automatically makes tears burn my eyes.

"I'm so happy for you," I say honestly.

Lunging forward, we wrap our arms tightly around each other, both of us breaking into a half laugh, half sob.

I faintly hear Gabe mutter, "Bloody women," and we both laugh a little louder. Pulling back, we wipe the tears from our faces and smile at each other.

"I'm sad that you'll be leaving, but I'm happy you've found your mate. And Roan is a good man. You deserve a good man, someone who will make you happy," I whisper.

Finan and his pack have to leave tomorrow. They have been away from home long enough and need to return. I know they will come running if we need them, but Kate has decided to stay behind for now. I don't blame her. She is making up for lost time.

My phone vibrates in my pocket, and I pull it out, my smile instantaneous. "Suzy?" I answer, accepting the call.

"Not Suzy," a deep rich voice hums through the speaker. Lukas stiffens behind me, having heard the voice.

"Stephan, why do you have Suzy's phone?" I growl, my stomach twisting in fear. I don't think the vampire would hurt Suzy, but I also can't be sure his intentions are true.

"Suzy is fine. We are actually having a coffee at Little Bites."

I relax slightly. "Wait. A coffee? You can have coffee?"

Stephan's rich laugh fills the line. "I have adjusted over time."

"Oh." I'm a little dumbstruck by this. Maybe it's the fact that I know little about vampires. Shaking my head, I get back on topic. "You haven't answered my question. Why do you have Suzy's phone?"

Stephan's exhale is for show, and I hear him mutter something to Suzy. At least, I assume it's her. I can't quite make out the other voice. "Suzy wanted to see you, rose sauvage. She misses her friend."

Zee, who has been leaning against the railing, straightens, his brow lowering as he makes no attempt to hide that he is listening.

"When?" I ask, flustered. Stephan is working an angle, and he's using my friend to make a point. I am going to find something very pointy and stab him with it if he isn't careful.

"Tonight. At a bar called Breakers." His tone is relaxed and almost playful. He knows Lukas must be listening. Stephan is playing with fire.

Indeed, I feel Lukas's body tremble in a silent growl, and the hairs on my arms stand on end. Breakers is a vampire bar. The reputation isn't the best. But before I can respond, a piercing scream breaks through the air, all of us jumping to our feet. *The kids.*

I drop my phone and leap down the stairs, bolting for the river, the others right behind me. Lukas overtakes me in his wolf form. I see Alex change in the span of one leap next to me. The urge to shift myself is strong, but I push it down. I don't want to be stuck in my wolf's form like last time.

Another scream tears through the air, but this one is one of rage. We finally see the children. Noah and Liam are in their small wolf forms, standing guard in front of Astraea, their hackles raised, heads lowered, and ears pinned back. I stare beyond them, scanning the river for threats. *Who screamed?*

We reach the kids, making a circle around them, the five of us on high alert. Lukas, Zee, and Alex are in their wolf forms. Gabe and I remain as we are.

"Do you see anything?" I ask the others.

'*No,*' Zee replies. His gray wolf is standing beside me, muscles taut, his head high on alert.

Lukas lets out a loud growl from deep in his chest. '*Something isn't right. The air smells rotten.*' He huffs a breath out of his nose, shaking his massive head.

NATASHA MADDEN

Turning around, I face the children, squatting in front of Astraea so I'm at eye level with her. "Sweet girl, who screamed?" I ask, taking hold of her shoulders gently.

*'The shadow,'* is the nervously whispered reply in my mind.

"What shadow?" I brush the hair off her face. Noah and Liam push in closer to us, their small wolves pressing tight against Astraea's body.

*'The one that always watches us.'* My head jerks back, startled at her response. I quickly stand upright, scanning our surroundings. So, I'm not the only one who has been seeing the shadows move.

A loud crack sounds in the air and static pricks at my skin. Something just came through a portal. Something bad. I push Astraea toward Alex. "Get her out of here, Alex."

My friend nods and lowers herself to the ground for Astraea to climb on her back. From the corner of my eye, I spot a dark shape taking form at the edge of the river. Lukas and Zee leap forward, their massive forms covering Alex, Astraea, and me. Gabe moves to stand by my side, facing whatever is across the river. We watch as the shadows grow and expand, becoming solid. Lukas prowls forward with Zee at his side. Both have their ears erect, hackles raised. A snarl rumbles from Lukas as his lips pull back, his incisors on display. He seems almost to grow in size, and I can feel his anger and protective instincts take over. It is flooding our bond, his feelings overwhelming me. Closing my eyes, I feel for our bonded link and put a metaphorical blanket over it to muffle his feelings so I can focus.

My eyes widen as a barely visible form steps out of the haze of shadows. "Emerson?" I whisper as I take a step forward, bumping into Lukas, and sink my fingers into his warm, soft fur, hoping it helps center me.

She looks different, her beautiful red hair, a shade brighter than mine, still falls in waves around her shoulders. But her eyes are different. They are amber instead of green. I recognize those eyes because I stare at them every day in the mirror. "How?" I whisper, my hand absently moving to my face.

Emerson looks at me and only me as she steps forward. Lukas growls in warning, but she pays him no mind. Her focus is fully on me.

*'Is this the Emerson who helped you escape?'* Lukas asks.

"*Yes,*" I reply through the bond, studying Emerson. Her clothes are dirty and torn, there's blood on them. I must have been staring, because she looks down to see what I'm looking at, noticing the blood.

"It's not mine," she says, shrugging her delicate shoulders.

I frown at her blasé tone. "Whose is it?"

She waves off my concern. "Never mind that. I've come to warn you."

"Warn me? Why are your eyes different? Who are you?" I'm throwing out too many questions, I know, but I'm so confused. I don't want to believe what my gut is telling me. That this is Leila.

"That's not important. The–"

"I think it is," I interrupt, moving toward her past Lukas and Zee. I feel a hand on my leg and glance down. Astraea is right there with me. Glancing back, I see Alex moving the boys up the hill. Good.

"Nesrin, I can't get into that right now. The Order has released daemons and monsters that will come after you. I just disposed of one that was lurking across the river hunting the children."

Not that I'm ignoring what she's saying, but I have to know. "Leila?" I ask quietly, and Emerson's body stiffens as she looks away. I watch as she visibly swallows before looking back.

"I need to go. I need to alert someone about what's happening. Be on the lookout." She turns her gaze to Lukas. "Keep them safe." Then she steps back, the mass of shadows swirling around her. Zee leaps forward, stopping a foot away from Emerson . . . or Leila. I'm not sure anymore. He tilts his head, studying the shadows as they converge around her. He seems to search for something in her gaze, but she just stares back, a blank look firmly in place. Just before she disappears, I see it—a single tear slipping down her face as she looks again to Zee. Then she was gone.

I shake my head as an ache starts in my chest, my shoulders dropping. Could it be? Is she my sister? And if she is, why wouldn't she tell me? Why would she stay with the council, be a part of that? I forgave Emerson for torturing my mind, but Leila? My own sister? I feel sick. As I turn my back to the river, a silence falls over the woods, and a dark, ominous feeling creeps into the air. Pinpricks of awareness scatter over me. Something is watching us. My insides twist as the grim feeling increases. Something is about to happen. I can sense it deep down in my bones. Fighting the chill that sweeps over me, I step closer to Zee and let my hand brush along his back.

A savage growl erupts behind me, the kind that has the blood draining from your face. My stomach drops, and I feel as if I am free falling as I spin, searching for the source. I come to a halt as my gaze collides with six glowing crimson eyes staring at me from down the river.

"What the fuck is that?" I say to everyone and no one. Stepping out into the open is a pure black beast the size of a horse with three gigantic heads all snapping and growling, saliva dripping from their fangs. This is what I felt come through the portal a few minutes before, not Emerson.

Shit. Is that . . . Cerberus? I instinctively take a step back, my hand reaching for the dagger I keep strapped to my thigh. Not that it'll do much damage, not to this beast.

*'Fuck!'* Lukas's voice is hard and pissed. Dread fills me. We won't be able to defeat Cerberus. He is known for his strength and brutality. His owner is the god of the underworld, for shit's sake! Cerberus makes sure that no dead soul escapes, and no living man enters the realm of the dead. *How are we supposed to defeat him?*

Its three massive dog heads, which resemble cane corsos, snarl and snap in my direction as it draws closer, saliva dripping from each of the mouths. His pitch-black body is corded with muscles. He is as gorgeous as he is absolutely terrifying. Lukas and Zee stalk past me, effectively blocking Cerberus from reaching me easily. They growl in warning, but they won't be enough. More howls rise from the house, the pack answering Lukas's call to arms.

*'Get out of here, Nesrin. Take Astra and go. We will hold it off,'* Lukas says into my mind, his worry seeping through the bond. He recognizes this as a fight we might not win. I turn and notice Gabe's eyes glowing a bright whitish yellow, almost as bright as the sun. He shifts and I stand there gaping. I've seen his fox before, of course, but this is not the same fox. I blink several times just to make sure I'm actually seeing what stands in front of me. Gabe's fox has three tails, all swishing back and forth. Each has a beautiful pure white tip, and on his head is a white diamond. He is absolutely magical. As he prowls forward, the glow from

his eyes grows brighter. Then I notice the river. A whirlpool is forming in the middle. My eyes dart back to Gabe. *Is he doing that?*

'*Go now, Nesrin,*' Zee urges.

Not wasting another second, I turn, looking for Astraea, but come up short. She's gone. Where is she?

Panic fills me and I spin around, searching. "Where's Astraea?" I shout, and all heads turn my way.

I hear the water from the river come crashing down as Gabe loses his focus. Movement up on the hill catches my attention and I see Alex come bounding down the hill with Roan's gingery wolf by her side. Finan, Kate, and some others are following close behind, all in their wolf forms. I glance back at Cerberus and my blood freezes at the sight in front of me. Fear tumbles through me and a scream leaves my mouth. Without thinking, I run forward. Astraea is now only a few feet from Cerberus.

"Astraea. NO!" I scream, but she pays me no mind. She moves a step closer. Damn it. I'm too far away. I won't reach her in time. Gathering my magic, I prepare to encase her in a protective bubble that I'm not sure will even be able to fully protect her from a beast of Hades. My steps falter as I watch Cerberus sit on his massive hind legs in front of Astraea. I slow my steps. My magic is humming under my skin, a warmth filling me. Astraea tilts her small head. She looks so small next to this creature. Cerberus tilts all three of its massive heads, copying her. I take one slow, careful step, not wanting to startle the beast. I can see the others around me spread out, all waiting, doing their best to avoid provoking Cerberus into attacking with Astraea so close.

"Astraea," I whisper, knowing full well she can hear me. All three of Cerberus's heads snap up and snarl, but just as quickly, they stare back down at Astraea. Surprise rolls through me as I watch the massive beast lower himself to the ground, resting one of his three heads in his paws, giving her what looks like puppy dog eyes, as if she scolded him. One of the other heads looks like it's smiling, and the last is tilting its head in confusion. *Well, that makes two of us, buddy.*

Astraea moves the last step forward. My breathing hitches. Reaching out her small hand, she pats the guardian of the underworld on the head like it's some normal-ass dog. One of its tongues snakes out, licking her across the face. A giggle breaks free, and my shoulders slump in relief, the feeling making me queasy. Bending, I put my hands to my knees, breathing deeply. *Fuck.* I'm either going to pass out or puke. I'm not sure which it will be. A warm hand rubs circles on my back and I peer up at Lukas.

"What just happened?" I croak, getting light headed.

"Our star just tamed a beast," Lukas replies warily, looking over at Astraea, who is currently sitting in front of the three-headed beast clapping her hands. I slowly stand up straight, and Lukas grabs my hand so we can take slow, measured steps toward Astraea and the beast. Cerberus lifts his crimson eyes to us, the hackles rising on its back.

Turning, Astraea smiles at me. '*Puppy dog,*' she says, and I choke on a laugh.

Shit. I swallow hard. "Astraea, honey. That's not a puppy dog." We are less than a dozen feet away now, and Cerberus is so much scarier up close. I swear I can see the pits of Tartarus burning in his eyes.

"Astra, can you come to me?" Lukas asks, reaching out a hand. Standing on her little legs, she turns to us but stops, giving

Cerberus a hug, her arms nowhere near wrapping around its thick neck. I notice a slight stir of wind around my head and turn slightly to see Nissa landing on my shoulder, her violet eyes wide in disbelief.

"Is that?"

"Yep."

"How in the world did Astraea get that close to a hellhound?" she asks, her voice sounding squeaky. Poor little sprite looks utterly horrified, holding her hands clasped over her heart.

Exhaustion is creeping in now as the adrenaline fades. "I don't know." I sigh, rubbing my temples.

Cerberus stands, following Astraea over to us. I inhale sharply, coming eye to eye with the crimson eyes of the middle head. The other two heads are watching the wolves very closely. Lukas has gone as still as a statue, the kind of stillness that is unnatural, his concern bleeding through the bond.

Cerberus's massive head leans in closer. I hold my breath in anticipation, trying not to cringe away when a sloppy tongue rolls out, licking my face. Startled, all I can do is stare. Astraea laughs and the tension in the air dissipates. If only slightly.

The hound's head pulls back and starts panting excitedly. Swallowing my fear, I reach up and run a hand over his head, and he leans into the touch. I smile. "Thank you," I whisper. He tilts his head. The other two heads swing to glance at me with what I would call shock. "Lukas, let's see if we can find somewhere for Cerberus to stay until we can figure out how to get him home."

Lukas's head swings my way in disbelief. "Can't you just send him back?"

"No, only the summoner can do that." It also isn't something I ever learned. It's dark magic, a magic that steals a little piece of your soul each time.

"Well, that's just great. What are we supposed to do with the hound of hell?" Zee snaps, shifting back into his human form, but makes no move to get closer.

"Feed it and find it somewhere to sleep," I reply, taking turns patting each head. The tongues each loll out, a dopey expression on its faces. He doesn't seem all that threatening anymore. Don't get me wrong, I'm still terrified. But whatever Astraea did to get this creature on our side, I'm grateful.

Cerberus abruptly spins around, startling me, his jaws snapping in the direction of the road as a blur comes at us fast. "Uh, Lukas. What is that?"

All the shifters snarl and snap, standing in front of us as the blur halts not twenty meters away. "Stephan?" I choke out.

Stephan stands straight and adjusts his suit, looking at the situation with cold, calculating eyes. He takes in Cerberus and raises an eyebrow in question. "Got a new pet, my rose?" he asks.

Before I can answer, Lukas steps forward. "Why are you here?" Straight to the point, good.

"I heard screams and snarls through the phone and I wanted to make sure everything was okay." Stephan's stance is casual, but I can sense his unease. He did come on to pack land uninvited and is surrounded by shifters.

I raise an eyebrow at the vampire. "Really?"

"Yes. Don't sound so surprised."

Lukas moves in front of me, blocking my view of Stephan. "We don't tolerate vampires on pack land," he snarls.

"Very well aware of that, alpha."

"So, it's time for you to leave," Zee snaps, strolling toward the vampire. His massive shoulders rolling back as if itching for a fight.

Stephan smirks, cocking his head to the side as he stares at Zee. "Down, boy." He turns his azure gaze on me, as I inch around Lukas. His voice is silky and rich as he says, "I just wanted to make sure my rose sauvage was safe and sound."

Lukas snarls, the sound animalistic. I place both hands on his back before leaning in and placing a kiss there. He is extremely tense. I know this isn't sitting well with him, having a vampire on his land. I'm not exactly comfortable with Stephan's interest in me either, but he risked coming onto pack land to make sure everything was okay. Lukas relaxes his stance.

Cerberus, on the other hand, stalks forward, its three massive heads lowered and snarling. I swallow over my fear and move to stand at Cerberus's side. "Everything is fine. Thank you, Stephan."

"Leave!" Lukas barks, a scowl etched into his face.

Stephan remains quiet for a moment, then his voice reaches me. "Very well."

As I stared at the three hundred fifty pound, three-headed dog rolling around in a stack of hay, I wonder if I'm dreaming right now. I feel like I'm dreaming. I could be dreaming, right? Calmly, I reach my hand up and pinch my arm. "Ouch. Okay. Not a dream, then," I murmur, not taking my eyes from the dog.

Cerberus, having heard me, stops rolling around and launches to his feet, padding over to me where I sit next to Astraea and Nissa on a bale of hay. Both of them watch the dog with wide, expressive eyes.

"His eyes are quite unnerving," Nissa says, shifting on her feet.

"I'm getting used to them," I say, rubbing along his side, Cerberus's long tail coils around my leg.

"It's only been twenty minutes. How can you be used to it already?" she huffs, crossing her tiny arms and lifting off her feet to flutter in the air.

I smirk at her. "Come on, Nissa. You're not scared, are you?" I tease jokingly.

"No, never. I just feel uneasy with such a beast around," she grumbles, her wings beating quickly with agitation.

"Are you a beast?" I ask Cerberus in a baby voice, earning a playful stare from each of its heads. His long tail uncoils and whips back and forth as his legs bounce off the ground playfully. "Oh yes, you are. You are a big bad beast," I say, throwing my head back and laughing. Cerberus nudges me with one of its heads, sending me tumbling to the ground. "Ouch!" I chuckle, rubbing my elbow as I sit up amongst the hay. Looking up at the beast towering over me, I'm not afraid. I can't help but admire the friendly giant.

'Can we keep him?' Astraea asks, her tiny voice hopeful.

My eyes whip to her and I balk. "Keep a hellhound? No, Astraea. He is not a pet," I say, all humor vanishing. Her face drops and I feel terrible. "Astraea, you cannot keep him, but maybe we can look into getting you a pet. Possibly one that won't mind being around a pack of shifters." I cringe because that will be hard to find. Astraea nods, her body deflated, obviously thinking like me.

I rub the back of my neck, standing up. "Okay, let's get our guest settled and head back to the house, sweet girl."

We get to work feeding Cerberus and settling him down for the night. It is dark by the time we head back up to the house. I'm halfway to the house when a playful bark sounds behind me, and I grin at Cerberus's attempt for attention. Cerberus is such a surprise. Behind those terrifying, glowing red eyes and enormous sharp teeth is a sweet, adorable puppy who is currently jumping around in our barn, enjoying the softness of the straw. With Astraea and Nissa racing back up the hill to the house, I slow my pace, taking my time to enjoy the cool night air on my face. I close my eyes, tilting my head up to the sky and taking a few deep calming breaths.

"I can do this," I whisper to myself.

# CHAPTER THIRTY EIGHT

S miling to myself, I walk back to the house and push through the door. Several sets of eyes swiveling toward me, all reflecting a variety of different emotions. But there is only one set of eyes I want to see right now. I realize it should be Lukas's, but instead I turn to find Zee leaning back against the far wall. I make my way over to him. He looks so lost.

"You know Emerson?"

Looking taken aback, his head hangs. I rest my hand on his shoulder, squeezing.

*'Zee?'*

When he lifts his head, there is a glimpse of sorrow on his face, and my stomach twists. I hate that look.

"I met Leila about three years ago," his voice is deep and gruff with emotion. "She showed up and saved my life from a bunch of wraiths on a trip to Pittsburgh. We ended up getting close during my stay. Then she disappeared. I tried searching for her, but there was no sign of her anywhere."

A small huff escapes my mouth, tears welling in my eyes. He knew Leila. She was in Pittsburgh, too? If she knew about us, why not say something? This explains why he was so mad when he found out about my missing sister. I wrap my arms around him. He lifts his arms, hugging me back, both of us clinging to each other.

"I'm sorry, Zee," I say quietly, pulling away. I reach up to wipe the tears off my cheeks.

"It's okay, honey. It was a shock to see her."

"We will see her again."

Distracted, Zee nods his head, lost in his own thoughts. I turn to face the room, my eyes immediately focusing on Lukas. Taking in his disheveled hair, I smirk. He is leaning against the kitchen counter, a thoughtful look on his face, his powerful arms crossed over his chest. His eyes meet mine, a tender expression softening his face. This man is gorgeous even when he's worn out. A wave of calming energy and affection floats down our bond followed by, *'I love you.'*

A small smile pulls at my mouth and his own twitches in return. I walk over to him, his arms opening for me, and I bury my head in his chest as his strong, warm, safe arms wrap tightly around me.

"I love you, too," I breathe into his chest. Realizing it's extremely quiet in the kitchen, I turn in Lukas's arms, resting my back against his chest, his arms once more coming around my body, hugging me close to him.

Kate, Alex, and Gabe are seated at the table. I look around for Grace, but don't see her. She must have headed back into town. Finan, Roan, and Merve stand at the entrance to the hall, speaking in whispers.

A moment of panic hits me. "Where's Astra?"

"Nissa took her upstairs to get ready for bed," Merve answers as he comes into the kitchen. I exhale and give him a small smile. He has been such a great friend throughout all of this. I glance around the room, feeling extremely lucky to have all these wonderful people backing me. Not one of them has faltered in any of this.

Finan enters the kitchen behind Merve. When he speaks, his voice is deceptively calm, but his eyes are like chips of ice. "We can stay longer, Nesrin. There's no way I can leave tomorrow like I planned. Not with a hellhound here."

"If what Emerson said is true, there are more monsters and daemons on the loose. You need all the help you can get," Merve points out, agreeing with Finan.

But I can't ask that of him. Yes, he has become part of the family, they all have, but his own pack needs him home. The alpha needs to be with his pack.

Shaking my head, I voice my worries. "Finan, you need to take care of your pack. Go home. Regroup. You've been gone long enough. We can handle this."

"She's right, Finan. You need to get back to your pack. If we need you, we can send for you," Lukas adds. I shiver as his warm breath skates across my ear, desire curling in my belly. Through the bond, I sense amusement and desire mirroring my own. All I want to do is drag Lukas upstairs to our bedroom.

"Keep thinking like that and I'll be dragging you upstairs, sweetheart."

I turn my head, looking up at him, a roguish smirk on his face. "Promises, promises," I taunt and his eyes flare with surprise as his arousal hits me with full force down the bond.

"Are you two even listening to me?" Finan's voice raises, drawing my attention.

"Sorry," I mutter, feeling like a scolded child. I forgot how on edge everyone was with the arrival of Cerberus.

"It could be too late by then," he argues, his arms crossing over his wide chest.

I understand his hesitancy to leave. I really do. Things have gotten messy. He's only just found Astraea, and Kate is planning on staying for a while herself.

As if voicing my concern, Kate pipes up, "I will stay. I was planning on staying for a bit longer, anyway." She shrugs her delicate shoulders, a small smile growing on her face, making her blue eyes sparkle. "Plus, I've never seen anything like I have today. I'm curious what else is going to pop up."

Finan growls in warning at his sister. "This isn't to be taken lightly, Kate."

Kate merrily shrugs before sipping at her drink.

Alex pushes up from the table, casting Roan a quick glance. "I will stay until this is over. I can't leave now, not when I'm needed," she says almost apologetically.

"That could be a while. You should go," I say, making sure she realizes this isn't something that will be finished by the end of the week. It could take months to track down the leader of the Order.

"If Alex stays, so do I," Roan chimes in, receiving a glare from his alpha. But Roan only has eyes for Alex, whose answering blush has joy spreading through my chest. She deserves happiness.

"Fine. Kate and Roan will stay for the time being," Finan says, relenting. "I will take the others and go home to make sure things are stable there. I want daily updates, though," Finan demands, turning the last request to his beta.

Roan nods, his red hair looking awfully vivid tonight under the bright lights. "Of course," he replies.

Finan's arctic blue eyes turn to me. My breath stalls at the harsh look. "Be careful. Listen to your instincts. Do not hesitate to call me, you are like a sister to me, and I hate the thought of leaving you—all of you." He looks to Lukas, a silent exchange passing between them.

Lukas nods. "I will protect them with my life."

"As will I," Zee agrees, pushing off the wall and striding toward Finan. He holds a hand out to the alpha. Finan's eyes look down at the hand offered and he knocks it away, pulling Zee in for a bear hug instead. I hold back my giggle. Zee looks so uncomfortable, but the Viking gives wonderful hugs, and Zee definitely needed one.

Merve moves in front of me. Worry lines every inch of his body. I've never seen him so serious. "This is going to get worse, Nesrin. So much worse, I fear. But remember, you have so many allies who will come if you ask."

My brow furrows in confusion. What allies? So many thoughts are running through my head it's hard to stay focused on any one thing. I see Gabe move to sit at the table, and like water dripping from the tap, I blurt out my next thought before I can stop myself.

"Is anyone going to mention the fact that Gabe has three tails?"

Gabe's hand is halfway to his mouth to take a bite of a sandwich when he freezes. Lukas's warm chuckle sounds from behind me as everyone stares at me.

"What?? I can't be the only one who noticed."

Gabe puts his sandwich down and turns those almond eyes on me. They flash like lightning, and I'm mesmerized. He would never hurt me. I'm not afraid of that anymore. I trust Gabe.

"I'm a *Yasashī Kitsune.* We can have up to nine tails, usually one every hundred years."

I jerk in Lukas's arms. "You're *three hundred* years old?" I exclaim loudly.

Laughing, Gabe shakes his head. "No, I'm not even thirty yet. I don't know why I have three already," he replies.

"Are you . . . " I trail off, not sure how to put my thoughts into words, but Gabe seems to understand where I'm going and answers anyway.

"I'm one of the good ones. I have an affinity for my elemental magic, which is water, or more accurately, river. With age, my powers will grow. I haven't trained much in my magic, though. It's hard when I'm the only kitsune around. I prefer to use my time training more in combat than magic."

"Why didn't I see three tails when you led me away from the fight in the woods?"

"I had them hidden."

"How?"

He shrugs his shoulders, picking up his sandwich again. "I can choose what people see when they look at me."

A loud crack sounds through the room, making everyone stop what they're doing. We listen as another crack sounds. My eyes fly to Lukas.

"The dragon," I exclaim, pushing out of Lukas's arms and dashing for the living room. I skid to a stop on my knees as I reach the basket. Tiny cracks fracture across the surface of the egg. It starts splitting as the others file into the room behind me.

I can't take my eyes off this egg, though. As I watch in wonder, the shell slowly breaks apart. One tiny claw grabs the edge of the shell, pushing it and breaking it away, leaving a tiny hole. I bend forward to get a closer peek. The egg wobbles, tipping. I quickly grab it, holding it steady. A gasp leaves my lips. I'm absolutely speechless. The baby dragon has made a small hole.

One small, golden eye blinks up at me from the shell. "Hello, little one. It's okay. It's safe to come out. I promise," I whisper gently. I let my magic flow through me and into the egg, showing the baby dragon I'm harmless. It makes a soft chirping sound that ends on a growl as it pushes against the hard shell of its egg. The shell finally breaks apart in my hands, leaving a small green dragon amongst the broken pieces of shell, my hands still there in the position they were when holding onto the egg. I sit back on my heels, my hands coming to rest on my knees.

"You're beautiful," I whisper, studying the small dragon in amazement. There are flecks of iridescent blue and purple mixed in with the green scales. Big golden eyes blink up at me, and the baby dragon tentatively moves closer to me. The others are whispering excitedly behind me. I tune them out as I concentrate on the small creature in front of me. The dragon climbs onto my legs, huddling into my stomach, making my heart clench. I slowly reach my hand up and run it along the dragon's back, taking in the small translucent wings that would grow and become stronger as it aged. The dragon turns its head, looking up at me as it makes that odd noise again.

"My name is Nesrin. Your mother asked me to watch over you," I whisper softly, hoping it can understand. The dragon makes a rumbling sound that comes from his throat, and his tiny body vibrates. Then he snuggles back into my body. Glancing up, I almost laugh at the wide-eyed looks of my friends. Lukas moves to sit next to me, but changes his mind and stretches his long body out beside mine, propping his head on his hand as he stares at me. "You are amazing," he murmurs, his hand coming up to tug on some of my hair, making me smile.

Then, reaching over, he runs his hand over the dragon, a slight smile pulling at his lips. The baby dragon lifts its head and blinks wary eyes at Lukas, then nudges his hand with its nose, giving it a small sniff. Lukas moves his hand away, and the dragon lurches forward so fast I swear my heart stops. The baby dragon darts toward Lukas, snuggling under his arm, and along his torso. My eyes meet Lukas's and we share a smile.

"What should we name him?" I run my fingers over the warm scales, finding them surprisingly soft to touch.

Lukas's eyes sparkle with emotion. "Whatever you like, sweetheart." The warmth in his smile makes my tummy flip and my face heat. Clearing my throat, I turn my head to ask the others for suggestions, only to notice they've all wandered back into the kitchen. All except Merve.

"He is beautiful, Nesrin. Don't worry about a thing, you are more than capable of raising a dragon. Kaida couldn't have chosen better," he tells me before turning to follow the others out of the room. Emotions well up inside of me at the thought of Kaida and all she gave up in setting us free. I really hope she wasn't wrong in trusting me with her baby, but I clench my jaw, holding back those feelings. A warm hand covers mine and I glance back at Lukas. He looks so handsome laying there on his side, head propped up on his hand and a baby dragon snuggled up against him.

"So, a name then." I clear my throat.

"Yes, did you have any in mind?"

"No, I wasn't sure how long it would take to hatch, so I didn't even want to think of names yet."

"Hmmm. Arlo. Or Kade?"

I shake my head "Nope."

"Okay, what about Samuel?"

I scrunch up my nose at the name, and the dragon lets out a little chuffing sound. We're clearly in agreement. "Don't think he likes that one," I say, pointing to the dragon.

"Well, judging by the face you pulled when I said it, I don't think you did either," Lukas laughs, the sound doing crazy things to my insides.

"Well, it's your turn, then. I'm clearly terrible at names." Lukas grins, motioning for me to continue.

I stare down at the dragon, at his beautiful scales. "What about Malachite?"

Lukas looks down at the dragon and runs his pointer finger along its back. "Huh. Malachite. I like it."

"What about you, buddy? Do you like it?" I ask, poking the dragon lightly. It blinks its tired eyes at me, then surprises me by nodding its head and letting out a high-pitched sound. Laughing, I scoop the dragon up in my arms and hug it close to my chest. My heart is full of happiness. The dragon has hatched and is okay. I have been so worried. I'd never admit it out loud, but I was so scared it wouldn't survive the escape. All that time in the freezing cold. "Okay. Malachite it is. Let's take you upstairs with Astraea and get you settled in," I say, giddy with excitement. Astraea is going to be beside herself when she wakes up in the morning.

Lukas and I grab the basket and some blankets, getting the new addition to our family settled in with Astraea and Nissa in the room across from ours.

We shut the bedroom door behind us, and Lukas's firm hands land on my hips, pushing my back into the wall, his head bending to nuzzle my neck. Heat flows through me at his touch and I bite my lip. Clenching my hands in his shirt, I pull him closer, my lips skimming his neck where my mark is. A low guttural sound rumbles from his chest, every nerve inside me winding tightly at the sound. His lips move up, taking my earlobe in his teeth and tugging gently. I melt like butter into his touch as his hands roam over my hips and around to cup my ass.

He moves to lift me when an ominous feeling sweeps over me, my instincts flaring as the hairs on my neck stand on end. I push Lukas back and spin around, darting toward the stairs at the front of the house.

Flying down the staircase, I skid to a stop at the bottom. Lukas, nearly running into me, places his hands on my shoulders. Shadows are gathered in the entryway in front of us, all converging at the front door. I can sense the others coming to see what the commotion was, seeing the dark shadows. They brace themselves for whatever is going to come out of it.

Lukas moves around me, coming to a stop at my side, our arms touching in silent unity. I can feel Zee's hope that it will be Leila, but this shadow isn't like hers. It seems thicker, a heaviness present that is hard to explain. The shadow solidifies and a tall figure steps forward. Power seeps from the tall, formidable stranger, the shadows fading behind him until only he remains. Startled, my eyes clash with his. The grin he sends my way has me on alert.

There is something . . . off about it. Something not quite right, unnatural. I feel like prey.

Fear and shock ripple through the room, through me, at the sight of the newcomer. I faintly hear the others behind me changing form, their wolves growling long and low. I barely hear Asena's warning hiss as she stalks forward, her lynx sleek and stunning. Lukas's warm hand lands on my stomach as he moves closer to me, ready to push me behind him at the first sign of things going severely wrong.

I don't take my focus off the man in front of me, if that's what you would call him. He is dressed impeccably in an expensive black suit that has been tailored to perfectly fit his lean, muscular build. His midnight hair is slicked back off his face and his eyes are unique. A shade of dark golden with flecks of black through them. Lethal and dangerous are my first thoughts. This man is emanating so much power, more than I've ever felt before. At my appraisal, the man before me raises a brow. It's such an odd move, something so simple, that I am struck speechless with the reminder that he is anything but human. His eyes begin to glow like liquid gold.

My breath falters, but my magic does not. It rushes to the surface so quickly that my body jolts and starts to glow. I know my eyes are glowing when a white haze coats my vision. Lukas's hand spasms on my body. "Easy, sweetheart."

But the stranger doesn't seem all that fazed. "No need for that. I'm not here to harm you. Or your pets," he states, looking down at the wolves.

Anger at his blatant disrespect has me opening my mouth to refute, but Lukas's voice in my head stops me. '*Nesrin, Astraea is upstairs.'* I flush with shame at almost letting my mouth get away from me.

"Who are you? And why are you here in our home?" I demand, a knot forming in my throat at the smirk that is shot my way.

The man takes a step forward. "You don't know who I am?" He sweeps his arms out wide.

I shake my head. "If I did, I wouldn't be asking, now, would I?" Lukas stiffens beside me. Oops.

The man in front of me laughs. The sound runs over my skin like spiders, setting my nerves on edge. This man is dangerous. His golden eyes meet mine. There is amusement there, but also a hardness.

"I believe you have something that belongs to me?" his lips twist into a smile that is harsh and cold. A shiver dances down my spine as confusion rolls through me. I have nothing that could belong to this man. But I am cursing myself for not doing what I should have done as soon as I was back on pack land after my escape. I really should have put on that necklace. Althaea said it offers some protection and warnings against danger, along with helping me channel my full power. Why haven't I put it on yet?

I blink, not replying.

Tilting his head, he studies me. "You really don't know who I am?" he sounds perplexed. "Huh, I don't know if I should be offended that none of you know who I am."

I open my mouth to reply, but before I can, he adds, "I'm Hades, my dear. And I believe you have my dog."

# EPILOGUE

## Lukas

I scan the forest floor, letting my nose guide me forward. Gaining speed, I weave through trees and bound over fallen logs and streams. The wind shifts, and I pick up a familiar scent. Veering left, I follow the scent for ten minutes. When the trees clear, I glance up at the moon, taking in the sight. We don't have the same pull to the full moon as werewolves, but it still calls to us. The animal part of us needs to run with a pack during the full moon. It triggers the need for emotional grounding. Wolf shifters are more in tune with our animal side at night, and symbolically linked with the mysterious, the occult, and all things hidden. The other shifters in my pack—the bears, large cats, and badgers—don't feel the need to run through the forest during the full moon, but they do join in the gathering beforehand.

I leap over some boulders, my giant black wolf form quick and agile. My paws are silent as I dart through the trees. I catch a glimpse of Zee up ahead, his gray wolf stalking a rabbit. Though we don't eat the animals, we do enjoy using our instincts to chase them. I watch as Zee creeps closer to his prey. A twig snaps under his paw and the rabbit darts off.

*'You always were the loud one.'*

Zee spins and trots over to me. *'Can't all be good at everything, alpha,'* he retorts, his tongue lolling out. I huff out a breath, rolling my eyes. Zee is my second in command and, although he isn't my brother by blood, he is my brother in heart. We grew up together, and when my parents moved to Europe, I opted to stay here with Zee and his family. Zee knows me as well as I know myself, sometimes more than I like.

Feeling a slight shift in the trees, I tilt my head skyward as a delicious scent drifts on the air.

*'Do you smell that?'*

Zee lifts his head, sniffing the air. *'No.'* Turning in a circle, he sniffs again, his head snapping in my direction. *'Wait. Witch?'*

Witch is not what I smell. The smell of rose, jasmine, and lily, with a hint of coffee wraps around me, pulling me toward the hiker's path.

I nudge Zee. *'Let's check it out.'*

Before I have a chance to tell the others through the pack's link, a howl rises from the direction of the enticing scent and panic hits me in the chest. Shifters and witches do not get along. We never have, and a lot of my pack will take this as an act of rebellion and disrespect.

*'No one is to touch her,'* I send out the order to my pack. I will not have them running off half-crazed, causing trouble.

Zee and I break into a run, and within minutes, we have caught up with the pack. Up ahead is a young woman running down one of the trails. Picking up speed, I run by her side, easily keeping up. I watch her in amazement. She has guts. She almost looks as if she is enjoying the chase. I would believe that if I couldn't smell her fear and desperation. Her long auburn hair streams behind her and all I want to do is wrap it around my fist as I drive into her from behind. *Fuck.* It has been a long time since I thought about a woman like this. I need to get laid. I'm just not that kind of guy who enjoys casual sex. This little witch has drawn my curiosity. I want to learn everything there is to know about her.

I see one of my wolves get too close and snap. *'Back it up.'*

They all fall back, content to simply chase her out of the forest. The full moon was our night, and the coven members knew that. I'm still keeping pace with her as she runs through the barrier. She slows a little to see if we will follow.

*'Stop!'*

I feel my pack stop and fall behind, waiting on the barrier lines, their growl erupting in the night air.

*'Head home. I will meet you there.'* Howls fill the air as they turn to leave.

Zee's voice filters through my mind. *'You sure?'*

*'Yes.'*

Shifting, I step out of the forest. Adrenaline is still coursing through my body from the run, the excitement of the chase. I stand a few yards away from her, my eyes tracking her movements. As if sensing my gaze, she spins, scanning the area. Her eyes stop on me and widen, the brightest amber I've ever seen. Fucking beautiful. I watch as her pink lips part in surprise and her hand drifts to grip the hilt of her dagger on her thigh. A gentle breeze rose around us, picking up strands of her loose hair and tossing them around her face. I catch a whiff of her scent again. Rose, jasmine, and lily, with a hint of coffee. It was all her. Warmth infuses my entire body as I stare at her. Attraction bubbles to the surface, and I feel a pull in my chest. Need. Possession. Perhaps she can cast a spell with a glance, because I feel hypnotized by her. As we continue to stare, held in that moment, something absolutely powerful lights my veins. Maybe she is a temptress. I tilt my head, narrowing my eyes as I scramble for any semblance of common sense. What she has me feeling isn't at all possible.

Before I can speak, she spins, jumping into her old piece-of-shit car. Disappointment hits me harder than I thought it would. I shift and trot back into the forest, looking over my shoulder one last time before the forest engulfs me. Zee and the others are waiting when I get back to the house.

"Well?" Zee asks as I come to a stop in front of him and shift. He hands me a bottle of water, and I shoot him a grateful look.

"She is no threat," I reply before gulping some water.

One of my more outspoken shifters, Ryan, steps forward. His wolf is small, but he makes up for it with ferocity. "We need to track her, teach her a lesson about who this forest belongs to."

A growl rumbles from my chest, and I snarl, spinning on him. He drops his gaze to the ground. I rarely have to assert dominance, but this time it's a reflex.

My gaze moves over all of them. "It belongs to the animals and creatures who live there. We take care of it, keep the peace, keep it safe for magical creatures. It doesn't belong to us. And she isn't to be touched. Understand?"

Ryan's expression hardens ever so briefly before he nods in acceptance.

"The witch is off limits to everyone. She is under my protection." My voice is low and controlled, and I infuse it with my alpha's magic. I will have none of them going after this girl. A thought floats through my mind. *'She's mine.'*

Everybody turns and leaves, heading either to their cars or the house they have on the pack lands. I turn to Zee, who has been silent this whole time. And I know my best friend when he is silent, he is thinking. Zee is watching me carefully. I realize he can sense something is up. Absently, I reach up, rubbing at my chest, a weird sensation coming over me.

"Who do you think she is?" I ask.

He stares at me a beat longer. "Holy fuck."

"What?"

Zee shakes his head, running a hand through his hair, a smirk pulling at his mouth as if he knows a secret I don't. I growl in annoyance. "What?"

"This is going to be fun." He laughs, clapping a hand on my back and walking away. "So much fun, my brother." I frown at my friend as he disappears into the forest, shifting.

# FINDING SANCTUARY
# NOVELLA

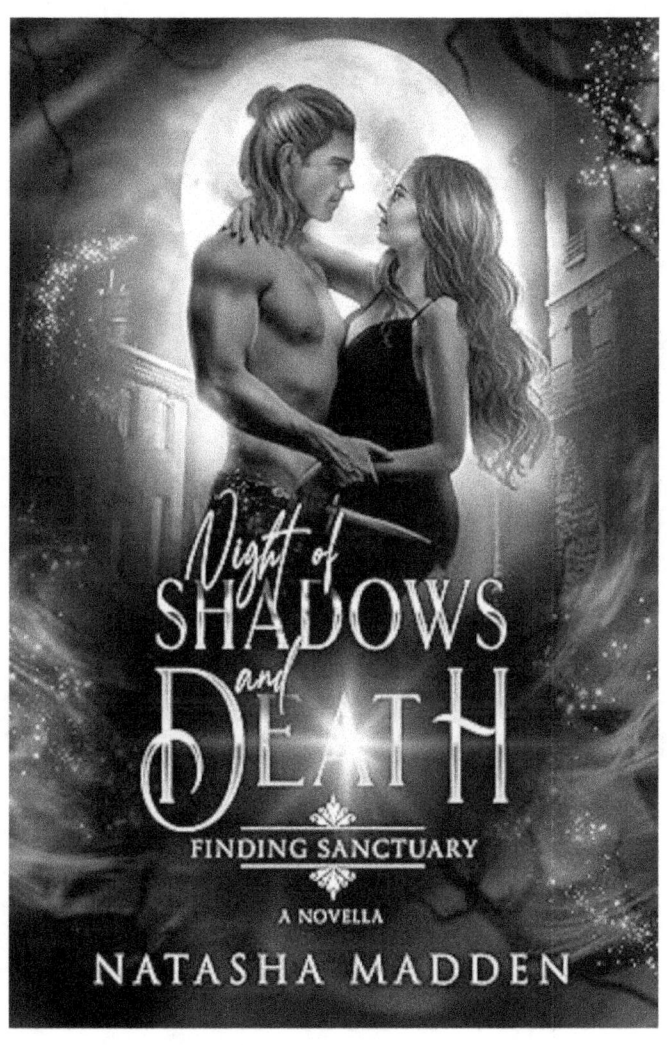

BEST TO READ AFTER
CHOSEN BY DESTINY OR MARKED BY THE GODS

# ACKNOWLEDGMENTS

I would first of all like to thank you all for taking a chance on this book. This is my debut novel and I have enjoyed every moment of this journey. I hope you all enjoy it as well.

I want to thank my family, especially my husband for all the time he put in helping me, and the love and support he has given me. Thanks, mum, for always pushing me and believing I could do this, it's an amazing journey to go on. If you hadn't pushed me to do it in the first place, I probably never would have.

I'd like to thank my friend Siobhan for being my beta reader and helping me when I needed it. You've shown me so much and I appreciate all the support you've given me. I also want to send out a huge thanks to the best cheerleader of all. Sanela, without you this story would have taken me a lot longer. You inspired me, you boosted me up when I needed it, you were there for me, cheering me on the whole way. You were so enthusiastic about my characters, and their journey. It was truly amazing having you there, your feedback and opinions were invaluable.

# About Author

I have been book obsessed since I can remember. It all started with The Saddle Club, Goosebumps, Babysitters Club and then anything fantasy or adventure from the school library. I went through a massive faze of King Arthur and tales of the knights. I dreamed of being a female knight, keeping my identity hidden. Falling in love with a prince and saving his life. To raising dragons and running with wolves. I have lived so many of my dreams through books. Authors sending me on a journey with their words.

I have always had an active imagination and my mum has always told me write! *Write it down!*

From my thoughts, my dreams and experiences. For years, and I mean years, I was like no that's silly, I can't do that. No way! Now at 36 years old, having written three books, in eighteen months. Loving every minute of plots, research and drafting. It's taken me along time to start writing, it's taken me a long time to admit to others I've started writing. I needed confidence and belief in myself, I'm working on it. I'm super excited to share my work with you all!

This is my debut novel and I hope you all love Nesrin and Lukas as much as I do.

www.ingramcontent.com/pod-product-compliance
Lightning Source LLC
Chambersburg PA
CBHW060812120726
47909CB00006B/1888